THE GIRL
IN THE EAGLE'S
TALONS

THE GIRL
IN THE EAGLE'S
TALONS

A LISBETH SALANDER NOVEL

Karin Smirnoff

Translated from the Swedish by Sarah Death

VIKING

VIKING

an imprint of Penguin Canada, a division of Penguin Random House Canada Limited

Canada • USA • UK • Ireland • Australia • New Zealand • India • South Africa • China

Published in Viking hardcover by Penguin Canada, 2023.
Originally published in Sweden as *Havsörnens skrik* in 2022 by
Bokförlaget Polaris, Stockholm.
Copyright © 2022 by Karin Smirnoff.
This translation is simultaneously published in the United States by Alfred A. Knopf,
a division of Penguin Random House LLC, New York, and in Great Britain by MacLehose
Press, an imprint of Quercus Publishing Ltd, London, in 2023, by agreement with Norstedts
Agency. Published by arrangement with Quercus Publishing PLC (U.K.).

Translation copyright © 2023 by Sarah Death

www.penguinrandomhouse.ca

*Publisher's note: This book is a work of fiction. Names, characters, places and incidents either are
the product of the author's imagination or are used fictitiously, and any resemblance to actual
persons living or dead, events, or locales is entirely coincidental.*

LIBRARY AND ARCHIVES CANADA CATALOGUING IN PUBLICATION

Title: The girl in the eagle's talons : a Lisbeth Salander novel / Karin Smirnoff ;
translated by Sarah Death.
Other titles: Havsörnens skrik. English
Names: Smirnoff, Karin, 1964- author. | Death, Sarah, translator.
Description: Series statement: Millennium series ; 7 | Translation of: Havsörnens skrik. |
"The Girl with the Dragon Tattoo Returns".
Identifiers: Canadiana (print) 20230144381 | Canadiana (ebook) 20230144861 |
ISBN 9780735246652 (hardcover) | ISBN 9780735246669 (EPUB)
Subjects: LCGFT: Novels.
Classification: LCC PT9877.29.M57 H3813 2023 | DDC 839.73/8—dc23

Book design by M. Kristen Bearse
Cover design by Keenan, based on an original design by Peter Mendelsund
Cover images: (feather) © schankz / Shutterstock

Printed in the United States of America

10 9 8 7 6 5 4 3 2 1

Penguin
Random House
VIKING CANADA

Now do I see
the earth anew
Rise all green
from the waves again;
The cataracts fall,
and the eagle flies,
And fish he catches
beneath the cliffs.

"The Wise-Woman's Prophecy"
The Edda
(Translated by Henry Adams Bellows)

CHARACTERS IN THE MILLENNIUM SERIES

LISBETH SALANDER, an exceptionally talented hacker with tattoos, piercings and a troubled past.

MIKAEL BLOMKVIST, an investigative journalist at *Millennium* magazine. Lisbeth assisted him with one of the biggest stories of his career, about the disappearance of Harriet Vanger. He later helped to vindicate Lisbeth when she was on trial for murder.

RONALD NIEDERMANN, Lisbeth's half brother, a blond giant impervious to pain. She arranged for his murder at the hands of Svavelsjö Motorcycle Club.

CAMILLA SALANDER, Lisbeth's estranged twin sister. The head of a criminal network in Russia. She killed herself after a final violent confrontation with Lisbeth.

ALEXANDER ZALACHENKO, once the head of a criminal empire but also the father of Lisbeth Salander, who as a teenager tried to kill him with a Molotov cocktail for the violent abuse of her mother. Ultimately he was finished off by Säpo, the Swedish Security Police.

HOLGER PALMGREN, Lisbeth's former guardian, a lawyer, now deceased. One of the few people who knew Lisbeth Salander well and whom she trusted. He was murdered as part of the cover-up of Lisbeth's abuse by the government systems meant to protect her as a child.

DRAGAN ARMANSKY, founder of Milton Security and now Lisbeth's business partner. One of the few people she trusts.

PERNILLA BLOMKVIST, Mikael's daughter, who as a child helped him solve the Harriet Vanger case, but does not spend much time with him.

ERIKA BERGER, editor in chief of *Millennium* magazine, Mikael's lover on and off over the years.

ANNIKA GIANNINI, Mikael's sister, a lawyer who represented Lisbeth Salander when she was on trial for murder.

SVAVELSJÖ M.C., a motorcycle gang closely associated with Zalachenko, which has had several run-ins with Lisbeth.

SONNY NIEMINEN, a member of Svavelsjö M.C., part of a plot to try to kidnap Lisbeth. She leaves him incapacitated.

HACKER REPUBLIC, a coalition of hackers, among whom Lisbeth, who goes by the handle "Wasp," is the star. Includes the hacker Plague.

HANS FASTE, a police officer formerly with the Stockholm force who has clashed with Mikael and Lisbeth in the past for his unscrupulous leaking of information in the murder investigation of Lisbeth Salander.

THE GIRL
IN THE EAGLE'S
TALONS

1

The Cleaner keeps an eye on his watch. From the moment he baits the feeding tray with hunks of meat it takes forty-one seconds for the first eagle, a female, to land.

He can never tell exactly where it has come from. It could have been perched in a nearby tree. Or sailing a couple of thousand feet above. With eyesight like that, two hundred times sharper than a human's, it can zoom in on prey from several miles away. He is sitting fifty yards from the bait, well concealed in his hiding place, following the meal through his binoculars.

Fourteen across, "raptor treats," ten letters. *Eagle candy.* The tenderness he feels for the birds is not fatherly love, for what does he know of that? And yet he cannot help thinking of them as his children.

He thinks about them before he goes to sleep. The moment he wakes up. As he goes about all the essential chores like chopping wood, preparing their meals or lighting the fire, he thinks about them. Have they mated? Have the young survived? Can they find enough to eat? Will they make it through the winter? Yes. With his help and a decent year for voles, they will pull through.

He rubs his knuckles over his eyes. The sun has risen higher now and is warming his back. Maybe for the last time this autumn. It doesn't matter. This house is in a corner of the world forgotten by humankind. Although "house" is a bit of an exaggeration. A log hut that has stood empty since the last foresters left in the early 1960s and the area was designated a national park.

This is rugged country with its irregular structure of ancient forest, meres, bogs and mountains. There is no proper road leading to it, either. Apart from animal paths the only visible markers are the faint traces of an old forest track that nature is busily reclaiming. The only way to get there is on foot or by quad bike, and you have to know the route.

It's a good five miles from the nearest public road, and he limits his movements to a radius of a couple of miles around the hut. When he first came here, he marked directions with branches so he wouldn't get lost. This local territory provides him with a stream to fish in, fallen trees for his woodpile and convenient clearings where he can look out for birds and smaller game.

The hut is his sanctuary. Minimally modernized with a diesel-powered generator that he uses for charging his phone. Here he is no one. A man with no name, background or future. He simply is. Lives each day as it comes. Gets to sleep early. Wakes at dawn. Does what he has to without dwelling on whether it is good or bad.

There are dates carved into the log walls. And names. Messages to the future from other solitary men. Olof Persson 1881. Lars Persson 1890. Sven-Erik Eskola 1910. And so on. But what is solitude if not relative? Months can pass without him talking to anyone but himself, birds, trees and even rocks. Yet he feels less alone than ever. It is as if his childhood has caught up with him. Day by day he is getting closer to the boy who took refuge in the forest. The boy who learned how the world was constructed by sitting stock-still and watching the mating dance of black grouse in the spring. Following the progress of the vixen as she cared for her growing offspring, of the wood ants taking their shift in the heap or the bark beetle burrowing its way through the spruce.

The boy has a father. A strapping devil with arms that reach everywhere. The boy has a mother. Nobody takes her into account. The boy has a brother. Run, he says when their father gets home, and the boy makes off into the forest.

He catches a slowworm. When it sheds its tail, he catches it again. Pulls his knife from its sheath, severs the head from the body and everything falls silent. He is the silence.

The boy places the slowworm on a rock. Leans against the trunk of a spruce and wipes the knife blade on his trousers. Scrapes it against a fingernail. Along its sharp edge there is freedom. Nobody can take that from him.

Another eagle is coming in. This one is a young male. He hasn't yet got the white belly feathers of sexual maturity, or the yellow beak. Presumably born last year. Two years old max, he writes in his notebook. It is unusual, but it happens from time to time, he adds, that young eagles stay where they were born instead of moving south. Possible defect or sickness. Question mark. Keep an eye out. Exclamation mark.

The female is so engrossed that she doesn't bother to look up when the young male, which has first circled the meat, dares to come in to land. There are mostly just bits of bone left now. She lets him get on with it. They tug and tear until the sinews come free and slip down their throats like spaghetti.

Within a few minutes, the day's climax is over. He tucks his notebook and flask in his backpack. Pulls the strap of the rifle over his shoulder and crawls out of his hiding place. His right leg lags behind, as usual. He has to turn it manually in the direction of home. His route takes him along an animal path. Birch, alder and willow have already lost their leaves. He grabs a handful of lingonberries and pulls a bittersweet face. Bittersweet also describes the smell of the lumps of meat left in the lidded plastic drum. Well camouflaged under a spruce, but still. He should throw it all onto the feeding tray at the same time, but he just can't. His time with the eagles means everything. It is for them that he breathes, eats, sleeps, shits. Tomorrow he will come here again. And then his phone rings. There is only one person who has this number. There is only one person he rings.

"Yes," he says. "Right. Tomorrow morning. OK."

It is a colder morning than usual. He adds a couple of extra logs and warms his hands around a coffee cup. If he wants to get out to the road on time he will have to set off soon. Things could happen on the way. The quad bike could break down. The ground could be waterlogged.

He walks the first few miles, to the place where he keeps the quad bike hidden. Purely as a precaution. If anyone were to find it, unlikely though that is, it would be impossible to link it to the hut or to him.

As he walks, he keeps a lookout for sea eagles. One of the nests is over this way but there are no birds to be seen. Pity. It would have given him a good feeling, something to live on. Not that he is dreading it, but still. A sea eagle is a sign. A good one.

Once he gets there he brushes the spruce twigs off the machine, puts his backpack in the carrier in front and sets off for the meeting place.

The ground is dry enough, everything goes to plan. He gets there with ten minutes to spare and stays well hidden from the road before driving up to the barrier and turning the quad bike around for the return trip.

The car is already parked there. It's always the same person who makes the delivery. The Cleaner knows him as the Delivery Man. The Delivery Man knows him as the Cleaner. They don't know each other. Exchange only a few words.

"Who do you take orders from?" he asks.

The answer reassures him. The shorter the chain of command, the fewer the links.

This time he's asked for some things he needs. A bottle of whisky and a few items of fresh food. And the newspapers, as usual. He jams them down into the carrier and goes back to the car.

The Delivery Man pulls his delivery out of the back seat.

A woman, which is unusual. Her hands are tied behind her back and there's a hood over her head. Inarticulate sounds indicate her mouth is taped. At least he won't have her idle chatter to contend with.

"Do whatever you want with her," says the Delivery Man. "You have a free hand."

Whatever he wants, as long as he does his job.

The individuals who come his way have earned their fate. To that extent, his conscience is clear. He is no sex killer or psychopath, even though the rest of the world would probably view him as a murderer following his baser instincts.

He and his employers have a deal. As long as they keep their side of the bargain, he will keep his.

"What did she do?" he asks for once. Maybe because it is a woman. Maybe because the Delivery Man is the first person he has spoken to for a long time.

"I don't know," says the Delivery Man, and the Cleaner believes him.

He climbs onto the quad bike and the Delivery Man helps him position the body in front of him. Body sounds better than woman.

"Strap the belt on, too," he says. "That's right, isn't it, cutie pie? We don't want you falling off."

He raises his hand in farewell and drives back toward the hut.

While he is camouflaging the vehicle, the body is on its feet, tied to a tree. It's not completely silent. It makes faint whimpering sounds, like a sick cat. Sick cats have to be put down. Still no sea eagles in sight.

"Off we go," he says, and shoves the body ahead of him. He notes that it is not as fit as he is. On the last stretch he has to kick its hind legs to keep its feet moving.

Normally he never takes bodies into the hut. This is an exception. He pushes it onto the bed and takes the chair for himself.

"Pleasure before work, will that be alright?" he asks the body. "And maybe put some more wood on the fire. Don't you think it's cold in here?"

The cat whimpers. He feels himself go hard. A woman is a woman, after all.

He peels off the body's trousers and knickers. He is excited to see what she's got under her wrappings. It's a fairly young body. Thirty-five, maybe. Forty, max. Age makes no difference.

He starts out thinking he will take his time, just enjoy the view so to speak, but he's too aroused to be patient. He tears off a length of plastic wrap, fuck knows what shit she might be carrying, winds the plastic a couple of times around his erection and adjusts the body so it is lying at a perfect angle for penetration.

"You can stay in the hut for a few days so we can cozy up," he says, and fumbles like a virgin at church camp. He doesn't even get it in before he comes.

Once his breathing calms and his desire goes flat, he sees that the body has wet itself.

Wet his bed, which decides everything.

"No more cozy," he says, then does up his trousers and gets the body ready for departure.

The body can barely walk. It is on the verge of passing out, so he doesn't take it as far as he had planned. Ties it to a tree for a second time and unties the cord of the cloth bag where he keeps his gun.

He contemplates the beautiful machine. Screws on the silencer and holds the pistol between both hands as a consecration of the action it's about to perform.

Meow. Kitty won't have to suffer anymore.

2

They've been sitting in the cold car for more than half an hour, waiting for a sign that the house is empty.

The car is parked a little way along a side road leading down to the river. It is out of sight of the house, behind a barn. But they have a good view of anyone driving in or out. First the woman drove off with the child in the back seat and now he is leaving, too.

This is not the first time they have sat here.

Every time they drive back into town with their assignment not carried out, Svala can breathe again, even though they drop her a good way outside Gasskas and she has to walk home. Home to Mammamärta. Home to a missing Mammamärta on Tjädervägen, where her grandmother has moved in instead.

There is nothing wrong with her, really. She does things that Mammamärtas never do. Cooks, cleans and fills the flat with her chatter. This is standard procedure. Mammamärta sometimes disappears and comes back a few days later without saying where she's been, but this time is different. It's been nearly a month since she put her handbag over her shoulder, kissed Svala on the head and said, *I'll be right back, my little swallow. Just going for some cigarettes.*

Svala asked Grandma not to touch anything in her room. Not to clean up or collect dirty clothes into a pile while she's at school. This room is the only place left untouched. As Svala lies down on the zebra-striped bedspread, Mammamärta is there again. As she sits at Svala's desk, pretending to correct her homework. Stroking her hair and saying: "When I get paid, we'll do something fun."

Fun can mean going to Jokkmokk Winter Market and buying colorful socks and sweets.

Fun usually means a pizza at Buongiorno. They've brought in a pizza chef from Naples. Mammamärta bets he's from Syria.

"Who cares?" Svala says. "I'm having a Vegetariana."

. . .

The cheese is hot. It burns the roofs of their mouths. Svala gets another Coke. Mammamärta a second glass of wine. She's at her best after one glass and a couple more gulps. She jokes about the people around them. Talks about things that happened long ago. Like the old Lapp who walks into a restaurant and orders grouse. Sticks his index finger up its arse and claims to be able to tell where it was shot. Maybe Arvidsjaur. She can't exactly remember. But when Svala fills in the gaps, Mammamärta gets cross. Her eyes narrow even more than usual as she grips Svala's hand and squeezes hard: "You're Sami, you know. Not a bloody Lapp. Don't you forget it. You ought to be proud of your roots."

Which are what? A mother who's missing, a dead dad. A grandma with angina. No siblings or close relatives. At least, none who want anything to do with her.

"Except Lisbeth," says Grandma.

"And who's Lisbeth?"

"Lisbeth Salander. Your dad's half sister."

"Nobody's mentioned her before."

"Your mum didn't want anything to do with the Niedermanns," says Grandma. "And that's understandable."

"Why?" Svala asks, but gets no proper answer.

"It was all a long time ago, not worth talking about," says Grandma, indicating that the conversation is over. Instead she traces the lines of Svala's palm with her finger.

"You're going to have a long life," she says. "At least three children. Somewhere there's a break. After that, everything will be fine."

At least three children. Bring new Svalas into the world? Not if she has anything to say about it. But the break . . .

It feels to Svala as if the break is already here. The autumn trees have burst into flames. She wants to paint their fire. An eye can perceive ten million shades of color. She wants to capture them in brushstrokes around a leaf.

She has no idea what their names are, those shady customers in the front seat. But she knows who is behind it all: Pap Peder. Her own worthless step. She would never honor him with the suffix "dad" or "father."

Although he's not been living with them for several years, he's still lurking there like a starving pike in the reeds. Especially lately, since Mammamärta went missing.

The woman from social services said Svala ought to prepare herself for her mum having died.

"What of?" Svala asks.

"Your mum had her problems."

"My mum hasn't gone missing of her own free will."

"We don't always know everything about our parents."

"Well, maybe you don't."

The car's front door slams, the back door opens. She has company.

"Are you scared?" he says.

"No," she says.

"Does this hurt?" he says, twisting her arm.

"No," she says.

He shifts closer to her, puts an arm around her shoulders and pulls her to him.

"Shame we're short on time, I get the feeling you're good at one thing and another. A bit scrawny, that's the only thing," he says, and squeezes her shoulder. "But quite cute."

With his other hand he grabs her by the chin and turns her face to his. She does her best not to meet his eye.

"You know what happens if you fail," he says, and runs a finger across his throat. She holds her breath to avoid the smell of his. Like all the Peders and their disgusting crew, he stinks of unbrushed teeth, ammonia and smoke.

Her heart is ticking, her mouth is sticky, her lips are dry and smarting from the winter cold. Which is just as well. She might be powerless, but she has two advantages. The second-best thing is that she feels no pain. They can hit or burn her as much as they like. Snap an arm or break a leg and get no reaction from her at all. Not even a stranglehold causes her any discomfort.

The best thing about her is something that cannot be explained, it is simply there. As if she knows the answer before the question is even asked.

You didn't get your eyes to see with, Mammamärta says. You got them because you can see.

Not all of the days at Buongiorno have been double fizzy drinks. She has worked as hard for her pizza crusts as the tall Lapp girl at the funfair.

Roll up, roll up: Christina is already seven foot two and still growing.

Roll up, roll up: Beat Svala at Rubik's Cube and win a thousand kronor.

Svala never loses, but the best show is about something else entirely.

The pizzeria does not look like normal pizzerias, with plasterwork around the door frames and humming drink fridges. The theme of Buongiorno is the world of the American mafia. The walls are hung with framed pictures of Al Capone, Johnny Torrio, Lucky Luciano, Joe Masseria and other gangsters, along with film stills, clothes and old guns with plugged barrels.

In one corner there is a safe, used not for money and diamonds but for plates and cutlery.

It is Pap Peder who comes up with the idea. The only present he has ever given Svala is precisely that: a safe. It's not large, but heavy. And the main thing is it's locked.

"I have no idea what's in it," he says, "but if you crack the code, you can keep the contents."

She is ten years old and knows he is lying, but still she cannot resist having a go. There is something about her fingers and there is something about her brain. The figures flicker before her eyes like balls in a raffle drum. That is how she sees it. Or feels it. It takes a few attempts to get the information into order. Pap Peder shifts his feet impatiently beside her.

When she senses that the code has slotted into place, she turns to Pap Peder and says, "No, I can't do it. I don't know how."

Anything at all could happen now. He could lose his temper and shout at her, which is the usual thing. He could slap her. That happens less often these days. Or he could slam the door behind him, creating enough pressure in the air to make the hall light hit the ceiling.

She sits still and listens. Once she feels sure he really has left the flat, she opens the door of the safe a little way.

There is money in the safe. More money than she has ever seen.

But as she sits counting the five-hundred-krona notes, he is suddenly standing in front of her.

By this stage he knows that physical violence will get him nowhere with Svala. It doesn't hurt her enough. But it hurts Mammamärta all the more.

"You realize I have to punish you," he says. "Putting your hands over your ears won't help."

He has the great idea about the safe in the pizzeria a few years later.

The guests choose the code and Svala cracks it. Sometimes she gets a coin or two for herself. Or a tip that somehow escapes Pap Peder's greedy eye. She keeps the money in the shaggy toy monkey on her bed. She unpicks the seam, pulls out a bit of the foam filling and sews it back up.

3

Well, what the hell did he expect? When they announce for the third time that the train to Sundsvall, Umeå, Luleå and Kiruna, due to leave at 6:11 p.m., is delayed and now has an estimated departure time of 7:34 p.m., Mikael Blomkvist finds a seat in Luzette Brasserie and orders a beer.

Whiling away a bit of time at Stockholm Central could be quite relaxing. Sitting in your own bubble. Watching the flow of people. But not this evening. He is too tired to take any interest in his surroundings. Tired for a variety of reasons, most of them familiar. Too much work. Too much hassle at work. Late nights, too little sleep and a deadline that is genuinely dead.

Always this *Millennium*. His lady above all ladies. The one who always draws the longest straw in the battle with family, friends and girlfriends. Now that she is dead, he has to ask himself if it was worth it. Yes. An unhesitating yes. *Millennium* is the air he breathes. The blood that runs in his veins. Not everyone can be a perfect husband and head of the family. There have to be others, and he includes himself, who have to tell the perfect husbands and fathers what the world is actually like beyond the well-raked drives of their nice detached houses.

This is what makes it so hard to comprehend that it's over. The evil, the injustices, all that shit still has the same grip on society, but no one has the energy to care. They come home after a day at the office, pour a whisky, check their e-mails, have dinner, play a game of padel and go to bed. That goddamn bubble is inhabited by most of the people he knows. They're stressed by their lives. They can only cope with caring about those closest to them, and sometimes not even that. Being a servant of justice in addition is simply out of the question.

He scrolls down his list of chats. Still not a word from Erika Berger. Or from anyone else on the editorial team.

Mikael Blomkvist is not alone. But he feels alone. This is new.

When he's finished his beer he goes over to the Pressbyrån, where he buys a to-go coffee and the *Morning Star*. He gets engrossed in an article about a British mining company's bid to establish itself up in Norrbotten County. It takes him a few moments to respond to the voice.

"Mikael, hello, Mikael."

He looks up. His sister, Annika. "What are you doing here? Aren't you supposed to be in Åre?" he asks.

"I was, but something happened at work and I had to catch the train back. I just got here. What about you? Are you waiting for somebody?"

"My train's delayed," he said. "I thought I'd go up a bit early. When are you all planning to head north?"

"The rest of the *famiglia* is heading up in a few days," she says. "I'll have to come up and join you later. I haven't even met Pernilla's fiancé yet."

"None of us has, I don't think. Is anything wrong?"

"No," she says. "Well, yes. But I can't talk about it."

"Oh, come on," he says. "Surely you can say something?"

"Oh, it's nothing. Only a politician who messed up."

He waits for more but nothing comes. And because he knows his sister, he knows that nothing can make her talk if she's decided to keep quiet.

"You'd make a good spy," he says.

"Would I?" She laughs. "Why a spy, specifically?"

"If they tortured you, you wouldn't say a word."

In silence they watch a man walking past with all his possessions in a grocery cart. He has some kind of back problem. The cart also serves as a walker.

"Did you know that for an hour every night the security guards send out all the people sleeping on benches while the place is cleaned?" Annika says. "Can you imagine how long that hour must feel? And incidentally, what a scandal that society can't find anywhere for these homeless people to live," she goes on. "Some of them are only here because they have bad credit."

"Which politician is it?" interrupts Mikael.

"Stop that," she says, and gives him a hug. "You'll see it in the press soon enough. Give Pernilla my love," and then she has to rush off.

The train is only minutes from departure as he struggles into the compartment with his case, instantly regretting that he didn't treat himself to a first-class ticket or at least a three-berth sleeping car. In the chaos as six men try to sort out their sheets, he throws his case onto the middle bunk, takes his shoulder bag and makes his way through the swaying carriages to the restaurant car. He buys a beer and a sandwich and heads for a seat the very moment it is taken by someone else.

"Just my bloody luck," he says out loud, and feels a tug on the sleeve of his jacket.

"There's room for you here. We're in the same compartment," says the man he recognizes from the bed chaos. The one who offered him a dram. And Mikael had said no thanks. In an unnecessarily brusque tone to keep his distance.

"IB," he says, holding out his hand.

"MB," Mikael replies, peeling the plastic wrapper off his sandwich as he asks how far IB is traveling, in the hope that he might be getting off as soon as Gävle.

"Boden," he says, raising his glass. "Where are you off to yourself?"

Why the devil is it such a hard name to remember? Norrbyn, Sjöbyn, Storbyn—*Älvsbyn*.

"Älvsbyn. My daughter's getting married. She met a guy from Gasskas. A man from Gasskas," he corrects himself. Henry Salo does not look like a guy.

"If you're heading for Gasskas, then you ought to get off in Boden, too," says IB. "It's the quickest way. The railbus runs direct."

"I'm getting a lift from Älvsbyn," says Mikael, and then buries himself in his phone.

Much has been written about his future son-in-law Henry Salo. Head of the municipality of Gasskas. Relatively new to the post. The type who wears a broad smile in every photo and seems popular. Well, it's her choice. He's OK, no doubt. Good-looking. Perhaps a bit *too* good-looking. Not that there's anything wrong with Pernilla, far from it, and it isn't Salo's face that disturbs him per se, but his demeanor, his body language. His way of ensuring he's always at the front of a photo op, whether he's congratulating a young grant recipient or opening a park.

He's good with Lukas. She says it every time they speak on the phone. And Mikael always replies, *I believe you.* But after they hang up he feels unsure. The boy. His grandson. Mikael had spent hardly any time with him. Until last summer.

First he says, "No, I don't have time to look after a child," but Pernilla sticks to her guns.

"I've hardly ever asked you for anything," she says.

This is true. He has never been particularly involved with his daughter. Something always gets in the way. Usually *Millennium*. So when Pernilla asks him to look after the boy for a fortnight because she's going on a course down in Skåne and Salo is at a conference in Helsinki, he turns her down flat. It won't work. He doesn't have the time. He's got a deadline next Thursday. He isn't used to children.

Yet here is Lukas, disembarking at Sandhamn while Pernilla heads straight back into town on the same boat.

Two weeks later he's hugging a boy who would really rather not leave. Or is it him, wanting to hang on to Lukas? The place is going to feel empty. He has taken up space. Pushed aside the persistent gloom that has squatted in Mikael's body like some kind of flu these past few months. Simply by being a child, following his spontaneous need to wake early and embark on a new day of possibilities. *Zest for life, Mikael Blomkvist. You could do with more of that yourself.*

"We'll see each other again soon," he says to the boy, and then, "Wait!" He takes off the necklace he was given by his own grandfather long ago and has worn ever since, a cross, an anchor and a heart on a simple silver chain, and puts it around Lukas's neck.

"It's yours now," he says. "It will protect you against most things."

The boy's answer is still hanging there: "But not everything."

Mikael scrolls through the newsfeed of the local paper, *Gaskassen*. A name as good as any other, he supposes, and smiles at the headlines. ELK PRESCHOOL SELLING HAMA BEAD PICTURES. ALL PROCEEDS TO UKRAINE. DEFEAT AGAINST BJÖRKLÖVEN. GOALIE SENT OFF. A grim-looking Salo in the VIP stand surrounded by other grim-looking guys. Community bigwigs. Do they still call them that these days? Men of great importance for their locality's and their own best interests.

Then a headline grabs his attention. Not in *Gaskassen* but in another paper: MIMER MINING CLOSE TO QUARRYING PERMIT.

In the smaller picture, Salo's satisfied mug. In a bigger one, protesters with placards.

"Do you know about this?" asks Mikael, holding up the picture.

"Of course," IB says. "My dad worked down the mine, like most other men in Gasskas. The mountain was meant to be another Kiirunavaara but the iron ore ran out back in the seventies and they filled the mine with water. They didn't even bother to salvage the machinery from the sites."

"So why do they want to reopen it?"

"There's no plan to reopen the old mine. The British are doing test drilling in an area a few miles away, where they want to put in an opencast mine. So far the County Administrative Board has said no, which is entirely understandable. It would lead to the destruction of lakes, Gasskas's drinking water would be at risk and the reindeer herd owners would come off worse, as usual. But as always when there's big money involved, nobody takes no for an answer. Apparently they've now rejigged the composition of the board and Mimer's had advance notification of a positive outcome."

"As simple as that," Mikael says.

"Gasskas is a real nest of gangsters, in case you weren't aware," says IB. "Well, Gasskas municipality is, anyway." He takes a few swigs of beer, wipes the foam from his beard and drinks some more. "A total shithole for crooked opportunists," he adds, then lets out a couple of belches, drains the bottle and opens the next one. "The municipality gives its blessing to most things and the mine isn't the only thing in the pipeline. The next project is the biggest onshore wind farm in Europe, however the hell that's supposed to happen. We're talking a vast area of land, tens of square miles, that will virtually become an industrial park."

Mikael Blomkvist smiles. Malmö is a shithole. Stockholm, too. Gasskas, with its twenty thousand or so inhabitants, is more like the lamb pen in paradise by comparison.

"Why Gasskas, specifically?" he asks.

"Good electricity supply," IB says. "Municipalities with cheap, reliable electricity are the rulers of the global market, didn't you know? There's a long list of foreign companies keen to establish themselves in the area."

"Yes, I know, but it must be good for Norrland if people are getting jobs."

"I can tell you're from the south. You lot are still living with the myth that Norrlanders have to move south to get work. But there are quite a lot of job opportunities. In some places there are more job vacancies than we have labor to fill them. Besides, it won't be the locals who benefit if the Gasskas mine opens, but underpaid labor from the east and Stockholmers commuting home for the weekend and not bothering with local parish registration," mutters IB, shifting his eyes to the countryside rushing by.

Mikael sees this as a chance to take out his Mac and open the screen to put a reasonable barrier between them.

The latest issue of *Millennium* has come out, not just the latest but the last. He opens the pdf and stares at the black-and-white front page with no pictures or advertising. Like a front page from 1939, which is the intention. Sparse text and a single headline: AN EPOCH IS OVER BUT THE WAR GOES ON.

Thirty-one years in the service of investigative journalism. Even Mikael Blomkvist had to admit that it was the end of an era.

A print magazine goes to the grave and rises again as a podcast. A podcast! A word that can't even be said without a snort. The written word is out. Now they'll all have to talk over one another, including him. The very thought is exhausting.

You're getting old, Mikael, was how Erika Berger put it. *Old and grouchy, like a billy goat. We won't just be making podcasts. We'll be blogging and vlogging as well.*

And what was his response? It was that an old ewe like her should know that social media can never replace proper journalism. *What the hell are you thinking? Can't you see how bloody pathetic you are? Hipsters make podcasts. Self-absorbed twenty-year-olds talking makeup and eating disorders.*

They've had no contact since. And he won't be the one to make the first move; he wants her to be very clear on that point.

"Here you are," says IB. He's fetched a couple more beers and holds one out to Mikael. "Drink plenty and you'll find it easier to sleep."

"Lousy connection," Mikael says, jabbing a finger at the keyboard.

"Sorry, but you do know this is the Norrland train, right?" IB says.

Mikael stuffs his laptop in his bag and makes to get up, but the man opens his mouth again.

"There are weird things happening in Gasskas," he says. "People going missing. Men go out to get the newspaper and never come home. Boys walk to school and . . ." He does not complete his sentence.

"That isn't exactly unusual. They say ninety-five percent of all disappearances are voluntary."

"Maybe," IB says, "but what about the other five, then?"

They look at each other across the beers.

"I don't know," Mikael says eventually. "What's your view?"

"Money. It's all about money. How you get it. Spend it. Make it grow. Hide it. Get into debt. Mess up. Get into even more debt. Disappear."

"Are you talking drugs here?" says Mikael.

"Not only," IB replies, "although Gasskas is starting to look like Järfälla. The youngsters are doping themselves to death and the police haven't a clue what to do."

"Very sad," says Mikael, swallowing the last lukewarm drops of beer.

"It's going to get worse, believe me," IB goes on. "When the money moves north, the rabble follows it. We've already got a biker gang, a direct import from Stockholm."

"Hells Angels?" Mikael asks.

"No, they've got some other name, something else biblical. Abaddon? Gehenna, Hades . . ."

"Svavelsjö?"

"Yes, that's what they're called, Sulphur. I knew it was biblical."

Mikael is beginning to realize this IB guy could be right about Gasskas. Svavelsjö Motorcycle Club, unbelievable. They ought to have been expunged from the face of the earth long ago. He quickly checks out the name on his phone. The latest news item is from the summer: MOTORBIKE RIDE FOR CHILD CANCER FUND.

"Smart bastards," says IB. "They rode in procession around the town and charged for each circuit. The municipality topped up with double the amount they raised. It came to a hundred and forty thousand kronor, which they donated to children with cancer. Sweet of them, eh!"

"Really," says Mikael, trying to zoom in on faces concealed by helmets and sunglasses. Presumably most of this lot will be new. Maybe only the trademark name has lived on. He really hopes so.

"What line of work are you in?" he then asks.

"None. I've been retired for a couple of years now."

"And before that?"

"Psychologist. For the last twenty years I was with the Security Service."

"What does a psychologist do there?"

"Oh, various things," IB replies evasively. "Mostly criminal profiling."

Mikael knows how forthcoming the Security Service can be. Which is to say, not at all, and IB is no exception.

"After I retired I met a woman in Uppsala. We're a couple but we live apart."

Not much more is said after that except good night, nice to meet you, and thanks for the beer.

It's been a long day. There are even longer days to come. Mikael keeps his clothes on, puts out the light right away and closes his eyes. Not that he thinks he will be able to fall asleep. Yet he does seem to have been asleep by the time Security Service IB closes the compartment door and climbs up to the bunk above his.

"Are you awake?" he says. Mikael does not know what to answer but nonetheless grunts a "Mmm, yes."

"I have a daughter," he says. "We like to go fishing in summer and hunt ptarmigan in winter. She's always been a daddy's girl. She likes doing things with her hands. She was only fifteen when she started her summer job at the cabinetmaker's."

"Well, er, that sounds great," says Mikael in a neutral tone, hoping to discourage the family saga.

"Yes. And there's nothing wrong with her brother, either, but there's something special about Malin. She's, how can I put it, good-hearted. She must have let herself get forced into some infernal business just to be nice. From one day to the next she changed completely. Gave up on school, even though she only had a term to go until she took her leaving exams. Gave up seeing her friends. Wouldn't say what the matter was, not even to her brother. She would go to Luleå or Kalix. Call sometimes and need a lift home. I thought I'd give her a taste of her own medicine. Left her to get back as best she could. When she didn't come home, I lay awake night after night. Kept calling her, reported her missing, searched all over. I got her back for a few days before she disappeared again. A couple of weeks later, a card came from Stockholm. 'I'm fine,' she wrote. 'I'll be back when I'm ready.' After that we had no contact until she turned up in Gasskas again, out of the blue. She signed up for adult education so she could finish high school. Took up hockey and was back to her old self."

The man falls silent. Even the snoring around them stops. The Lappland Arrow bellows like a wild animal through the night and finally Mikael says: "What happened then?"

"She vanished. That was two years ago. Nobody's heard anything since. Not a trace, until yesterday. The police rang. A hunter has found human remains. They think it could be Malin. I'm on my way to give them my DNA."

4

The text message comes in the morning. <Churchyard 3:30 p.m. Be there. Or else.>

Or else what? She doesn't know.

It started just after Mammamärta went missing. Svala opens the door and a couple of heavies barge in. In the past year or so they've added a leather vest to their uniform, with SVAVELSJÖ M.C. on the back. In summer they go around on American motorbikes but now it's winter. They've left their Dodge Ram idling on the street.

You don't get what an honor it is to be allowed into Svavelsjö. It's a club with class. Completely separate from the Harley-Davidson clubs. They do their own thing. For them, the club is the only thing that matters.

And they work as youth recreation leaders, says Svala.

Exactly, says Pap Peder. Honest guys with regular jobs.

Svala sorts Pap Peder's associates alphabetically. Not on the basis of their proper names but chronologically, as a list of letters, depending on when they came into her life.

With the precision of a secretary, she enters them into an exercise book. These two fine specimens of complete shitbag are old acquaintances bearing the letters E. and F.

The exercise book goes back over a period of at least seven years, but it has changed over time. Back at the start she would write things like "E. and I went to Frasse's" or "F. is nice when we're on our own." Now she keeps strictly to the letters and specific distinguishing features. F., for example, has a little mauve birthmark on his left temple. E. has no hair growth anywhere and is unfeasibly fat.

E. pushes her down onto the sofa, sits next to her and puts his arm around her, sweaty armpit included.

"How's my little darling, then?" he says.

"Fine," she says, holding her breath until she has wriggled out of his grasp.

"The thing is," says E., "we have a problem in common. Your mum. You've got your wits about you and we reckon you know where she is."

"I don't," she says, which is true. She does the rounds in the evenings. Starting at Buongiorno and ending at the City Hotel, but nobody has seen Mammamärta.

Recently she has widened her radius. Straight after school she goes down into town. Zigzags between the shops, through the Åhléns store, over to the town liquor store via the library and down to the OK petrol station.

Sometimes she imagines that she has seen her. The relief spreads through her body, as does the disappointment when she realizes she is mistaken.

"Märta owes us money," he says. "A lot of money."

"So?" Svala says. "What's that got to do with me?"

E. pulls her to him again. "Do you remember when we went to the sledding hill in Kåbdalis?" he says.

You do a bit of sledding, then, eh? There are a couple of things I need to sort out. I'll fetch you later.

"I like you, my little darling, you know that, but a debt is a debt. It isn't only income that gets inherited. If your mum's gone missing, then you've got to pay. You can see that, surely?"

"I haven't got any money," says Svala. "And I'm not your little darling."

"No, no, of course not. Big girl now," he says, and pinches her cheek. "But the other thing about big girls is that they're ready for work. You'll have to take over your mum's job, that's all there is to it. Once the job's done, the debt's paid."

Now they are waiting in the car. According to F., the house has no alarm.

"What am I looking for?" she asks.

"What do people keep in safes, darling? Valuables, maybe. Take the lot. We're going to check every single inch of your body, so don't try to be clever. Money, jewelry, anything at all."

Svala closes the back door of the car as quietly as she can and moves cautiously toward the house. A couple of ravens track her from tree to tree, which is good. The ravens will sound the alarm if a car or a person happens to turn up.

She does not know who lives here, but the house and everything around it looks expensive. Not like your average red-painted Gasskas houses with their white corners and rowan hedges.

Below the house, the river sweeps over steep black rocks and goes into free fall. The garden is more like a park. Although autumn has now pushed into late October, there is still the odd rose in bloom.

She passes her hand over the cold head of a lion, goes up the wide steps and rings the doorbell. That is the plan. To ring at the front door. Make sure there's nobody home. Sell raffle tickets for the ice hockey club if somebody is there after all. Break in and follow the hand-drawn map D. gave her.

No one comes to the door. Svala checks it. Locked. She walks around to the back and checks the door from the terrace. That's locked, too. She continues to the western gable end of the house, where there's a door to the cellar. That door is also locked. She runs her hands along the recesses of the outside steps.

I'm doing it for you, Mammamärta. Please let me get in.

The door has a window divided into smaller panes. Big enough for a girl's arm. She pads her hand with the sleeve of her jacket and breaks the glass. Splinters pierce the fabric as she feels around for the handle on the inside. Blood feels sticky on the lining of the sleeve. She finds the key, turns it and lets herself in.

Her eyes get used to the dark. Slowly she goes up the stairs. Takes a long pause by the door at the top of them before she steps out into the bright light of the hall. Spots of reflected sunlight play on the marble floor. She takes off her shoes and gets out the rudimentary map they've given her, a few sketchy marks on the back of an unopened letter from the enforcement officer.

The room is upstairs. Looks as if it's been cut out of a magazine, an "At Home With" feature on Jan Guillou. Taxidermied animals in neat rows. Most of them on the walls, others standing on the floor or on shelves, their empty eyes following her. For the second time she runs her hand over a lion's head.

The safe is in a wardrobe. She pushes aside some suits and kneels down.

Apart from the color, it's like the one in the pizzeria. No digital functions to decode. Only numbers and letters.

She fingers the buttons. Closes her eyes and visualizes herself standing in the middle of a maze. Seen from above, the maze could be interpreted as convolutions of the brain with their rooms and chambers. Most of the passages are dead ends, others lead in circles. A few will lead forward.

All her senses are successively disconnected: smell, hearing, feeling and the part of her sight that looks outward. Her heartbeat slows, her pulse is reduced to a minimum.

If anyone asked, she would say it was logical. Instead of the energy being evenly distributed across the senses and organs of the body, it is concentrated in a single place: the eye's ability to see inward.

The same person would very likely question her theory and dismiss it as a vivid fantasy, but the fact remains: it works. The inward gaze requires no keys. No empirical proof or research team. It is independent of all things worldly and is directed only by the host animal of the eye. In this case, Svala.

The door of the safe gives a click.

She does not move, but listens. The house is still silent. If somebody comes, then that's that. She is only a thirteen-year-old committing a burglary. The worst that can happen is that she's sent away somewhere. Which might not be such a bad idea.

Within a minute or two she's got the door open.

The safe is empty.

No bundles of banknotes, diamond necklaces, tiaras once owned by a queen or gold bars. To be on the safe side she runs her hand around the interior of the safe. As empty as a drained can of Norrlands lager.

She pulls the safe door closed, puts the suits back as they were and searches through the jacket pockets. A few coins, a scrap of paper with a foreign phone number on it, a snus tin, and that is all. She puts the finds in her own pocket and moves on to the desk. It's the same there. Nothing of any value.

They're not going to believe her. In fact they'll claim she's hidden the money in the forest or some other stupid thing.

E. and F. are among Pap Peder's business acquaintances, as he ludicrously refers to them. Along with other losers they constitute a tier in the hierarchy that starts with men with no names and ends with . . . Well, she doesn't really know. People like her perhaps, or small-fry pushers with bumfluff.

She has seen these types for as long as she can remember. She has always done her best to keep out of the way when the sofas are full of drunks and dopeheads, or for that matter, just Pap Peder. The way out has always been the way in. The ability to shut out sounds and voices. And Mammamärta, of course. Like a wall between them and her. Sometimes, anyway.

I'm doing this for you. When it's all over we're getting out of here. You can decide where we're going to live. But don't forget, Svala. I'm doing this for you.

Svala is not vindictive, but she does have a sense of justice. No one should ever underestimate a child. The child collects words. Writes them down. Makes columns for dates, events, names and places and sews the exercise book into a toy monkey's arse.

One day she will find a way to betray them all. Get Peder Sandberg put away. Hatred is unnecessary, it makes people weak.

They say that Svala's real dad is the worst of the lot. A legend, his name only mentioned when something truly diabolical is being described. With every tale he grows taller and bigger. But Svala still finds it hard to believe anything can be worse than Pap Peder.

Not now. But soon it'll be your turn. The thought calms her.

Svala is on her way out of the room when she hears a sound. She stops and listens. Damn. Footsteps coming up. She turns on her heel and hurries back to the dead animal collection. Pulls the wardrobe door closed, slips in behind the suits and muffles her panting breaths against the sleeve of a jacket until her pulse subsides.

The steps are clearly audible now. Quick, decisive steps heading, oh God, for the wardrobe. She sinks into a squatting position, makes herself look small, like something crumpled up, right at the back.

Please, Mammamärta, help me one last time. Then I'll leave you in peace, wherever you are.

Between the suits she catches glimpses of a figure, a man. A memory comes back to her, there in the wardrobe. They have met before, so long ago that she ought not to remember.

Svala is sitting on his shoulders. Mammamärta is happy. They walk down toward the bathing beach. She is given an ice cream. Somebody calls out. She recognizes the voice. The voice is angry. Pulls Svala down to the ground. She hits her head on a stone. A hand grabs her, carries her like a beaten rug toward a car. She screams. Mammamärta breaks into a run. A car pulls away.

She shuts her eyes until the memory fades.

Fingers are pressing buttons, entering the safe code. The door opens. The door closes again and the footsteps recede.

She must get out of this house right now. Let the men in the car do their worst. She struggles out of the jungle of suits. One step at a time she moves toward the stairs. Stops. Listens. The house is empty, she is almost certain. So empty and silent that she . . .

Don't do it. You've got to get back to the car. They'll kill you.

Yes, and if they kill her, who is going to find her Mammamärta?

She returns to the safe. Taps in the code and prays for some booty. Still no bundles of notes. A single envelope. A solitary, stuck-down envelope with something hard inside and her own name on the front: TO SVALA HIRAK. She tears open the envelope. A key. She makes a ball of the envelope and stuffs it into her pocket.

She cannot go back empty-handed. Even so, she pulls down her knickers and inserts the key as far as she can. She is taking a risk. There is no guarantee they won't search there.

Only when she's standing in the hall does she remember her shoes. Neatly placed sneakers that do not belong in this house. He must have seen them. *Men don't do detail. Never ask a man to look for anything. They're useless at it.*

In Mammamärta's eyes, men are useless at most things, but she still seems to need them near her.

If you chuck out Pap Peder, you won't have him getting on your nerves.

You're too little to understand all that, my little swallow, responds Mammamärta, and don't call him Pap Peder. Not when he's within ear-shot, anyway.

Back down the cellar steps. Broken glass crunches beneath the sole of her shoe. She rounds the end of the house. Makes sure the yard is empty and runs toward the car. Slows when she reaches the barn. Tries to catch her breath and gather her thoughts.

There are no alternatives. She will have to tell the truth, that the safe was empty. Things will have to take their course; she is prepared.

5

They have edged the car forward slightly and they haven't yet seen her. E. winds down the window and lights a cigarette.

"Agreed. The kid already knows too much."

She can't hear what F. answers.

"Yeah, but still," says E. "You can have the honor, just not here. Guess we'll drive up to Vaukaliden."

Vaukaliden is the Gasskas equivalent of the Stockholmers' concrete overcoat in Nybroviken Bay. Pressing herself close to the barn wall, Svala moves step-by-step away from the car. She is only a yard or so from a place out of their sight when the car moves forward again and switches its headlights on, full beam.

Her first impulse is to shield her eyes from the glare. Her second is to run. A hare has an undeserved reputation for timidity. On the other hand, it is very good at running away.

The hare turns and jumps over a ditch, trips on a low-hanging branch, gets up again and hurtles on into the forest, up toward the mountain.

A car door slams. Rapid steps across the gritted road. She stops. If she moves, he will see her. If she does not move, he will catch up with her.

The hare runs. A shot whistles past her shoulder. Another misses her right leg by the length of a bobtail.

There's a shortcut through the forest. A track. A connecting path between villages. A route to school for a grandma who was scared of the dark, before the roads existed. Valerian, Saint-John's-wort, marsh Labrador tea, chamomile. That was a long time ago. Perhaps in another life.

Darkness protects, sounds betray. He's getting closer. Twigs snap. There are panting breaths right behind her. Her own lungs fight for air. She feels along the ground. A fallen branch and a loose stone. *Your last chance, little hare. Then you're dead.* F. is slowing. Listening. She waits.

He takes a few steps. Listens again. Soon. Soon. She opts for the branch. Puts the stone down by her foot. Stands up slowly, gripping the branch in both hands. It is heavy. Heavier than she thought.

"Die, you devil, die," she yells as the branch hits his head with the full force of a warrior's hand. Once, and again, and then she has to drop the branch.

And if he does not die? The hare runs. The moon sweeps the treetops. In the distance she can make out the silhouette of Björkberget. She sets her sights on the mountain, runs, stumbles, gets up again. The skirts of the spruces get tangled around her legs. She should reach the path soon. *Run, little hare, if you want to live.* Does it? She runs. Moss turns to bog. It squelches beneath her shoes. She feels herself sinking. The bottomless bog is where the spirits dwell. Horsetail, yellowing sedge, marsh saxifrage, bog myrtle. The water rises to her knees. Her strength ebbs away. Hanging on to a birch sapling, she manages to drag herself out before the water of the bog pulls her down. She negotiates a final ditch and emerges onto the path.

She slips behind the trunk of a pine tree. Gives herself a few seconds to get her breath back. Listens for footsteps, but the forest is silent. Raindrops fall onto leaves and brushwood. The moon wanders across the indigo sky.

Keep your brain busy so you don't lose your way. Scrape off a bit of resin and you've got yourself some chewing gum.

It is too dark to look for resin. She pulls off a few spruce shoots and exchanges the taste of blood for the bitter conifer tang and goes on walking.

There is supposed to be a house around here.

Poor Marianne, she hasn't had things easy, says Grandma.

Why? asks Svala.

She lost her children.

There's a light on downstairs.

"Who's there?"

"Svala," she says. "I was taking a shortcut home."

"Through the forest in the dark, in the pouring rain, are you stark staring mad? In you come."

The woman takes Svala's jacket and hangs it over a chair in front of an open fire. She stuffs newspaper into her shoes and sets them beside the chair.

"Take off your clothes," she says. "Underwear, too."

She waddles into the bedroom and comes back with a pair of worn, faded jeans in a small size and a woolen sweater with leather elbow patches.

"I daresay these will fit. Maybe not the latest fashion, but you'll be dry and warm, at any rate." Something catches her eye and she pulls Svala's arm toward her. "You're bleeding," she says and now Svala, too, sees that it is not just the rain making her sleeve wet. In her mind she is back in the house by the broken cellar window. She must have left bloodstains behind her. Damn. She ought to go back and clean up, but the woman's hands are dry and warm. She smells of bread and the house is benign.

"Doesn't it hurt?" says the woman, scrutinizing the wound, which is gaping open like fillet steak cut by a knife.

"No," Svala says. "Have you got a Band-Aid by any chance?"

"It needs stitches, really," she says, rooting around in a kitchen drawer. She comes back with antiseptic and a bandage. "This is going to sting." She sprays the liquid onto the wound.

Stinging is an alien concept to Svala, but she says nothing. She quietly lets herself be patched up with surgical tape and a bandage on top, probably quite unnecessarily. It feels homey. It is a long time since she has eaten anything. What she would like most of all is to get some sleep.

"Do you live in town?" says the woman. "Maybe you ought to ring home."

"There's no need," says Svala.

"Oh, isn't there?" says the woman. "Whose girl are you, then?"

"Märta Hirak's," she replies.

"Märta," says the woman, stirring the contents of a saucepan. "She was often here as a child. I don't know what happened after that. Anyway. It was a long time ago," she says, and puts a bowl of soup in front of Svala without meeting her eye.

Afterward they spear bits of coffee cheese on forks and dunk them for just the right amount of time to make the cheese soft.

"Do you live here by yourself?" says Svala.

"Yes," she says. "I was even born here."

"It's a cozy kitchen," says Svala, and gives a yawn.

"Lie down on the sofa for a while," says the woman, and Svala does not say no. She is oblivious to the rug being spread over her, as she is to the woman making a phone call and the person knocking at the door a while later.

She wakes to the sound of voices. The woman, Marianne, and another woman are each sitting in an armchair with pieces of paper in front of them and their glasses on.

"But, Marianne, they can't force you," says the younger one, who seems to be called Anna-Maja.

"Those men at the top can do more than you would ever suspect," says Marianne.

"Yes, but not absolutely anything. If you don't want to sell, then you don't want to sell."

"I'm going to live here till I die," she says. "They'll just have to shoot me if they want the land before that."

When they notice that Svala is awake, they go quiet. Gather up their papers and take their coffee cups over to the sink.

"Are you talking about the wind farm?" says Svala, sitting up.

"Märta Hirak's daughter," says Marianne, nodding at her.

"Well, I never . . ." says Anna-Maja. "I haven't seen you since you were born. And yes, we're talking about the wind farm. Not that we've any-thing against it. Not on a modest scale. But people shouldn't be forced to hand over their land. Should they, Marianne?"

"But if everyone says no," says Svala, "what happens then? Wind power has to be better than nuclear, after all."

"Oh yes," says Marianne. "But the forest is big. They're building where they can earn the most money, not where it's most appropriate. I've stayed on here all these years for the quiet, and for the forest, of course. They'll build it anyway, no matter what I say, but I have the right to decide about my own land. Full stop."

"Yes, and amen to that," says Anna-Maja. "I can give the girl a lift home if she wants."

They sit in silence virtually all the way into town before Svala plucks up the courage to ask.

"Do you know my mum?"

"Not really. She's a few years older, but I know who she is. I heard she'd gone missing or something. Or is she back now?"

"What isn't stolen always comes back," Svala says. The thought takes her to the key chafing uncomfortably between her legs. A key that could lead absolutely anywhere, but nobody keeps a key in a safe if it isn't important. Before long she will sew it into the monkey, her very own safe.

"Take care of yourself," says Anna-Maja as Svala hops out of the car.

"Tell Marianne thank you," says Svala. "I think I forgot to say it."

It is past midnight when Svala unlocks the front door of the flat. She cannot get the door open very far and has to squeeze through the crack.

The body is lying on its side. The skirt has ridden up over the varicose veins. She looks neither hurt nor afraid. Svala rolls her onto her back and rings the emergency services. She may have just fainted.

Does she have a pulse? She can't tell. Is she breathing? No. Her lips are a bluish color. Her skin is gray.

"Grandma," she says, shaking her shoulder gently, but Grandma is picking daisies along a well-worn forest path.

Loves me, loves me not.

"I think she's dead," says Svala. "In fact I'm sure of it. My grandma isn't in her body anymore. Maybe you could come and fetch her?"

"Fifteen minutes away," says the emergency services hub.

She looks into the hall mirror and sees the room reflected behind her. The Swiss cheese plant on the TV table where there is no longer a TV has tipped over. *Repot it in spring and give it some food. You've got green fingers,* says Grandma. Not that hard when they only have one potted plant.

Someone has been here. She follows the trail from room to room. Clothes pulled out. Wardrobe doors left wide open. Everything that was in its place is now in heaps on the floor.

The monkey is perched safely in its corner. Her anxiety subsides. Everything else is chaos, but it can be tidied up. They came looking for something and now Grandma is lying dead on the hall floor.

She stands the plant up. Gathers up the DVDs and books lying strewn around the living room floor and shoves them under the sofa. Closes the doors to the bedrooms and checks the line of sight from the hall.

The state of the place might make them contact the police. The police are the last people she wants coming here. They would take her away somewhere. She's only a child, after all.

But I'm not a child. Am I, Grandma? She strokes strands of her graying black hair into place and straightens her clothes.

She knows so little about her maternal grandmother. Still less about her wider family.

"To hell with them," says Mammamärta when Svala asks. "They've got their business and we've got ours."

"You ought to teach her the language," says Grandma.

"What would be the point?"

"So she can choose for herself."

But Svala cannot work out what she would be choosing between. So she stops asking.

"Is there anyone you want us to ring?" the ambulance man asks.

"There's no need," says Svala. "My aunt's on her way."

"Loneliness" is a strange word. So ugly and yet so beautiful. She locks herself in her room and pulls the chest of drawers in front of the door. Two stories up. If worse comes to worst, she'll have to jump.

The night passes uneventfully. As dawn breaks she dresses in warm clothes, locks the door and sets off on foot toward Björkberget.

In the cover of the trees she passes Marianne Lekatt's house and continues to the start of the path.

A black grouse flies up from its hiding place. The ferns are nodding with nighttime frost. At the ditch she scans the bog. She finds the driest tussocks where knotty birches are clinging to dry ground and jumps her way across.

She lets instinct guide her, keeping the high ground behind her and the sun to the east. The heel of a boot is the first thing she sees.

Do you remember when we went to the sledding hill in Kåbdalis?

He is lying on his back. His head is a mess of blood and crushed bone. He still has the gun in his hand. First come the crows, the wolverines, the rats and the raptors. Last of all come the maggots. She works the gun out of his grasp, turns and sets off for home.

Still no sign of genetic freaks in cowboy boots and leather vests. She makes tea and a couple of sandwiches. Retrieves the exercise book from the monkey's backside and enters a new column under F.

Deceased.

6

With the train being late, it is almost light when Mikael Blomkvist gets off in Älvsbyn. He walks toward the station building, keeping an eye out for Pernilla.

She has a red car of some sort. There's no sign of any red car.

Something jeep-like turns into the parking area and brakes to a halt beside him, its window wound down.

"Well, hello there, Father-in-law," he shouts. "Jump in, for Christ's sake."

Mikael shoves his case onto the back seat. No Lukas. Just Henry Salo.

"I had some things to get in Älvsbyn anyway," says Salo. "And Pilla forgot the boy had a dental appointment. She says hi. Fantastic weather, even though it's October. How was the journey? Did you get any breakfast?"

"You call her Pilla?" Mikael says.

"Yep, like the alpine ski racer, remember her? They look very alike, don't you think?"

"Not exactly," Mikael says. "She's rather . . ." He has no time to say more before Salo pulls away on a sightseeing tour that lasts all the way to Gasskas and covers everything from species of pine, motor vehicle inspection sites, military areas, old girlfriends and ski slopes to fishing waters and the best berry-picking bogs.

At the falls at Storforsen they stop for a coffee. When they are back in the car, he casually throws in the fact that this is where they're holding the wedding.

"The chapel is the building you saw down by the river, but we're having the ceremony up by the falls. If I get to decide, that is. And the reception will be at Raimo's Bar. You know, where they filmed *The Hunters*. We've rented out the whole place. Pilla would rather we were at the hotel, but Raimo's is, er, more like the real thing, you might say. At my wedding we're going to eat, drink and dance. Do you want to drive, by the way? I've just got this one. Brand-new Benz, not some ghastly electric. Shit like that doesn't cut the mustard up here. Well, except for work, where you have no choice if you don't want the eco-nazis after you."

"No," says Mikael. "You drive, you know the way."

Salo gives him a sideways look.

"You do have a license, I suppose?" he says. "Pardon me asking but, you know, Stockholmers." And he laughs again.

Just before Gasskas, Salo slows down for reindeer in the road. A little further on, a group of people in high-vis vests have assembled in a parking area.

"It's the Missing Persons lot," says Mikael. "Who are they looking for?"

"You tell me. Probably some drugged-up kid who's lost his way in the forest."

"Are there so many drugs around here?"

"Do berry pickers shit in the woods?! But we've been spared gang shootings, at any rate. It's too bad that the police can't catch a few beardy dudes and send them back to Talibanland."

"Aren't you confusing two things here?" says Mikael.

"No, I'm not, and don't tell me it's Swedish kids running around with guns loaded with live ammunition."

"Most of them are born in Sweden," ventures Mikael, but Salo interrupts him.

"It's a fucking epidemic," he says. "And the police just stand there like morons and don't get it. It's obvious all they need to do is lock up the bastards and throw away the key."

When Mikael cannot bring himself to answer, Salo changes the subject.

"Welcome to Gasskas, I suppose I should say. The little town with big vision."

"Is that your town slogan?" asks Mikael.

"No, but you might be onto something there. We should have a new slogan. A competition maybe, with swanky prizes. Free tickets to ice hockey or dinner at City Hotel."

"The little municipality with the big boss," suggests Mikael, already tired of Henry Salo.

"That's not bad at all." Salo chuckles. "Here are the new public baths. We had the official opening only last week. And on your left we have the holy of holies."

"The church?"

"The municipal council building. This is where everything starts. The heart of the community."

"The Salo Building, you mean," says Mikael with a sideways glance at Salo. He is tempted to wonder what Pernilla sees in him. The man is a virtual parody of himself.

"That's given me an idea," says Salo. "Much obliged! This weekend we've got the opening ceremony of the indoor market. It hasn't been named yet, so what do you reckon?"

"Not the market hall but the Salo Hall?" says Mikael.

"You've got it! Without me it wouldn't have happened. Heh," he adds, "I'm only having you on. Our ventures involve a whole host of people, not only me."

"Like in the mine?" Mikael asks, and Salo's face lights up.

"Exactly," he says. "Exactly. You've read about that, I assume. A great project that could make a real difference to the area. The bedrock is rich in rare earth metals. And not just the bedrock but the slag heaps left from earlier mining operations, too. The whole world is short of that stuff and surely it's better to deal with the problem on home territory than to buy the crap from developing countries where people die like flies in the mines? Yes," he says, answering his own question. "We have to hope the eco-nazis come to their senses. I mean, we can't let billions run through our fingers for the sake of a few mangy reindeer."

"No, you wouldn't want that," says Mikael and lets his thoughts wander to IB. One man gives his daughter's hand in marriage while another searches for his missing child.

He had intended to say something to IB that morning, but by then he was in a hurry to get off the train. He proffered a dog-eared business card bearing the *Millennium* logo and suggested they meet up for a beer sometime. The sort of thing you say because it sounds good but is likely never to happen.

7

Marcus Branco doesn't like the cold but he likes the view.

"Open," he says, and the door opens. His wheelchair glides out onto the terrace and he takes several deep breaths.

Below him the expanse of landscape stretches away. In the distance, the bare tops of the high fells stick up like innocent hillocks. Streams meander like knots on the river as it gently flows on its crooked way east.

It is not by mere chance that the house is located here. He, they, spent a long time looking for the perfect spot, the perfect mountain. He imagines Hitler must have thought the same thing as he stood on the Obersalzberg making plans for his Eagle's Nest. The sightlines had to be open. The rock had to be suitable for bunkers and underground escape routes.

The bunker. Almost thirty thousand square feet divided between four halls linked by tunnels, steps and a number of side rooms, plus the land, have been in his ownership for several years now. The house, blending ingeniously into its mountain surroundings and as invisible to the world as the bunker, is a later addition.

These days the Branco Group is as white as its name implies. He has done his years of slog. Built up a comfortable fortune that will soon start to breed like salmon on the ladder, and all within legitimate areas. Well, sort of. Some money is simply too ludicrously accessible to resist.

He glides back in again. It soon gets cool around the legs. Nobody would be so bold as to point out that he doesn't have any.

In a little over an hour, the Knights will have their morning meeting. This is not the first time he has laid out his plans. Today he just has a few figures to show them. He takes the lift down to the conference room and puts the water on for tea.

Here, a long way underground, the military would probably know exactly how deep, twentieth-century Russophobia is on its way to being transformed into the twenty-first century's *high-tech dream of a green revolution*.

Unlike Boden Fortress, a little way to the northeast, these rock shelters are unknown to the outside world. No itchy-fingered museum curators have tinkered with the locks to let the public in. Nor has the National Property Board lovingly tended it as a cultural monument. It is a hidden place. Condemned as of no further military interest and sold off to a farmer in the early 1950s for forestry, 5,200 acres which he tended until his death.

The new owner of the property, Marcus Branco, is now sitting in an exact copy of Stephen Hawking's wheelchair feeling very well disposed toward life. To the extent that he can afford to reward himself.

He feels stirrings in his groin. It has been some days now since the last one had to walk. Well, not exactly walk. She'll be worse at walking even than he is right now.

One by one, the Knights assemble around the semicircular conference table. Mild as Jesus he lets his gaze sweep over them. Yes, the inner circle: Järv, Varg, Björn, Ulf and Lo. Wolverine, Wolf, Bear, Fang and Lynx. His trusty gang from Långgatan in the Umeå suburb of Teg.

Branco loves giving lectures. It is speaking the words that brings them to life.

"Before, it was the paper mills. Now the stink is the stale sweat of stressed council officials and politicians suddenly having to deal with multinational mega-companies knocking on the door of Norrbotten County. But it doesn't smell bad. It smells of money! Gasskas and the surrounding area provide the perfect conditions for us to be as successful as we deserve. The European market is working well. Industrial concerns are ticking over nicely. But there is a storm cloud on the horizon and you all know what it is: energy supplies."

He glides across to a flip chart and folds over the first page.

Within him there is a mental process that has been going on for many years. The part of the country that formerly went by the name of Norrland has suddenly acquired a clearer identity and Marcus Branco wants to know why.

Gone is the derogatory description of the taciturn, solitary, hard-working, hooch-drinking bachelor who refuses to move south. It has been replaced by the overexcited council official literally promising the world gold, and green electricity. And the world is catching on. Perhaps it started with the building of the Facebook server halls in Luleå in 2011, but that is not important; now everybody wants to go there. A rumor goes around that Facebook gets its electricity for virtually nothing and suddenly the lemmings migrate north.

One of the world's largest battery factories is built in Skellefteå. At around the same time, all the steel firms and mines give notice that traditional steel production is to be phased out and replaced by so-called green steel. Instead of coke they will use hydrogen to separate the liquid iron from the oxygen. It remains to be seen whether the CEO of Swedish Steel will drink the residual product, which is not only iron but water.

Branco looks at the Knights. "Are you keeping up?" he asks.

Yes, of course.

"When the directors of the various companies have expounded in several miles' worth of columns on the importance of the state supporting fossil-free industry, which they are in complete agreement with, they'll all be left trying to answer the same question: what's going to fuel all this? Because they're all greedy consumers of electricity. And we're not talking a few percent above the total generation of electricity, but needs that far exceed what we today consider the top limit. Electricity, what's more, that will have to come from solar, wind and water power."

Branco folds back a few more pages and bounces his pointer across the figures. Varg stifles a yawn. Lo tries to smooth a broken nail against her trouser leg.

"Sweden's total electricity production is 166 terawatts, divided between seventy hydroelectric, fifty-one nuclear, fifteen cogeneration, fifteen solar power and twenty-seven wind power, plus a few other minor power sources.

"This new industry, so-called green industry, needs an additional fifty-five terawatts in round figures. The question is where to get them from.

"Nuclear power is beyond the pale, so forget that.

"Hydroelectric power has been expanded as far as it can go, so forget that.

"Solar power in a country like . . . forget that.

"Which leaves wind power. Because the wind does blow. Sometimes."

He returns to the central problem: "The large-scale industry that's going to supply the world with batteries and construction steel still needs to find fifty-five terawatts of wind power. That is to say, twice as much as Swedish production currently."

"Excuse me," says Järv, "but where do we come into the picture? If wind power's so unreliable, why would we put our money into it?"

"I was just coming to that," Branco says. "If there's no wind, then there'll be no electricity, no matter how many wind turbine power stations get built. And when the wind blows, the electricity has to be used right away, because it can't be stored." He pauses briefly for effect. "But hydrogen can. So when the wind is blowing hardest," he goes on, "we can manufacture hydrogen and store it—yes—in our excellent underground bunkers."

"Hydrogen is one of the world's most flammable gases," points out Lo. "I assume you've done a risk assessment?"

Branco folds back another sheet and writes "Risk Assessment?"

"Nobody can assess the risk entirely accurately because there is no comparable large-scale storage anywhere else in the world," he says. "But someone has to be first. The technology isn't new, it just needs scaling up by a few hundred thousand geometric cubic meters."

"The whole of Norrbotten would be blown to kingdom come if things went wrong," says Lo.

"There are plenty of ways to die," says Branco. "Being blown to smithereens can't be the worst."

The land, the underground complex, the situation, the time we live in with its energy crises and rising electricity prices. This is where Branco has identified his chance to make himself legitimate in a way that society will thank him for.

He will get into electricity production, and not any old electricity, but wind power, which will make him an even more select person. The kind of person who takes radical social responsibility by investing his private fortune in the future. A visionary, a likable individual who would be admired by everyone around him.

But he has no intention of taking it that far. Marcus Branco has got a long way by being nonexistent and invisible.

Norrbotten's gas and hydrogen will be sold like gold to the highest bidder. The world is standing in line. As foul and filthy and evil as ever, and stuffed full of green arguments that even the most basic advertising agency could come up with.

Branco, too, has a way with words.

"Those Swedish politicians, with the Socialists and Greens taking the lead, have stood on their heads to satisfy the environmental movement. Nuclear power gets decommissioned and up go the windmills. But before the international companies that own the majority of the wind farms have even built them, the electricity's been sold abroad. Deal done and paid for. Although it looks good on paper, of course. Good little Sweden, protecting the dirty world around it. Viewed strictly from a climate perspective, it's better for clean electricity produced in Sweden to be used for the benefit of countries that normally burn gas or coke. The fact that it's the Swedes themselves who have to pay for the party through inflated electricity prices because there simply isn't enough electricity in the country for them as well . . . Well, that's a minor matter."

Branco is not political in any way. He gets worked up about how dumb people are, that's all, not least the politicians. For his part, he sees any kind of energy crisis as nothing but positive. The day work starts on his wind farm construction project, he'll be the one who sets the rules. It's his, as far as he's concerned at any rate. Ask Henry Salo whose wind farm it is and Salo answers. What a patsy. And speak of the devil, it must almost be time for their one-on-one.

"For us it makes no financial difference if the attempt to store vast amounts of hydrogen goes up in smoke," says Branco. "If we miss out on one opportunity, there are thousands of others standing in line. If we don't want to sell Power Purchase Agreement raffle tickets to the mega–power companies, there are alternatives."

The municipal councils with their front doors wide open to foreign businesses who are queuing up for a plot of land in return for unlimited access to electricity, even if some of them should probably only be let in through the basement. If at all. This is where Marcus Branco gives a final polish to his arguments. The Branco Group is basically a security company, after all. Few are as well placed to dish the dirt on countries and their inhabitants as Branco and his Knights. He himself would function as some kind of green-dipped Saint Peter at the Pearly Gates. Some people simply don't get in.

Obviously there are problems. Stroppy landowners and plotting competitors, but nothing that cannot be solved by capital. Marcus Branco has thought of most things and feels more than satisfied. Then there are other parts of the plan that he is not yet prepared to share, not even with the Knights. The thoughts are itching inside him like lice. He can't get them out of his brain. They make a deep impression on him, touch a part of his life that he doesn't control but that can be summarized in a single word: *revenge.*

The stars will be aligned for the next phase, too. The signs are already visible, there is no doubt about it. Branco is not alone in having grown tired.

"OK," says Ulf. "That sounds like a long-term plan, but what do we do about the rest?"

"Svavelsjö takes over all distribution in the north of Sweden. They've shown themselves reliable in other situations. We speak the same language, as it were."

"Yes, I know," says Ulf. "The Svavelsjö guys are the least of our problems. Sandberg's a bigger one. He and his crew haven't raised any objections to the merger, but what we're hearing from the bikers is that he's freelancing in the eastern areas."

"Clearly getting greedy," says Branco, and swings his wheelchair irritably. This is exactly the sort of thing he wants to get away from and he thought he'd achieved it. Grubby problems created by insignificant pieces of shit. Parasites who never generate, only consume.

"In that case, I think we'd better tidy him out of the way," he says.

"I'm happy to take on the job," says Varg. "Be nice to get out for a bit."

"Unfortunately we still need him," says Ulf. "Don't forget, he's king on his home turf."

"Then we'll have to talk to him," says Branco.

"We've tried that. He was accommodating and promised to fold his existing turf into Svavelsjö, which he duly did. But meanwhile he's been reaching new agreements with the Finns. Maybe the Russians, too."

Now Branco is not just irritable, he is angry and he needs to think. His best thoughts are born out of anger, or his worst, depending which side you're on.

"Has he got a woman?" he says.

"Most likely."

"Kids?"

"A stepdaughter."

"Are they close?"

"Unclear."

"OK," says Branco. "Find out everything about Sandberg's cutesy family life and there'll be a way around this."

8

"Decent shack you've got here," says Mikael, looking up at the old wooden house. "Is this Salo's parents' place?"

"Hardly," says Pernilla. "He grew up in a hut in the forest. His mum still lives there, in fact. Not all that far away," she says, pointing to an area of dense coniferous forest that should have been thinned years ago.

"Have you ever met her?"

"No. They have no contact. She wasn't much of a mother, as I understand it. Not the same way you were a useless father; it was more a mental illness thing. Henry doesn't want to talk about it. And I've stopped asking."

Mikael dusts off a wooden bench with the sleeve of his jacket and sits down. He cannot decide whether there is any accusation in what she says. Or whether it's just a bald statement of fact. He could hook into the conversation, tell his side of the story. But he has no idea where he would start if he did.

"Things feeling OK generally?" he says. "The wedding and so on?"

Pernilla takes her time to answer.

"Until a few weeks ago it all felt fine." She looks out over the river rather than meeting his eye. "I mean, we've been together for a while now. Henry is how he is, as you must have noticed, but there's more to him than that. When we met I wasn't in a great place. Henry was like a door opening to let the light in. Without him, I don't know where it would have ended. I barely wanted to live. He took care of me in a way no one ever has before. I feel safe with him."

"So what are you doubtful about?" says Mikael, and gets only a sigh in answer. "Have the two of you talked about it?" asks Blomkvist the therapist. The king of all relational conflict anxiety, the man who likes to leave the room when the uncomfortable questions start.

"Of course. He says he's stressed, but then he always is. Though now he's not so much stressed as paranoid. He asks me weird questions about people I meet at work. Checks the door's locked. Keeps watch out the window. I don't know what to make of it," she says.

"It sounds as if he's scared," Mikael says.

"I think it must have something to do with his wind farm project," she says. "It's crazy, if you ask me. Nobody wants that complex so close to town, but he's managed to get the politicians on board. That's the most important thing for Henry: everything connected with the municipal council. It's almost as if he's running his own business."

"Yes, he does seem incredibly tied up in it. But what about you? How's work?"

"Depends which work you mean. I started a new job in the spring."

"So you're not . . ." He realizes he scarcely knows what she does. Some kind of youth work, possibly? Or music?

Bingo, Mikael Blomkvist.

"I'm standing in as a welfare officer at Youmo. We'll have to see how long it lasts."

"Sorry, where?"

"Youmo. Young People's Guidance Center."

"Oh yes, that," says Mikael.

"Never mind that," says Pernilla. "Do you want to see the pool out back? We had it put in last year and we must have used it all of twice."

She links arms with him and leans on his shoulder.

"It's great to have you here, Dad."

Dad finds he has tears in his eyes. She usually calls him Micke.

They round the corner of the house and Pernilla stops short. There's broken glass on the steps down to the cellar door and on the grass above.

"Must be a bird," she says. "Odd that Henry didn't mention it."

Mikael picks up the shards he can see. A couple have dried blood on them, but he says nothing. It could just be a bird.

Cranes flying south. The sun on its way down. The air is growing cold.

"Listen," Pernilla says, "here comes the school bus."

The boy's body has no time to feel shy. Before he knows it, he's in Mikael's arms.

"Grandad! There's something I want to show you."

Together they take a shortcut down to the water.

"I think I'd better hold your hand so I don't fall in," Mikael says.

The boy's hand is warm.

Mikael holds it tightly, all the way down to the riverbank.

9

Henry Salo at home is a different person from the one who met Mikael off the train. There's no gush of words as he takes him around the house. Pernilla has already shown him the ground floor and the room where he'll be sleeping. Upstairs the house is divided between a private bedroom area and Salo's office.

"Take a seat," he says, "and you can taste the best whisky in the world. I got it from a business acquaintance. It's not the Scots who win prizes these days, it's the Asians."

Mikael sits down on a dark green chesterfield and sips his drink. Whisky is not his thing, he prefers beer, but it slips down well enough and Salo pours him another.

"What a room," says Mikael, his eyes scanning the walls. "It looks like Leif G. W. Persson's place. I didn't know you hunted."

"You bet I do," he says. "Hunting is a good way to open doors. But you have to be sure to hunt in the right company."

"How do you mean?"

"Hunting and business, business and golf. A skillful hunter or a golfer with a low handicap is always at a premium. Everybody wants to hang out with a winner—that's just the way it is, no matter whether you're buying or selling."

"Which category are you in yourself?"

"If you mean as municipal council chief, it's a seller's market. Everybody wants to come here. I've got a long list of enterprises just waiting for the go-ahead. Notionally we can pick and choose among all these multinational mega-companies who've spun their money globes and put their finger on Gasskas."

"Well, that sounds great," says Mikael. "Is it your charisma that attracts them?"

Henry Salo's boastful side is waiting in the doorway. It only needs to be called in.

"I'm handsome alright," he says, flashing his most blatantly handsome smile, "but there are businesses here in Gasskas that are even more attractive."

"And whose are they?"

"It's watts, not whose. Electricity," says Salo with a chuckle. "Without our unlimited electric power resources, Gasskas would be like any other landlocked dump, devoid of industry and jobs. Electricity in Norrbotten is what oil was to the Norwegians. And now that the world has painted itself into a corner with overpopulation and the eco-nazis are screaming that the end of the world is nigh, Norrland has emerged as the new Klondike. All it'll take is for Putin to choke off the gas supply and its good fortune will be complete. Electricity out in the world costs the shirt off your back, but not here. Everybody wants to come to the promised land of hydroelectric and wind power. And what's more, it often means they can stamp their products as environmentally friendly, too."

Mikael has obviously been aware of rocketing electricity prices and greenwashing, but he hasn't taken a close interest. It is not a subject that immediately shouts "Scoop!" Nothing about the climate movement is sexy. It is solid, holier-than-thou and full of lobbyists.

"Unlimited electric power resources," he says. "Is that possible?"

"Absolutely," says Salo. "Not without investment, of course, but yes, in principle they're unlimited. We drew a winning lottery ticket years ago, when Vattenfall dammed the river and paid compensation to the municipality. The hydroelectric power is stable but like everyone else we naturally have to complement it with other things, like wind power. I'll take you out to the proposed wind farm site one day soon. If everything works out, it'll be able to claim the title of biggest in the world. I promise you'll be impressed. The groundwork outside Piteå can kiss its own arse."

They get no further because Pernilla is at the bottom of the stairs, calling that dinner is ready.

"You go on down," says Salo. "I've got a few calls to make and then I'll be with you."

Pernilla has set out napkins and the best china. The chairs are upholstered. There are lighted candles on the table and the chandelier is dimmed.

"You've done it so beautifully," says Mikael. "I feel like a guest at some grand manor house."

"I liked our old kitchen better," says Lukas. "It was nice and snug."

"Snug but poky," says Pernilla.

"It was just right for us," says Lukas, helping himself to potatoes.

"He means our flat in Uppsala," Pernilla says. "The move here hasn't been very easy for him."

"I still don't want to move," says Lukas.

"But we live here now, you know that," says Pernilla, pouring wine into Mikael's glass.

"I can live at Grandad's," says Lukas.

"But your mum would really miss you," says Mikael. There is anger in the boy's voice. Mikael's not convinced Pernilla can hear it.

The sauce is spicy and the meat is tender. They've had the starter and half the main course before Salo comes to the table. He doesn't want any of the starter and takes only a few mouthfuls of the casserole.

"Delicious," he says as his phone rings again. "Bloody people—can't they ever leave me in peace?"

He listens but says only, "Good, thanks, so that's agreed."

His face smooths out, he says yes to dessert and kisses his fiancée on the hand.

"Did you know Pilla was such a good cook?" he says, and Mikael has to admit yet another embarrassing gap in his knowledge of his daughter. She is his child, his only child as far as he's aware. But he knows a good deal more about his female acquaintances than he does about her.

He puts his arm around her chair. Somewhere down there, buried deep beneath layers of neglect, there is a tenderness. An urge to get to know her properly. If she wants. He can't tell.

"So, the big day approaches," says Mikael. "Will I know any of the guests apart from my sister's family?"

"You know Mum, of course," says Pernilla. "Other than that, it's mostly people Henry knows, except for a couple of friends of mine. We tried to keep it to a reasonable number."

"We don't want it getting too expensive for you, Father-in-law." Salo grins and thumps Mikael on the back.

Lukas slides off his chair and over onto Mikael's lap.

"Will you read to me?" And Mikael obliges.

He must have fallen asleep reading to the boy and wakes to the sound of voices.

Voices shouting over each other. Howling words like slaps in the face.

"I'm so goddamn tired of your nagging," says Salo.

"But how about taking a bit of notice of us for a change?" Pernilla snaps back at him. "The only thing you can think about is your damn wind farm."

A door slams. Then another. Lukas turns over in his sleep. Mikael listens.

When the house has fallen silent he tucks Lukas in and goes downstairs.

Salo is sitting on his own at one end of the dining table like an abandoned king.

"I thought you were asleep," he says.

"Where's Pernilla?"

"Sorry, we don't usually have rows. Not so other people can hear, anyway. She went out for a bit. Needed a breath of air, I expect."

"Maybe the two of you should think about the boy," Mikael says. "He found it hard to get off to sleep. Children don't like rows, do they?"

"Don't you start sounding like some interfering old woman, too," says Salo, getting to his feet. "Come on, time for you and me to take a sauna."

10

The sauna is on the bank of an inlet of the river. From the sauna building, a jetty leads out into the water. A rowboat is waiting to be put into hibernation for the winter. The wood-burning sauna heater has been lit for a couple of hours. The intense warmth hits them like a hot mist, contrasting with the cold light of the full moon outside. Mikael sits on the mid-height bench. Salo takes the top one, opens a couple of cans of beer and passes one to Mikael.

"What happened to your hand?" he asks.

Salo twists and turns his left hand, as if discovering for the first time that he is missing two fingers.

"When I was a kid," he says, "we didn't have central heating or running water. Barely any wood, either, come to that. Not that there was any shortage of forest, but my dad was a lazy bugger. He was the foreman of a lumberjack team but not even up to making sure his own family had enough wood. He was away all week. From Friday to Sunday he was drunk. 'Make sure you look after your mother,' he would say each time he left. Other than that, he didn't say much, good or bad. We did the best we could, my brother and I. Felled small birches with a handsaw and axe. Gathered sticks whenever the ground was clear of snow and begged floor sweepings from the sawmill. But it still didn't get us very far through the autumn. Sometimes the electricity was on. Then Mum would yank up the heating as high as she could, but we generally had to freeze. The summer I was turning ten and my brother nine, Dad had got his hands on a pile of timber and had it dumped in our yard. He was away on a job up in Ligga and wouldn't be back until later in the autumn. We were left in charge of crosscutting the timber and then chopping it into half-yard lengths. A neighbor helped us with the crosscutting. He even brought over a wood splitter and would probably have done the rest of it for us, too, but he got sick. We spent a large part of the summer splitting wood and stacking it in the cowshed. We only had a fraction left to do when a fucking twig snagged on a chunk of wood and dragged my hand with it into the circular saw. Thanks to my brother diving for the emergency stop button, I didn't lose my whole hand. He stemmed the bleeding with his shirt and put the fingers in a bag of ice. Then we got on our bikes and went down to the local hospital. And they took us to Boden by ambulance. There they were able to sew a couple of the fingers back on but somehow social services got wind of the situation at The Holt. Mum was admitted to the psychiatric clinic. My brother and I ended up in different foster homes. That was the last time I saw him."

Mikael moves down to the bottom bench. The sweat is running down his thighs. Salo stays on the top, unfazed by the heat. He beats streaks into his skin with the birch switch and wonders why southerners never learn how to do saunas.

"Here," he says, passing down a birch switch.

"I'm good, thanks."

"Well, beat me instead, then," he says, turning his back to Mikael.

The twigs leave white impressions on the hot skin.

"So you lost your mother, your brother and your fingers all on the same day?" says Mikael. "That must have been devastating. Even later on, I mean."

"You can say that again. Most of all being without Joar. I missed him so much it settled in my fingers like a phantom pain. It still hurts sometimes, even now. But," he says, throwing on a scoop of water, "I ended up with Mr. and Mrs. Salo and I was alright. They had no children of their own. When Dad died of a brain hemorrhage a few years later, they adopted me, even though Mum was back at The Holt. I don't know what she thought about it all. I met her once afterward. We ran into each other outside the shop. She put down her shopping bag and looked at me as if I was a piece of filth. 'You should have taken better care of your brother,' she said. Then she was gone. And it's just as well," says Salo. "She wasn't much of a mother, after all."

Yet he remembers what happened next as if it were yesterday. He ran through the forest and did not stop until he reached the rocky outcrop above the house. From there he could see her coming on her bike. She walked it the last little way up the hill, the Coop carrier bag dangling from the handlebars.

As for him, he had his hand on the sheath of his knife. Pulled it out and crept from tree to tree until he was right up close.

She was sitting on the front porch. The carrier bag had toppled over. Some green apples and a plastic tube of pea soup had rolled down the steps. In that moment it was not his mother he saw. It was a human being. His mother was already dead. He slowly put his knife away and ran back to the village.

"Pernilla says she's still alive," says Mikael. "Haven't you ever thought of looking her up?"

"No, never."

"And your brother, do you know what happened to him?"

"Not really. He kept being moved between foster homes. I tried to find him, but the trail went cold. Maybe he didn't want to be found. Anyway, I've put my childhood behind me. The years at The Holt, at least," he says, and drains his beer. "But there's one thing I can't get over," says Henry, studying his maimed fingers. "It's that we never got to enjoy the heat from all that chopped wood."

"That's a sad story," says Mikael, struggling to breathe. His skin is turning sausage pink; he badly needs to get out.

"What kind of a weakling are you?" says Salo in a different sort of voice. "Only kids sit on the bottom bench, but OK, never mind. It could be time for a dip."

Outside, the weather has changed again. The moonlight has gone. It is raining. It is cascading like a bathroom shower and Mikael does not bother with the dip. Salo takes the steps down into the river. In seconds he has vanished into the darkness.

Underwater there is no room for reality, neither the present kind nor what is in the past. One day he will disappear without a trace, like the eels heading for the Sargasso Sea. But not tonight. He still has things to do. He swims a couple of strokes and pops up on the other side of the jetty.

"Christ," Mikael says. "You scared me. I was beginning to think you'd . . . I couldn't see you."

"Bullshit," Salo says. "They always find you. If nowhere else then in the sluice gates come the spring."

Mikael is shivering. The sauna opens its warm bosom. He risks the top bench and finds a fresh beer in his hand.

"How about you, then, Mikael Blomkvist? Who are you? The celebrated journalist or a boy who doesn't want to grow up?"

"Maybe both," says Mikael, "or nothing at all. Professional successes come with sell-by dates. No man on the street remembers yesterday's news. And *Millennium* doesn't exist any longer. Well, only as a podcast, but it's not the same. I'm wondering whether to do something different."

"Like what?"

"I don't know," he says, and honestly he doesn't. Chasing news is his only skill. Acquaintances of his are making fresh starts as gardeners and sommeliers, programmers or carpenters, but he has no secret calling or special interest to propel him into anything. He isn't even a closet crime writer. He's just a journalist. A bloody lonely one, too, he has to admit, since the permanent editorial team dispersed and went freelance.

So now that he has started this mental list of all the ways in which he's useless, he might as well continue.

The fact that he lives on his own is no great surprise. He falls in love. She falls in love. She wants more. He wants less, and then it's over. Friends, family and so on, it's the same. All the second chances he's offered and doesn't take. People he lets down. Feelings he hurts. Not to do deliberate harm, but because there's a higher purpose, a calling that always takes precedent.

It is only *Millennium* that genuinely means anything. Without *Millennium* he is nobody. A bewildered has-been, paralyzed into inaction and refusing to move with the times. A denier of progress. A sad sack reading the evening paper with other sad sacks over a beer at the Loch Ness Tavern to make him feel less lonely. A nonentity.

He doesn't know if it's the heat or just the mood of the moment. But here and now, in a sauna five hundred miles from home, in the company of an individual who veers between macho talk and the most naked honesty, he begins to weep. The worst of it is that he cannot stop.

He weeps as Salo chucks on more water. Weeps and moves down to the middle bench. Weeps so hard he can barely drink his beer and weeps until there are no more tears to shed.

"Good. Just let all that shit out," Salo says, and thrashes him with the birch twigs. "A man with a sauna never needs a goddamned psychologist!"

11

The next day Salo wakes up on the sofa in his office, fully dressed. Someone, Pernilla, has spread a blanket over him. If only she would stop being so hellishly kind and be a little more like himself. For the sake of balance. But no. If a creature is bleeding, she will protect and nurture it. Cooks great food, listens without interrupting, looks at everything as soberly as the teetotaler does the Communion wine.

I am a bastard. The bastard gets into the shower and tries to remember the night before. They were in the sauna, but then? He was just going to have one last drink. Then . . . Christ . . . he sent a long text message to Märta Hirak. When she didn't answer, he sent another and then another. In the end he called her switched-off phone and left a voicemail. He can't remember exactly what he said. The bastard punishes himself with a cold shower, which at least dispels the worst of his hangover.

In a couple of hours' time he will meet the third of the parties showing serious interest in the wind farm. A global company with a Swedish owner, Marcus Branco, about whom he does not know very much.

Obviously he has familiarized himself with the company's financial situation, scrutinized its results and discussed references with the council's legal officer, Katarina da Silva, but until now their contact has been through intermediaries.

There are many Marcus Brancos in the world, but none of them that fit this context, discovers Henry Salo when he googles the mother company's CEO. According to the company presentation they've been given, he's an anonymous figure, successful in various lines of business, property and security among them. A ghost, never seen in pictures or self-promoting on social media, which is not unusual in itself. But it is a little odd, all the same, that he's not able to dig up anything at all about the man.

He dresses carefully. Combs his hair back like Prince Daniel and goes downstairs to the kitchen.

"Good morning," he says, and kisses his fiancée on the head.

"Good morning," says the hack. The boy looks away.

"If you're heading into town, could I come with you?" Mikael continues.

"Sure," says Salo and checks the time. "Five minutes."

"So," Salo says once they're in the car, "were you hoping to see the tourist sights of Gasskas? In that case, I thoroughly recommend the mining museum. It's a proud part of Gasskas history."

"I need to buy a couple of things and go to the library."

"Hah, Pernilla's clearly a chip off the old block. She must have the all-time borrowing record, for crime fiction at any rate. I prefer biographies myself. Right now I'm reading one about Elon Musk. What a guy!"

"It's mainly the newspapers I want to read."

"No need to go to the library for that. We get *Gaskassen* delivered."

Salo drops off Mikael Blomkvist and drives on to the council building. He zigzags around people who need to discuss things with him; they will have to wait. Märta is still there like a persistent headache and a stomach in urgent need of the toilet. He dissolves three Treo Comp in a glass of water and tries to collect his thoughts ahead of his meeting with Marcus Branco. He would have preferred to have the whole project group with him, or da Silva at the very least, but Branco has been clear. Nobody but the two of them.

Britta's Treehotel is half an hour away, in Harads. To be on the safe side, he has booked a private room, lunch included, but that plan disintegrates the instant he arrives. Marcus Branco is a wheelchair user. In place of legs there are stumps that he has neither disguised with prostheses nor covered with a blanket. A dark-skinned man in a wheelchair. An adopted child, possibly. Does he even speak Swedish? Salo's stomach is calmed a little by the man's physical disadvantage.

"Nice to meet you," he says, and apologizes. He had no way of knowing, after all.

"Don't give it another thought. I rented out the whole place," says Branco, and enters by way of the access ramp.

There's nothing wrong with his Swedish, certainly. Even Britta seems to have made herself scarce, though it is lunchtime and the place is normally full. The table is laid for two. The food is under domed covers.

Branco parks his wheelchair at the head of the table and takes out a sheaf of papers. Maps, sees Salo, and the prospectus. As if to show that he, too, has done his homework, Salo produces a folder, a pad of paper and a pen bearing the council logo. Onward and upward. *Come on, Henry. Onward and upward.*

Branco unfolds the map on the table. Apart from a small section on the western side, he has striped the entire area with red felt pen.

"What's this?" Salo says.

"The area where Branco Group is going to construct the wind farm," he replies. "Most of it, as you know, is land owned by forestry companies or the municipal council. I assume the other owners of the land have given their consent?"

That old hag and those fucking Lapps, thinks Salo for the umpteenth time since waking up that morning.

He clears his throat and opens his own folder.

"As things stand, there are three companies, including yours, who will be able to divide the wind farm between you. We've drafted a proposal for how it will be divided up," he says, drawing his finger across the map. "Under that proposal, your company would be in phase two, with a planned construction start date of 2025."

"We want to come in as the sole interest," says Branco, pushing the folder back to Salo.

Salo looks out the window. Sleety rain runs down the glass. A squirrel jumps to another branch. A workman's van comes slowly up the hill.

He is tired. Bone tired. He tries to muster his thoughts and say the right things. Branco Group has capital, but so do the Finns. The Dutch could buy the whole of Norrbotten and not even blink. If anybody pulls out, the Chinese are next in line. He has to put his cards on the table. Play a little dumb, perhaps.

"I understand you, but the council members have made a formal decision, based on the advice of our own economists, that the area be divided into three. We make that clear in the prospectus. If Branco Group is still interested," he says, taking out the map of the geographical division, "then this is the land that will be at your disposal." He runs his finger around the boundary.

"Do you have a family?" says Branco.

"Why?"

"I was just asking. Purely out of courtesy. I have no family myself. Branco Group is my child, my parent, my sibling and friends. It matters immensely for us to get the undivided rights," he says. "And while we're on the subject, have all the owners of the land agreed?"

"Not yet," says Salo, "but it's only a matter of time."

"A little bird whispered in my ear," says Branco.

They look at each other across their folders, maps and briefcases.

"It told me there's a woman living on the most crucial stretch of land who refuses to hand over her property. Same with the reindeer herders, the Hiraks. They claim the wind farm will disturb the reindeer's grazing territory. What are we going to do about that?"

Salo gives up. He cannot summon the energy to go on pretending. "The old girl will give in, I promise," he says. "We just need a bit more time."

"And the Lapps?" says Branco.

"Well," says Salo, "I'm sure they need money, same as everyone else."

"It sounds as if it's going to take some time, but I have a suggestion," says Marcus Branco, borrowing Salo's pen. "We'll take this part," he says, indicating essentially the whole area, even if he generously chooses to broaden the western zone slightly. "The others will still have room for at least fifty wind turbines each. If you agree, the municipality won't have to worry about either the woman or the Sami. We'll handle that ourselves. They'll be as keen on the idea as Catholic priests on choirboys."

It seems an odd choice of simile. The situation is starting to develop in a direction Salo had not reckoned with. If it was only about Branco, he would have agreed right away and got the problem solved. He wouldn't even have had to know how they dealt with Hirak and Lekatt.

Personally, he couldn't care less who pays for the windmills, but the Finns and Dutch have been in on the project from the beginning. Established companies with a long-standing involvement in the Swedish energy market, unlike Branco Group, which no one has heard of. Salo has more power than most council bosses can dream of, but bypassing the politicians is out of the question. Not even a democratic decision at the next lodge meeting would alter that. And even if he could get Olofsson and the gang on his side, transparency, eco-nazis, competition laws and other crap would put a stop to Branco Group's plans.

"There is an upside," says Marcus Branco, and he scribbles something on a piece of paper.

"A lot of zeros," says Salo.

"Directly into the pocket of your Dressmann suit."

Salo folds the paper and puts it into his jacket pocket. "Nice try," he says. "I think we'll leave it there for today. I'll discuss the matter with my colleagues and get back to you shortly."

"Good," says Branco, "but you didn't answer my question."

"Which was?"

"Whether you have a family."

Salo stands up and puts the folder in his case, pushes his chair in and looks down at the man in the wheelchair.

"Everyone has a family," he says.

"True, so we have to take care of those we have."

Salo is on his way out when he suddenly turns and goes back to the man in the wheelchair.

"If that was a threat, I just want to tell you that I don't like threats. I will do my best with the division of the land, but threats won't get you into the VIP lane. Because even if you threaten me and my family, it's democratically made decisions that determine the outcome, not me personally."

Salo, dear boy. I may have no legs, but my arms reach a long way. If only you knew how much a security company can dig up from the past.

Which is roughly what Salo himself is thinking. He has neither the present nor the past on his side. Soon he won't have anything else on his side, either.

He drives back into town. Picks up a Maxi Meal on the way and shuts himself in his office. He has hardly taken the first bite when Branco makes contact again. This time by proxy. A pleasant woman, at least initially. A well-toned body and shamelessly attractive. Definitely a model to his taste.

"Sorry to interrupt you in the middle of your lunch," she says, "but I thought I ought to bring you the good news right away."

"I'm glad you people have reconsidered," he says. "I mean, it's advantageous to you, too, for the wind farm to be divided between various companies. Anything can happen. Next year's election, for instance. Or a sudden overproduction of electricity that brings the prices down."

"Our decision remains unchanged," she says. "Ninety percent to the Branco Group, five to each of the others. And that's generous. We could have insisted on the whole cake, you know."

Who the hell does she think she is?

"So what's this good news, then?"

"Check your bank account. You won't be disappointed."

"Have you put money in my account?" He reaches for his Coke, in need of something for his dry mouth.

"We have. Enough to settle old gambling debts with crippling rates of interest and a bit more besides."

"But . . . how can you know . . . ?" His head is spinning. There is a rank smell of sweat from inside his jacket.

"Don't worry, I promise not to blab to Pernilla."

Pernilla.

"No, you can't do that. I don't take bribes. I never have and never will. My credibility. My reputation." He is too tongue-tied to go on and his stomach loosens again.

"See it as a gift from friends," she says, "even if the police might not share that view. Or the municipal council, for that matter."

"The police are precisely the people I'll take this to," he says, and his stomach settles a little.

"We wouldn't recommend it. Nice boy you have, by the way. Very well behaved. More people ought to teach their children manners, don't you think?"

Lukas.

"What the hell is it you really want?"

"Nothing impossible. Only ninety percent of the land and the agreement of all those who currently own it."

12

The balance is 614,305 kronor. Salo stares at his account page on the bank's website. There are council officials who have had to resign for a few free sessions at the golf club. Should he throw in the towel right now? Transfer the money to Lucky Strike, take a gamble and hope to win? Make himself scarce, leave the country?

Pernilla and Lukas.

He simply can't. He has to find a solution. Problems exist to be solved. Isn't that what he always says in team meetings? No problem is so large that it cannot be solved. Let's celebrate that. Slap on the back and pat on the backside.

This is an entirely different league. *Do you have a family?* He has to go to the police. The police and the executive committee.

You have seven days. The clock is ticking.

He is seeing da Silva in the morning. That will be a good start. She's smart and she knows how to keep quiet. And will doubtless suggest a solution. But if she doesn't keep quiet? She is the council's legal officer, after all, not his.

No. He can't. He's a fly swimming alone in the soup. The rise and fall of a council boss. He's not going to let the hack enjoy getting stuck into that. Salo is a man of action. Aside from an initial bit of bad luck in the genetic lottery, which is not a unique problem, things have gone inordinately smoothly for him and he intends to keep it that way. Millions in project funding are jingling into the municipality. With a firm and expert hand he's able to pull most projects off, sometimes in spite of the negativity of the politicians. Sooner or later they tend to come on side. If you're not in, you're out. Compromise is the name of the game. Some padel courts in exchange for an indoor riding center, another indoor ice rink for a cultural center, eighteen holes on a Bronze Age Sami site for a market hall. Yet this is all peanuts compared to what's waiting around the corner. If Salo gets what he wants, at any rate.

The plans for the mine lie further into the future. He has time on his side, time to turn public opinion to his advantage. High inflation, rising interest rates and spiraling house prices are not exactly political Viagra, but the more people are worried about their jobs, the closer he will get to his grand dreams. A mine creates job opportunities. At least on paper. The fact that it ultimately benefits foreign labor is hardly his fault. If the unions can't be realistic in their wage demands, then English with an Eastern European accent will be the official language in all branches of industry. That's not his problem. No, the problem with the mine is the problem that always afflicts everything up here: reindeer and eco-nazis.

He pours himself a small whisky. A solitary ice cube clinks against the crystal.

Back to reality. He's got to think clearly. To focus on the future instead of the present is tempting but deceptive. The politicians are one thing, as are the council officials. No contracts have been signed yet. They'll follow his line and let the Branco Group get what it wants. He just needs to fine-tune his arguments a little. That leaves the owners of the land. The old hag and the bloody Lapps.

With a certain symbolism, the window that has been ajar slams shut. The rain drums on the windowpane. The wind is getting up.

It's a bad idea. An extremely bad idea, in fact, given that he's been drinking, but it's the only one he can come up with.

He heads off in the car and turns left a few miles before Gaupaudden.

Just below the house he slows down and rolls down his window. The puffball heads of the cotton grass are drooping in the rain. The field scabious is spreading across the patch of farmed land. The barn roof has fallen in. At the edge of the field, the scythe-bar mower stands like a skeleton in the dusk.

There is movement inside. Salo goes up the steps and rings the doorbell. The bell doesn't seem to work. He knocks instead and takes a step back.

When she opens the door, they stand there in silence.

"And what might somebody like you want?"

"Only to have a little talk," he says.

"Well, come on in, then, so the heat doesn't escape."

She runs water into the coffee pan. Puts in a few scoops, but hesitates over the last one as if reluctant to waste too much coffee on an unwelcome visitor. "Let me guess," she says, before he has time to answer. "You want to persuade me to hand over my land to the wind farm. But I'm not going to. If it's the last thing I do in my life."

Which it very well might be.

"You've made it nice for yourself here," he says, looking around the old-fashioned kitchen with its cast-iron range and log basket. Rag rugs run across the floor. The windowsills are crowded with geraniums. *Suddenly he is there in the doorway. Just roused from sleep. Hungover. His eyes are bulging in his florid face. His eyes scan them. Eeny meeny miny moe. If they run she will be left there alone. If they don't he will catch them all.*

She slings the cup, milk carton and sugar bowl onto the table. The teaspoon rattles against the saucer.

"I've no buns or cookies," she says. "Poor pensioners have to ration their treats. But I don't suppose you know anything about that; you'd rather spend your money on ice rinks and mines."

"It's the politicians who decide that, not me," he says, trying to cast himself in a better light.

She gives him a look. *Don't come here and bullshit me,* it says. *I know all about it.*

"I'm surprised you hadn't come sooner," she says. "You only live a stone's throw away, don't you?"

"Out at Gaupaudden," he says. "Been there a couple of years now. My wife—that is, my fiancée—has always dreamed of living in the country. She's from Uppsala originally. Our son's nine and likes fishing, so a house by the river is ideal for us."

He babbles away about the family. Confidences. Isn't that what women like?

"You said you were here about the land?" No superfluous chitchat here.

"That's right," he says. "Everything's in place for the construction work to start. Europe's largest wind farm. Loads of job opportunities. Money rolling into the area. Unlimited electricity."

"And so on," says Marianne Lekatt.

"And so on, if it weren't for the fact that you're making things difficult."

"I'm not making things difficult," she says. "I don't want to live in an industrial complex. I want to hear the wind in the trees and the sound of water from the river. Not the whir of eleven hundred windmills. I'm completely within my rights to decide for myself. And however keen you are to build the wind farm to make yourself look like a big shot, that has nothing to do with me. I live here. I intend to live here until my dying day. And I will not allow a wind farm on my land."

"You'll still hear the windmills, though," he says. "You only own a tiny patch of all this."

"It's not just me refusing, you know that," she says.

"It's you and Hirak against the world. And you can hear how it sounds. Your share would earn you at least a hundred and fifty thousand kronor a year, possibly more. Just think what you could do with the money. You told me yourself that it isn't easy to get by on a pension."

"Don't you get what I'm telling you? Some values can't be traded for money. Anyway, I think you should go now. If that was all."

How easy it would be. A pair of hands around her scrawny neck. The body in the boot of the car. Dump it in the falls, as soon as it gets dark. No, even better. A log, a blow to the head. Then into the falls. No suspicion of murder the day she floats up, just an everyday accident.

And the Hiraks? The farm shared between three siblings. Märta. Has he got to kill them, too?

"Thanks for the coffee, then. I hope you'll think about it even so. I know what land means, but at least consider the future and all the children who'll have to grow up with the climate crisis we've caused. Do it for them, if for no one else."

13

"What's your name?"

"Why do you want to know?"

"Just wondering. It was nice talking to you. See you another time, maybe." He puts his hand on hers. She removes it just as swiftly.

"Don't think so," says Lisbeth Salander, and she gets to her feet the moment the FASTEN SEATBELTS sign is turned off. She pushes past a family with children and joins the stream of people going through the gate.

She's traveling light. A few changes of clothes are crammed into her backpack along with her laptop and assorted chargers, her exercise gear and a pair of sneakers, the leather cracked and the soles worn smooth. If the need arises, she'll have to buy things along the way. An unseasonably warm October sun greets her. The air is clear. She can breathe.

As soon as she has checked in at the hotel, she logs into the Milton Security intranet. Answers a couple of pointless e-mails from an exceptionally dim colleague. Perhaps not surprising; this is a person employed to keep paper in order. She throws in "Have a nice weekend" and assumes Carina Jönsson's will be as dreary as usual.

Small talk has never been Lisbeth's strong point. But since she's been part-owner of the company, she's become aware of increasing demands on her social skills. Especially if she has to go in on a Monday. Staff trickle in, pour coffee and say more or less the same things as they did the previous Monday.

For Carina Jönsson, life seems to revolve around being conspicuously normal. Picking mushrooms, cleaning the house, going to the theater, making a special breakfast, going to IKEA. She is fond of the notion of treating oneself. *I treated myself to a new dress. Sometimes you have to treat yourself to eating outside. It's important to treat yourself to some of the good things in life.*

"As if you know anything about life. I was born older than you are today," mutters Lisbeth.

Personally she has nothing to contribute to the post-weekend conversation, either to Carina or to any of the other nerds. She's a lone wolf and she likes it that way. In the eyes of the Milton staff, it's self-inflicted. They have stopped asking whether she wants to come along to *Lord of the Rings Live* or the tech meetup at the Hilton. She doesn't say no to be unpleasant. Decoding the human factor is not like identifying a data breach. It requires something different. The ability to read between the lines, perhaps.

With very few exceptions, relationships with other people take too much energy. Most people who give something want something else in return.

Every day looks the same. She works, and when she isn't working she exercises or sleeps. She has no specific partner. No children. No pets. Not even a potted plant. So she doesn't even try. Has nothing unnecessary to say about herself, beyond the fact that she works and exercises.

"Are you still going to that boxkicking?" asks Carina in such a friendly tone that Lisbeth has to give a friendly response. "It's called kickboxing," she says, and she can't be bothered to say that she's now doing karate and it's all the fault of that goddamned Paolo Roberto. Not because she cares who he sleeps with, but when you're a hero in a trafficking racket one minute and a frequent customer of sex workers the next, it just gets to be too much.

This weekend, however, she's doing something completely different. Something basically one hundred percent against her will.

She looks in the minibar. No Coca-Cola. Opens a beer instead and drains it in one draught. Her head spins in the nice way that only a beer downed in one can produce.

A hundred percent against her will—is that true? Even if she counts all the logical reasons for not wanting to get on a plane to some dump in Norrbotten, she still has to take into account the fact that she's actually here. No one has forced her. No one has put a gun to her head or lured her here with fat rewards. So there's something inside her driving her choice.

Isn't that precisely what she loathes about people? Emotion-based decisions. Lack of logic.

Give her mathematics any day. Quite apart from its anxiolytic effect, which beats Valium by a mile, it can fill an uneasy mind with outwardly simple theses that could still take an individual human thousands of years to work out.

Lisbeth has got caught up in the missing link in Goldbach's conjecture. His assumption that every even number greater than two is the sum of two prime numbers is perhaps true because no one has succeeded in proving the opposite. But it could also be false. The answer would then be found in the presumably infinite chain of prime numbers, not within a capricious human psyche.

So she's looking for patterns. Spending nights and sometimes days in the clarity and safety of numbers. Not to get one over on Goldbach. No, it's the very possibility that he could be mistaken which is significant. And if the counterargument were to manifest itself, against all her expectations, then it would be utterly pure. Liberated from human fancy and subjectivity. The truth is a safe sequence of figures that arrange themselves in line, one after the other, until one jumps out.

It's that damn psychotherapist's fault, she thinks. Kurt Ågren, whom she has swiftly rechristened Mrs. Ågren.

With his smooth voice, his clumpy, hand-thrown pottery teacups and his unfeigned empathy, he lures her into a state of openness. Makes her tell him things. Things that were buried long ago and ought not to be reawakened.

Afterward she feels totally drained. Picks up a pizza from Little Harem and goes home to sleep. On the dot of four she is woken by the voice of anxiety asking what she said and why.

Mrs. Ågren thinks it's time for Lisbeth to step out of her comfort zone, as he calls it. Even though he is by now aware of quite a few of the uncomfortable zones in which she has found herself and still does.

"That's exactly why," he says. "The world isn't as evil as you think."

The world is more evil than you can imagine, Mrs. Ågren, and in the end she couldn't do it. Something would have to be reordered inside her. Memories would have to be erased and replaced by new thoughts.

The first session is a disaster. He just sits there waiting for her to say something. When she doesn't, he makes tea. They drink tea in silence. The clock on the wall is the only sound to be heard. Ticktock for forty-five minutes. Then she pays nine hundred and fifty kronor and goes home and e-mails him.

"Give it one more try," he says. "You're the one who decides what you want to talk about, not me."

At the next session he makes tea again. His Knulp slippers creak as he balances his way across the parquet with the tray. She gets to choose which chair. He asks her why she chose it.

"So my back isn't to the door," she says.

"Explain," he says. And like a river when the ice melts in spring, the words come gushing out of her. Over a year ago now.

I don't go north of my own free will, but I go. I don't go to therapy of my own free will, but I turn up. Not because the world is good—it's fucked— but I have to go.

And that is where she runs out of self-psychoanalytical steam. To have time to compose herself and to talk herself out of it, she has come up a couple of days early. Paid a lot of money for the hotel's only suite, which has actually fulfilled her wish for sparse furnishing, bare walls and a hard bed. Right now, she is feeling inclined to retreat. Check out, catch a plane south and return to normal life in Fiskargatan.

Her phone vibrates on the table. She recognizes the dialing code. Nobody but public organizations and old people call from landlines, and she doesn't know any old people anymore. She accepts the call but says nothing, letting the voice go through its hello, hello before she says, "Yes."

"Oh, there you are, Miss Salander," says the woman and introduces herself as Elsie Nyberg. "How are things?"

"Fine," she replies.

"Good, good," says the parrot and asks if they can meet up briefly.

"The meeting isn't till the day after tomorrow," says Lisbeth.

"I know, but something's come up," the woman says. "I'd prefer not to do it over the phone. Would it be possible for you to come here?"

"No," says Lisbeth, "but we can meet at the hotel." She runs her hand through her dirty hair and sniffs her armpits. If it was for anybody else, she might take a shower.

14

Lisbeth Salander pours herself a free cup of coffee from the thermos in the lobby. It's lukewarm and has a metallic smell, but it eases the pressure in her head.

She sits down in an armchair. No frumpy social services types as far as the eye can see.

There's no mistaking them, thinks Lisbeth as she surveys her surroundings. The suits are crowding around the bar, a gang of sports jackets are playing shuffleboard, office blouses are having after-work drinks and . . . There she is, on her way in through the first set of entrance doors. A female exemplar of the social worker species. Indeterminate age, gray-blond hair, a worry line across her forehead. A Kånken backpack, the original model, with a folding umbrella sticking out of the side pocket. Around her neck an ID lanyard she forgot to take off when she left the office.

When the woman stops, looks around, spies the after-work blouses, smiles and heads over to them, Lisbeth is taken aback. So shocked by her own misjudgment that she doesn't have time to register the man who has materialized out of nowhere and is now holding out his hand to her.

"Erik Niskala," he says. "Elsie Nyberg didn't feel well so I'm filling in for her. Can I get you anything?" he adds, and suggests a beer.

Lisbeth nods. A few minutes later a beer and some peanuts appear in front of her.

Niskala hangs his overcoat over the chair and sits down, with some effort. He is big and overweight. The shirt buttons are straining around his belly beneath his cardigan, but his eyes are sharp. She notices that, too.

"Well," he says. "I had to be briefed on this case in rather a hurry. And cheers, by the way, welcome to Gasskas. This IPA is brewed locally and they even sell it at the liquor store. Give it a try and you'll detect distinct notes of pineapple." He looks at her over his tankard and takes a few good swigs. Wipes the froth from his beard and ends with an, "Ahhhh, I've been looking forward to that all day. An ice-cold beer in a proper glass."

Then it's as if he catches himself. The undesirability of drinking at work. The fact that he has business of a formal nature. He fishes his glasses and a plastic folder out of a battered leather briefcase and leans back. Puts on the glasses and then takes them off again. Leans forward as far as his belly will allow and regards her with the sort of look that a teacher might give a pupil who has done something unexpected. Not necessarily good, not necessarily bad.

"It's about Svala," he says. "Your niece, if I understand rightly."

"Ronald Niedermann's daughter," Lisbeth replies. "She and I have never met."

"No, I realize that," he says, "but you're down as Svala's emergency contact. With no name or phone number. It's evidently taken them some time to find you, but you're here now."

She tries to probe him on how they went about it, but he doesn't know.

"I'm just a basic child welfare officer," he says, "not some hacker."

Lisbeth takes a few gulps of beer, too. Bloody pulse. Bloody headache that won't let up. And bloody Niedermann, who should never have had a child before he died. How was she supposed to know? And even if she *had* known, would it have made any difference?

It was him or her, it was that simple. He was the one who came after her, not the other way around. Apart from that last time, perhaps. It's still a favorite memory. Niedermann's gigantic body, hoisted up in chains like a masochist at some S&M club. His rage, then his empty eyes and some mumbled German. The sound of motorbikes approaching. Lisbeth riding back to town, tasting freedom on the dark red Honda.

Conclusion: Of all the bad things she has done to other people, Niedermann's death is up there with the best. She regrets nothing. Not even for the sake of an orphaned child.

"Do you know anything about her father?" says Niskala.

"No," says Lisbeth. "I never met him."

"So you don't know how long he was on the scene?"

"No," she says again.

Lisbeth Salander pins Niskala with her stare for so long that he is forced to look down.

"Alright," he says, fingering the file. "I'll get straight to the point. We need an emergency placement and Svala has suggested you."

"Me?" says Lisbeth. "I can't look after a child. I won't do it. I agreed to meet her, but that was all." Right now she has no recollection of why. "She's got a grandmother. Isn't it best that she lives with her?"

"That's exactly why we had to see you today. The problem is, Svala's grandmother died this morning. It was the girl who found her."

"Shit," says Lisbeth. "What did she die of?"

"I don't know," Niskala replies. "A heart attack, presumably. She was lying dead on the hall floor."

"Shit," she says again, but she's thinking, *Fucking hell!* If there was a chance of wriggling out of all this, that's now gone. Of course she could say no. Social services would come up with a foster home and Lisbeth wouldn't have to give it another thought. But social services is too damn good at messing up. They'd probably place the kid with some local pedophile.

"Naturally, we're working on finding a permanent family home for her," says Niskala.

"How long?" says Lisbeth.

"Hard to say. We've got various suitable families in the area. It could all happen quite fast."

"No," she says. "I just can't. I have to get back to Stockholm," she adds, which is a lie. She comes and goes as she wishes. She has no need of an office to do her job. But a child. A teenager. No. She wouldn't even agree to a stick insect.

He opens his folder to leaf through his papers.

"There's nothing wrong with the girl," he says, looking for a suitable passage to read out, but then he changes his mind and passes the whole file over to Lisbeth. "Take the evening to think it over," he goes on. "It's meant to be a confidential matter, but I daresay we can make an exception," he chuckles. "You're in the security business, after all."

15

Katarina da Silva is already in the office. She sets out the coffee cups and cuts slices of bun loaf.

"You think these people like to eat buns?" says Salo.

"Cinnamon softens people up. We might well need that. Do you know what they want this time?" she asks. She is not exactly happy about having to interrupt her weekend for Henry Salo's business acquaintances.

"An assurance that I'm on their side, I presume."

He's told her about the meeting at the Treehotel and Branco Group's ambition to appropriate the bulk of the wind farm and leave only small areas for everyone else.

He does not mention the threat, if a threat is what it is.

"I'm glad you're here," says Salo. "It all looks good on paper, but there's something about the owner, Marcus Branco. I think we need to sound him out. One of our conditions is for some of the electricity to stay in the region, otherwise the whole thing is off. Gasskas is attractive enough already because of the hydroelectric power, but for future projects to go ahead we have to be able to guarantee much greater capacity."

"I know that already," says da Silva. "What do you know about the Branco Group—the company itself, I mean?"

"No more than what has already emerged. Basically it's a security firm that's invested in mines, property and the manufacturing industry. Center of operations in Umeå. Plenty of capital."

At five minutes to one, Salo goes to the main entrance to let them in. On the dot of one o'clock, Marcus Branco comes gliding in with Lo in his wake.

"A new face," says Salo, pretending they've never met. "Welcome to Gasskas Municipal Council building. I thought we could use the conference suite. Please come through, and then we'll go to the right."

"And you're the lawyer?" says Branco, looking at da Silva.

"I'm the council legal officer. Retired. I come in when needed. Like today," she says, untying the tape from around the folder. "We've discussed your proposal, brought it before the politicians and concluded that the original decision still stands. Three operators dividing the land equally between them."

Branco says nothing. He pauses theatrically and looks out over the town, the river, the police station and the enforcement service. He's not annoyed, merely expectant.

"Excuse us, ladies, I'd like to talk to Henry Salo alone," he says eventually.

There's a feeble protest from da Silva. Then she gets up and turns to Lo.

"We can go and sit in the staff room for a while, I suppose."

"I understand you know Märta Hirak," says Branco when they're alone.

"Yes," Salo says. "Why?"

"We want to talk to her about something, but we haven't been able to track her down."

"I heard she disappeared, left town," says Salo. "But what's it got to do with me?"

"We've done a bit of investigating. You and Hirak were an item. A teenage love affair that came to a sorry end."

"That was thirty years ago. Get to the point."

"If I understand my source correctly, you're still seeing her?"

"I still don't know what you're driving at," says Salo.

"My source is pretty sure you still care about her. Maybe more than you do about your fiancée. It would be a great shame for you and for her if anything happened. Wouldn't it?"

His entire body, every single sense, his intuition and everything else is impelling him to get up and yell: *Out of my life. I don't give a damn about your fucking wind farm. Leave me in peace!*

"I want to make this very clear," says Branco. "Guarantee the land, otherwise Hirak will be gone for good. And then there's your official family, too, of course. Your future wife, Pernilla, for example. And it's lovely, isn't it, that Lukas's grandfather—Mikael Blomkvist, isn't it?—is so attentive to the boy."

"Thank you," Salo says, "that's enough." One of the few things he credits himself with is the ability to stay cool when his soul is on fire. Now he's supposed to judge the circles of hell. Weigh one person against another.

Märta Hirak . . . They wake in the Treehotel's Bird's Nest room. Hours have passed, though it feels like minutes. He is still lying there, his legs entwined with hers. If he holds on to her tightly enough, perhaps she will stay.

"I've got to disappear for a while," she says. "I'll be in touch."

Two words are all he has had since. *Miss you.* He is still living on them.

"You can do what you like with Märta Hirak," says Salo, "it's not my problem. I'm afraid I can't help you. Rules are rules. If that's all, then perhaps we can finish here."

Get the guy out before he says any more.

But Marcus Branco just glides off without thanks or goodbyes.

16

Erik Niskala takes his leave and Salander stays in her seat. She opens the file and closes it again. Tries to marshal her unruly thoughts but gives up. She stuffs the file inside her leather jacket and goes to the bar.

The place has been steadily filling up with people celebrating the start of the weekend. This time she orders a Coke with lots of ice. She has had only one sip when some stupid idiot bumps into her and the glass is knocked to the floor.

"Oh dear, I'm so sorry, are you soaked? Wait a minute, I'll get some paper towels," says someone.

Someone is a girl with red hair and red nails. Red nails bitten short, notes Lisbeth, a leather jacket pretty much like her own, black jeans and the same boots.

"Oh dear," she says again. "We must buy our clothes in the same place, you and I. What are you drinking?" she asks. "It looked like rum and Coke. Let me buy you another one."

"Sure," says Lisbeth.

"Jessica," says the girl, holding out her hand.

"Lisbeth," says Lisbeth.

"You're not from around here, are you?" Jessica asks. "Or I would have seen you before."

"Right," says Lisbeth. "And you?"

"Yes, I'm from here. Never got any further than Skellefteå. Met my husband there. He was from Gasskas, like me, and when we had children we moved back home."

"So you're married," says Lisbeth, to have something to say.

"Divorced."

They stand in silence for a while, watching the bartender as he shakes cocktails with muscled arms beneath the sleeves of his T-shirt.

"We were at school together," says Jessica, nodding toward the Tom Cruise look-alike. "There are only two types in this town. Sporty types and those who go along to support them."

"Which type are you?" asks Lisbeth.

"The second, I guess. My ex is an ice hockey player. But I've had enough of that world. Maybe I'll have to invent a new category. Workaholic, for example. Or stressed-out mum. Which type are you?" she asks Lisbeth.

Avenger, hacker, murderer. "Workaholic," she says. "And sporty. I exercise and do my job, that's all."

"No kids, then?"

"No, no kids."

"Or man?"

"Is it obligatory?"

"Definitely not," says Jessica. "A cucumber works just as well. At least they don't play hockey."

"Or talk," says Lisbeth.

"Want to dance?" says Jessica. "The dance floor's downstairs."

"Dance?"

"Yes, you know, wave your arms in the air and swing your hips a bit. Saves you having to talk, as well. Come on," she says, and takes the clip out of her hair, letting it fall loose down her back.

It's not that Lisbeth hates dancing. It's just that it's been such a long time.

The music is loud and the dance floor cramped. No great stylists on display. It's more like a group ritual with a booze-fueled crowd of happy people jumping up and down, shrieking along to the chorus.

You know where pike swim in the reeds
And the fox sneaks on the porch
And the hooch is on the bubble in the garage
That's the place I damn well want to call my home

In the billowing crowd, Jessica grabs hold of Lisbeth and shrieks along, too.

Because who wants to live in an anthill
Where the people are so stuck-up and so evil

And they panic when they see a flake of snow fall
Shitting bricks as they all flap at the mosquitoes

Her hair swings into Lisbeth's face. Stroboscopic flashes turn the red to violet and make the contours of her face as sharp as slates.

Like a witch, a fiendishly tall and sexy witch. Lisbeth pulls her closer. Takes in the scent of dance sweat and perfume, the pressure of her hip bone, the freckled lower arm and hand firmly clasping her own. But as the music subsides and the crowd disperses, Jessica takes a step backward. She pins her hair into its clip and says she needs something to drink.

They have a drink. Jessica banters with Tom Cruise and Lisbeth can do nothing but stand on the margins like a forgotten child.

Of course she can do something, though. She can go up to her room. Read through the file and work out how to say no. No no no. She doesn't need a teenage girl in her life and she doesn't need any other girl, either. And yet there she stands until Tom Cruise is claimed by other customers and Jessica turns to her.

"You're still here," she says. "I'm going home now, but it was fun meeting you."

The intimacy of the dance floor is gone; there is dismissal in Jessica's voice, but Lisbeth takes a chance. People avoid risks, she thinks. They rarely follow their instincts. Sometimes they need a bit of help along the way.

"I'm staying at the hotel," she says. "If you want, we can have a drink in my room and I'll ring for a taxi later."

Jessica gives her a long look. She gets out her phone, sends a text and drinks the last drops of her wine with what looks like ceremony before she answers.

"No," she says. "I've only got my babysitter until twelve."

17

It is a quarter to five when a white Transporter pulls into Fridhem Refugee Center for unaccompanied children and young people, just north of Gasskas.

It's not here to make a delivery. More of a collection. Filling an order, to put it simply. Issued barely an hour ago.

A couple of children of primary school age are playing ball against the wall. The daytime staff are just leaving and Frej Aludd has the evening shift. A perfectly ordinary day. A Friday.

The ball lands at Varg's feet. He puts one foot on it, whisks it up into the air and kicks it as far as he can.

"Nice shot," says Björn. "Give those little brown bastards something to run for."

They walk to the reception area. A cube with curtains drawn across the windows and a door that generally stands open.

"Hello there, Frej, it's been a while. You working overtime?"

Frej instinctively cowers behind the desk. Closes his laptop and pulls the phone toward him as if caught out by burglars.

"What do you want?" he says. "I told you there wasn't going to be another time."

"But we're here now," says Varg, casually shuffling the files on the desk.

"If you don't leave, I'll ring the police," says Frej.

A sense of relief, a lightness spreads through Varg's body. The situation is under control, so now he can just lean back and enjoy himself.

"I doubt that," he says. "Not unless you want us to contact your wife. Although, oh yeah," he smacks his lips, "we've already spoken to her. She says to tell you she'll keep the house and demand sole custody of the children. Bye-bye, kids. No great loss for them, I guess. Who wants a pedophile for a father?"

"What do you want?" says Frej in a voice that is cracked and pitiful.

"Same as last time. No more and no less. Preferably under eighteen, and a black girl."

"I suppose you know how wrong this is," Frej pleads.

"No more wrong than you being paid for them."

"You've got to stop," says Frej. "I'm the manager, not a pimp."

"You can always try explaining your bank statement to the police. Chop-chop, we haven't got all night. Where should we start?"

The younger children's rooms are nearest to reception, then the older boys and at the far end the older girls. That is where they're heading, with Frej in the lead. A reluctant Frej, dragging his feet to win time.

Varg smiles as he walks along just behind him. Frej Aludd's body is screaming for a way out. His spidery legs are tripping over his own feet and his bulging hamburger butt looks just too good to resist. A perfectly aimed kick pitches Frej several yards forward to land on all fours like a dog.

"Please," it whimpers, "don't kick me. I'll do what you say."

"There's no other way out," says Varg, hauling him up from the floor. "So get on with it."

He knocks at the door of the first room. A voice calls, "Wait."

"Wait for what? We're going in." The girl has just come out of the shower and does her best to cover herself. Her eyes dart anxiously to Frej.

"Sorry," says Frej. "We didn't mean to come barging in like this."

"Too skinny," says Varg. "Next room!" He yanks open the door without knocking and slams it shut in equal haste.

"Is this a refugee camp or a fucking AIDS clinic?" he says, twisting Aludd's arm. "Last chance, or we're going to the kiddy section."

"Ow, no, ow, stop," he mews, now sounding more like a tortured cat. "You've got to believe me, there aren't any more girls. Maybe you can find one down in town?"

Varg kicks the cat ahead of him. The two middle rooms are empty. The last one is locked.

"I haven't got a key," says Frej. The Frej neck is puny. The hand is heavy. The corridor wall hard.

"Open the door, you little jerk," and the jerk opens it.

"Ha ha," chortles Varg. "I can see why you wanted to keep this tasty morsel out of our sight."

"Not Sophia," Frej says in an attempt to stop them. "Let me at least talk to her first," he suggests and sits down on the bed.

"What do they want?" says Sophia.

"Just to talk," says Frej. "I think it's something to do with your family. Perhaps they have some new information."

"About what?" she says.

"I don't know. They want you to go with them to the police station."

"They don't look like police."

"Police don't always look the same," says Frej.

Her skin, her hands, her lips, her eyes, her light. Frej tries to hold his voice steady.

"Just do as they ask and you'll be home by bedtime," he says, putting his arm around her. "There's no need to be scared."

No more coddling. A wrist is broken. A heart is crushed. Two soldiers and a girl take the back way out.

A few minutes later, everything is back to normal. Dinner at six. Film evening at seven. A white Transporter with fake plates drives north.

18

The first snow is just as amazing every year. Even though Jessica Harnesk has never lived anywhere without winter.

Suddenly it is simply lying there, always first thing in the morning. White paint brushed over the autumn that has long since left its glorious color behind and switched to brown.

The neighborhood is silent beneath the snowflakes. Cars glide past on their way to work. This is exactly how she wants things. Restful.

An even week in the calendar. That's to say, Henke's week with the children and what the hell was she thinking when she went out dancing on Friday night? It was spontaneous. Hanna rang and asked if she needed a babysitter. What won't we do for a little sister who wants to earn money? We say yes, and call a date. The fact that the date doesn't turn up is another matter, even though it was just as well. A mate of Henke's. What was she thinking? She wasn't.

The hatred in his eyes. The things he calls her.

"By the way," he says when they're standing in the hall for the handover, "I met Hanna in the shop. Are you so desperate that you have to go out even when it's your week?"

"That's none of your business," she says, although it is. As the children's father and so on.

She chooses not to contradict him. There's something in the children's eyes these days, and something even worse. Entreaties. A desire to make peace between their parents.

Henke shuts up when he meets no opposition. Instead Jessica gets a text message that she doesn't answer.

She brushes the snow off the car. God, what a relief to be able to go to work.

Others find Mondays give them stomach cramps. For her, it's Sundays. Either the children are leaving. A whole week until they see each other again. Or they're coming back from Henke's. Bursting with restless fury that sometimes takes days to neutralize.

Things aren't like that at his place, of course. No, the children are so happy to be with him again.

"Maybe I should have them full-time?" he says.

"Maybe you should," she retorts.

People get divorced to make more time for themselves. What bullshit. Then her phone rings. At work she's simply Harnesk.

"Are you on your way?" asks Birna Guðmundurdottir, who for practical reasons is known as Birna.

"I'm just turning into the garage."

"Good. Have you had breakfast?"

"No. Didn't manage it today, either."

Gasskas Police Station is among Sweden's smaller ones, although it has grown in recent years. When Jessica arrived, eleven years ago, it had twenty police officers. Now they've reached about thirty and there should be even more. If anyone is off sick, their absence instantly makes itself felt.

"Simon's on child sick leave, Tanja's at the dentist's and Monika's husband has had a heart attack. Though it can't have been a very serious one," says Birna. "She's coming in later this afternoon. I've rung Pipsqueak as backup. He's at his gran's in Kåbdalis, but he'll come in if things get critical. We've got to assist with a mental health detention this afternoon. Maybe he could tag along for that."

Pipsqueak is Serious Crime's latest trainee. At least twenty-three, though he looks about twelve. What's more, his parents have blessed him with the name Klas-Göran. An impossible name for a twelve-year-old.

Birna has laid out a bit of a spread: home-baked Norrland flatbread, butter and cheese.

Jessica tears off a bit of the soft, chewy bread. Dips it in her coffee until the cheese melts. She still feels a sense of discomfort after her morning run-in with Henke. She quickly tucks the bread into her napkin and pours her coffee down the sink.

"Right, meeting time," calls Faste, even though everyone is already there. He sits down in Jessica's seat, which he has made his own, and leans back.

"So, another Monday," he says. "How's the weekend been?"

"The refugee center called in," says Birna. "They've got a person missing." She puts a transcript on the table.

"Has she got permanent leave to remain in the country?" asks Jessica.

"Yes," Birna says. "She's in her last year at high school. Ambitious girl. Just got a flat. She's moving in at the end of the month."

"Bet you she's gone off with some boy," says Faste.

"And if she hasn't?" says Birna. "She went missing on Friday. Her roommate rang on Saturday morning, but we were short-staffed. The official opening of the market hall and the Gasskas-Björklöven derby were seen as more important, so this hasn't been followed up yet."

"I still think a boy is the most likely explanation," says Faste, "but by all means you and Harnesk go over there."

Jessica inserts her first snus of the day. The snus sets off her stomach, despite her failure to get the bread down. She sits on the toilet and tries to plan her day in her head.

Ping. <Can't you even remember to pack a change of clothes? You're bloody useless.>

Ping. <Why the hell didn't you remind me it was parents' evening on Tuesday?>

Ping. She turns off the sound.

"How long can we put up with it?" asks Birna.

"Henke?"

"Him, too. But I meant Hans Faste."

"We've no choice, as far as I can see. He has his long experience, his time with international crime divisions, no young children, et cetera, et cetera."

"He's just so repulsive," says Birna. "Have you heard what he calls Tanja? 'Pussycat.'"

"I'll have a word with him," says Jessica. "Unless she's spoken to him herself."

"She has. Now he calls her 'She-cat' instead."

They drive over the river and turn off toward Jokkmokk.

Fridhem Refugee Center is housed in a former home economics college ten miles or so north of Gasskas. The overnight snowfall is already melting. Water is dripping from the roof. A cat runs across the courtyard.

"It's good that you could come," Frej Aludd says, and invites them to take a seat in his office. Or the admin area, as he calls it. "I'm from Motala," he says with a shiver. "Haven't adjusted to the cold yet."

"The best season is just beginning," says Birna, which makes Jessica smile. Inwardly, at any rate. A southerner's first Gasskas winter is no laughing matter. Birna wishes twenty-five below on him for at least three weeks and a snowstorm just as the first spring flowers push through and the amateurs think winter is over.

But then summer, thinks Jessica, is hardly child's play, either. As soon as it gets warmer, the mosquitoes hatch. Once the mosquitoes have sucked all the goodness out of people trying to enjoy the mild evenings, the horseflies come along. Horseflies are ruthless. They see every living creature as sirloin steak. And once the horseflies, mosquitoes, wasps and other airborne invaders have decided to leave humanity in peace, the blackflies arrive. There is no pen or spray that can repel blackflies. They love eyes. Crawl into the corners, suck on tears and lay eggs in the sticky yellow matter.

"Nothing can be worse than ticks," says Frej, and he's telling them in detail about his brush with Lyme disease down south when Jessica interrupts him.

"The girl," she says. "Sophia Konaré. Do you think she went of her own free will?"

"We don't know," he says. "I wasn't working last Friday. According to her roommate, it was their turn to cook dinner but Sophia didn't show up."

"Are they free to come and go as they like?" asks Jessica, who has never been to the center before.

"Oh yes," says Frej. "We keep a closer watch on the younger ones, of course, but Sophia was of age."

"Was?" queries Birna in her suspicious way. That's just how she is. Direct and a bit brusque. Born of an Icelandic woman whose look could solidify lava.

She is well liked and considerate. Yet Jessica knows hardly anything about her beyond that. She has a way about her that blocks intrusive questions long before they're asked.

Birna reminds her of that other woman. Lisbeth, in the hotel bar. Jessica is still thinking about that evening. They danced and then . . . well, she took a taxi home to the children and thanked her lucky stars for it. Anxiety is the last thing she needs. Henke has eyes everywhere.

"*Is* of age," Frej corrects himself, clearly bothered by Birna's comment. "She was very much alive when she rang me on Friday, anyway. We talked about her move to her own flat, which is coming up. I offered to take her stuff over in the car."

"That was nice of you," says Birna.

The room is small. There is just about space for a bed each, a shared bedside table and wardrobe, and a drawer each in the chest of drawers. Not that they need more space than that for their things. Apart from clothes for different seasons and their schoolbooks, the room is as bare as a cell.

"Can't you have pictures on the walls?" says Birna. "Or a rug on the floor, at least?"

"And perhaps a spa in the basement?" says Frej.

"We need a word with her roommate," says Jessica. "Is she in the building?"

The manager looks at the clock. "No," he says. "Fatma goes to the high school in town. I expect she'll be on the four o'clock bus."

"Then we'll come back," Jessica says.

"By all means," says Frej.

"Bye for now, then. Thanks for the help, Frej," says Birna.

19

The doll is sitting on the edge of the bed when Marcus Branco wheels in from a side door. She has been told to take off the bathrobe and lie down. But she is still sitting there, hugging herself.

He smiles his best smile. Really cute, he thinks. Nice firm flesh, no doubt. An advantage to black girls. This tasty little number is on the well-padded side. Is there anything better than sinking into the yielding flesh of a woman and being held in motherly arms?

His smile grows even broader as the doll with the blinking eyes becomes wide-eyed with terror.

Just you wait, he thinks, *until I let my robe fall to the floor.*

"Do you have a name?" he asks. She whispers something inaudible. "There's no need to be timid with me," he goes on. But it is the timidity that turns him on. Assertive, self-satisfied women with loud voices are something he would rather leave for others. She is like a little rabbit, there on the bed. A captured wild rabbit trembling with the knowledge that it will never regain its freedom and the uncertainty of how it is going to die.

"Just tell me what you're called, my doll, and everything will be just fine."

"Sophia," she says finally. "Sophia Konaré."

"I don't care about the surname, but now that you've told me, I have to ask whether you are related to Alpha Oumar Konaré."

She does not know which answer she's supposed to give.

"Konaré was a great man," says Branco. "A visionary who unfortunately took a wrong turn, but let's not talk about him now. Let's talk about you. How old are you, my little honeybun?"

"Fourteen," she lies, in the hope that lowering her age will help her situation. He realizes that she is making an appeal to his loftier moral side. A child is a child, after all. And a hole is a hole as long as it isn't in a pig.

"You know you'll have to take your things off whether you want to or not," he says. "If you make up your mind to want to, everything will be easier, for both of us."

She loosens her grip and then hugs herself again, as if she is hesitating. Presumably because she thinks there are alternatives. And there are, in a sense. He can dispatch her to eternity right away. But if she's lucky, she'll be as wonderful as he imagines and will get to live a little longer.

It is all to the good that she's stupid enough to think she can buy time by being compliant. She slowly removes the fabric and gets under the quilt.

His penis is bulging under his silk robe. He will undress in a moment. He loves the doll's initial reaction. The widening eyes. The shock when they see the lack of legs. The contrast between the stumps and his magnificent erection.

"It doesn't matter," he says. "You're not the first person to be scared of me. It's big but not dangerous. If you could move in a bit," he says, and heaves himself over onto the bed. He has no use for legs. They disappeared along the way, a few weeks into pregnancy. He has long since stopped crying over spilled breast milk. He only uses the prostheses as a last resort. This is not a last resort. His arms, by contrast, more than compensate. Now he uses them to force the girl's head down to his crotch.

"Now, my doll, stroke my legs, it's so nice." The old jokes are the best.

Tears are running down her round cheeks. She doesn't seem to have much of a sense of humor.

"Shush shush, doll, don't cry. Daddy will comfort you. Mmm?" The more she cries, the more eager he grows. He knows he has her in his power. She will do whatever he wants.

She has already calmed down. Shifted position so she can reach more easily.

"There there, doll, now it's Daddy's turn to enjoy himself." But just as everything is going so well and the girl has learned what she must do, there's a knock at the door.

"Go away," he says. "I'm busy."

"It's important. Can't wait."

He looks at her. The doll has closed her eyes. Maybe she's asleep. Sexual gratification can exhaust you like that, after all.

Sophia shuts her eyes to keep reality at bay. It is almost evening. The village is doing what it normally does at that time of day. It is full of women and children who have come home from work and school.

When the soldiers march in with loaded Kalashnikovs in their hands and cartridge belts slung around their bodies, it is already dark.

They ask no questions. They do not request a meeting with the elders or offer any explanation. They shoot. They unreflectingly shoot everything that moves.

Sophia is sitting beside her aunt. When her aunt is shot, the body falls on top of Sophia.

There is blood running over her face. Into her eyes.

"Don't move," mumbles her aunt. "Play dead."

It is the last thing she hears anyone say.

She must have fallen asleep. The sun has risen. From under her aunt's arm she can see soldiers who are also waking up. Eating what is left in the dishes. Poking dead people with their rifle barrels to make sure. Even children. Even Joseph. His body is a bloodied mess with no discernible life, and yet they shoot again. He twitches. He was alive! Her little brother was alive.

Shoot me, too, she says, but nobody hears.

Her aunt's body is weighing her down. She wants to close her eyes but forces herself to see. Who else will tell the story if she doesn't?

For the first time, she pays attention to the way they look. She runs her eyes over faces, uniforms.

Some of them look as they usually do. Compatriots. Some younger than she is. Children. But the others. Foreigners. Uniforms without flags. Big bodies with red, sunburnt skin.

Boots come toward her. She shuts her eyes.

Boots kick her aunt's body. Sophia tries to roll with the blow. Ends up on her side. He is so close. He bends over her. Puts his hand on her cheek. Two fingers against her neck. Anything. She is ready.

For a second, their eyes meet. He closes her eyes with his hand. "Stay dead," he says. "Stay dead."

. . .

Branco hauls himself out of bed and into the wheelchair.

God created the sun to shine on Lucy, the first woman on earth, the primal mother of humankind. Her dark skin glows in the last rays of the afternoon sun. No doubt he'll be back later this evening. That is how it will have to be.

20

Darkness is falling over Gasskas and the days are now shorter than the nights. With every day that passes, several minutes darker.

Those who live here deal with winter in different ways. Many adore it. Snowmobiles are revved, skis are waxed and sociable fires are lit around barbecue hearths.

When the days are shorter than the nights, the snow comes to the rescue. It provides its own kind of low-vision lighting and makes people say things like *Down south it's even more hellish. At least we've got the snow.*

A month or so before all this, Märta Hirak kisses her daughter's hair, nods to her mother, shuts the door behind her, pulls the hood of her jacket over her head and sets off on foot for Berget industrial park.

She has decided to give as good as she gets. To obliterate Peder Sandberg and leave Gasskas. She is prepared. No one can say otherwise. Ten years. At least.

She will have to live with the fact that everyone, including the girl, will think she is dead. It's for the girl's sake she is doing this, but she has got to do it in her own way. With patience.

It all starts well. Better than she expected. She has learned from the best. At least by Gasskas standards. First she cozies up to the vice president of Svavelsjö M.C., even though she finds the prospect nauseating. *Close your eyes and think of England,* isn't that what the British say? *Hold your breath and get it done* works just as well. Sonny Nieminen is in love. She is . . . supportive, you might say. Allows him to cry on her shoulder when nobody's looking. Builds up a sense of trust. Like a prompter she whispers everything he ought to do and lets him take the glory. No one knows the market better than she does.

But she also keeps close tabs on everything Peder Sandberg is doing. The target itself. He worships Sonny, the way boys always look up to the big guys. She has allowed for the fact that he's going to tut about their relationship. Because although he doesn't want her, he doesn't want anyone else to have her, either. But as it's Sonny, he's prepared to forgive. Peder even moves in at Berget. Good! The only question is where she can hide things that belong to her and nobody else. Apart from Svala, that is.

Rapid rewind: Svala inherits a few thousand kronor when Niedermann dies. Märta knows that Peder will spend the money. So instead of putting it in a bank account, she buys Bitcoin. Not that she has a clue what it is. Totally hammered, she teams up with some computer nerd at Buongiorno who comes home with her after a drinking session. The next day she regrets it. They need money for the rent. But instead of six thousand in the bank she has a log-in to some account. The only problem is, she can't remember the password. Shit happens. Her default on the rent is referred to the enforcement officer and she gets another strike against her.

That was 2010. One Bitcoin was worth barely a krona. Fast-forward to 2021. One Bitcoin costs $68,408. Multiplied by six thousand. Märta isn't even sure how to say a number like $410,448,000.

Anyway. When the computer dies, she takes it down to GameStop. To get some help with transferring the contents to an external hard drive. There are photos she wants to save. That's her only reason. She has long since forgotten about the Bitcoin account.

Remarkably, everything falls into place. Peder Sandberg moves out. Takes with him everything of value including the TV and the girl's stamp collection. And . . . the external hard drive. It is only then that Svala's inheritance comes back into her mind. And evidently into Peder's, too. The world is full of discarded hard drives with Bitcoin accounts on them. Lucky the creep has no idea what kind of sums are involved.

One night the idiot is so wasted that he falls asleep on the floor and she sneaks up to his room and goes through his things . . .

Although winter has only just begun, it is cold. She walks fast to try to keep warm. Every autumn she thinks it must be time to get a thicker jacket, and then puts it off.

It is more of a problem for the girl. She's still slithering around in ankle socks and her fake white Converse with the soles flapping loose. Not that she looks out of place. Sami boots with curled toes and fleecy linings are well and truly out. And she never complains. She sort of floats above them all, like a being who doesn't really belong in the world. If she'd made more of a fuss she might have got some new footwear.

Märta Hirak has many reasons for feeling guilty where her daughter is concerned. First and foremost the fact that she was born at all. If she goes back to the sperm's encounter with the egg, the cardinal error is the sperm owner's, but she is by no means blameless. It takes a serious talent for willfulness to fall in with Ronald Niedermann.

But, but . . . She was young, wanted to get away from her family, and then it went the way it did. She has sealed in the mental scars as best she can. As for the physical ones, she has systematically covered them with new tattoos.

Thank goodness the girl is not like him. And thank goodness he went and died. Compared to him, everything since has been a minor problem. With the exception of her daughter, that is: Svala Inga-Märta Niedermann Hirak, who demands neither food nor clothes, but whose brain demands a constant supply of nutrition.

In an educated family, or in any family of a better class, she would have been declared a genius by now. Been allowed to skip a year or two at school, found her place among like-minded peers and been encouraged by dedicated specialist teachers, but as it is she happens to have been born into a completely different environment and has to make do with what's on offer.

Märta is not oblivious to her daughter's gifts. She just doesn't know what to do with them. She finds it hard enough sorting herself out.

She checks the time. She looks around. Does an extra circuit of the pond and stops behind a tree to make sure nobody is following her.

They always meet on the same bench in the park by the old mine.

Over the years, crack willows and hawthorn have wreathed it in invisibility. Even in winter you have to know it's there to be able to find it. Märta is almost there. She slows down and lights a cigarette.

"Hello. There was something you wanted to talk about," says a voice.

Märta looks around. Darkness has its advantages and disadvantages.

"If it happened to come out that I was dead . . ." she says under her breath.

"As we've said, we can protect you."

"Yeah, sure," Märta says, "but you know you can't."

"In that case," says the dim figure, "why are you telling me?"

"You already know. Peder Sandberg," she says, "if you know who he is. My ex."

"Yes, I know," the woman in the darkness says, writing something on a pad. "What about him?"

"He's hopped on the gravy train," says Märta.

"We already have that information. But as you know, it isn't against the law to ride a motorbike."

"You can't seriously believe a whole biker club moves up to bloody Norrland because they fancy some fresh air?" says Märta.

"No," says the other woman, "but have you got a better explanation?"

Märta could tell her about a person with no name who directs everything from above. She could also tell her about the usual old drug dealing. The sort handled by regular family men who put their children to bed with one hand while killing other people's with the other.

"There's snow in the air," she says, shaking another cigarette out of the packet.

"Come on, Märta," says the woman. "You're the one who wanted to meet."

She's had plenty of time to think out a plan. Since he took his goods and chattels and moved out, she's been on his tail. Little leads have led to assumptions. For now she's only prepared to share the shadows. In the shadows, Peder is king. It would help them all if he got nailed.

"Peder's joined forces with Svavelsjö. So far they're not doing much except polishing their bikes, but the plan is to take over the drug trade in the whole of Norrbotten. The thing is, he can't settle in his place in the Svavelsjö hierarchy. He's doing his own stuff on the side."

"You sound as if you want to sell him out."

"That's right," replies Märta.

"Why?"

"To protect my daughter."

"What's special about her?"

"Nothing to do with you."

Svala is different. Ever since she was little, Peder has been trying to get at her brain. He has exploited her for his own profit, yet still managed to miss the point. She is much more than a memorizer of figures and a solver of the Rubik's Cube. She is . . . *illuminated* is the word that presents itself, even if it's not quite the word she's looking for.

When Peder moves out, Märta makes sure to get herself into debt. She pays down the debt by doing favors. It may be a stupid plan, but step-by-step she's drawing closer to the inner circle. The one that Peder the fucking loser and Svavelsjö all work for.

His advancement, from minor dealer to organizer, as he calls it, is not a step up toward the top as he no doubt imagines. The small fry he supplies with drugs, and their trade, which they conduct in the belief that they have a whole region in their grip, are merely a screen. Behind the screen there is a whole other world; she knows that. Being local, knowing people high and low, has its advantages.

"If you don't mind my saying," says the other woman, "that sounds pretty diffuse."

"Doesn't make it any less true, though. They've got something brewing," says Märta, and she stuffs a slip of paper into the woman's coat pocket.

They part where the streetlamps begin. The other woman heads for her car. Märta is in no hurry. She wouldn't mind dropping in for a drink somewhere. For the girl's sake she has tried really hard. Only had a bit of wine occasionally, but no spirits. She has earned a beer tonight. Earned a bit of time to sit and think. The alcohol will open up her thoughts, make her sharper.

If she is to pull off her plan, she has to take it the whole way, but there is an X-factor, several in fact. That bastard Peder is the easy part. He isn't stupid, but he has a tendency to fall on his arse, however well gritted the path. A psychologist would call it low self-esteem. Deeply rooted self-loathing compensated for by thinking unnaturally highly of himself. Hubris.

Ten years with him, if not more. Although it's all basically about a debt. Not a monetary debt. A moral one. It was Peder Sandberg who helped her leave the girl's father. Without Peder and the others, she would be dead.

All these years he has never stopped reminding her, forced her to be grateful.

In what has become some sort of tic, she keeps staring at her hands. On the toilet, under the bedcovers, in the shower. They are still strong and smooth. If the future lies in her hands, it looks good. Up to now it has been in the hands of others. In powerful male fists that casually bruise her soft parts, just because they can. But that's all over now. She has made up her mind. Märta Hirak can be a stubborn devil when she wants to.

At first, a few individual snowflakes fall and die on the tarmac. But the wind suddenly picks up and the air is thick with falling snow. She stops under a streetlight, looks up at the light and opens her mouth. A fleeting sense of happiness runs through her, a few joyful seconds. That is all it takes.

In the roar of the wind she hears the car too late. It stops just behind her. Something like a delivery van door swishes open.

The blow rings in her ear. Her saliva tastes of blood. She feels her wrists as the cable ties are tightened, the tape as it is wound several times around her mouth and eyes. The smell of new car and something else. Coffee.

Märta reckons the drive lasts half an hour or so. Initially she finds it easy to maintain her sense of direction. Föreningsgatan down to the main street. Then right, so they're driving west. They stop at a set of traffic lights. If they are at Max Burger now, they'll only be able to go straight ahead. They turn left. That means the last set of lights on the main road before it ends and turns into a timber track. Across the bridge and then a right. They're driving along the western bank, but hang on a minute. They turn left where the main road leads to a residential area and reaches a dead end. On for a bit, then another left and immediately right. She no longer knows where they are or what direction they're going in. The van accelerates. They're out of the town. They drive at high speed. Eventually they slow down. They slow even further until they're just crawling along. The van stops. Someone gets out and then back in again. Five minutes later they're there. God knows where.

21

Varg opens the side door of the wheelchair-accessible vehicle. Pulls Märta Hirak out onto the ground and hauls her to her feet. They haven't really hurt her. Merely rendered her harmless.

That's the way Branco's orders work. With the same efficiency every time. The second the order is given, it is being put into effect.

Find the woman Sandberg used to live with and voilà, here she is.

Varg presses his finger to a fingerprint reader and taps in a code. A few minutes later they shove her into the arrival area and ask Lo to call Branco.

The arrival area is next door to the bunker's conference room.

It can hardly be called cozy, but the chairs are comfortable. Varg deposits the woman in one of them and sits in the other.

She hangs over one side. With her eyes and mouth concealed by silver duct tape she is a body, not a human being. They have taken her pulse and her heart is beating. They followed the instruction: take her alive.

They wait. He waits. Tears a page off a pad and folds a paper plane.

It misses, sailing over her head. He makes another. Gets her right on the nose. He laughs out loud and is about to make another when there are sounds at the door and Branco glides in.

Varg knows Marcus Branco as well as he knows himself. Probably better. Every shift in his mood, every fraction of a change in his tone of voice, whether he is glad, annoyed, cross or furious, Varg registers its pitch perfectly.

Right now he is annoyed.

"And this is?" he says.

"The Peder Sandberg woman," replies Varg.

"That was quick," says Branco, two-tenths less annoyed. He glides over to her. Removes the tape from her mouth and looks at it for a while.

"Mouth sore. Yuck." He backs away a few yards and gives Varg a nod. "Ask if the mouth can talk."

He asks if the mouth can talk, but all it wants to do is lick the sore and ask for water.

"Not interesting," says Branco. "If you haven't got anything more exciting to tell us, we can remove you right now. Your choice."

Lo comes in with a pot of freshly made tea and a plate of cookies.

"The thing is," he says, "you interrupted me in the middle of something important. I was about to . . ." He breaks off and pours tea. Brings the cup toward him and inhales the fragrance of the steam.

"The Chinese are good at a lot of things. Executions, compulsory sterilizations, pirate copies. But when it comes to tea," he says, "they're masterly."

He takes a good sip, gargles it around his mouth and swallows it with an audible *ahhh*.

"Oolong from Anxi County in the southeast of Fujian province. One of the world's most perfect teas, if you ask me. But sorry," he says, "I would have let you taste, of course, if it weren't for . . ." He pats his mouth delicately and turns to Varg.

"She's got exactly one minute."

"Your beloved husband," says Varg, "has made a fool of himself."

She clears her throat. Her lips are sticky but she knows what she has to say.

"He's set up his own show," she says.

"We already know that."

"Yes," she says, "but not in the way you think."

"What do we think?"

"That he's gone in with the biker club. But in fact he's freelancing out east. Isn't that why you picked me up?" she says. "To put pressure on him."

Varg and Branco exchange glances. This looks promising.

"Go on."

"Can I have some water?" says Märta.

Branco picks up the teapot and brings it over. He raises it above her head and lets the boiling liquid run down over her face.

She screams, tries to get out of range by throwing her body from side to side. Branco has no legs, to be sure, but there is nothing wrong with his arms.

"How sad," he says. "When Heaven rains tea, the poor man has no cup. Do you know why we brought you in?"

"For information about Peder Sandberg," she says.

"That's hilarious," says Branco. "We already have the information we need. No, it's a bit less fun than that for you, in fact. We're chiefly thinking of how he'll suffer if anything happens to his beloved Märta. Mmm? Don't you think?"

"We're not together," says Märta. "Sonny and I—"

"Well, that's better still," interrupts Branco. "He could do with a reminder of who he works for, too."

The plan she had, the words she had carefully thought out, the plotting that ought to have worked, they are all obliterated.

To win time, she jabbers on about the factory repurposed as a lab, where Peder's chefs cook meth like some communal kitchen churning out pea soup. About their plan to supply the whole of Norrland with first-class methamphetamine, heroin, cocaine and all the other fucking crap there is.

It doesn't sound particularly credible. If only she could get rid of the duct tape over her eyes. Talking into the darkness without seeing who she's talking to makes her unsure. And what the hell do they care about some shitty little lab where other junkies can blow themselves sky-high at any moment? She needs to give them something else. The only thing she can think of is Henry Salo.

"What's up with 'im?" says Varg.

"Him," says Branco.

"Head of Gasskas municipality."

"We know who he is."

Damn.

"I know him personally," she says. "He's told me about the plans for the wind farm."

"Excellent," says Branco. He puts his hands around her neck and squeezes. Neither too little nor too much. He hawks up a perfect gob of spit. "You only get one chance."

"A chance in return for doing what?" she tries to say. A gesture to Varg and the duct tape is straight back in place over her mouth.

"She can sleep in the cushion room."

He makes it sound nice and snug. A room of cushions and padded walls. And it *is* snug. Cuddly, you could almost say. Other potentially useful individuals have found their last rest there. Märta Hirak is at least guaranteed a few more hours' survival.

"Link me through to Sandberg via Squad," he says once they've locked the cushion-room door and returned to the conference room. "And make sure you locate the daughter."

Märta Hirak can scream as much as she likes behind duct tape and padded walls. No one will hear her and no one will care.

Eventually she lies down. Decides to conserve her energy. If only she had stuck out her tongue when he spat at her.

When Heaven rains gobs of spit, the poor man has no tongue.

22

"There you are! Nice of you to make time for us. We've got a special visitor with us this evening."

Peder Sandberg waits. Branco's pause is deliberate and for effect.

"Anyone I know?"

"Yes, very well indeed. Märta Hirak. Unfortunately, she isn't available to join us. She's—pardon my language—fucked." He holds up his phone so Sandberg can see the bundle sitting on a chair, its head hanging like a prisoner of war. "She had some interesting things to tell us. About you, among others."

"Women like talking about me," says Sandberg, leaning back. "She can't get enough."

"Cut the crap. We hear you've turned east. And I assume that doesn't mean Mecca. In other words, you're breaking our agreement and will be punished accordingly. Or your nearest and dearest in the first instance."

Sandberg laughs. "Nearest and dearest. Do what you like with the whore. I'd do the same."

"Interesting," says Branco. "I don't think Sonny would appreciate that."

"If you take things that belong to other people, you have to be punished. Get your hands chopped off."

"Even more interesting. But to go back to you and your little hobby lab at the fish factory. How did you see that going?"

"Oh, that," says Sandberg with a relieved sigh. "That closed down long ago."

"Burned down, you mean. Such a pity. But never mind, you can have one more chance."

"Oh?"

"Henry Salo. Sound familiar?"

"Everybody knows him, don't they?"

"Good. So you know his mother, too?"

"I wouldn't say I *know* her. I know who she is."

"And where she lives?"

"I suppose I do."

"Brilliant. You've got two days. Then you're back in with us and we let bygones be bygones. But one more thing before you go. The whore, as you call her, said she'd taken back something that belonged to her. What's this exciting thing she's pinched?"

Sandberg hesitates. On the one hand, he's happy that she's feeling the heat. She doesn't get how much he's done for her and her revolting brat. The fact that she's in Branco's clutches is almost comic. She's going to suffer, alright.

"An external hard drive," he says. "A long time ago I invested some savings in Bitcoin. The bitch took the hard drive and that's a fact. I haven't kept track of how much it's worth, but I'm sure it's a pretty sum."

Branco *has* kept track.

"Including the password?" he says.

"No bloody idea what that is, but we can always get a new one. Or ask the kid. She's a wiz with numbers. I've tried to get hold of her. Just for a little chat, I mean. Slippery devil. Too clever for her own good."

23

In the top-floor suite, the only sound is the hum of the ventilation system. Lisbeth stands at the window and looks out over the town. It looks the way dumps usually do. A central hub with rented apartments in three- or four-story blocks. Areas of detached houses on square plots. Some kind of water, maybe a river, and in prime position with the best view: a factory.

People are staggering home along the pedestrian street after closing time.

She ought to sleep but she can't. The disappointment clings on like chewing gum stuck to her heel, even though there's not that much to be disappointed about. A girl who doesn't fancy going to bed? No, it isn't about the sex. It's more like . . . the least attractive word of all: *loneliness.*

Loneliness can also be solitude, a place of refuge when she chooses it herself, which is to say three hundred and sixty days of the year. It's when she elects to step out of it into some kind of communion that it changes color. Like tonight. For once it was easy to talk. She could have said absolutely anything. Rambled on about herself or not at all, but what the hell . . . She gets undressed, shoves an armchair aside and counts to fifty. She has only reached thirty-eight when it starts getting tough. Thirty-nine, forty, forty-one. No, she can't do it. Her arms are giving out. She has to keep going, two more, four, eight, twelve and *bang,* her nose hits the floor.

She lies there for a while. Gets her breath back and lets her lactic acid levels fall.

The kid.

She can check out and take the first flight back.

The kid.

She can meet her, sit down for a coffee and a bun and explain why she, Lisbeth Salander, is an unsuitable person to live with. The list is endless. She can't cook, has scarcely any friends, has routines that are sacrosanct, is always working, hates people, never does housework and to crown it all she as good as killed the girl's father.

The kid.

Lisbeth stands up and goes to the middle of the room, bows, positions her feet slightly apart and clasps her hands. In an even flow with just enough *kime* for a Friday night she works her way through kata after kata. From *Heian shodan* to *Kanku dai*. Then she goes back to the bed and the kid.

There are similarities between the girl's life and her own. A mother who doesn't know how to set boundaries. A bastard of a father. A stepfather who's been suspected of crimes and cleared of them. Few friends. A loner who fights when she has to. There was an incident in the file in which a classmate ended up with a broken nose (which he probably deserved). Not bullied. But not included, either.

Yet she can't be a total freak, either, thinks Lisbeth. High marks in all subjects except maths, despite a lot of absence. No known drug problems. Keeps her room neat. *Keeps her room neat.* What utter bullshit. These blessed guardians of authority are always the same.

No contact with her biological father.

Be glad of that, my girl.

Suffers from Vittangi disease. Hereditary sensory and autonomous neuropathy type 5. A congenital defect that makes her insensitive to pain, heat and cold, which increases the risk of accidental self-harm.

Lisbeth stops reading. Vittangi disease. Insensitivity to pain. Niedermann must have had the same thing. That was why the meat mountain barely reacted to violence that would have paralyzed anyone else. Knives, shots, blows or kicks. Nothing worked on that monster. She reads the sentence again as her life flashes before her eyes. Parts of it, at any rate.

Conclusion: There is nothing seriously wrong with the girl. It is Lisbeth who is wrong. As five o'clock comes around and she hasn't yet been to sleep or made a decision, she gets out her laptop.

Wasp to Plague: <Can you check out someone in Gasskas? Peder Sandberg. Probably born in the 1980s. Lived in Tjädervägen until a few years ago. Nothing in particular to go on. Just curious.>

Plague to Wasp: <Is Gasskas a place? Sounds like some kind of vomit. Will fix.>

Peder Sandberg is very likely also a kind of vomit, she thinks. Tucks herself under the covers and waits for an answer.

A few hours later she's woken by a knock at the door. She looks at the time and realizes she has to be at the social services meeting in half an hour.

The chambermaid apologizes and Lisbeth throws on her clothes. She runs her fingers through her hair, sniffs her armpits, which now smell of dried disco sweat mixed with men's deodorant. Roots a stick of gum out of her backpack, having left her toothbrush at home by mistake, and checks her phone. An unrecognized number has rung twice. She'll have to deal with it later. She connects to Plague's server once more. He has replied.

<Sandberg has only minor convictions. Will be in touch if I find out more. Look after yourself.>

In the taxi she decides not to decide. She'll have to see how she feels.

Five minutes late, she takes a deep breath and rings at the entry phone.

24

Several minutes later, Lisbeth is still cooling her heels outside the social services entrance. She fancies a smoke even though she gave up long ago and almost walks away several times. If they can't even open the door, then what's the point? she tells herself. *OK, I'll let fate decide.* She rings one last time and gives them two minutes.

"Welcome—sorry you had to wait," and other polite phrases to which Lisbeth does not respond, but she says yes to a cup of coffee.

"We'll go in to the others shortly," says Elsie Nyberg. "But I wanted to give you a few updates first. Svala is still living in the flat. She refuses to go to an emergency placement and we don't have the resources to move her until after the weekend. That's to say, we don't want to subject her to any compulsion. She can't be in the best of states after what's happened."

"Alright," says Lisbeth. "So?"

"Regardless of what you decide in the longer term, we were wondering if you would be prepared to sleep there for a few nights."

Lisbeth immediately says no. It's her instinct to say no if she hasn't got things under control, and she hasn't. The whole situation is telling her loud and clear: *Go home! Grab the first available taxi to the airport or the station or all the way down to Stockholm, but go home!*

"Think about it for a minute," says the social services woman. "It would be good for Svala to have a relative with her."

"We've never met," Lisbeth says. *And it was me who killed her dad,* she doesn't say.

"I am aware that you don't know each other, but sometimes family means something, even so," she says, and describes a reunion of cousins who had not met for thirty years but still knew almost everything about each other.

"I have no cousins and I know nothing about the girl," says Lisbeth. "Any more than she has the faintest idea about me."

"You share your DNA, at least," is Elsie's final argument as they're on their way along the corridor to the visitors' room.

Not necessarily, thinks Lisbeth without answering. She could deliver a whole lecture on deoxyribonucleic acid if she thought the woman had the capacity to understand it.

But yes, there is a likeness, shudders Lisbeth when she sees the girl for the first time. The same blond hair and sweet-as-sugar features. Born, dead and buried. Resurrected from the netherworld, sitting at her father's right hand to pass judgment on the world. Camilla. Zalachenko's favorite daughter, her own twin sister. Even the voice is the same when she opens her mouth and says a husky hello.

How the hell is this going to go?

Apart from the hello, she says nothing as the social services people run through the current situation and what the plan is for her. She is holding a key ring and on the key ring there's a miniature Rubik's Cube. She barely needs to look at it. Her practiced fingers move over the colored squares. In a minute or so she has solved it and starts again from the beginning.

When Elsie Nyberg finally asks the girl what she thinks of the plans, she looks up and asks her to repeat the question. She doesn't say *Eh?* like any other teenager, but "I'm sorry, I didn't catch the question."

"What do you think of these plans?" Elsie repeats.

"You already know what I think," Svala says.

"Not me," says Erik Niskala, maneuvering his bulk into a more comfortable sitting position.

"You'll have to ask your colleague," says Svala. "She seems to have done her homework."

"I'll go get us some more coffee," says that colleague. "Try to get to know each other a little. Lisbeth, why don't you tell Svala something about yourself?"

"Does martial arts, works for a security company, owns a Honda 350, lives in Stockholm," says Svala. "On Fiskargatan. In Södermalm."

They look at each other across the table. Even the color of their eyes is the same.

"How do you know that?" asks Lisbeth.

"I've done my homework."

"Good," says Lisbeth. "That's all you need to know."

"No, it's not," says Svala. "I need to know whether you can come and stay in the flat for two nights so I don't have to have a babysitter."

25

They take a taxi to Tjädervägen. They're still a block away when Svala starts looking out for the car. Discreetly, so her aunt won't notice. She has to keep all the others on the outside. This is Svala's problem and nobody else's. And besides, it's her only inheritance from Mammamärta. As far as she is aware. According to Grandma, there's a document. A will, written on the back of a Buongiorno menu, but it hasn't turned up yet. In any case, it's not going to contain unheard-of riches or anything else of financial value. Mammamärta was chronically broke. And anyway, she isn't dead; she can feel it.

The rent is paid to the last day of October. Then she has to get out of here and go to the home of some family of strangers who have been on a course with social services that gives them the right to look after other people's children for money. It's like being sold at a child auction. *Unfortunately the Nygrens turned her down; they would prefer a younger child. We had the Nilsson family lined up, but they didn't feel they had the capacity to accommodate a teenager just at the moment.* And so on.

She still has no concrete plan, but she's not going to some family. Right now, Lisbeth Salander is her shield against society and will have to play that role until she knows what she's going to do. She will cope on her own; she always has.

The car is parked in Pappy Peder's old spot. Tinted windows and behind them a couple of the ugliest mugs that genetics ever created.

The question is whether they'll make a move while her aunt is there. Should she call her that? Surreptitiously she studies Lisbeth. The side bangs fall across half her face. Apart from the kohl that makes her eyes even darker, she is without makeup and her skin is virtually white.

She looks strange. Like a child with an adult face, thinks Svala. Gray hoodie under a black leather jacket. Black jeans and white sneakers. From behind she could be any fifteen-year-old.

Svala pulls the sweater with leather elbow patches more tightly around her and sinks lower into her seat. She asks the taxi to drive right up to the entrance of the building, where she hopes they will be hidden by the bike shed. She doesn't look toward the parking lot as they get out.

Damn. She forgot the rug her grandma's body was lying on. The bladder that emptied itself and perhaps something worse. She rolls it up and apologizes. Holds her breath through the living room, pauses for a few seconds before opening the balcony door, and throws it out. Everything is quiet in the back courtyard. Neither children nor bandits.

"There's no need to apologize," says Lisbeth. These are the first words she has spoken since they left social services. "We'll clean up. I can scrub the floor."

Scrub the floor. Has she ever scrubbed a floor in her entire life? She doesn't even own the kind of mopping bucket Svala fetches out of a cupboard and fills with water and liquid soap. The most she ever does is run the vacuum over the floor of her flat, whenever she remembers that people sometimes do that kind of thing.

"What do I do?" she says, and finds herself on the receiving end of a hard stare.

"Dip, twist and then mop," says Svala. "It's not hard."

Dipping, twisting and mopping has been Svala's job since forever. As have vacuuming, washing up and doing the laundry, taking out the rubbish, clearing out the fridge, cleaning the stove and picking up after Mammamärta and that pig Pap Peder. For her trouble she gets a bit of pocket money, but she would have done it anyway. She hates them together. Together they are Botticelli people in Dante's hell. She draws them in secret. Naked, repulsive, with snakes coiling around them and into their drunken pig-pink bodies. Each time she feels guilty afterward and crumples up the drawing. It isn't Mammamärta's fault. She loves her child, doesn't she?

Lisbeth mops and Svala vacuums. Not because the flat is dusty but to bury herself in the noise.

She hadn't been intending to cry over Grandma's death. Especially not in front of someone. Everyone has to die sometime and Grandma was old, at least sixty.

She pulls the vacuum into her room, closes her eyes and lets the tears flow. That's the way she cries. In silence so nobody can hear. A valve that opens, lets the excess pressure hiss out and then closes again.

When she opens her eyes, Mammamärta is sitting at the desk.

Hello, she says. Why are you blubbering?

Because I won't get through this. They're after me now.

You have the key, don't forget.

The key to what?

To everything.

26

After cleaning comes sunshine. Lisbeth empties the dirty water down the toilet. The green soap has got rid of the reek of pee. Her stomach is growling for food. Hot, sticky cheese burning the roof of her mouth. Dough cooked brown and crispy at the edges. An ice-cold Coke to go with it.

The girl seems hungry, too. She stares into the fridge, goes to the pantry and then back to the fridge.

"Ketchup and macaroni, will that do?"

"Or pizza," says Lisbeth.

"There isn't one around here," says Svala, putting a pan of water on to boil. As long as they stay in the flat they can simply not answer the door or even ring the police at a pinch. Outside, they haven't got a chance.

Her plan is to climb down via the balcony when Lisbeth Salander has gone to sleep. The flat below is empty, so nobody will see her. From the back of the flats she can make her way via the basement to block five. You can see the parking lot from there. Hopefully they'll have grown tired of waiting and left. Even monsters have to sleep from time to time. Then she'll cycle down to the bus stop across the park. The last bus to Boden leaves just before midnight. After that she will have to improvise.

"There's always home delivery," says Lisbeth, getting out her laptop.

Pizzeria Buongiorno is only a block away. The girl is lying. Lisbeth thinks it must be to do with the car. The door that opened when Svala got out of the taxi. The man who drew back when he saw she was not alone.

Vigilance comes as naturally to Lisbeth as eating, shitting and sleeping. Without even turning her head, she scans her immediate surroundings and stores the impressions in the brain file labeled "information for survival." She scans people the same way. Registers their character traits, idiosyncrasies, appearance, voice and behavior.

No one escapes her scrutiny. Svala is no exception. The girl is frightened. Possibly both frightened and sad. She is probably grieving for her grandmother and mother and hoping that no one will notice. The idiots of this life have long since taught her the definition of strong and weak. Strong is someone who never shows their feelings. Pretty much like Lisbeth herself, she admits. Weak is someone who shows their vulnerability. But it is one thing to be conscious of your failings, another to be thirteen and surrendering to heredity.

She sits on the sofa with the computer on her lap and pretends to google takeout. In fact she needs to pull herself together, come up with a plan and get them out of there.

Step number one is to persuade the girl to open up. If she's got herself into some sort of trouble, Lisbeth needs to know why. It could be some minor crap that can be sorted out with money. But it could also be something else, beyond simple solution models.

She swears to herself. Should have got Plague to check on the mother, too.

"What sort of pizza do you want?" she calls to Svala, who has gone into her room.

"Vegetariana, please," she calls back. "And a pizza salad, if that's alright?"

If that's alright. Polite little thing, this one. Lisbeth goes for a Capricciosa with extra everything and adds extra everything to the girl's order, too. She looks as if she could use some proper food. She rounds off the order with double portions of Carbonara, a couple of extra pizzas for emergencies and a big multipack of Coke. They could find themselves stuck here for a few days. *Special delivery instructions: Use back entrance!*

Wasp to Plague: <Märta Hirak. Same address.>

She could have done it herself. Getting into the police DUR-Två system is a piece of cake, but to get out again she would have to generate a crash. As she doesn't know quite how the day is going to develop, there's a risk of running out of time. Better to go via Plague.

<Reported missing. She has a history of disappearing and no criminal involvement is suspected. No further action recommended.>

<Any convictions?>

<Yes. Care of Abusers (Special Provisions) Act §4 but a long time ago. A few other bits and pieces. Possession of firearms. Concealment of a criminal. Possession of drugs. Assault and battery. Yep, that's it.>

Then the doorbell rings. Pray God it's the pizza delivery.

27

How do you talk to a teenager? thinks Lisbeth, cutting herself another slice of pizza. The only teenager she has for reference is herself, which is not a great deal of help. Lisbeth Salander, aged thirteen. Who was she? Until Mrs. Ågren came into her life she has been sending her memories to the refuse heap of her brain. The problem is that they never decay. They can be activated at any time and spread as contamination. Like now.

In what little she knows of Svala, largely from the social services reports, she realizes that they are different in many ways, but alike in certain others. Not alike in external ways like appearance and voice. No, the similarity is at a deeper level. More or less like stones that are worn smooth in identical ways, due to the geographical conditions.

She must find her way through to the girl. Win her confidence. She will never reveal anything otherwise. Neither about her mother nor about the men outside in the car. There are only two approaches available. The other is menace.

"What do you like doing?" she asks.

"Don't know," says Svala. "Reading. Drawing, maybe."

"Can I see one of your drawings?" asks Lisbeth the after-school club leader.

"No," Svala says. "I never save them."

"Have you got any other interests? I saw how quick you were with the Rubik's Cube."

"That's not an interest," says Svala. "That's just something I do."

"I watched a documentary about the Rubik's Cube world championships," says Lisbeth. "Have you seen it?"

"No. We haven't got a TV," she says, a fact Lisbeth has already noted. She has no computer or recent model of smartphone, either. Hardly any clothes in the wardrobe and few personal possessions. If Märta Hirak earned money from selling drugs and her job as a personal care assistant, it most definitely wasn't to shower the girl with frivolous gifts. The whole flat smells of poverty.

They have almost finished eating when there's another ring at the door. Svala drops her piece of pizza and leaps to her feet so fast that she knocks over her Coke can.

"Wait," says Lisbeth, taking hold of her arm. "Is it those guys from the parking lot?"

They hold each other's gaze for a few moments. Svala will have to make a choice.

"Why do you think that?" she says, to win time.

"Doesn't matter," says Lisbeth. "Who are they?"

"I don't know," she says in a voice that may possibly have decided to tell things the way they are. "Mammamärta owes them money. And when I was going to—"

"OK," interrupts Lisbeth, pushing the girl toward her room, where they can talk without any risk of being overheard. "Listen to me. We won't open the door. We won't go anywhere near, got it?" And the girl gets it. "Do you know anyone in this block?"

"Only Ingvar," says Svala. "He's old."

"Good," says Lisbeth. "Have you got his phone number?"

"No, we usually only see each other in passing."

I heard your mum went missing. You must be upset about that, he says.

She'll be back, says Svala. What about Malin, has she come home? He shakes his head. They sit quietly and watch the pied flycatchers flying in and out of a nesting box in the birch. He's good at being quiet. That is the best thing about him.

"Surname?" says Lisbeth.

"Bengtsson. He lives at number four."

"Now this is what I want you to do," says Lisbeth, holding out the phone. "Ring him and tell him to come downstairs to the second floor. Then he needs to tell those guys outside the door that nobody lives here anymore. That social services took you away and your grandmother's dead."

"That won't work," says Svala. "They saw us arrive."

"Not a problem," says Lisbeth. "They'll come back, of course, but they don't like an audience."

"And if they hurt him?" says Svala, sounding like someone speaking from experience. "Perhaps I should just go with them."

"Certainly not. I'm responsible for you for the next two days."

"And what if he rings the police?"

Blessed kid, so practical. "They won't get here in time," says Lisbeth.

"He's going to ask questions."

"Say you'll explain later."

Svala rings. They wait.

"Stay here," says Lisbeth, and she sneaks to the front door. She can hear voices. Not exactly what they're saying, but voices. She approaches the door. Puts her eye to the peephole. No. How can that be? Peepholes can distort faces, but she'd recognize dregs like that even if they had plastic bags over their heads. When one of them shifts his focus from the neighbor to the door it feels as if he's staring straight at her. Her pulse races. She can hardly breathe. Svavelsjö Motorcycle Club. How the fuck can they have risen again from the bubbling swamp of purgatory?

If it's the Svavelsjö bikers who are after the girl, then they really are in hot water. Not that they're particularly smart, but they're completely unscrupulous. And clearly they don't even draw the line at children.

She leans toward the door again and shudders. Cloned in a directly descending line from the devil's gene bank. New guys, but the same lank ponytails and greasy mustaches. The same leather jeans and the same vests.

The clatter of cowboy boots fades. She can breathe again. The stairway is empty. They have won a short respite.

Lisbeth googles car rentals. Dismisses the big companies and rings Rent-a-Wreck.

"I'll give you three thousand extra if you deliver it here. Leave it in the disabled-parking area at the back and put the key on the front wheel."

"Five. And if the car gets stolen, you're buying a replacement."

"Text me when you get here," says Lisbeth. Then she turns to Svala. "You can decide where we're going."

"Rovaniemi," says Svala. "In Finland."

"Do you know somebody there?"

"Not exactly."

"OK," says Lisbeth. "*Perkele* Rövaniemi, here we come."

"Rovaniemi," corrects Svala.

28

As if they haven't already had enough to contend with for one day, it starts to snow. First lightly, then more heavily and finally coming down in such quantities that they can only crawl the last ten miles or so.

The girl struggles against sleep, drops off and wakes up when her head bangs against the window.

Lisbeth has tried to wheedle more out of her about her mother. She is plainly practiced at being on her guard. She has not really said any more than Lisbeth already knows.

"I can drive if you like," says Svala.

"Oh sure," says Lisbeth.

"Seriously," she says, "I'm used to driving," and what can one say to that?

Lisbeth pulls into a lay-by and turns to Svala. "Do you know who these Svavelsjö guys are?"

"Some of them. They teamed up with Peder's lot a year or so ago."

"Do you know their names?"

Whatever happens, whoever asks, say nothing.

"You don't get it," says Lisbeth. "Svavelsjö isn't any old biker club. They beat the Hells Angels any day. They live off other people's misfortune. Stick in their ugly mugs the minute they sniff violence or money. Preferably both at the same time."

She has got to make herself clear and the girl has got to talk.

"They'd kill a homeless man for a few lousy kronor," she says, "so you've got to tell me. What hold do they have on you?"

"Even if I tell you, what are you going to do about it?" says Svala with a meaningful look at Lisbeth's body, which barely reaches the top of the steering wheel.

"I don't know yet," she says. "But you can't get away from them without help—you can see that, right? If they've got something on you, they'll stick to you until they find what they're looking for. So what are they looking for?"

Whatever happens, whoever asks, say nothing.

Lisbeth sighs and drives on. She understands her, would probably have done the same herself. But Svavelsjö . . . what are the odds? Five hundred miles from Stockholm. They must be working up to something big.

"If you wanted to make yourself useful, you could look for a hotel," says Lisbeth. "At least four-star and with a reception desk open around the clock."

Svala goes on a booking site. But after a while she puts down her phone and slumps against the window.

"How's it going?" says Lisbeth.

"There's no point," she says. "We won't be able to afford it in any case."

"Don't worry about the money," says Lisbeth. "Social services has given us a nice fat sum for entertainments."

"Yeah, sure," says Svala. "All the social services cases in Gasskas get to go to Rovaniemi once a year. And to Majorca in the summer, as long as they send a postcard."

"Generous, isn't it?" says Lisbeth. "Have you found a hotel?"

"Yes. Five thousand a night."

"Ring them," says Lisbeth.

"Seriously?"

"Seriously."

"This is Svala Hirak. I'd like to book a room for . . ." She turns to Lisbeth. "Two nights, thanks. Preferably a cabin, thanks. With sauna, thanks."

"And a minibar," says Lisbeth.

"Minibar, yes, thanks. Card payment?"

"Cash."

"Cash, thanks."

Svala looks sideways at Lisbeth. Further thanks are written in her face.

Lisbeth turns up the volume on the radio. The music sounds familiar but she can't quite place it. Music has only incidental access to her life. Mostly she prefers silence.

"Can I turn it up?" says Svala.

"Do you like music?" says Lisbeth, and the girl turns off the radio.

The wipers thump against the windscreen and the fan whirs.

"Stop trying so hard," says Svala. "My favorite food is potato dumplings. I'm the library's best customer. I play hockey with the Gasskas Junior Ladies. Or used to, anyway, until nobody bought me skates anymore. You don't need to ask me if I like music just because I want to turn it up."

"Sorry," says Lisbeth, realizing she's the one at a disadvantage. The girl is not a child in the sense of the child Lisbeth sees as she watches the thirteen-year-old struggling to stay awake. Just like herself, she's formed by circumstance. An individual who has grown up too fast and developed a survival strategy. Part of it is not being easy unless she has to. Quite the opposite, she thinks, and turns the radio back on.

"If you don't like the music, you'll just have to put up with it," she says, and starts singing along.

Svala turns up the volume even higher.

"I like his voice," she says, filling in wherever she can.

"He's Danish," says Lisbeth. "Unfortunately, he's dead."

"Mum may be dead as well," says Svala, "but I don't think so."

"Then I don't expect she is," says Lisbeth. She slows and checks the GPS one more time before turning off into a parking area and looking around her.

"What is this place? Santa's very own hell?"

Colored lights are festooned between the trees and wherever you look there are Santas, Santas and more Santas and when it isn't Santas it's reindeer, presents, Christmas trees and all the other trappings of a Christmas nightmare.

"He lives here," says Svala.

"He must be totally fucking psychotic in that case."

"You do swear a lot," says Svala quietly. "Father Christmas is a lovely person."

"Father Christmas isn't a person, he's a myth."

"No, he exists."

The hotel lobby is possibly even worse. In addition to varnished log cabin walls decorated with reindeer antlers and a stuffed reindeer with a sleigh full of parcels and another bloody Santa, there's festive music sucking up the oxygen supply like a moldy carpet.

One hates Christmas and the other loves Santa. How is this going to work out?

When they're welcomed by an elf rather than a receptionist in traditional black and white, Lisbeth has had enough. She hands her wallet to Svala and sinks onto a red-and-green-striped sofa with glittery cushions and itchy reindeer skins.

"Have you got a cold beer, at least?" she calls. "Or something stronger. Preferably the strong stuff."

"Do you have to drink?" says Svala, giving back the wallet. Only minutes ago she was grown-up. Now she is little. A child with restless eyes. A thirteen-year-old on her guard. An eight-year-old who locks herself in the bathroom to escape wandering, drunken hands. A five-year-old who is left alone when her parents have business in town.

Damn. Insensitive fucking Lisbeth, who hasn't realized the gravity of it until now.

"Sorry," she says. "I'd like a Coke, but it can wait until we get to the room."

They are both traveling light. Most of the space in Svala's backpack is taken up by her monkey.

For a child who had only ever stayed at a youth hostel, if she was lucky, their chalet is an orgy of luxury. This self-restrained girl, old beyond her years or somehow simply old, cannot help herself. She frolics around their two rooms and the bathroom and sauna like a heifer at its first summer pasture and doesn't stop until she has inspected every last corner, including the wardrobe.

Lisbeth wants only to sleep. She cannot be bothered to get fully undressed, merely pulls off her jeans and lets her body sink into the quilt.

"Come here," she calls to Svala. "Have you seen? The whole roof is made of glass."

Unlike Lisbeth, Svala has changed into her nightdress and cleaned her teeth when she climbs under the quilt with her monkey and switches out the light.

"There's another bedroom if you want peace and quiet," says Lisbeth.

"Thanks. Same to you," she says.

The vast expanse of sky through the roof is a grayish-black mass with no falling meteorites or twinkling stars.

"Do you know anything about black holes?" asks Lisbeth.

"A bit," says Svala. "Gravitation stops the light forcing its way out."

"Exactly. Imagine you're an astronaut falling into space and coming up to a black hole."

"The event horizon, you mean?"

Bloody kid has done her homework. "Yes."

"I only wanted to check you didn't mean singularity," says Svala, "because then I would have been dead long ago."

"Like the snowflakes when they hit the glass roof," says Lisbeth.

"But that's not the same thing," says Svala, and then she yawns and turns over. "Anyway, any dummy can google black holes. The first things that come up are gravitation and singularity. To me they mostly just sound like neat words. Can we go to sleep now? I'm tired. Monkey is, too."

So much for that bedtime story.

29

Hotel breakfast, is there anything worse? Lisbeth gets in the line for the coffee machine. By the time she reaches the front, the coffee has run out.

Hordes of strangers who insist on saying good morning are winding like a sluggish grass snake around the cold meats and cheeses. To make matters worse, the place is full of Santas, both the living and the model variety, even though it's only October.

An overfriendly elf chats with guests in several languages as she refills the platters. Then she puts her arm around Svala and points out the waffle iron while Lisbeth looks for a table as far as she can get from elves and families with children, which proves impossible. Nor is there any way to escape the fact that Bing Crosby is oozing out of the loud-speakers like earwax softener.

Everybody seems to have woken up at the same time. There are no vacant tables. The best option is to sit with a guest who is talking loudly on his phone in Chinese, sitting with his daughter.

"Please," he says in English, gesturing that there's space.

To be sure of avoiding any exchange of pleasantries, she picks up a copy of *Helsingin Sanomat*.

"Do you read Finnish?" says Svala, tucking into sausage, scrambled egg, waffles, cream, several kinds of bread, pastries, dessert cheeses and doughnuts.

"No, but the photos are good," says Lisbeth, her gaze coming to rest on the Swedish minister for families.

She feels it may be time to mouth the words *Shut up*. As the elf goes by on the lookout for plates to clear, Lisbeth asks her to translate the headline.

"It's something about a data breach," she says, making a grab for Lisbeth's coffee cup.

"At the family minister's?"

"And his wife's."

"Christ," swears Lisbeth, and checks her phone. Out of battery. How the hell has that happened? Someone like her, always online, never without power. "I need to make a call," she says, getting up.

"Have you seen?" asks Lisbeth when Dragan Armansky picks up.

"We were informed on Friday," he says. "I thought you had enough on as it was. The situation is under control. When are you back in town?"

Lisbeth looks out over Santa Land. The whipped cream looks freshly piped over the roofs. Santa is always awake.

"I don't know. A few problems came up along the way."

"I can imagine. How are things going with the girl?"

"Uh, yeah."

"Which means?" he says, and Lisbeth sighs.

"We're in Rovaniemi."

"In Finland?" says Armansky, and laughs. "Have you seen Father Christmas yet?"

"Multiple versions, plus his flirty elves and mangy reindeer," says Lisbeth, and asks him to get to the point.

Dragan Armansky, majority owner and founder of Milton Security, slurps his morning coffee and looks out over the city. For just over a year Lisbeth Salander has been part-owner of the company and nobody could be happier about it than he. On her own terms, naturally. Physically in the office once a week, preferably less, her own room, daily reports and full insight into all her colleagues' projects.

In their eyes, Lisbeth is a strange bird. In his, a rare and unique species.

Milton installed the beefed-up security for the Ministry for Social Affairs that autumn at the request of the government offices' own IT section. The project ended a few weeks ago and was assumed to have been completed successfully.

"So what's happened?" says Lisbeth. "Have Dick and Pick messed up or is there something else going on?"

Pick's actual name is Patricia, but because she works in a pair with Dick she has to be Pick. In Lisbeth's address book, at any rate.

"We're in the dark," says Armansky. "We don't know any more than the whole of Sweden does by now, namely that the minister's wife has red hair up top and down below. And her lover is a Turk with a murder sentence who should have been deported years ago, which is pretty comical in itself, seeing as de Deus is known among other things for his tough line on crime and the immediate deportation of immigrants with criminal convictions. Haven't you read the papers? You're usually up to speed; the girl must be a big distraction." He does not say it in a nasty way, but rather with hope in his voice. Lisbeth knows he is worried. He's always inviting her to his nice house in Nacka, where his pleasant wife, Nadie, makes good, nutritious food. Lisbeth generally declines politely.

"It's not good to be on your own. Families are the best defense a person can have."

"Really?" says Lisbeth.

"I don't mean parents, but a family of your own. A decent man, a couple of children to bind you together, a place to live."

She usually tells him to shut up when he starts playing the family waltz, which is scratchier than Evert Taube on an old 78. She has made her choice and will stick with it. Relationships are tiresome. She doesn't know if she is even capable of feeling anything warmer than horniness. In any case, she has no intention of finding out. Life has more to offer than people. Prime numbers, for example.

"Send me what you know and I'll get back to you later," she says. "Wait, one more thing. Was it you who gave social services my number?"

"I'd never do a thing like that."

"Are you sure?"

"Sure," he says, a fraction of a second too late.

She locks the chalet, one of a hundred identical chalets nestled in among timberwork, hotel, restaurants, designer shops and—perhaps a newsagent? Although she gave up smoking so long ago that she can't remember, she occasionally still buys cigarettes. Keeps them for a few days and then throws them away.

"Did you know this shop was built for when Eleanor Roosevelt came to visit?"

The Chinese breakfast guest is there on the same errand. Evidently he has to talk, too.

"No, I didn't know that," says Lisbeth. "Did she come to see Santa Claus?"

"Ha ha, not exactly," he says. "Santa didn't move in until later. This was a few years after the war. The Germans burned down the whole town in 'forty-four. Only a few buildings were left undamaged," he says, appearing to get wind in his sails from Lisbeth's attempt to look interested. "The Russians forced Finland to forgo Marshall aid but the U.S. wanted to make a contribution anyway. So when Madame Roosevelt decided to come and visit they built the chalet and put it on the Arctic Circle for the sake of a good story, even though the Arctic Circle is a bit further south. Then she sat in here and wrote a postcard to Truman."

"Dear Harry," says Lisbeth, "Santa Claus does exist."

"Your daughter tells us you're from Sweden," says the man.

She decides to make no comment on the mother-daughter assumption. It's none of his business.

"Isn't this a wonderful setup?" he says, indicating the whole complex with a sweep of his arm. "But excuse me, I should have introduced myself. Kostas Long. I was here with my son many years ago. Coincidentally I had the opportunity to invest in the area, so now I bring my daughter, Mei, here as often as I can. It may sound childish, but I love Christmas. Don't you?"

"No," says Lisbeth.

"And Finland," he says, "what a country, what people! Have you two done anything nice yet?"

"No," says Lisbeth again.

"Then perhaps I could show you around?"

"I don't know . . ." says Lisbeth.

"So, I took the liberty of booking you in for a few activities," he says, and gets a sour look for his trouble.

"Kostas," says Lisbeth. "Are you Greek?"

Now it's his turn not to answer.

"Your daughter and Mei are keen to go for a ride on a sleigh pulled by reindeer," he says. "You're very welcome, too, of course. You can rent ski suits from reception. You maybe hadn't bargained on it being winter up here?"

"Thanks," says Lisbeth. "We'll have to see what we can come up with."

An hour or so later Lisbeth nonetheless finds herself standing in the reception area with Svala and a group of Japanese ladies taking selfies in their borrowed pastel-colored ski suits.

"No way," says Lisbeth. "I'd rather freeze to death. We can go and exercise instead. Any self-respecting Father Christmas surely has a dojo?"

Svala's eyes keep flitting to the happy band. Lisbeth would have been the same. Although it was a long time ago, she recollects with the sharp edge of a diamond cutter the way the ordinary world was out of reach. With its unmistakable message, it could be glimpsed on TV or through the window of the clinic. *You are a freak, Lisbeth,* it said. Freaks are not allowed to join in.

"Come on," she says to the girl. "There's a sports shop over there. We might as well buy warm clothes. Choose what you want and don't worry what it costs. Social services has sent through another payment."

"Things are looking up," says Svala, running her hand over quilted jackets in assorted colors and styles.

It is only now that Lisbeth thinks about how the girl dresses. Well, that's a slight exaggeration. She had her thoughts when she saw the gaping sneaker soles and jeans that only came down to her calves, and supposed young people's fashion was merciless.

"These could be good, too," she says. "And these."

Memories come raining down like becquerels dropping on Chernobyl.

"You can never have too many pairs of jeans, and sweaters. Do you need a sweater?"

"I'll have to get back to school soon," says Svala. "We've got a test."

"What on?" asks Lisbeth.

"History. Norrbotten history."

"Do you like history? Orders of succession, warlords, dates?"

Svala looks as if she doesn't understand the question. "History is probably the most important of all school subjects. How do you think people can understand the future if they don't know their history?"

"Wise words," says Lisbeth. *That kid can't be thirteen. More like thirty-three.*

"You need a computer, too," she says, "and a new phone."

"I'd like a computer, but this phone's fine."

"Everything's still there if you swap. Even photos."

"I'd rather keep my old one."

30

"I'm popping out for a while," says Svala, and leaves her aunt engrossed in figures and symbols rolling across a computer screen.

The snow is still falling thickly and she plows her way over to Santa's post office.

I'm not freezing. Not even my feet.

Not that she normally feels the cold. Putting her hand on a boiling-hot stovetop is no problem, either. But people around her, those who appraise her from top to toe, can see a pair of decent boots now. Not outgrown sneakers with a sole flapping loose even in subzero temperatures. Somebody has taken the trouble. It means everything.

The post office is full of people squeezing cuddly toy animals and buying postcards. She loiters for a while beside an Italian party with their guide. At high school in Gasskas, German is the only additional language option. That's why she's doing Italian, Spanish, Chinese and Russian via an app. So far she has only covered the basics, but she still manages to catch the odd word. She does her best to blend in. Maybe she's even here with her family.

"Excuse me," she says to the elf at the till. "All the letters that come in for Father Christmas, where do they end up?"

"Did you write to him yourself?" asks the elf, but Svala does not answer. "They come here," says the elf. "Santa and his workshop elves read all the letters. Then we put them in a special cupboard. What country are you from?"

"South Africa," says Svala, and the elf points to the glass-fronted pigeonhole for South Africa.

"I'm afraid the cupboard is locked, but perhaps you can catch a glimpse of your letter," she says. "Or write another one."

She doesn't want to do that. She just wants to be sure that Santa's post office exists and that the letters get read. Then she moves on and follows the arrows to the Christmas House.

The wooden staircases wind their way to the upper floor. Even though she's not a child, never has been, she still feels a little nervous at the prospect of meeting Father Christmas. There's something special about it.

Yes, she would like her photo taken and to have the conversation recorded and saved on a memory stick.

She sits on the chair beside him. They sit in silence for a moment. She is very small compared to him. He has a cold.

"I always write to you," says Svala. "Maybe you know who I am, Svala from Sweden." A stupid question, a complete long shot, but Father Christmas nods.

"I know who you are," he says. "Father Christmas knows everything."

"Like God," says Svala.

"Like God," he replies.

"Then you know that my mum has gone missing," she says, and he nods again. "And maybe you can tell me where she is. Or at least whether she's alive."

"When I was little, just a tiny elf, my mum disappeared, so I know how it feels."

"Did she ever come back?"

Father Christmas takes his time answering. "I never stopped hoping," he says, "and suddenly there she was, back home again."

"Where had she been?"

"On a long holiday. Perhaps your mum has gone away on holiday, too?"

She knows full well that Father Christmas doesn't know where her mother is, but it still feels good to talk to him. She thinks about her next question. He blows his nose.

"Can I ask you something?" she says, putting her hand in her pocket.

"Of course. When you visit Father Christmas, you can ask for whatever you like."

"I want to give you this," she says, taking out a rectangular parcel wrapped in homemade Christmas paper. "It's for you, but you mustn't open it until Christmas."

"Of course not. I am Father Christmas, after all. I'll put it here with these other parcels for now."

"No, I want you to take it home with you. I've written to you so many times and never had an answer. So, like, you owe me."

He squirms. Blows his nose again and has a drink of glögg or whatever it is Father Christmas drinks.

"OK," he says, "that's agreed. I promise. On my honor."

Svala knows a good deal about honor. A hint of threat never hurts, as Pap Peder likes to say.

"I've got you on film should you happen to forget." Then she stands up, pats him on the shoulder and says she hopes he gets better soon.

The funny thing is that he really does know who she is. This is his first autumn as Santa Claus. Every holiday while he was in high school and all through his journalism training, he's had a part-time job at Santa Land. Generally opening letters, reading them and occasionally answering. Because his father is Swedish, he's in charge of the letters from Sweden.

Contrary to what most people think, more adults than children write to Father Christmas. Sad tales of poverty and divorce, incurable illness and loneliness, with Father Christmas as their last hope.

He answers them as best he can. Says it will all sort itself out. You have to never stop hoping and wishing for everything to be alright in the end. That's all you can do.

But the girl's letters are different from the rest. She doesn't write letters. She writes poetry.

The poems make him laugh and cry. Above all it is her language, as if she belongs in a volume of literary history. She writes so well; he can see that as an amateur poet himself. If only he could have answered the letters. She always ends with "Svala H." Never with her address.

And that is why he's taken certain liberties. Taken photos of the poems and passed them off as his own under the pseudonym Svala H. Initially only individual words and phrases, but then, over time, whole poems. He has even—and he feels so ashamed at the very thought that he has to take a break and go to the toilet—translated them into Finnish, sent them to a publisher and had them accepted. In just a few weeks, the poetry collection will be in the shops. And Christ, it's getting pretty sweaty inside his costume all of a sudden. His beard is all itchy and the frames of his glasses are digging into his temples.

He is a fake. A total idiot who stole a girl's poems and made them his own. He slams the bathroom door and pelts down the stairs and out into Santa Square, but there is no Svala H. in dove-gray quilted jacket and pink woolly hat among the tourists in their borrowed ski suits.

"Hello, Santa, be in a picture with us," calls somebody, and he has definitely missed his chance to find her. Father Christmas may well be a myth. A make-believe figure from childhood who flies across the world in his sleigh to deliver presents. But in Santa Claus Village he is very much alive. He stands in the middle of the shot and puts safe arms around little shoulders and smiles paternally into the camera phone.

Just as Svala's asked him to, he takes her parcel with him at the end of the working day. Eeli Bergström could open it and perhaps find an address, but he decides not to pass it along. He will have to take the consequences of his actions. Let the poetry collection come out. Hopefully only in Finnish.

Svala watches him through the window of the Marimekko shop. Sees him fly down the steps with his Father Christmas jacket fluttering like a skirt. He's looking for someone. And she makes sure to keep out of the way, in case he's changed his mind about the parcel.

31

Mikael Blomkvist gets himself a ten-krona coffee from the vending machine and makes a mental note to have a word with Salo about the library.

For a municipality of twenty thousand inhabitants, soon to be thirty, it is ludicrously small. A history section with local reference books. A section for novels that also includes poetry, essays, biographies, short stories and fantasy. Separate, larger sections for crime fiction and romance. The rest, at least half, consists of books for children and young people, and that is only right. Plus half a shelf of LGBTQ+ books. The whole lot crammed into a space no larger than a smallish living room.

Things look a little better in the newspaper section.

As in all libraries, people are scattered around at tables and in armchairs, absorbed in news items and magazine articles. Mikael Blomkvist snatches up the only Stockholm paper and sits at a table with a view over to the river and the police station.

How gray can a day be? How small can people seem, how big can council offices be built and how the hell can anybody live here, he thinks as he sips his coffee and watches everyday life outside the window.

A woman emerges from the police station. He keeps his eyes on her. The wind plasters her hair around her face. She digs into her pocket. Tames her hair into a severe bun. Skids on a patch of ice, regains her balance and takes out her phone.

Is this the way it is in small places? No one can be anonymous because everywhere there is some bored bastard in a café, petrol station, car or library studying the world around them under a magnifying glass, as if it were a rare stamp.

He looks around. Presumably nobody has overlooked the outsider with the brown bangs falling over a finely scarred right cheek. His way of pushing his hair out of his eyes, his corduroy jacket that is too thin for this weather and his Böle Tannery bag that cost him half a month's wages and is the only luxury purchase he has ever indulged in. He and Göran Persson, former prime minister.

A woman in a gray coat goes into the police station. A man in a gray suit comes out. *Wait a minute.* There's something familiar about him. Mikael Blomkvist dredges his mind and memories return. Some make his muscles hurt. Others make his balls ache. Make his arms itch. His cheeks redden. His back stiffen. The man on the street is of the itchy-arm variety.

Hans Faste, probably one of the worst police officers in Sweden. He comes strutting out of police HQ with a smile on his lips. He does not hold the door open for the woman going in, most likely does not even see her, and walks briskly toward the car he has discourteously parked in a handicapped space.

Hans Faste. Colleague of Sonja Modig, Jan Bublanski and what was his name? Curt something. Svensson, maybe.

Yet they are only the advance guard for another person entirely.

She's not a police officer.

Never will be.

Hates society the way a vegan hates a meatball and is forever bound up with his past: Lisbeth Salander.

To begin with, he sent at least one e-mail a week. When the daily grind started getting in the way, maybe one a month. Nowadays he only sends one on Christmas Eve. She has never answered. That's not to say he doesn't think about her. He catches sight of a back. Is reminded of her hair. But it is never her. This couldn't be her.

Rather than opening the newspaper, he sends a message.

`<Hi Lisbeth, it's been a long time. Am in Gasskas in Norrbotten and just saw Hans Faste. Thought of you. What are you up to these days? Love/M.>`

When the phone pings only seconds later he is genuinely surprised.

`<Best of luck with that moron. Laters. Lisbeth>`

Well, what had he expected? Nothing, really. His forefinger is itching to send another, but he restrains himself. At least he knows she's still on the same pay-as-you-go phone number.

She's out there somewhere. Perhaps that's all he needs to know.

"Oh, hello. Fancy seeing you here."

Sober, with a fresh haircut and gloomier than ever. IB from the Security Service.

"Oh, hello," Mikael says. "Good to see you. How are you doing?"

"So-so," he says. "Mustn't complain."

Gray can evidently get even grayer.

"It wasn't Malin they found, by the way, so now we're back to square one."

"Still sounds sort of positive," says Mikael. "At least there's a chance of her still being alive. Have a seat. You want a coffee?"

"Yes, please," says IB, turning the newspaper around. He laughs out loud.

"They never change," he says.

"What's happened?" asks Mikael.

"Nothing new, that's for sure, but Thomas de Deus seems to have messed up. He and his wife."

Mikael has only had time to read the headline. So they were the ones involved, but who the hell cares, at the end of the day? Since the Sweden Democrats made their entry into Swedish politics, the bar is set as high as it possibly can be. Taking part in street assaults on "baboons," their choice term for refugees from Africa, and then being put in charge of the party's justice policy doesn't raise an eyebrow. Going straight from your Hitler salute at a party at your house to being responsible for schools is equally unproblematic. Nobody knows how they get away with it, but just as Donald Trump can lie and slander and even get a mob to storm the Capitol without being there himself, the SD progresses by denying everything point-blank.

It was not a Hitler salute, I was reaching for something on a high shelf. I did not punch an unarmed refugee to the ground, I was ice cold with fear and thought I was going to die. Pure self-defense.

Yet they're not the worst offenders, because he can sort of understand them. They have a calling, a single cause that they're passionate about, even if it is loathsome. The worst offenders are the others, the mainstream politicians. The established parties that keep their promises for about as long as it takes to draft a new one.

We will never work with the Sweden Democrats. Yeah, sure!

And although he understands that politicians can never afford to take the long view or be reflective when the population bases its opinions on a finger stuck up on social media, he can't help grieving over their incontinent neediness. They ought to be more hardened. A bit more like himself, refusing to subscribe to every newfangled idea.

The headlines in the paper are about the lover shared by Christian Democrat Thomas de Deus and his wife, Ebba. They circulate photos between them, which have been intercepted by a hacker who threatens to pass them to the press if payment is not forthcoming. Mr. de Deus opts to pay because he's a little closer to God than other people and doesn't want to risk getting stuck at the Pearly Gates. Which in his earthly life would mean losing his position as a pastor and his credibility as an MP.

The hacker blithely takes the money and forwards the pictures to the Truth of the Day website, which publishes them and paves the way for the rest of the media.

The lover is quite something, too. De Deus has made a name for himself as a proponent of tough measures against criminality and strict quotas on refugees. The lover, it turns out, has been convicted of murder and is to be deported and banned from the country for the rest of his life, yet he's still in a comfortable top-floor flat in a newly built high-rise in Kista.

"Pathetic," says Mikael. "How lazy can you get? If they'd dug a bit further, about ten Google searches and a few phone calls, they could have built a much fuller story than this. De Deus was on the carpet fifteen years ago. That time it was rape. The girl took her own life and de Deus walked free on the grounds of lack of evidence."

"You're a journalist, I take it," says IB. "So you think you're better than this lot?"

"No, but I make sure I've got more meat on the bones. Not just scraps."

"Yet you've missed what's going on right in front of your nose," says IB.

"Oh yes?" says Mikael. "That sounds exciting."

"Henry Salo. I don't know why nobody's nailed that clown. And not only him, but all the other corrupt politicians and officials in Gasskas who are lapping sour cream out of his dirty hand."

"You sound angry," says Mikael.

"I am angry," says IB. "Eleven hundred windmills will be whining right across this community if he gets his way. This whole forest, where Gasskas residents have the legal right to roam, is going to be turned into an industrial site. We will mobilize all our resources to protect green industry, the politicians chorus. Salo goes so far as to profess his love of mines. It's not just that he sees them as a necessary evil—he loves them. For Salo and his cronies, it's about so much more," IB continues. "They want to write themselves a place in history as the men who cleared the way to a new Norrland. But it isn't a new Norrland. Sorry, Salo, there's very little new under the sun. Today it's the same old exploiters, extortioners and mercenary colonizers shouting loudest as it was five hundred years ago. The only difference is that the king doesn't care about silver, reindeer skins and salmon fishing. In his case, environmental issues lie closest to the heart. Such a crying shame he has no power anymore."

"Are things really that bad?"

"No, they're worse. But maybe you don't read the Flashback Forum?"

"Occasionally," says Mikael. "But it can't be Salo's decision alone to exploit the public land? That's not how municipal politics works."

"No? OK, then," says IB, "how does it work?"

"Well, by political decision-making. Officials put forward proposals, which are approved or turned down by the municipal councilors, that is, democratically elected politicians. Singling out Salo as a dictatorial ruler seems a bit far-fetched," says Mikael.

"But if the politicians, officials, businessmen and bankers all belong to the same gentlemen's club where they tie things up, wouldn't you say the word 'corruption' springs to mind?" says IB.

"What are you talking about?"

"The Tigertooth Order. Have you never heard of it?"

"No," says Mikael. "The Lions' collection of old glasses and out-of-date medicines, perhaps, but not the Tigertooth Order."

"I gather Salo is your future son-in-law," says IB, making it sound like a swear word. "He's one of the highest-ranking members, possibly the highest of the lot. Ask if you can go along to a meeting. They sometimes invite aspiring members. And speaking of Salo," he says, "I'm sure as hell he has something to do with Malin's disappearance. I can't prove it, but I know I'm right."

IB is not just anybody. He has recently retired from the Security Service. Knows people in the police. Or he could simply be a deeply unhappy father who wants to find his daughter and is clinging on to hope.

"What would your criminal profile for Salo be, then?" asks Mikael.

"Corrupt, low self-esteem, dual personality, empathy deficit disorder."

Mikael whistles. "My daughter seems to have found a real winner."

"Make a joke of it if you like," says IB, "but let me give you a lead to follow up. It's about Malin, but not just her, actually. Quite a few young people have gone missing these past few years. Several months after she disappeared, Malin's aunt found a phone that she handed in to the police."

"Did she give it straight to the police, or to you?" asks Mikael.

"Alright," says IB. "To me, and I passed it on to the police."

"And where does Salo come into the picture?"

"The phone had a message on it with coordinates that matched the location of Salo's house. He had already bought the place but not moved in."

"So that makes you assume Salo had something to do with Malin's disappearance?"

"Exactly. It can't be a coincidence. I think there's something fishy about Salo. His hands may very well be scrubbed with Dettol."

Mikael checks his watch. He's due to have lunch with Pernilla in ten minutes.

"Do you still have the coordinates?"

"Yep."

"That's a good book you've borrowed, by the way. Stieg Larsson and Mikael Ekman's *Sweden Democrats: The National Movement*. I thought they'd taken that one off the shelves long ago."

"It's as topical now as it was then. And we've got the election next year, besides. I'd bet my bottom dollar Sweden Democrats are going to get onto the municipal council."

Or into the government.

. . .

A text message from IB pings into his phone as he sits at the taco bar in the indoor market to wait for Pernilla. He finds the council offices' phone number and asks to be put through to Salo.

"Hi there. Just wondering . . . your businessmen's club, the Tigertooth Order, has its next meeting soon, doesn't it? Is that something I could tag along to?"

"No. You have to have two personal recommendations."

"You and . . . ? I'd enjoy spending some time with men again. I've really missed it, to be honest."

"OK, OK," says Salo, sounding stressed. "Got to go. I'll see what I can do."

Mikael Blomkvist has found something to poke around in, even though it's unlikely to lead anywhere. And he may get a foot in the door of the power and the glory, Amen.

For the first time in ages, he feels a slight sense of exhilaration.

32

Svala has evidently found a soulmate, Lisbeth notes, watching the girls snuggle together under the reindeer skins in the sleigh. They are the same age, and Mei, as the other girl is called, does something to Svala. She gets her to talk. Lisbeth does her best to eavesdrop. They're not talking about boys or music or anything else that teenagers presumably talk about. They're discussing books. Or maybe not even books. Literature.

"I thought it was a bit too long," says Mei, referring to *Anna Karenina*.

"Me, too," says Svala. "But just imagine if the book had been too short for some of those incredible sentences."

"There's that, of course," says Mei, and passes her half a Finnish chocolate wafer bar.

"Xiè xie," says the kid in reply, because naturally she has learned Chinese in an afternoon, thinks Lisbeth, pulling the rug over herself and her Greek-Chinese companion.

It's a squeeze. Their legs are pressed together. Or rather, he does his best to make sure they are.

"Smart daughter you have there," says Long, and Lisbeth still cannot face explaining her position in the family tree. Truths generate questions. She is glad to be spared them.

"First tour of the year," the sleigh driver calls out to them, a young man with a knife dangling from a wide belt.

"Are we going on a bear hunt?"

"I'll take you on a ride of about forty-five minutes," he says. "My tip is to sit quietly and just enjoy the scenery."

The snow has eased off, to be replaced by a cautious sun that will soon be setting. Kostas Long seems to have a vast range of words for beauty and it sure is as pretty as a postcard, but Lisbeth thinks about her job and when she's stopped thinking about that, she thinks about the message from Plague.

<Did some more digging. Peder Sandberg saves pictures to a cloud. He seems to like taking photos.>

```
<Child porn?>
```

```
<No, a different kind of gross. Pain turns him on.
```
Other people's, that is.>

```
<Is there a young blond girl who looks just like
```
Camilla in the pictures?> she writes, but deletes the message without sending it. `<Copy the files>` she writes instead.

```
<Done.>
```

Lisbeth looks at Svala, who is looking at Mei. All at once, that serious face breaks into a smile that transforms her into her very own self, not a copy of Camilla. An individual who may never find her place among ordinary mortals, but hopefully not among social outcasts, either. It is a balancing act, as she has learned from personal experience. When life becomes a matter of life and death, backing out is not an option; she knows that all too well.

Did you realize what a commitment you were making? comes Mrs. Ågren's question from far in the future. *No,* she is going to reply, *but I had no choice.* So there she is again. First she was the girl who played with fire. Now she's the girl who had no choice. Pathetic.

A sleigh ride with reluctant reindeer does not go fast. It goes so slowly that the Lorentz factor in $E = mc^2$ does not apply. Lisbeth has all but dozed off when she feels a hand stroking her leg.

"What are you doing?" she says, not removing it.

"Rest for a while if you're tired," he says, continuing to run his hand slowly over her body.

"Think of the girls," whispers Lisbeth. "The closest they've come to this in biology is some sea god who gets seduced by a siren."

"I recommend the Peking duck," says Long a couple of hours later when they're sitting in a Chinese restaurant with the menus in front of them.

Lisbeth dismisses the suggestion. "If they can't serve a proper pizza, then at least I can have an entrecôte with chips and béarnaise sauce," she says. "And no bloody garlic butter."

They are like two separate parties who have been placed at the same table.

"Your daughter is beautiful," says Long.

"Yours, too," says Lisbeth. Politeness must rub off. "Perhaps they'd like to sleep in the same chalet," she says. "We have two rooms at ours, so you can take one."

For Christ's sake, Lisbeth, you don't even want this.

Maybe not, but I want an escort.

After a taxi stop for crisps, sweets and fizzy drinks, they say good night to the "daughters" and lock the door.

"Do you fancy a Finnish sauna?" asks Lisbeth, fiddling with the heater controls.

"Why not?" says Long. "I've never tried one."

While the sauna is heating, they share a bottle of champagne. That is, Lisbeth makes a genuine effort but then opens a bottle of Coke instead.

"Champagne's overrated," she says.

"So is Coke," he replies, and asks what line of work she's in.

What line of work is she in and how private does she want to be? Dentist? Easy enough to fake. Everybody knows what a dentist does. But then this guy would turn out to have been a goddamned dentist in an earlier life.

"Programmer," she says. *Near enough to the truth, anyway.* "I develop updates for Microsoft. Word is my specialty." *Was that necessary?*

Lisbeth gets undressed. First her jeans, then her T-shirt and finally her knickers all land in the same pile. She has not bothered to put on a bra.

Her companion unbuttons his shirt and hangs it on a coat hanger. He folds his trousers neatly along the creases and arranges them on a reindeer-skin pouf. He puts his socks neatly on top so as not to lose them. And his underpants on top of the socks.

Shut up, Santa, don't laugh.

Their skin burns against the sauna bench. They have been there only a few minutes before Long has had enough.

"If you don't mind," he says, "perhaps we could . . ."

She can see he's suffering. She thinks he can suffer for a while longer.

"Taking saunas is healthy," she says. "Good for the heart."

"Excuse me," he says, and staggers out.

For the sake of appearances, she sticks it out for a few minutes more before she goes to take a shower.

He is lying on the bed and looks as if he's dead.

"Are you alive?"

"I think so."

"You're not exactly a tough guy, are you?" she says, and lies down beside him. Turns off the light and switches on the stars.

"Incredible. Now I see why the roof is made of glass. We should have had the daughters here," he says. "I bet they can spot all the constellations, no matter where they are in the world."

"I'm not Svala's mother," says Lisbeth.

"I know. Mei told me." Hair that has been neatly brushed back falls in a soft wave over his face. She has barely looked at him. Only as a body. A potentially acceptable body.

"What?"

He strokes her temples with gentle fingertips.

"Nothing."

Out of the corner of her eye, she sees something spreading like spilled watercolor across the ceiling of glass.

"Look," she says, turning his face to the sky.

"Incredible," he says, propping her against his shoulder. "Shall we make love under the Northern Lights, or shall we just watch?"

"Watch."

"Alright," he says, pulling her closer to him.

There is something about the smell of him. She inhales it like fresh air. And there is something about his hands. They are attached to arms that have worked hard. She mentally notes tattoos and registers his ring, but what the hell? Tonight, he could be a married assassin for all she cares.

Were it not for the kid's parting words: *Don't do anything stupid.*

She pushes away his hands but they're instantly there again, and not only the hands. *Come here, little girl with the dragon tattoo.* Mouth, tongue, teeth, cock. Has morality ever won out over sexual arousal? He turns her onto her stomach and bites the back of her neck. Holds down her arms. Drops his full weight onto the dragon's back before he pushes into her with a lion's roar. He is the owner. She is the property.

. . .

The next day the Northern Lights have been replaced by a sky as gray as granite. The lion is a castrated domestic cat. Not that she cares. He was just a body.

"I apologize for yesterday," he says, twisting his wedding ring. "Too much champagne, I'm afraid." Thank God he's not going to tell her about his long, dull marriage.

When he finally leaves, she does twenty extra push-ups and a hundred sit-ups. Four katas and *kihon* to second black. She comes to a decision. Whatever the kid has done, or her mum, she has had enough. Financially speaking, they could live with Father Christmas until they die, but Lisbeth has made up her mind. She can't shackle herself to a teenager, however charming it may sound. She can't wait to get home. Home to her 3,500 square feet of solitude, free from furniture, teenagers, Greek-Chinese men and all manner of Christmas clowns.

33

"You slept with him?" asks Svala in the car on the way back to Gasskas.

"None of your business."

"He has a wife."

"That's his problem."

They sit mutely all the way to the border crossing between Torneå and Haparanda.

"Did you girls see the Northern Lights?" says Lisbeth, to relieve the silence.

"Of course. But you probably don't even know what makes them happen," says Svala tartly.

"No, but I'm sure you do."

"Yes, I pay attention in physics lessons. Aurora borealis is formed when charged particles, mostly electrons, reach a certain speed in the magnetosphere and crash-land in the atmosphere, where they collide with molecules and atoms, which in turn get energy from the electrons."

"Electrons on speed," says Lisbeth. "Any idiot can google that, I daresay."

Svala looks at her and shakes her head. "Anyone would think I was the adult in the car, but OK, then, we'll use your metaphor: when the speed wears off, photons are formed, if you remember what they are."

"Japanese beds."

"Photons, spelled 'p-h-o.' Want me to explain or not?"

"Go on."

"A photon is the smallest possible particle that can be transferred by magnetic radiation, and it appears when, for example, an atom moves from higher to lower energy. It is in that process that the different colors of the Northern Lights are formed. To reference your world, we might say it was reminiscent of strobe lights at a rave party. Blue is extremely rare, so I hope you weren't concentrating on anything but the sky last night." Even though she is in a sulk, she cannot contain her excitement about the blue light. "Moskosel, 2010," she says. "That was the last time anybody saw the blue. It's not that far from Gasskas."

"Speaking of Gasskas, I've been thinking about your mum's debt. What do you know about it?"

"Nothing. Those goons showed up when she went missing. They made me break into a house, but when I got the safe open it was empty."

"Seems fishy. Why would they get you to do a break-in if the safe was empty?"

"How should I know?"

"It sounds like a made-up story. Safes don't just open like that."

"It's to do with numbers. I look at them, somehow. Or feel them. I can't really describe it. It's like being in some kind of altered state."

"Odd that you only got a C in maths, then."

"My teacher thinks I ask annoying questions. So I pretend I can't do it."

A little school visit might be in order. Ram the calculator down the fucker's throat.

A couple of decent pizzas (with extra cheese) later, they continue toward Gasskas. The Kalix River winds slowly beside them like a crocodile. Solitary houses sit on little islands where the river widens. Red dolls' houses with white-painted corners and outhouses. The perfect hiding place. A clear view and no contact with land.

"What was my dad like?" says Svala. The question comes out of nowhere, but it is not unexpected.

"Big. A man of few words. I barely knew him. How about you?" she forces herself to say. "Do you remember anything about him?"

"Think so," says Svala. "He used to carry me on his shoulders. I held on to his hair. It was black."

"White," says Lisbeth. "Like yours."

"I suppose it must have been white, then" she says. "He vanished when I was two."

More like before you were born.

And while they're sloshing about in the mud of the family album, she wants to know what "Grandad" was like.

A psychopath. Someone who reveled in violence. A swine who should have been suffocated at birth.

"My parents got divorced when I was little," says Lisbeth. "He came to visit occasionally."

"You think I can't google?" says Svala. "Half your life's there to follow, like an online box set. I get that you don't want to talk about him, but I'd still like to know how it felt."

"How what felt?"

"When you threw the petrol bomb at him."

"You want to do the same to Peder Sandberg?" says Lisbeth.

"Maybe," says Svala.

For the second time on the journey, Lisbeth swings into a lay-by and turns off the ignition. Snow soon covers the windscreen. Twenty-five degrees. Dark, even though it's only just past five.

"OK," says Lisbeth. "You googled, but not everything online or in the newspapers is true."

"Of course not. I'm good at treating my sources critically."

"Alright, then," says Lisbeth. "Most of what's been written about Zalachenko is true. Your grandfather . . . my father . . . abused my mother at the drop of a hat. Turned up whenever he felt like taking out his anger on someone, in this case Mum. He hit her so often and so hard that she suffered brain damage, while my sister and I sat in the room next door, hearing it all. That's the short version."

Thin ice. But the girl isn't just anybody. *How did it feel to pay him back?* "I did what no one else was prepared to do: I tried to save my mum. I don't remember how it felt. Necessary, I'd say. Something I had to do, although I might have hoped there'd be another way of resolving it. It's hard to explain. Social services may be better at helping families these days." Empty words in a car that will soon be snowed over. "*And,* whatever you were thinking as far as Peder is concerned," she adds, "there are other ways of getting your revenge, if that's what you want."

"Such as?" asks Svala.

"The police, the criminal justice system." Even emptier words in a rapidly cooling car. She turns the ignition back on. The tractor-trailers thunder past. The radio starts up. Svala switches it off.

A stray reindeer passes them on the wrong side of the game-proof fence. A car pulls in behind them.

"It's the same for me. It isn't revenge in itself that I care about. I've just got to save my mum."

"What from?" says Lisbeth, approaching the heart of darkness.

"I think she's trying to frame Pap Peder to save me."

"It doesn't seem to be going too well."

"No."

It is only a few days since she came north, but the City Hotel bar feels very distant. The redhead in the hotel bar equally so.

They check in to the same suite as before. The bar is empty. Svala slouches listlessly after her.

"OK," says Lisbeth. "Life sucks cock but there's always exercise. Have you ever tried karate?"

"Could you stop swearing and using disgusting words, please? And no, I haven't."

"OK. Rule number one. All karate begins and ends with a bow."

"Was it Long who taught you?"

There's a preachy old lady living inside that kid.

"The Chinese do kung fu. The Greeks, I don't know. Retsina, maybe."

Heels together. Feet turned out. Arms at your sides. Look respectful. And bow.

An hour later, Svala has learned four striking techniques, *tsuki*, three defensive techniques, *uki*, and two kicks, *geri*, plus the most common stances, *dachi*.

"I can already count in Japanese."

Of course she bloody can.

Tonight, Svala chooses to sleep alone. She shuts herself in her room without saying good night.

The restlessness is in Lisbeth like the itch of lice. She needs a plan. Or does she? Can't she just leave the kid with social services and go home? She's already done more than could have been expected. The girl got to meet Father Christmas. Bathed in luxury as a temporary respite from her shitty life. Made a new friend and saw the blue Northern Lights. No, Lisbeth doesn't owe her anything. But perhaps the lice are not only restlessness? The girl is like a bridge to back then. The bridge that she herself blew up long ago.

It is not Lisbeth who is the girl's only living relative. It is the other way around.

She opens a Coke, plumps up the pillows behind her back and carries on with her reading of the wad of papers from social services. There is so much that isn't right. The girl is a genius, for Christ's sake, but they're squandering her gifts with comments like "Seen by some of her teachers as provocative and prone to dissent" and "Difficulties with social interaction." Throwing her to the wolves hurts more than Lisbeth had anticipated. She mulls over the alternatives. Take her back to Stockholm. No. Leave her unprotected in Gasskas in some family home where the sole aim is to turn children into a source of income? No, that won't do, either.

She browses through the file. Mother. Märta Hirak has family somewhere nearby. Reindeer-keeping Sami. Two brothers and a sister. Their father has been dead for about two years. Their mother, Svala's grandma, that is, seems to have shuttled between Märta and the others. Hordes of cousins and other relatives, presumably. Surely some of them could take pity on Svala?

"We've tried to make contact with them," says Erik Niskala as they sit in the social services office the next day. "Most recently was three or four years ago, I suppose. They made it extremely clear to us that they don't want to have anything to do with Märta, or her daughter."

That daughter looks out the window. Apparently taking no interest in the conversation going on around her. She has brought her computer and has it on her lap. Every so often, she types something.

"Is it entirely out of the question for her to stay with you until we find a good alternative?" he says.

Lisbeth looks out the window, too. She does not know what to reply.

"And if I say no?" she asks finally.

"We hope we would be able to find her an emergency placement. If all else fails, she'll have to stay at Himlagården for a few weeks."

"And what's that?" says Lisbeth.

"Residential care for children and young adults," Svala pipes up. "It'll be terrific, I'm sure. I'll be able to learn to do drugs and get better at breaking and entering."

"That sounds like an interesting complement to the elementary particle physics."

"Yes, quarks and leptons are a bore. Time to take it to the next level."

"You'll get your own room, all your meals provided and help with your homework," tries Niskala.

Lisbeth and Svala subject him to a stare that is both amused and aloof. They do not look alike, but still they somehow melt into each other. As for Niskala, his authority melts like ice cream in a sauna. In their eyes he's presumably nothing but a sad social worker with limited resources. Rather as he sees himself. Especially since Marie moved out. He wonders where she is and who she's with. Someone better, of course. Someone who does carpentry around the house and sticks to a moderate half a bottle of red with his Friday steak. Exercises four times a week and comes in the top two hundred in the grueling Vasaloppet ski race.

"I'll do my best to set up an emergency placement," he says. "But for now we can organize a flat."

"In Svartluten?" asks Svala.

"Yes," he says. "How did you guess?"

"People who read Tolstoy usually end up there."

"Fuck that," says Lisbeth. "We'll stay on at the hotel."

34

Lisbeth makes it into the convenience store just before they close. Five minutes later she's mixing ranch dip with sour cream.

"They've got *Kill Bill 2* on channel four," says Lisbeth. "Have you seen the first one?"

"Don't think so."

"Let's watch that for starters, then. The hotel's got Netflix. Beatrix Kiddo."

"And she is . . . ?" says Svala.

"Immortal."

"But not Bill?"

"No, not Bill."

Svala keeps one eye on the film and the other on her phone as she texts.

Something good is happening. Her face takes on a softer expression.

"You look pleased," says Lisbeth.

"Mmm. I'm texting with Mei. They might be coming to Sweden after Christmas."

"But not to Gasskas, I hope," says Lisbeth, and gets a hard stare.

"Mei and I can't help the fact that you two screwed things up," she says.

Lisbeth would like to know what is special about Mei. In view of how mediocre her father is. Svala doesn't seem to have any pals. Boyfriend?

"None of your business."

"You're right. But for your information we slept in separate rooms. Like you say, he's married."

"Sure you did," says Svala. "Did you know, by the way, that they gave sick people sheep's blood in the seventeenth century?"

"No, I somehow missed that nugget of information."

"Well, they did, or the blood of the young, which was considered rejuvenating, until the patients suddenly died. Today they know there are more than a hundred different blood types and they're identifying new ones all the time. Do you know what yours is?"

"Something common. How about you?"

"Something unusual, I think."

"Have you ever been in hospital?" says Lisbeth.

"Only for fractures. Collarbone, ribs, thigh bone, wrists and skull." She makes it sound like part of everyday life. "I've got this condition."

"Vittangi disease," says Lisbeth, "it's in your file."

"You've read my file? I thought that sort of thing was confidential."

"Oh, sorry," says Lisbeth, switching off the TV as the credits roll. "I wasn't exactly planning to publish them in *Gaskassen*."

She checks the time. It isn't late and Thursdays are a kind of Saturday, after all.

"I'm just going out for a bit, if that's OK?"

"Of course," says Svala. "Be home by twelve at the latest."

"I promise. Call if you need me."

"Likewise."

35

Lisbeth takes the lift down to the bar. Life has been upended. And not just life, but her whole existence.

Before, she only had herself. Having another person in your life pushes other things to one side. Like work.

They are not buddies, obviously. If Lisbeth plays in the regular Hockey Allsvenskan, Svala plays in the elite SHL league. That's what the kid thinks, anyway, and sure. She knows so much, sucks up knowledge like a whale swallowing plankton. But she's young. Inexperienced. Not everything in life is theoretical.

It can be erotic, too.

The hotel bar is already heaving. The sound of hot-blooded young male voices must have exceeded the comfortable decibel level some time ago.

She stands at the far end of the bar and tries to make eye contact with Tom Cruise's colleague. Tom himself seems to have a night off.

She checks her phone. Yet another way for the transformation from lone wolf to overprotective mother to express itself. Dare she have an alcoholic drink? What if the kid were to ring all of a sudden?

Fuck it. A few more weeks and she can go back to Stockholm. Maybe the girl can come and visit now and then. She would be amazed by the city. The flat. The view. The dojo. The pizzas.

She would sigh at Lisbeth's austere solo life.

She reads her text from Micke B. one more time. `<Am in Gasskas in Norrbotten . . . Thought of you.>`

Every time he messages, usually around Christmas, she's pleased at first and then . . . furious.

Memories check in. Ask for the royal suite and stay until they're thrown out. She cannot do as other people do, put things behind her and forget. As soon as she sees his name, the shame is there. She wanted him. Was prepared to take a chance. But just when she had plucked up the courage to go and see him, he emerged from a front door. Arm in arm with that woman from *Millennium*. Erika Berger.

It's an integral part of your personality, says Mrs. Ågren. Some people find it harder to forget than others. You probably have an exceptional visual memory, too, he says. The two usually go together. Brilliant brains find it hard to forget. They have to approach their demons differently.

She is aware of the perfume a few seconds before she feels a hand on her shoulder. But still it makes her jump.

"Oops, hello, it's only me, Jessica. If you remember me."

She looks different. No-makeup different. More vulnerable. More open.

AI robot Lisbeth Salander scans Jessica Harnesk for a few seconds. Newly washed hair, no nail polish, worn jeans and a casual, perfectly tucked-in top with baggy sleeves. Boots, the same ones as last time, a necklace with small vertical name tiles, most likely her children, a leather bracelet with silver embroidery, probably Sami. Small handbag, contents unknown, and an oversized parka which she hangs on a hook under the bar and then tries to catch the bartender's eye.

"I took a chance," she says. "Wondered whether you might drop by. What can I get you to drink? G and T?"

Lisbeth is about to say Coke, but has second thoughts. "A beer," she says. "As long as it's big and cold."

"Big and warm can be quite sexy, too," says Jessica. "Sorry," she adds, and blushes for the first time in at least fifteen years. "The work banter must be getting to me."

"What's your job?" asks Lisbeth. This time she isn't going to gamble away her cards by behaving like any man she can think of.

Take an interest in your surroundings! Ask questions! Follow up with more questions!

Shut up, Mrs. Ågren, she says, and reaches for her glass. *Give it a rest for tonight.*

"Cheers," says Jessica. "Let's play guess the profession."

"Librarian?"

"Dyslexic."

"Hairdresser?"

"Close. There's a fair amount of cut and thrust."

"Stockbroker."

"I could certainly do with the salary."

"OK, then, the public sector. Nurse. Prison warder. Social worker. Traffic warden."

"Make a cocktail out of all those and you'll have your answer."

An uncomfortable feeling is growing inside Lisbeth. They are nearing an inescapable conclusion. How the hell? It must be the kid making her lose her judgment.

"You're a police officer."

Jessica nods.

No, it won't do. Having to collaborate with social services is bad enough. And now a police officer. She stretches her sensibilities even further. Going to bed with a cop? It's like sleeping with the enemy.

"I understand if you're not a fan of the police," says Jessica.

"No, you misunderstand," says Lisbeth. Her whole being wants to get away from there, but Jessica insists.

"Don't go," she says. "I'd like you to stay. I haven't been snooping. I didn't even know your surname. I googled someone else and your name came up. Name, pictures . . . and I admit: I read everything that's up there, including Flashback," she goes on. "No secrets."

No secrets? Sure. Do you really think everything about me is in the public domain? They are getting close to the essence of Lisbeth's aversion to the police, and not only the police. The authorities. Lawyers. Psychiatrists. People who think they know anything about her, even see themselves as specialists, and here's another one. A googler snacking happily on bits of her life. Enlarging images of the poor victim. The child outside the law. The angry girl. The even angrier woman.

Jessica puts a hand over hers and Lisbeth removes it.

Stay in the feeling. Be present in the moment. Mrs. Ågren won't give up.

She doesn't want to feel. She wants to have sex with a tall redheaded woman with Barbie legs and then go home. But the object turns out to be a police officer.

They stand there saying nothing. They finish their beers. Order a couple more.

"I hoped you would be here this evening," says Jessica. "Ever since we met you've been on my mind."

"It isn't mutual," says Lisbeth.

"No, OK, maybe not. I go by my own sense."

"Sense of what?"

"Of people who interest me. It doesn't happen that often. I live a pretty pared-down life. Go to work, pick up the children, come home. Make dinner, tuck in the children, watch some TV series and go to bed. When Henke's got the kids, I do overtime. Come home, watch some TV series and go to bed. I see my sister sometimes. Very occasionally my dad."

Minus the children, not entirely unlike Lisbeth's own life. "Who were you googling when my name came up?"

"My boss, Hans Faste."

"Hans Faste, that old jackass," says Lisbeth.

"The last one had a stroke. I've been standing in since then. So I applied for the job. Faste got it and started this autumn."

"And?" says Lisbeth.

"Sigh," says Jessica. "Maybe. I don't know. I'm sure he's good at what he does. The problem is that our section's used to everyone speaking their minds and no one pulling rank. For Faste, it's all a matter of prestige. He makes fun of any opinion that doesn't come from his own mouth. He wants to be the great paternal leader, but he comes across as a tired old man. I've decided I'll try to warm to him for a little while longer."

"Good luck, then. There's not much to warm to with that one."

"Possibly, but he's got a lot of experience, after all. Serious Crime is a new unit. They say we need a competent boss. One without small children. I'll have to put up with him until he retires. Why do you dislike him so much?" Jessica asks, mainly to get Lisbeth back on side. She already knows the answer.

"Because he's a misogynist and a racist," says Lisbeth. "Something he shares with plenty of people in your line of work, in fact. It seems to come high on the list of desirable qualities. Add a lack of intelligence and empathy, and you've got the prototype for a Swedish cop."

"It's not that bad," says Jessica, smiling at Lisbeth's categorical summary. "Not at our station, anyway. There's the bro-ish banter, of course, and a few guys who think they're tough, but the majority are just decent people trying to do their jobs. Racism and misogyny sound quite extreme."

"But it was still him and not you who got the job," says Lisbeth.

"How about you, what are you doing up here?" says Jessica, shifting the focus from herself.

Now it's Lisbeth's turn to sigh.

"Looking after a relative," she says. "A niece with a messy family setup. It's only temporary; I hope I'll be heading home soon."

"And where's home?" Jessica asks, and gets a strange look.

"Stockholm, naturally. Do you want another beer?"

"I'd love one," says Jessica. "Just heading to the ladies' first."

36

"Now I get it. You're the one fucking my wife. You might have thought she'd have better taste."

Lisbeth turns and looks up at a solidly built man with furious eyes.

"You've got the wrong person," says Lisbeth. "I don't know who your wife is, but she's not with me, anyway."

"No, she just went to the bathroom. She's my wife and not somebody who goes to bed with lesbian freaks."

The lesbian freak is initially speechless. Where the hell do these moronic, jealous husbands come from? Do they hatch them in a special factory and put them in strategic places to make women's lives a misery, or do they have the same defective gene that repeats itself over and over again?

"I don't know what you're thinking," she says then, "but regardless of any sick fantasies you may have, you can damn well stop telling me who to talk to. And if you want to keep your wife, I suggest you do the same with her."

"Former wife," says Jessica, back at the bar. "Where are the children, Henke?"

"That," says the man, grabbing Jessica by the chin, "is nothing for you to worry your little head about. It's my week, and the children are mine."

He is drunk. Answering back is only going to make it all worse. Years of practice have taught her never to lose her temper, never to raise her voice. He usually calms down after a while.

"Stop that," she says, removing his hand. When the hand returns, Lisbeth has had enough. In the crush and the noise of bawling voices and with the advantage of being short, she grabs hold of the Henke person's crotch—thank you, God, for making sweatpants the uniform of men with defective genes—and twists until he is standing on tiptoe.

"Where are the children, Henke?" she says.

"At hers," he says through gritted teeth.

She twists a bit harder. Right now, his physical build and his hockey-star status give him no advantages. From the depths of his pain he roars out loud and makes the security guard come running.

When Lisbeth lets go, he doubles over and mews like a cat that has been run over.

"Leave Jessica alone," Lisbeth has time to say before the guard drags him out into the street, "or I'll chop off the whole package next time."

She turns to Jessica.

"Autonomic pain reflexes are no joke," she says, and finishes her beer.

"Christ," says Jessica. "That was . . . Well, that was . . . bloody stupid. Now he'll never give up."

"Maybe it's time you started setting your own boundaries," says Lisbeth. "He exploits you because you're nice and don't retaliate."

"Sure, but it's not that easy when your kids are held hostage," she says, pulling on her parka. She takes a few steps toward the door and then turns and looks at Lisbeth.

"Are you coming?"

"He hasn't always been like this," says Jessica when they're sitting on the sofa with a cup of tea and Birna's soft bread, slathered in brown whey cheese.

Then she says it again. The pathetic phrase that is supposed to excuse his behavior. Because really, he's a wonderful person. Thoughtful and unselfish, the perfect man to have chosen as the father of her children and a great lover. Any questions?

"At least he'd put the children to bed," she goes on.

"But leaving them on their own . . . what normal person does something like that?" says Lisbeth. "It's bloody criminal." The name Svala flashes through her consciousness. She ought to check on her. Before long, at any rate. But Svala isn't a child. Or is she? Thirteen. Lisbeth wasn't a child at thirteen. The kid can cope for an evening without a babysitter.

In the gleam of the floor lamp, her hair is even more red. Lisbeth can't resist. She's got to feel the silk running between her fingers like the fringes of a satin tablecloth. To pull Jessica's head toward her and kiss her.

Kostas Long was the foreplay. The urgency of the desire catches her out, sends her hands roving over the woman's body, into curves, under clothes. Police officer or not. She wants to have her. To eat her up. To bury herself in her. To melt into her long arms and Barbie legs, slide over her sweaty skin like a seal basking on the ice, and exult in it.

Jessica responds by pulling her top over her head.

Jeans, socks, knickers, they all come off.

Mouths meet. Teeth clash. Tongue to tongue and practiced fingers finding sensitive points and thin, elastic flesh that is soon engorged and wet.

"Mummy. Mummy!"

"Damn."

"It's Jack," says Jessica, wrapping a blanket around her. "He must have woken up. Don't go anywhere, I'll be right back."

Lisbeth pours more tea. One by one the items of clothing go back on.

There is no sound from upstairs. She scribbles a line on the back of a receipt and shuts the front door behind her.

Outside, fresh snow is falling, covering the whole area in a layer of piped cream. There are lights shining in a few windows. She walks as fast as her worn Stan Smiths will let her. According to her GPS, she needs to plow her way west for 1.4 miles. She breaks into a run wherever there's tarmac showing through. Cuts across a park. Goes around the Åhléns store, ignores a red light at the pedestrian crossing and is almost run down by a motorbike whose driver clearly has not realized it's winter. She turns, keeps her eyes on the chopper and focuses on the back of the leather jacket. The Celtic cross and the axe. The insignia of Svavelsjö M.C. Evil has risen again. And in all the excitement, it felt like a change of scene and moved up north.

Herself. Micke B. Hans Faste. Svavelsjö M.C. They're all in the same place. Not in some district of Stockholm, which might have a natural explanation, but in Gasskas. A dump in the remote inland of Norrbotten with a population of 8.8 per square mile and nothing else but forest.

There must be some connection.

37

"Have fun at the old boys' club," says Pernilla, stopping outside a stone building a block away from the bus station.

"The Tigertooth Order has a women's section, too," says Salo. "It's up to you whether you want to come or not."

"To talk about home furnishings and make Christmas stars out of straw? No thanks, I couldn't stand the thrill. I'll pick you up at eleven. If you're any later, you'll have to get a taxi."

The building is newly plastered and the window glass is painted over.

Salo ought to be scared stiff about letting Blomkvist get acquainted with the inner circle; he's a journalist, after all. Nothing will make him drop a juicy bone once he's got his teeth into it.

Salo, for his part, knows he's taking a calculated risk. But he's a gambling man, after all, and the more he thinks about it, the better it feels. The hack can be unwittingly used to his advantage. With the media on his side, half the battle is won.

"You'll have to take it as you find it," says Salo, "but remember you're my guest. What's said in here stays in here. People feel safe in that knowledge. Or they have done for a hundred and ten years, anyway."

"How often do you meet?"

"Every other week. Anders Renstad and I have recommended you as a member. Recommendation by at least two members is a requirement. You should know it's unprecedented to propose a member from outside Gasskas. But as I say, tonight you're our guest."

"Who's Renstad?" asks Mikael.

"CEO of Municipal Gasskas Companies. Better known to the locals as Kommunala Gasskasbolagen, or KGB."

The Swedish Security Service and the "KGB" in the same backwater. Things are getting interesting.

The door closes on the world. Neither sound nor light penetrates the two-hundred-year-old stonework of what was originally the courthouse.

"Plenty of people tonight," says Salo. "Perhaps it's the weather." He greets fellow members as he moves through the crowd, shakes hands with some, nods and chats with a chosen few.

"Is it time for us to drink blood and wave skulls on sticks?" whispers Mikael.

"Sounds more like the Freemasons," says Salo. "We don't go in for that kind of thing."

"What do you do, then?"

"We meet and socialize. The showiest thing we have is the ring," he says, inspecting his hand. A signet ring with a stylized symbol presumably meant to look like a tiger's tooth. "I suppose it's a bit like being in a sports club or a free church," he says. "We dress sharply and meet as gentlemen. Other than that, there's nothing odd about us."

Lucky that Mikael had packed his suit for the wedding.

"So it's more of a gentlemen's club, really?" he says.

"You could call it that."

"But you don't take saunas together?"

"It has been known to happen," says Salo.

"I tried googling the Tigertooth Order and nothing came up. That's weird, isn't it?"

"A bit of mystique never did any harm. We're open to most, as long as he has the right attitude."

"But no women?"

"No, no women. Thank goodness. You said you were desperate for male company, I seem to recall. A bit less old women's gossip about how it feels and a bit more about how it's done."

"Some of my best friends are women." My best friend, at any rate, he thinks. Wherever she's hiding. He must have called her ten times since he came north.

Hi, this is Erika Berger. Leave a message and I'll call you back.

Hi, this is Mikael. Can we at least try to talk about it? Sorry. Call me. Kiss kiss.

"Men can be pretty pathetic sometimes, too. Women's topics of conversation are often more interesting," he says.

"Makeup and soft furnishings," says Salo. "Yeah, that really helps the world move forward."

"Maybe we don't mix with the same sort of women," says Mikael.

"I don't mix with women at all. Apart from Pilla, that is. She's different."

The assembled company initially roosts in the library, arranging itself among oxblood chesterfields and sofas with lion-claw feet.

"Isn't there any hierarchy?" says Mikael.

"Oh yes," whispers Salo. "You start as an apprentice and gradually work your way up through the ranks."

"And what are you?" asks Mikael.

"Crown prince."

"And that is?"

"High up."

The master taps his crystal glass and the buzz of voices dies away.

"Welcome, everybody," he says. "It's wonderful that so many of you were able to come this evening. By popular request we have Jens McLarsson paying us a return visit. This time we'll be taking a deep dive into the fine products of Speyside, Scotland's newest whisky-producing region. But first I'd like to introduce a guest. Mikael Blomkvist, the stage is yours."

"Er, hi," says Mikael, getting to his feet. "It's nice to be here this evening. Thanks to my future son-in-law, Henry Salo, who's about to marry my daughter, Pernilla. Anyway," he says, wondering what to talk about. "I'm a journalist. Paying a visit to Gasskas, with the intention of coming to live here."

What did he just say? Coming to live in Gasskas, this godforsaken little hole? Oh well, let them believe it. Corners of mouths are turning up, in any case. A Stockholmer with an urge to move north is an admission that there are worlds beyond the city limits.

"For a good thirty years I've been working at the magazine *Millennium*. It may not have made its way up here, but it was . . . is . . . a magazine that underlines the crucial role of investigative journalism. That is, worked-through articles that focus on topics like power structures, racism, neo-Nazism, unholy alliances between capital and politics. And one of our more recent subjects is global climate change." He can't resist a tease.

One person rolls their eyes, someone else yawns.

"*Millennium* only exists now as a podcast, so if you want me to send somebody here to do a live broadcast, just shout."

He means it as a joke. Nobody laughs.

Anders Renstad raises a hand.

"Members of the Tigertooth Order are generally politicians, leaders of business and other organizations, although we do have a few members on the cultural side as well. Like Jan Stenberg, editor in chief of *Gaskassen.*" He nods to Mikael. "The question is," says Renstad, "if we admit you as a member, what do you think you have to offer us?"

"Well," says Mikael, "that rather depends on what you're after."

"New networks are always a good start."

Perhaps he ought to just thank them and leave. Gossip and nepotism are not his scene, but there's something about the whole gathering that piques his interest. Sitting right here is the crème de la crème of the Gaskas elite. Directors, municipal officials, media, politicians and so on, scratching each other's monkeypox. With one foot in this association, he could doubtless flush out a few items of interest.

As usual, it's Salo who seems the odd one out. Pernilla says nothing and Salo just doesn't feel right. Mikael isn't quite sure why. For Lukas's sake he will try to find out more. A closed order that only accepts men who have taken a vow of silence is a good start.

"My networks look much like yours, with the distinction that they're largely in Stockholm and abroad. I don't know what else I can say, beyond the fact that investigative journalism is also a question of timing. Finding the right news story at the right moment is more or less like finding a business idea whose time has come."

He rambles on and it seems to hit the spot. There is a ripple of applause and he sits down. Half in.

"I'll hand over to McLarsson in a moment," says the master. "And after that we'll eat well and enjoy ourselves as best we can on this dark and dismal evening."

Six varieties of whisky later, the volume has risen to a comfortable level for those who don't want everyone to overhear. Mikael has Renstad on one side of him and the municipal council chair, Torben Olofsson, on the other.

"I'm not that familiar with the local politics of Gasskas," says Mikael. An open question, evidently with a simple answer.

"It isn't all that complicated," says Olofsson. "We have a stable Social Democrat majority, with experienced politicians working closely with trade and industry and other organizations. Unemployment is low, the schools perform very well when measured against other parts of the country, there's no shortage of housing and the hockey team is on its way into the elite league."

"Sounds like a textbook example of a well-run municipality," says Mikael. Still aiming to flatter and hopefully to appear more stupid than he is.

"There are problems, of course, but we solve those with swift, transparent decision-making," says Olofsson, gesturing toward the full room. "Politics isn't a separate entity, as it were, but everything that impacts citizens. The closer the contact with those citizens, the better the politics. That's the way I see it, anyway."

"But the people here can scarcely be said to represent the ordinary citizen," says Mikael. "Or am I barking up entirely the wrong tree?" he adds to be on the safe side.

"Not directly, but indirectly they do. They are employers, lenders, sports leaders, builders of housing and so on. If we can combine redistributive social democratic policies with the upper levels, it benefits the citizens. In my view, and in the view of the rest of my party group, I think I can say, we've come a long way in developing close ties with trade and industry. It doesn't look like Stockholm, I'm sure, but as I say, we're a municipality with low unemployment and a strong economy in relation to our population numbers. There are no alarming crime rates here, either. People want to do the right thing. Work and keep out of trouble."

"What about the Sweden Democrats, though?" says Mikael. "Are they on their way onto the council?" A question that makes Torben Olofsson laugh out loud.

"Gasskas is solidly Social Democrat, with a small contingent from the left and one or two Moderates. The Sweden Democrats are negligible. I don't believe we're wrestling with the same problems as down in Skåne. The refugee quota is modest and those who do come are well looked after. Crime is still at a low level compared with the rest of Sweden, so there's nothing for the Sweden Democrats to draw oxygen from."

"But," says Mikael, "how do you think it'll be once the billions start rolling into all the new industrial projects? The mine, for example, and the wind farm and so on?"

"We see nothing to indicate that industrial expansion will lead to an increase in crime. Just the opposite. People will come here to work, both the unskilled and the highly skilled. We're ready to take the next step in the municipality's development. Pernilla's very nice, by the way," he says, his voice taking on a different tone. "We socialize sometimes—as couples, that is. Pernilla and my wife are good friends. And soon there'll be the wedding. Not the best season for an outdoor ceremony, but Norrbotten folk are used to whatever the weather throws at them." He lowers his voice and moves a little closer to Mikael. "Salo settling down with Pernilla is going to be good for him. He's softened since he met her. Seems more sensible, somehow."

"That sounds positive," says Mikael, "but how was he before, then?"

"Decisive and energetic, just as he is now, but difficult. Or maybe angry is a better word, and one can understand that."

"Certainly," says Mikael, thinking of that evening in the sauna.

"We can drink to that," says Torben Olofsson. "*Skål!* See you at the wedding."

In the break between the whisky and the dinner, the attendees mingle. Exchange a few words and rotate onward.

"Networks," in the sense of spiders' webs, is clearly misleading. Spiders spin out their threads in a given pattern, not on the basis of who they want to catch in their webs.

If anyone were to map the lines drawn by members of the Tigertooth Order as they move, a clear pattern would emerge.

There are key people; Salo is one of them. The KGB boss is another. The lines converge on them like minor roads heading for a motorway.

"I suggest we revisit our decisions on the wind farm," Salo is saying. "Fortum is already a major player. And the Dutch. Personally, I think the third interested party would best suit our needs. They're ready to begin construction at the end of next year, whereas the others' start dates are at least three years from now. At the end of the day, the most important thing for the municipality is to secure the electricity supply. God only knows what Putin might take it into his head to do. Sabotage Nord Stream or something."

"Now you're exaggerating, surely? But the electricity is important, I totally agree."

On the outer edges, the stream of traffic is perhaps not as intense, but steady. This is where he has found Lennart Svensson, for example.

Then there are other people who are above the concept of "important person" and do not have the same level of traffic. Douglas Ferm, for example. CEO of Paperflow. The pulp mill with the prime lakeside location, which in turn is owned by Swedish Wood.

Ferm has nothing to gain from networking, be it with politicians or council officials, supply chain specialists or bankers. He has underlings to deal with that kind of thing. Alex Ljung, for example. Despite being the youngest person present with his twenty-three years, he has business owners buzzing around him like bees in flowering clover.

The biggest employer in the municipality apart from the municipality itself, handing out subcontracts to those who work best and demand least.

Douglas Ferm is more interested in esoteric values like art and culture. He makes a beeline for Mikael Blomkvist and wonders whether he would like to share a good bottle of red with him and discuss the final issue of *Millennium*.

"Gladly," says Mikael. "I must just pay a visit to the gentlemen's room first."

Pay a visit to the gentlemen's room. Whatever made him come out with such a ridiculous phrase? Perhaps it was Ferm's doing? The members of the Tigertooth Order are affable, locally rooted and not very sophisticated. Like people generally are. Douglas Ferm is something else entirely. Not only in his dress, his rings and his immaculately cut hair. He has charisma. The kind of charisma some leaders have. Those who are born to both setbacks and successes but do not have to take the crappy-job route to get there. Like Mikael, he is an outsider in this crowd.

Mikael shuts the bathroom door and takes out his notebook. He jots down names, appearances, sentences flying through the air, jokes. All things that will probably never be of any significance. And while he's at it, he googles Ferm. Just as well to know what they're going to talk about.

Born on Guernsey in 1964. His father was the founder of one of Sweden's largest paint manufacturers, with its head office and factory in Gasskas. Acquired in the early eighties, after which the factory moved to Estonia. Family: divorced.

CEO since 2017. On the board of Mimer Mining. Earlier career spent largely in the international mining industry.

By the time Mikael emerges, the starter has arrived. Kalix vendace roe on toast. Beer and schnapps for those who will. On his way to his seat he is intercepted by Jan Stenberg, the newspaper editor.

"Just wanted to say hello. Good talk, by the way. We had Jan Emanuel at the last meeting. What a guy! Totally undervalued in the Swedish debate. And incidentally, while we've got an ace journalist in town, maybe you could come to *Gaskassen* and give us a talk on investigative methods? Not that we're bad at it, quite the contrary. More to offer us some inspiration. I'll get your number from Salo. Enjoy your evening."

Shame they don't accept women. Then they could have invited Katerina Janouch as well. What a gal! Totally underestimated in the Swedish debate.

Ferm sticks to wine and water. This seems like a good idea. Mikael can still feel the slight unsteadiness in his legs from the whisky tasting. Ferm is also extremely knowledgeable about *Millennium*. He reels off the magazine's highlights and asks informed questions.

The most interesting of these is one they're both wondering about: where has Lisbeth Salander got to?

At 10:30, Mikael decides to call it a day. He texts Pernilla to say he can take a taxi.

<No, don't> she writes. <I'm coming.>

"How did your debut go?" she says. "Did you meet anybody nice?"

"Yes," says Mikael. "It was an interesting evening. Torben Olofsson sends his regards."

"Oh, he did, did he?" she says.

"Anything odd about that?"

"No. He's pleasant enough."

"You socialize with his wife, I gather."

"'Socialize' isn't quite how I'd put it. She's my boss."

"At Youmo?"

"Yes."

"How are things between you and Salo, then, really?" says Mikael with the self-confidence of alcohol.

"How do you mean?" she says.

"I don't mean anything in particular, I was only wondering. You seem to be having a few rows. I'm just a simple dad asking simple questions."

"Simple questions? To be honest, you've never cared much about how I was doing," she says.

"Maybe not, but I've always been there when you needed me. Financially, at any rate. I'm trying to do a better job with Lukas," he says, his mind on other things. Salander answered, didn't she? Maybe he ought to send her another text.

"Well, good night then, Dad," Pernilla says when they get through the front door, and gives him a hug. "Lukas is sleeping over at a friend's house. If you want, you can collect him from after-school club tomorrow." There are dark rings under her eyes. The look in her eyes tells him she wants sleep.

"I'd love to do that."

Like all dads, he wants to help his children. Like many dads, he does not know where to start.

She is grown up now. He holds her for as long as she will let him.

Before he goes to sleep he messages Salander again.

<Can we talk?>

38

She should have walked home, but instead she pulls her hood over her head and makes for Berget.

The snow creaks as she walks. It crunches beneath her feet and makes the going slow and slippery, but what you see in the snow can be lost in a thaw and if she's to find what is hidden, there's no time to lose.

When she reaches the first fence, she gets out her binoculars. She tries to remember all the details of the area from Google Maps. She would prefer to avoid using her phone for navigation. She's sure to need both hands if she is going to look for Märta Hirak. It's more than likely that anyone who has gone missing is in the clutches of those bike club bastards. Their lair is a good place to start looking.

There's a gate, presumably kept locked at night. Through her binoculars she can read the signs. Although this is an industrial compound with a number of different businesses, you might think it was some homeowner's private property. A paranoid homeowner afraid of being burgled.

BEWARE OF THE DOG.

THIS IS A CCTV SURVEILLANCE AREA.

NO UNAUTHORIZED ACCESS.

TRESPASSERS WILL BE PROSECUTED.

Plus one older sign with some of the lettering weathered away.

VISITOR PARKING TO THE LEFT. ALL VISITORS TO SIGN IN AT THE SECURITY HUT.

A sign left over from the days of the pulp mill, perhaps.

She cannot detect any cameras. The sign could be a bluff. The question is whether she dares chance it.

The alternative is to follow the fence around, cut an opening and go in from the back.

She'll just have to put dogs and other potential booby traps out of her mind.

Tell yourself it's a Labrador. Slobbery and lumbering, sure, but friendly.

She passes a row of dilapidated wooden huts inside the perimeter fence, on the side where it runs along the forest edge. She makes slow progress. This is hillside terrain and the ground is slippery with wet snow and rotting leaves.

She reaches the end of one hut and finds there is a long gap before the shelter of the next. She doesn't dare risk it. She takes out her wire cutters and makes a hole large enough to get through. She bends the fence back into place so it looks more or less as before.

At the end of the hut there's a door. If she can gain entry, she'll be able to get a better idea of the overall layout from a front window.

She gingerly feels the handle. The door seems to be unlocked. It budges at the top, but the bottom edge is stuck. She braces herself to get as much leverage as she can. The door flies open with a bang that resounds across the whole compound. She steps quickly inside and shuts it after her. Stands still and listens.

No barking of dogs. No voices. Only her heart, pumping with adrenaline.

Easy now, she tells herself. *Easy now.* She gets out her phone and lets its flashlight illuminate the floor for a few seconds.

Those seconds are long enough for her to appreciate where she would have found herself had she gone a couple of yards further in. In the bottomless pit of whatever was beneath a collapsed floor.

There are many ways to die. It's not death itself that scares her, or pain for that matter, but time. A protracted, pointless death, and all because of a mistake.

Presumably it is also a mistake to be here, but right now she has no alternative. Well, she could always ring the police—that is, ring Jessica, who won't reply in any case because she's sound asleep at home with her children.

This is her mission. If the kid's mother is in the compound, it is her job to locate her.

She switches on her flashlight again, shields the light with her hand and decides to keep to the front wall, where the floor might still hold.

She moves slowly forward, testing with her leading foot whether the boards will take her weight. After a few steps, she stops. The windows run along the wall just below ceiling height. No one can see her from the front, but she cannot see out, either. She bends down, runs her hand across the floor and sniffs her fingers. Sawdust.

The silence is still so total that all she can hear is herself, but soon she will be faced with a new problem. The morning light. She will have to get away from here, too, and preferably unseen. If there's anyone the Svavelsjö bike club members recognize, it is her.

They kept on looking for a long time. Forced her to lie low. But then the years went by. In the life of a criminal, cells are rapidly replaced. Many die. Others get life sentences. These are not necessarily the same people as before. A younger, keener generation could have done their own start-up. Bought the brand name, borrowed a bit of money from the mother club and found fresh new business ideas more in line with the times.

Like moving to Norrland and forcing a thirteen-year-old to break open a safe.

Rage propels Lisbeth onward. This is the way it has always been and will always be.

Rage has saved lives, hers and others, whatever Mrs. Ågren may say about it never being too late to get yourself a happy childhood. It would be of no use to her.

But isn't that precisely what you are *doing?* he says.

How does he mean?

By helping the girl, you're helping yourself. By taking responsibility for her, you're doing what others should have done for you.

A sound, close by. She freezes. The sound stops and then starts again. Comes closer, then moves away.

The wall is smooth. It has no knot holes or gaps. She turns on the phone flashlight one last time and then the battery dies. Her hand is white with plaster. She puts an ear to the plaster and hears the sound again. The sound, and something else. A voice. No, two voices. Two voices and some kind of motor.

". . . I've asked around. Nobody seems to know what happened."

"But you heard what Sonny said. Guess he'll have to put Peder on the job. She's his woman, after all."

"His ex. Sonny'll be back tomorrow. Make sure you find the whore before then."

No Märta, in other words.

"What about the kid, then? She ought to know where her ma's got to."

"Even if she knew, she wouldn't tell us. Not even torture has any effect on her, but sure. It might be worth a try."

"You've got to say, it was better before, when we didn't have the Svavelsjö lot up here. I miss the old gang. We've known each other since nursery school, for Christ's sake."

"On the subject of the old gang and the kid. There are rumors going around that you and Buddha tried to earn yourselves a bit extra. They're talking about a break-in at Salo's."

"Like fuck we did. He's the last person anybody'd bother with. Nice place, but a public service salary and a gambler. A shit combination."

"Ha ha, you might be right there. But don't forget to ring Buddha, there's a party on Friday."

"Sure. Expect he's tied up in a bit of dealing of his own . . ."

The voices fade. Daylight is filtering in through the high windows. Lisbeth gasps for breath.

Sonny. There can be only one. Scum, a woman-hating bastard and a murderer who should have been put away for life and buggered by other inmates and ultimately left to choke on his own excrement. But clearly he's alive and kicking.

She should have finished him off while she had the chance. *Sorry, Mrs. Ågren, but some people don't deserve a second chance.* It was her mistake that saved him. Or was it, really? She waited for ages and suddenly he was gone. Well, no point worrying about that now.

He isn't simply one pile of shit among others. He is more.

She moves toward the same door she came through, stops by the hole and peers down into the darkness. The ruins of some stairs leading straight down to hell.

Why can't life ever just let us be?

Wherever she goes, whatever direction she takes, that part of her past always catches up with her.

That's why you need to keep coming. You're not done with what happened back then, but I can help you.

Sorry, Mrs. Ågren, but right now I don't think your method is helping.

Prepare yourself for war, Lisbeth. Get the kid to safety and leave this place.

39

Wedding day. Time for a wedding. Salo's side of the bed is empty. Pernilla lies there for a while, waiting for emotion to arrive. It should be sitting on the edge of the bed, rejoicing. *I'm getting married today, hurrah,* but the quarrels of recent days are still hanging as thickly in the air as mist over the river. And perhaps not just quarrels. Suspicions.

His voice. Slurred and incoherent strings of words addressed to some Märta. *It should have been us.*

She has tried to find the right moment to ask, but it never presents itself. He would probably deny it point-blank, anyway. *Unfaithful? Me? Pernilla, my love, you must have misheard.*

She wakes Lukas and goes into the shower, where she sits on the floor and lets the hot water stream over her. There should be a law to say you should marry no later than a year after the first date, when love is at its height and the future feels bright. Before everything starts going downhill.

Guests. Parents, wider family, friends. Or, well, mainly Henry's friends. People they sometimes ask to dinner. Slow-moving hours with Gasskas municipality as their backdrop. Herself in the role of the thoughtful hostess. She can't back out now.

There is a knock at the door.

"Just a minute!" she says, wrapping the towel around herself. "What is it?"

"Just open the door."

Henry. He could have waited, couldn't he?

For the blushing bride on her wedding day, hip hip hooray, hip hip hooray!

Clutching the huge bunch of roses in her arms, she studies her husband-to-be. The hair that he has not yet tamed with wax. The tracery of scars, like brushstrokes across his back. The nape of his neck. The woodworker's hands. His smile as he stands there to pee, splashing droplets onto the toilet seat.

"How does it feel, Pilla? It's going to be a party nobody'll forget for a long time."

"Who is Märta?"

"Why are you asking?"

"Just answer."

"A love of my youth. We were neighbors."

"So not someone you see anymore?"

"It was years ago."

He shuts the lid with a crash, pats her on the backside and gets out his razor.

Are we aiming for the bride, then?
Depends how it goes. The kid is our priority.

The bridal procession winds its way like a serpent across the rocks until it reaches the furthest point of Storforsen. Here they are to be married, to the sound of thundering water. No one but the officiant will be able to hear whether they say yes or no.

For anyone who has never been to Norrland, and most people have not, the Storforsen rapids are the longest unregulated falls in Europe. Over a distance of three miles, the water thunders down a drop of two hundred and seventy feet. And although the spot is a real cold trap with temperatures falling to as low as minus forty in winter, it never ices over.

Back in the seventeenth century, people came here to transport timber along the Pite River on its journey to the sea. So that the timber was not smashed to pieces by the force of the huge body of water, a side channel was constructed. Döda fallet, the Dead Falls.

It is a beautiful place, with streams flowing around big blocks of rock and cliff faces as smooth as chamois leather. Pernilla imagines that they will be married at the Dead Falls. On a sunny summer's day with calypso orchids, lady's slipper and linnaea blooming in the crevices. But here she is, getting married on a gray October day on a wooden ramp designed for disabled access with a railing to separate the party from the violent mass of water below. It is a scary place. She tries very hard not to look down.

A typical Henry Salo solution. Breathtaking, as he puts it himself.

He drives out here as often as he can. Even every day. Climbs up onto the railing. Holds on with his legs, leans out over the sheer drop and lets his eyes suck him down into the surging torrent.

Pernilla turns her back to the rapids and pulls her hood over her wedding hairdo. Best get this over and done with.

"Do you take this man?"

She raises her head and looks. Lets her gaze travel over his combed-back bangs which are fighting for their freedom, over those eyes that are fixed on the foaming water, down over the unfeasibly handsome face and into his brain.

The boy within him. Is it the boy she is trying to find? The one she sometimes glimpses beneath the layers of glued-on personalities.

"Yes," she says.

"Yes," he says, and he means it. He turns to Pernilla and says yes again, to the woman who can see through him as if through glass.

That is his hope. To be exposed as the phony he is. To stop all the pretense at last. Give up and be allowed to journey back through the sewage tunnel of life and be washed out into a new childhood. With the same brother but different memories.

He is somewhere out there, Joar. Maybe a loner like Salo himself, in attractive packaging. The Bark brothers have always been good-looking boys. No childhood can take that from them. It is what is inside that's the problem.

Salo turns his head toward Lukas. He is doing his best to like him. But the boy is sensitive, and sensitive children come to grief.

Their father never hit them because he lost his temper or wanted to teach them a lesson. He did it as a pastime. To have something nice to do on the weekend.

Please, God, spare Lukas this hereditary weakness.

Ceremony over. They go back to the bus at five.

The reindeer fillet melts in the mouth like finely sliced butter, and the speeches are numerous. Now playing: the groom's speech to the bride.

"My darling Pilla," says Salo. "Finally we have one another. We have walked a twisting path where every stone beneath our feet has been worth the effort. You are not only beautiful, but as wise as an owl and a wonderful mother to Lukas. I hope we will have a long life together," and so on and so forth. The speech is only a google away, freely available for anyone to download. Pernilla smiles and everyone else smiles except for Lukas, who is not listening.

He was originally sitting beside Mikael, with his grandmother on the other side. Now he is on Mikael's lap, remembering that day they set out the nets in Sandhamn last summer. The sun is just rising. That's when the fish bite best. In the evening they fry the herring and eat them on crispbread. "Can we do it again next summer?" he says. "Can I stay with you for the whole of the school holidays?"

"Do you think your mother can be without you for that long?" he replies and watches Pernilla across the table. Her eyes are fixed on a point beyond the assembled company. She is oblivious to Henry as he downs his drink, puts the empty glass in front of her and snatches up her own, which she has barely touched.

The wedding would almost certainly have been a more casual affair had they held it at Raimo's Bar. Drinking and dancing are more Henry Salo's style, and not just his. His childhood friends, too, sit among the evening dresses and suits, all dressed up for the occasion and wishing they were somewhere else.

They have sacrificed one of their hunting weekends for Henry's sake. Not that they like him. He's a mean bastard these days. But since he was put in charge of the municipality, he's been bloody useful to know. Salo's the one to ring if you need a river berth for your boat or priority on the waiting list for a flat.

But sitting through the dinner has not been for nothing. Soon they will make the short trip up to Raimo's Bar. Only the cloudberry dessert to polish off now and the glasses to be drained of weak, girly drinks.

A pause. Pernilla heads for the bathroom but changes her mind and walks toward the exit. The venue is stuffy. She needs air.

We have eyes on the bride. On her way out. Boy also out. Do we take both?
Wait.

"Mummy," calls Lukas. "Wait, where are you going?"

"Nowhere," she says, enfolding him in the fabric of her dress. "It's so hot in there, that's all. How about a little stroll?"

"No," he says, "I'm too cold." She strokes his hair. The bitter wind has died down and the rain has stopped. The temperature has fallen and it is cold and clear. A sliver of moon hangs above the forest.

40

The dinner is coming to an end. In the past hour, Mikael has slipped off to the bathroom several times to get a few minutes' peace and quiet. He has rung Erika Berger but got no reply and spent most of his time chatting with Pernilla's mother about everything from arthritis to her divorce from Arne. In addition, he has made a speech.

How the hell could he have forgotten about that? The most fundamental institution in the patriarchal marriage system, apart from giving your daughter away to her future husband: the father of the bride's speech.

When his turn comes, it is impossible to get out of it without humiliating Pernilla. He talks appreciatively about how good she is with the boy, her musicality and her affinity with the written word. But when it comes to Henry Salo his mind is a blank. It makes no difference that they took a sauna together. Or that he was reduced to tears in Henry's presence. He doesn't know him. And what he *does* know feels a bit dodgy. *Millennium* may now be a closed chapter and he himself a nobody, a case study in avoidant personality disorder, but he has one thing that no one can take away from him: gut instinct. So far the feeling is faint and defined only by individual words or phrases, but it is there. Up to now it has never let him down.

He turns to Salo and spouts a few platitudes about love and security. Equality and understanding. Amen.

Polite applause spreads around the table. Pernilla looks at him with warmth and Salo knocks over his water glass.

While everyone's attention is directed elsewhere, Mikael fishes his notebook out of his inside pocket.

He starts with IB.

Strange things are happening in Gasskas. People are disappearing. Find out who.

The municipality: Henry Salo. Who is he? Background? Education?

*Order documents from the archives. Read articles. The mine. The wind
farm. Other projects? Talk to Salo's colleagues.*

He looks around the table. It is a motley gathering. Like a cross section of the social ladder, at least to outward appearances.

Talk to the guests is the last thing he has time to write before Lukas
once again insists that he should sit on Grandad's lap.

Black curls tickle his chin. He pulls the boy to him.

"Can we go fishing tomorrow?" asks Lukas. "You can borrow a rod
from him . . . Hen . . . Dad."

"I'd be happy to, but do you think we'll get any fish at this time of year?"

"That doesn't matter, does it?" he says, and taps his glass. When no
one heeds the chime, he taps it again, slips down from Mikael's lap and
waits until the table has fallen silent.

"I would like to make a speech," the boy says, and takes a bit of paper
out of his pocket. "Well, it's a poem, actually. To my mum," he says, and
looks at her.

> *It's only been you and me,*
> *Just us for quite a while.*
> *I really don't like Brie,*
> *You are pretty when you smile.*
> *I haven't got a wedding present,*
> *Just a stone I found by a tree,*
> *Grandad tied on a cord to make a necklace,*
> *Please don't forget me.*

He holds out his hand to Pernilla without looking at Henry. A small
piece of granite in the shape of a heart, threaded onto a red cord, curls
down into the palm of her hand. They look at each other earnestly. Pernilla puts the necklace over her head. If Henry had not started tapping
his own glass so insistently, the hall would have echoed to thunderous
applause.

Lukas sits down. Henry gets to his feet and raises his glass.

"A toast to us, the happy couple," he says. "And the party will continue at Raimo's. With an open bar!"

41

Mikael does what most of the others do when they get there. He goes to the bar and tries to order a beer.

In no time the noise level has risen from polite buzz to voices shouting over each other to be heard. It comes as a relief. In this hubbub, no one can demand that he take part. He can just watch the guests from the sidelines. The seating plan from earlier has broken up. People who know each other are forming groups. By their choice of dress and way of expressing and carrying themselves, they draw dividing lines between them. The council officials, politicians and business owners make one huddle. The hunters and workers do the same, along with assorted others in smaller groups that are harder to define. Pernilla's friends, perhaps, and relatives like Mikael's own sister and her family, finding safety in numbers. He can see Annika through the crush. She gets a phone call and moves toward the exit.

Bride's aunt.
Not of interest. Wait for further instructions.

"Having trouble getting your beer?"

Mikael turns.

"If you do get served, maybe you could order one for me as well?" she says, and holds out her hand. "Birna. Pernilla's friend."

"Mikael Blomkvist, Pernilla's dad."

"I know," she says. "You gave a speech. Not quite in Obama's league, but I get it. Can't be all that easy to find anything good to say about Salo."

"I don't know him," says Mikael.

"Me, neither. Only what I read in the papers. He might be the loveliest person in the world in private life. If Pernilla's marrying him, he must be."

"How do you and she know each other?" asks Mikael.

"We're in the same book group. We talk books for half an hour and drink wine for the rest of the evening. It's a good way to get to know new people."

"In birro veritas," says Mikael, passing her one of the beers that has appeared.

"Cheers. Here's to tipsy chats," she says. "Not that she ever has much to say about Salo. But she certainly talks a lot about you."

"Me?" says Mikael.

"Yes, or maybe not you as a person. She's writing a crime fiction novel, and it's damn good. She reads us a chapter every now and then."

"She hasn't mentioned that to me," he says. "We haven't had time for a good talk yet. I got here about a week ago."

"She told me," Birna says. "Is it true that you've slept with four hundred women but have never been married?"

His brain almost starts counting before he can collect his wits.

"Maybe more," he says. "I'm a notorious woman-eater. Better watch out."

"Consider me warned." She downs her beer in one, then says, "Do you fancy another?" before forcing her way through to the counter to whistle loudly for the barman.

"Nicely done," says Mikael. "There are advantages to being a girl."

"And disadvantages," says Birna. "At least *you* don't get a creeping hand around your waist and another on your arse."

"No, more's the pity," he says as the band starts up and people find dance partners as naturally as the newborn calf finds a teat.

To avoid having to dance, he excuses himself and heads for the bathroom. Checks his phone. No missed calls from Erika, or texts or whatever the hell he was expecting. Maybe that she would try to cajole him. At least take a stab at talking him around, even though he wasn't going to change his mind. He didn't want to be a goddamned podcaster.

"What do you want to do, then?" asks Birna.

They have retreated to a booth a bit further away from the dance floor. He hadn't intended to, but he gives her his account of *Millennium*'s rise and fall. The more he talks, the less appealing he thinks he sounds. Exactly like the pigheaded old conservative Erika claims he has turned into.

"Apply for a job at our paper," she says. "They're going to appoint a head of news."

"At *Gaskassen*?" he asks, and laughs out loud. "You're the second person this week to say I ought to work there. That would certainly be something to top off my career."

"Is there anything wrong with it?" she asks.

"No, apart from it being a local rag that puts the opening of the indoor market on the front page and devotes an entire supplement to ice hockey."

"But that's the whole point. As head of news you'd have opportunities to make a difference."

"You sound as if you work there."

"Ha, no, I don't. But look, it's time for the cake," she says, standing up. "Come on, I feel like something sweet. Then I'll tell you why you ought to apply for the job."

42

Just as Salo had hoped, the festive spirit is at its height. You can never go wrong with an open bar, especially at Raimo's. Its walls are steeped in tradition. He's even hired the Thai waitresses, who are kept busy refilling the whisky glasses. Not quite the done thing, of course, but a party is a party and Norrbotten is Norrbotten. Some sort of catharsis for men who have been forced to abandon their hunting gear and shotguns for another outfit. Not least himself. Rows of suits in a wardrobe don't make a civil servant. In his heart of hearts he will always be the wild man. A tamed circus bear longing to break loose from his chains. Alcohol is the civilized escape. Liquid freedom. Before the night is over, truths will come out, bets will be placed, some guests will be vomiting in the toilets and hopefully one or two punches will be thrown. If he could have his way, that is.

He looks around for Pernilla. She said something about wedding cake. The women have already started moving toward the dessert table. He can fulfill one last duty, no problem. Then he will drink himself senseless.

Check your masks. Don't get sloppy. Shoot if you have to.
Take X, kill Y.

Municipal council chairman Torben Olofsson is plowing his way through the gaggle at the bar with his sights set on Salo.

Fuck. Not him. Salo has been avoiding him all evening and all the previous week. He puts up his hand. "Stop," he says. "No shoptalk on my wedding day, thank you."

"In that case you'd better start answering your e-mails," he says. "This whole wind farm project is starting to feel like some kind of mafia stitch-up."

"Really?" says Salo. "Has anything in particular happened?"

"Things in particular keep on happening, if you ask me. Anonymous threats, for example. Is that anything you might happen to know about? We've passed them to the police, of course, but we can't go on like this. Threats to publicly elected officials are like threats to democracy itself."

Blah blah blah. Salo guides him toward the bathroom, where they can stand in peace.

"One more thing," says Olofsson. "Your name crops up in one of the e-mails. Sent to my private Gmail address. It claims you've received money under the table. Bribes, Henry. What the hell are you thinking?"

Well, what the hell is Olofsson thinking, then? A flat in a prime location overlooking the river, moorings for his boat just below it, hunting rights even though he owns no land.

"Now listen," says Salo. "There are no bribes. They're just trying to put us under pressure. I'll find out all I can and we can speak on the phone on Monday afternoon."

After that last meeting with the Branco Group, he has heard no more. Salo is still feeling pleased that he got the last word. Negotiations can be tough, but he's hardly a weakling. His are the hands that steer this municipality. The very same hands that will soon be steering the cake server through the cream gâteau. He just needs to pee first.

But what the hell is that? Surely not the fireworks already?

You wanted action, Henry Salo, *bang bang.*
You thought I was a cripple, *bang bang.*
This is just for starters, *bang bang.*
Happy wedding day, *bang bang.*

At last. Excitement bordering on sexual arousal runs through Varg's body. It's been a long time.

Once a soldier.

He pulls his balaclava into place. Runs his eyes over Järv and Björn, no mistakes. Nods to Lo.

Always a soldier.

The river roars in the background. The moon disappears between scudding clouds. A smoker puts out a glowing stub with a heel and goes back inside.

NOW!

The feeling is indescribable when Varg yanks open the door and kicks someone who was on their way out straight back inside. The AK5 nestles securely against his hip like a sleeping baby. Järv and Björn have his back.

The seconds before the guests realize what's going on, what words can he find for those? The transition from partying to petrified. From denial—*this can't be happening*—to a truth that makes everyone react in the same way.

If a behavioral scientist had been able to sit in a corner and observe the pattern of reactions, they could have written the thesis of the century about human flight behavior. Some scream, others run, push, fall. Stumble over legs, break wrists, trample children's bodies to get into the bathroom in the hope that they will get to live.

Bang bang, a couple of shots through the door. That's what an effective strategy looks like.

But this isn't about mass killing. Varg enjoys their fear. He is the one with the power over life and death. Their fear has a scent that forces its way through perfume and aftershave. It pisses itself, shits itself. Moves aside and makes way for the one in control.

Varg has control. From his first shot in Afghanistan right through to today he has had ownership of his life, his actions and his dignity. He does not regret a single day. Only longs for the next one. The next conflict, the next order that gets the adrenaline pumping like steroids through his blood.

Järv, Björn and Varg. The love that flows between them. The pleasure in which they share.

A tough guy in his best suit tries to shield his woman.

How beautifully a row of teeth would shatter if you saw it in slow motion.

A mother picks up her child and runs toward the exit.

A bit of a shame about that hair lying so attractively around her head.

It never fails. Another shot, fired at the ceiling. Björn shouts, "Nobody move!" and everything stops. Gives up. Capitulates. Pleads. Begs.

Phase two: You can almost hear their thoughts, all one note: *We won't move. Don't kill me. Let me live. I have children. I'm about to get my pension. My old mother needs me.*

Varg does not even have to use violence. Like a king he sweeps through the terrified masses, his focus on the boy. There he is. As terrified as the rest, he is standing there, stock-still. His eyes have understood. He will not protest.

Were it not for a woman who suddenly steps forward and puts herself in front of the boy.

She does not look frightened. Her gaze holds Varg's.

Respect. He gives her that before he strikes her in the temple with his gun and picks up the boy.

The boy does not even cry out. He hangs upside down like a rag doll with his head lolling against Varg's thigh.

Secure X. Y out of sight. Time's up. Get back.

It could end right there. Nobody moves. All Varg has to do is back out with a child under his arm to the mellow strains of *Smoochy Dance Songs, Volume 29.*

If only the child had not.

If only he had not, at the moment they reach the front exit, opened his mouth and yelled, "Grandad!"

Mikael Blomkvist does not think. He runs toward the exit, toward Lukas, toward the voice that keeps on yelling for him. Out the door, after the boy, down the steps that are as slippery as soap after the rain and subzero temperatures.

He runs by sound. They have a head start. He can't see them anymore. Can't see the boy and the voice has gone quiet. The earnest face. The cautious smile. Lukas! Once, several times more, and there. There they are again, he can see them. He can hear the boy. *Faster, you can make it, get the boy back, run like hell, Blomkvist, run!*

Bang
Bang

First the sound, then his body. Feet skidding. *Drat, these fancy shoes. Got to get up again. Lukas.* Mikael Blomkvist falls backward. Hits his head on the tarmac. The blood spreads like crimson across a wet water-color. He feels the warmth.

It is summer. The evening papers are on the table. Fourteenth of July. Nineteen hundred and something, there is a coffee cup covering part of the date. His ankles are dotted with mosquito bites.

Opposite Mikael sits his father, in swimming trunks with his top bare. His body is bright white, apart from the top of his head, which has readily turned pink. He has just come from town to join them. That is, his body has come but not his head. That is still in the office.

Mikael wants to go over and sit on his dad's lap but doesn't dare. Annika, on the other hand, is already there. She is little. Perhaps she doesn't understand that what envelops their father has to be shed first. She wants him to read. "Later, Daddy's got to rest first," he says, and lifts her over onto the chair. He sips a beer. Looks out over the sea, which has made itself as smooth as glass in honor of his arrival.

They are going to have dinner outside and here comes Mum with a tray. She sets the table with the best china that they usually keep for guests.

Mikael has caught the dinner. Some splendid perch, the perfect size, according to Grandpa. Not so small that they are hard to gut. Not so big that the flesh loses its elasticity.

This is what he wants to tell his father.

Perch fillet with boiled new potatoes, melted butter, thin crispbread and radishes from their own patch.

"Delicious fish," says Dad, poking about in the fillet as if it were full of bones. "Micke, you're speedy, can you run and get me a beer?"

He downs his schnapps in one. Pours beer from the new bottle and gives a belch.

"Now," he says, "I'm starting to feel human again."

There is some kind of spark in his eyes and Mikael starts to hope. He has missed him. Not nonstop, he hasn't had time for that, but on and off.

"Tomorrow we'll go out in the boat," he says, and Mikael can breathe again. He asks if he can leave the table and go down to the jetty. Lies on his tummy and stares down into the water. Under the surface, shoals of tiny sticklebacks are flickering by. He sticks his head under the water to see better. It is not deep, a yard at most. The boldest little fish brush against his cheek until all of a sudden they dart away. Initially he doesn't realize what the shadow is that has put the sticklebacks to flight but then he recognizes the inquisitive pointed head of a pike.

Its mouth opens wide. It swishes itself forward with its tail fin and takes his head in its jaws. He screams, but screaming underwater is impossible. Screaming inside the jaws of a pike is like screaming in a padded cell. No one hears him, no one sees the teeth of the monster pike mincing his body down its throat, inch by inch.

43

In the aftermath there is a form of chaos. By the time the final shots are fired outside the venue, the first text messages have already been sent to families and friends. <I'm alive.> <Don't worry.> <What do you mean?> <Where are you?> A special Gasskas button appears on Facebook: I'M SAFE.

And naturally the media is alerted.

As Birna sounds the alarm to the Gasskas police and demands reinforcements from the whole Norrbotten region, the *Aftonbladet* hotline at the tabloid's editorial office in Stockholm receives a confused call.

"A gang of fucking terrorists attacked a wedding party at Raimo's! It's totally sick."

"What's Raimo's?" asks the journalist through a mouthful of his evening sandwich. He can hear the clamor in the background and wonders if this is another shooting in the city.

"Jesus Christ, the municipal head of Gasskas got married today and the party was in full swing and suddenly these madmen came in and started firing all over the place. It's just happened, for fuck's sake."

"The municipal head of Gasskas? Are we talking Norrland? OK. Anybody dead?"

"Must be, but how can I tell? It's total fucking chaos here. But they took the boy. Those lunatics who were shooting, they took the boy."

"What boy? Take it easy. You told me they were shooting and now you say they took a boy?"

"The municipal boss's kid, they took him with them. Totally sick. I'll send the video."

Within eleven minutes of the first ring of the phone in Stockholm, they have agreed on a payment for the tip-off and the first news flash from *Aftonbladet* is going out nationwide via the website.

Aftonbladet:

WEDDING IN THE NORTH ENDS IN BLOODBATH

In the middle of a wedding party, masked men forced their way in and shot wildly in all directions in the little municipality of Gasskas in Norrbotten.

Witnesses have told *Aftonbladet* that the aim of the raid was to kidnap a child. The Gasskas police are not prepared to comment on the incident at present.

TT News Agency:

CHILD ABDUCTED FROM WEDDING

The Gasskas police have confirmed that a young child was abducted earlier this evening from a private wedding party in Gasskas in Norrbotten. The men fired a number of shots before leaving the scene. The police have not yet provided details of casualties. The perpetrators are still at large.

Gaskassen:

MUNICIPAL BOSS'S SON KIDNAPPED

The wedding of municipal head Henry Salo has ended in tragedy. Armed men gained entry to the wedding party and kidnapped his nine-year-old stepson.

"This is unbelievable. Who could wish us such harm?" Henry Salo said to *Gaskassen*.

One of the gunmen's victims was Henry Salo's father-in-law, the well-known *Millennium* journalist Mikael Blomkvist. His injuries are said to be serious but not life-threatening. Those with more minor injuries received medical attention at the scene and a number have been taken to hospital.

Flashback Forum:

SHOTS FIRED IN KIDNAP AT RAIMO'S—
WHAT THE HELL IS GOING ON?

What the hell happened at Raimo's tonight? If anyone was there, fill us in. Just been reading *Aftonbladet* and *Gaskassen*—couldn't they have killed off that damned Mikael Blomkvist once and for all? And why did they take the boy? I fucking bet the boy's dad is a black and he's behind this.

There's hardly any blacks in Norrbotten. Bet they were Russians. They know their stuff. But then they've got a competent leader.

Expressen:

CUSTODY BATTLE BEHIND VIOLENT KIDNAP?

Just as the nine-year-old boy's mother was married for the second time (her new husband is the municipal head of Gasskas), the perpetrators struck. Armed with automatic weapons they forcibly abducted the boy and are still at large.

"We've called in reinforcements from a wide area to ensure the swift arrest of those who committed this crime," said Hans Faste of the Serious Crime Unit in Gasskas.

According to *Expressen*'s sources, a custody battle may lie behind the violent shooting incident and the kidnap of the young boy in Gasskas in Norrbotten.

The Gasskas police are on their weekend, too. From the time Birna Guðmundurdottir raises the alarm, it takes thirty-five minutes for the first patrol car to get there. The ambulance beats them to it. Then the freelance reporters.

Amid all the chaos, the alcoholic haze, tears and panic, Birna does her best to offer comfort while also gleaning as much information from witnesses as she can.

"There were three of them."

"There were at least five of them."

"I heard them speaking Russian."

"The boy went along without any fuss. He must have known them."

"It's Salo's fault. I bloody bet he's behind this. He locked himself in the bathroom. Who the hell does that?"

"Three people. Dressed all in black, a bit like the Wagner Group. Two with blue eyes. One with brown. Russian automatic weapons, probably AN-94s, also known as the Abakan. Could also be the Swedish Army's AK5D or conceivably the American M4A1. But I don't rule out the Mexican FX-05, which has a different back section."

"You seem extremely well informed about guns," says Birna. "Are you a member of the armed forces?"

"No, I'm a librarian."

44

After questioning, several rounds of it conducted by different people, they are taken home. They are still in their wedding outfits. Her dress has a long rip, running down from the thigh. The fabric is as itchy as lice. Rather than asking Henry to help her with the zip, she tugs it down so violently that the seams come apart. She discards bra, tights and knickers in a heap on the floor. Stands naked, clasps tightly in both hands the stone heart hanging around her neck and looks at herself in the mirror. Barely registers Henry coming in. He holds out a glass. She knocks it away with her hand.

"Whisky," she says. "That's your answer to everything, isn't it?"

"I'm as sad as you are," he says, hanging his head. But sad is not what she is. Not right now. Other feelings have taken over. She is. Well, what is she? Hate-crazed, maybe.

His stooped neck, his combed-back hair that has lost its shape and is swinging across his cheeks. The arms that do not know what to do with themselves. Oh yes, he has mastered all the roles.

"Can't you at least take off that ridiculous suit?" she says and gives him a shove. Then another. He stumbles and flops onto the bed.

She is Pernilla. Good, levelheaded Pernilla. The one you can rely on. A woman to have at your side, a rock in stormy weather. She looks at him. For now, the words are only inside her: if you've got anything to do with Lukas's abduction, they say, I'm going to flay you alive. Not kill you first and skin you afterward, but the other way around. I want you to feel the same pain as I do. Like Lukas. No. Don't say his name. Just think coolly and calmly. Suppress your feelings.

This is not about them anymore, her and Henry Salo. Although they have not even been married for a day, she is sure it is over.

She showers, pulls on jeans and a sweater, twists off her ring, drops it into the toilet and flushes it away.

She has deliberately avoided Lukas's room, but she suddenly remembers what he was wearing. White shirt, black trousers, smart shoes.

She hung his coat on a hanger in the cloakroom at Raimo's herself. She glances at the thermometer outside the window. Minus eight. She shivers.

His door is ajar. His bed is unmade. They left for Storforsen in a hurry. She slips under his bedclothes. Hugs his toy rabbit and closes her eyes, knowing she will not be able to sleep. The fear, the horror, the images are still there, constricting her throat and making it hard to breathe. The scent of him is still in his pillow. Her boy. Her sensitive, lovely, clever boy. Already so clear and wide-ranging in his thoughts.

Please don't forget me!

Wasn't that exactly what she had done? Put her own needs first and forced him to come with her.

He hadn't wanted to move, never liked Henry. Was happy in Uppsala, at school, with his friends, close to Grandma. It's all her fault. She should have known better. Instead she plowed on, thinking that things would improve. Not even Henry's infidelity made her open her eyes. But now that they have been opened she is like the eagle looking down into the vole's nest, seeing everything in sharp focus. She has to find her boy. Nothing else matters now. Perhaps it is already too late.

45

When the boy wakes, it is dawn. The first thing he is aware of is the smell of smoke and he wonders if his grandad has made a fire to smoke some fish. That nanosecond of security is the only comfort he will experience for a very long time. For although the light barely outlines this place he is in, he knows he is neither at Grandad's in Sandhamn nor at home.

He is in a hut.

The walls are made of logs, with window openings and a door.

Beside the bed where he is lying there is a chair. A bit further away, a table and another chair.

There is a man sitting on the chair. The man has just got a fire of birch bark and kindling to light with a steel and flint. Now he is feeding the fire with chunks of birchwood. It is smoking. The boy goes back to sleep.

Almost a whole day and night have passed since the Cleaner picked up the boy at the appointed place. He has had no sleep since, even though the child is still lying in the same position with his breathing and pulse apparently functioning normally.

"A child. Why a child?"

"Does it matter?" asks the Delivery Man.

"I don't want him here," says the Cleaner. "This is no place for children."

"As I understand it, you have a task," says the Delivery Man.

"It doesn't extend to children."

"*No women, no kids, Léon.* I get it. I can bring you a potted plant next time, then you'll have the whole film. But the thing is, you have a contract. There's nothing in it about age or gender. And you don't normally have anything against women. But this kid is to be kept alive until we say otherwise. Do you understand? Alive."

He does not reply. Being alive is a broad concept. Was his own mother alive? Clinically, yes. Father? He came alive by robbing her of her vital spark. And for his own part? A human death ensures a sea eagle's life. And if the death of one is the life of the other, who has the right to decide which life is worth more? Ultimately it is circumstances that decide. Keeping a child alive is not a given. But right now and maybe for some while yet, the boy lives because it is part of the agreement. Alive. *Keep the boy alive.* Because otherwise. Otherwise is something he knows nothing about, and everything.

"He's got a name," says the Delivery Man.

"I'm sure he has," says the Cleaner, and drives away, back to the hut.

The devil only knows what they used to put the body to sleep. It slips off the quad bike and hits its head on a root and gets its foot stuck in the door, all without waking.

The body weighs no more than a fox. He puts the fox down on the bed, the only bed, and spreads the blanket over it, not out of consideration. Only the nose sticks out. Fifteen hours later it is still asleep and shows no sign of waking.

He checks the boy and locks the door of the hut. The sun has just come up. He carries the lidded pail with him, fills it with lumps of meat and goes down to the feeding tray. The closer he gets, the lighter his mood. The forest is deep, the trees have thick trunks. Some of the firs are several hundred years old. Here the forest has been thinned by human hand and has seeded itself. Mosses that have never been churned up by the tires of forty-four-ton machines extend like soft, fitted carpets over tracks and stumps. The remarkable mix of fungi and algae; the lichens hanging like fairies' hair from the trees, their delicate tints from pale green to black giving life to stones and rocky hillocks.

Unlike most people who think trees grow in straight lines, the Cleaner has the sense to appreciate this daily beauty with which he surrounds himself. He stops by a decaying tree brought down by the wind and pokes carefully inside the crumbling wood in the hope of glimpsing a resident. He is in luck. A dung beetle gropes its way to the surface, opts to go over his knuckle, loses its balance and ends up on its back, legs kicking. *Anyone who turns over a dung beetle that has landed on its back will be granted forgiveness for their sins.*

He goes on toward the eagle's nest. Sea eagles always build their nests in really thick old pines. From the ground it looks like a handwoven basket. Years of sealing with twigs, branches, feathers and moss create a safe place for mothers incubating eggs and, a little later in the spring, for their growing brood.

It is silent around the nest. Perhaps they have already caught the scent of meat, he thinks, and moves on toward the feeding tray. Even from a distance he can see that something is wrong. He puts down the bucket and runs toward the feeding area. "No, no, no, no, no," he says out loud. "Not you, you poor mite, you'd got better, hadn't you? It was all going so well."

One of the youngsters that hatched in the spring is lying lifeless on the ground. The Cleaner sinks to his knees in the damp moss. Strokes its head. Picks it up and rocks it in his arms.

This must have happened very recently. The body is still warm. There are no signs of external violence or sickness. The young bird's dark brown feathers have a greenish shimmer in the soft sunlight. He lays it down on the ground. Empties the pail of its stinking pieces of meat, picks up the body of the bird again and goes home.

Just below the hut, under a spruce with branches that form a hiding place, he makes a bed for the bird beneath moss, lichen and twigs. He tops off the grave with a few big stones and puts his hands together.

God, take my child unto You. Let it fly among the trees of Paradise forever and ever. Amen.

46

Lukas feels cold. He'd like to pull the blanket around him, but he doesn't dare move.

All he has done so far is open his eyes and then close them again. It's as if his body has understood that he has to go back to sleep to wake in a better place, so he makes an effort.

Think of the summer, like Mum says. Put the worm on the hook and cast the line. He waits. The sun burns his shoulders. Nothing is biting. It is the middle of the day. Not even the roach can be bothered. He puts his rod down on the jetty and looks around.

Don't look, just close your eyes again and think of . . . not Mum. She hasn't got time. Of Henry. Not if he doesn't have to. He runs through Ylva, who he plays with sometimes, his table tennis coach Åke, who has just taught him the smash, his grandmother, whom he doesn't know very well, and Daniel, who looks after the garden. But although he looks after the garden, he missed the bird that flew into the window in the cellar door. Lukas mends it himself with a sheet of chipboard and some nails.

Finally his thoughts arrive at Grandad and then he can't go on. Against his will, his eyes open wide and memory catches up with him.

"So you're awake now?" says the Cleaner, pouring water into a kettle on the fire. "Are you thirsty?"

He has to answer, although he doesn't want to. His mouth has never been so dry. He can barely open it. The mug is rusty and the water is cold. He sits up so he can drink. He tries to swing his legs around so he's sitting on the edge of the bed but he can't get one foot down to the floor.

"I think I'm stuck," he says.

"In a cable tie," says the Cleaner.

"It hurts," says Lukas, trying to pull his foot out of the snare.

"The more you pull, the tighter it'll get. And stop crying. You can do what you like. Scream or talk or keep quiet, which would be the best thing, but don't cry. Nobody likes tears. Not the sea eagles, and not me, either. Sea eagles have beaks like sharpened pickaxes. They can take dogs and even children if they're hungry enough."

Lukas stops crying. Instead he vomits up the water, the remains of the wedding feast and the fear that have combined into something like stewed liver in his throat.

"Good," says the Cleaner, "you're a quick learner." He goes over to the boy, folds the blanket and throws it on the fire. "The only problem," he says, "is that you'll be very cold now. There was just the one blanket."

When the water comes to the boil, he pours in a scoop of rice and takes the kettle off the heat.

Autumn brings the chill. Any day now, winter will be here in earnest, which has its advantages. Nature is his refrigerator. Once the cold has settled in, he will be able to store fish and game. Today they will have to get by with rice, potatoes and *gáhkku* flatbread.

He passes a bowl and one of the flatbreads to the child on the bed.

"Eat," says the Cleaner. "It's the only food you'll get today."

"I'm not hungry," the boy says, and looks away. "I want to go home."

"Where's home?" he asks and Lukas has to think. He misses how it was before they moved and has made an effort not to forget, not to like their new life on Gaupaudden.

"I want to go home to my mum," he manages to get out. But he can't stop the tears. At least they are silent.

"I haven't got a mum," says the Cleaner. You adjust. At first, your brain is inclined to think of your mother's gaze, of hair casually stroked, but the brain soon forgets. "Parents are so overrated," he says. "The quicker you understand that, the easier it will be."

He doesn't know what makes a child cry. He will have to think about it. He closes the door and sits on the flat rock outside.

Crying is presumably a child's way of getting attention. Whatever the hell it is he wants. He's got the only bed. The burning of the blanket was the kid's own fault. He refuses to eat the food. This is not going to work out.

The Cleaner fetches a saw and an axe and goes down to the edge of the bog where the right-sized trees grow. It takes most of the day to fell trees, trim them and strip off the bark and drag them up to the hut.

The hut has an outbuilding, another log cabin. The roof has fallen in, the top sections of timber, too. Shoots as big as saplings are growing through the earth floor, but the foundations seem sound and only need patching up in a few places.

By the time he's brought up the last load and hidden the quad bike under the spruce branches, the sun has set.

The boy is sitting up in bed, staring into dark eternity.

"If I don't cry," he says, "will you undo my foot?"

The Cleaner lights the paraffin lamp. A coziness spreads through the room. He carves off a few bits of dried meat and boils up coffee. The boy feels the warmth through the scoop-shaped wooden cup.

Just when they're nice and comfortable, the boy needs a wee.

They look at each other. Is it a trick?

"OK," says the Cleaner, and cuts off the cable tie. Instead he puts a rope around the boy's neck and leads him out like a puppy on its evening walk.

"Get on with it," he says, and gazes up at the sky. Tomorrow is feeding day. A moment to look forward to. If he'd had children himself, he would have taken them with him. Taught them everything he knew. Brought them up to love the eagles as much as he does. Unreservedly. With the same dread of anything happening to them.

He looks at the boy. The tender young back trying to shut him out.

If you behave, I'll take you along.

They go back to the hut. His moment of weakness is past. He puts new cable ties around the boy's ankles and reminds him that crying is not allowed.

His winter jacket comes into early use. He throws it over the boy. As for him, he lies down on an abandoned reindeer skin with his Helly Hansen jacket for a cover. It's been a long day. His muscles relax against the rough animal hide.

"Now we'll sleep," he says, and blows out the lamp.

47

The merciful feeling of unreality that makes Mikael Blomkvist fall asleep, wake and then go back to sleep again passes all too soon.

His shoulder aches but there is help with pain relief. That leaves the rest.

"What do you remember of the evening?" asks Birna Guðmundur-dottir. She has a Band-Aid on her forehead.

At first he does not understand the question. What evening? "I fell asleep and I've just woken up," he says.

"Don't you remember the wedding?" she says.

"Of course," he says. "I met you there, after all." *Ha ha, he's still got the old touch.*

"You did. But what about after that?"

He tries to find words for something that eludes capture, but his mouth gasps like a fish on dry land. He is a fish out of water and he's running out of oxygen.

"Here," says Birna, "have a drink of water."

Mikael sits up with a start. His water glass goes flying. He throws off his covers. Swings his legs over the side of the bed. Someone tries to stop him.

"Let go of me, for Christ's sake, I've got to find Lukas."

"Take it easy. Listen to me, you're in hospital in Sunderbyn. We're going to find Lukas. Everything will be alright."

"Let go of me, for Christ's sake," he shouts, louder now. "Nothing will be alright. I've got to find the boy. It took him."

"What took him?"

"The pike, of course!" he howls. "The pike, the pike, the pike."

He must have gone back to sleep. When he wakes, it is evening. A woman is asleep in the chair beside the bed. Her hair has fallen across her face. He recognizes her. They have met before.

"They're about to cut the cake," he says out loud. She is sleeping only lightly and his voice rouses her.

Pernilla is standing there with the cake server in her hand, waiting for Salo. She puts her arm around Lukas. Whispers something in his ear.

"You and I are over to one side. Because you're Birna, aren't you?" he says. "I didn't know you were a police officer. Why didn't you say?"

"You never asked."

"Well, anyway," he says. "It takes me a while to realize what's happening. It's crowded, people are talking in loud voices. A couple of children are playing chase. Then the shots ring out. First one, then another. Maybe a third. Women scream, a child starts crying. You push through the crowd to Pernilla and Lukas and put yourself in front of him. Why do you do that?"

"I made an assumption that the bride and groom were the targets," says Birna. "I was going on instinct."

"Three masked men," he says. "Wearing black. Two at the door, a third moving toward the cake. No, toward you. My legs are trapped, a woman is hanging on to me, I can't move. A blow to your head makes you stagger. He picks up Lukas and puts him under his left arm, keeping his gun trained on the people. When he's almost out the door, I hear the voice. *Grandad!* First quietly, then louder. *Grandad!* I work myself free, barge through the crowd, run to the door and out through it, lose my balance, get up again and run toward the sound. Then . . . Then I don't really know. A shot, maybe. Or do I slip?"

"You got shot. Just a fairly shallow wound to your shoulder, thank goodness."

"Good story to tell the grandkids," he says, and reality catches up with him again. "Lukas! I've got to get out of here and find him."

"All in good time," says Birna. "For now, you've just got to trust the police to get on with the job."

"And are you?"

We can deal with this ourselves. Trust me. Bloody Faste.

"One last thing," she says. "Do you remember anything in particular from just before you were shot?"

"It was a bright starry night," he says.

"Yes, but anything more concrete?"

"There was something about the stars. But I can't remember exactly what."

48

Ever since Svala paid a visit to the woman in the forest, she has been thinking about her. Her, and the dead body on the other side of the mountain, across the bog and through the forest. F., aka Buddha.

She cannot rule out someone stumbling across him. The autumn berry pickers may have gone home, but hunting is still in full swing. *The broken window. Her bleeding arm. There could be traces.*

Although it's been only a few days, she is uncertain. This was where he ought to be. It has both rained and snowed since. The path is barely visible, apart from the tracks of hare and capercaillie. Nothing. Definitely no body. Not even the branch she used to kill him with. She retraces her tracks. There's a light on in the house. She knocks on the door, which was once green, maybe blue. It takes a good while for the woman to come. Marianne Lekatt looks as if she's just woken up.

"My dear girl, is it you? Have you walked here all the way from town? Come in and I'll light the stove."

She is moving slowly. As if she has aged.

"Are you unwell?" Svala asks.

"Oh, no," she says. "It's just my aching joints. It's the weather. I could do with a holiday in the sun."

"You'll have to go to Thailand like everybody else."

"Have you been?"

"Me? No, but I've been to Finland."

"That makes two of us," says Marianne.

"I brought my computer," says Svala, opening her laptop. "It was what you said last time I was here, that you could do with a computer."

They sit down on the kitchen settle. Svala shuffles closer to her so she can see the screen.

"First you put in your password. Mine's 'ermine,' like your surname means. Don't tell anyone—it's secret."

"Right you are. I've forgotten it already. Can you get maps on your computer?"

"Absolutely," says Svala. "Which country?"

"Not a country, more like maps of properties."

"Let me check," says Svala, and links up to her phone. "National Land Survey, does that sound right?"

"Perfect."

"Looks like you have to put in the registry title," says Svala, "whatever that is."

"All land is owned by somebody," says Marianne. "Most of it by the state and the forestry companies, but not everything. Gasskasliden 1:13. Put that in."

"Your address," says Svala.

"Yes," says Marianne, pointing at the screen. "This is exactly where you and I are now. At The Holt, as it's generally called. I was born in the attic bedroom. My husband and I took over the farming when my parents died. I was only eighteen. A few years older than you."

"I'm thirteen," says Svala.

"And already so clever. I've lived in this house all my life. But now they want me out."

"Why?" says Svala.

"Because I refuse to let our masters build a wind farm on my land. But I want my forest left in peace. The trees and the silence. What am I thinking—we should have something to eat. You're hungry, aren't you?"

"A bit," says Svala. She tends not to think about it. Which makes things easier.

She stows the laptop back in her backpack and asks if she could possibly use the bathroom.

The bathroom wall catches Svala unawares. All around the sink, in fact basically everywhere, Marianne has pasted up newspaper cuttings. Most of the articles are about the wind farm and there are a few more about the mine.

Current affairs. A boring phrase that nobody in school appreciates, with the possible exception of Svala.

"But if the people who live around here don't want the wind farm or the mine, isn't it wrong to have them?" she asks her teacher Evert Nilsson.

"You can't say no to everything just because it spoils the view or means the fishing fans have to buy their salmon at the shop like everyone else. This place needs the jobs and the world needs electricity. Electricity and minerals."

"But still," she objects. "Shouldn't there be referendums on things like that? We live in a democracy, after all. I mean, you've told us yourself that democracy is about the right to have your own opinion."

"Democracy means letting the majority decide," he says, "but not always. In this case I think we have to put our faith in the experts."

"Who are they, the experts?" she asks, but gets no answer.

"That's enough for now," he says. "We have other topics to get through."

Svala assumes that one of the experts is a dark-haired man who is in virtually all the pictures on the wall. She knows who he is. The boss of Gasskas municipality. She checked out his address. Gaupaudden 7. Henry Salo. The guy she glimpsed between the suits, stirring vague memories. Or rather bits of one memory that she can't wholly retrieve.

She flushes and washes her hands. She's about to go back into the kitchen when there's a knock at the door.

"You again?" she hears Marianne say. "I thought we were through with talking, for this century at least."

But she lets the person in, whoever it is. It feels awkward to come out of the bathroom at that moment.

She can't hear what they're talking about until the visitor raises his voice.

"You seem demented. People with dementia aren't supposed to live in houses on their own. They need care. If people with dementia don't understand what's in their own best interests, then steps have to be taken to make them understand."

"I haven't got dementia, or anything else," she hears Marianne say. Her voice changes now, too. "If you think you can come in here claiming things so you can get at the land, then you're mistaken."

Their exchanges become inaudible again. She gently turns the handle, switches off the light and opens the door a few inches.

Through the crack she can see the man. He's taken a seat. He's hanging his head and looking miserable.

"You don't get it," he says, and his voice has changed again. "If I can't guarantee that construction can go ahead at Björkberget, it'll be the end for me and my family."

"Someone's pressuring you," says Marianne. She doesn't sound sorry for him. "Well, I'm sure you brought it on yourself. Made promises you couldn't keep. That you'd get me to agree, for example."

"Yes," says the man, and sounds pitiful.

"But I'm not going to agree," says Marianne.

Svala is almost beginning to feel sorry for him herself when he stands up abruptly, knocking the chair over, and starts to shout.

"You don't understand the kinds of people I'm dealing with. If you don't give in, they're going to kill you. Do you get that? Kill you. First you, and then other people. Innocent people."

He disappears from her field of vision.

Now all she can hear is Marianne. The cry and the thud of her fall.

The next second the man goes past, only inches from Svala. He slams the door shut. Then there is silence.

Svala stays where she is and waits until she hears the car drive off.

Marianne is sitting on the floor. Svala helps her up. Gets some paper towels for her to blow her nose on and supports her back as she hobbles to the settle and sits down.

"Did he hit you?" she asks.

"No, he just gave me a shove. How much did you hear, you poor thing? You must have been really frightened."

"Will you go to the police?" says Svala.

"No, I won't do that. I've known worse. All through my marriage, for example."

"Did your husband hit you?" Svala asks, and Marianne nods.

"It was complete hell. Nobody can imagine what it was like."

Except for Svala. She is an expert in this area. And from one expert to another, the darkness inside her clears. Maybe there is a way out, after all.

"I've got to get home now. Will you be alright or should I ring the homecare service or something?"

"Homecare? I'm not quite at that stage yet, love, even if he claims I am. But you could get me a glass of water. And if you wouldn't mind posting a letter for me, I'd be grateful."

"Of course," says Svala, and shrugs on her backpack.

Marianne reaches for her hand.

"You look after yourself now," she says. "You're welcome to come here anytime you like."

49

"So here you are," says Pernilla, "stuck in bed."

She had fallen asleep at last. Fully dressed in Lukas's bed. She had barely spared Mikael a thought. According to the police he was doing fine and so on. She made tea, watered the plants and decided to start with the hospital. Perhaps it was skidding on the bend just after Harads that brought her feelings back to life. The fear, the regret, the anger. Yes. Above all the anger. A year of anger. A whole life of anger.

"Will you sit down?" says Mikael, extending his hand.

"No," she says, not coming forward to take it. "I can't stay."

"How are you?"

"How the hell do you think? My child is missing. The police haven't got a single lead, but maybe you have?"

"I realize you're upset, but why should I know any more than they do?"

"Because with you it's only ever about getting a scoop. You think I don't know that you're trying to hang Henry out to dry? It's obvious that was why you wanted to go with him to the Tigertooth Order! I get that you don't like him—that message has come through loud and clear—but it's despicable to make your living from him. Is Lukas part of the story you're chasing, too?" She is shouting through tears.

"Now stop it," he says, shuffling himself upright. "Lukas is my grandson. Don't you think I care about him? I'm just as shocked by his abduction as you are!"

"Yes, I think you care, but he's not only your grandson, he's unwritten words on your laptop, too. I know exactly what you're like. As soon as they let you out of here you'll start grubbing. The municipal boss whose stepson was abducted. You're worse than fucking *Expressen*! Every time we meet it's about your job. The big, celebrated journalist needs a hand and I come dribbling along like some idiot to help you. You never call unless there's something in it for you. Have you ever thought about how that might feel for me? I'm the superfluous daughter you found yourself saddled with and never took any notice of."

"I know I haven't always been—"

"You've never behaved like a proper father. Lukas has no father, but he has got Henry. And the fact that you now think you're so important to Lukas just because he spent a week at yours is more to do with your warped self-image than with anything else. It's your hubris, do you hear, you fucking stupid old man?"

"That's enough, damn it," Mikael shouts back. "I'm no saint, but I'm not evil fucking personified. Unlike your saintly Henry Salo, who's got his dirty fingers in most pies, I'm doing an honest job of journalism. Do you have any idea what he's up to, what risks he's exposing you and Lukas to, now he's set on being some local government bigwig? And who ran after them and took a bullet? Henry? No, he was in the bar trying to impress the waitresses."

"You prove my point exactly. You're not listening to yourself. Lukas is gone, they carried him out like a sack of potatoes and here you are lying in luxury with a graze on your shoulder whining about your journalist's integrity. It's my child they've taken, my *child*! Christ almighty!" says Pernilla, her eyes streaming. She heads for the door and turns. "I've packed your things. You can find somewhere else to stay. And don't forget to ask them for a fresh Band-Aid. I'm sure they've got some with teddies on."

50

"You got a good roasting there!"

Mikael Blomkvist hasn't noticed that another patient was wheeled in overnight. They are separated by a curtain. A hand draws it aside. "Are you OK?"

Is he? No. Not even close. His head is pounding from Pernilla's words and his own fury. The worst thing is, she's right. Ever since he woke up in hospital he's been toying with the outline of an article about the way municipal council business is being conducted and how it can be linked to the kidnapping. The fact that he got shot is an added bonus.

"My daughter has a hot temper," says Mikael, though he has no idea why he says this.

The man extends his arm as far as he can reach. "Per-Henrik Hirak."

"Mikael Blomkvist," says Mikael, copying the gesture. "So what's happened to you, then?"

"A little hunting accident," says the man, "nothing too serious. I was jumping over a fence and I managed to shoot myself in the stomach. I've been in another ward for about a fortnight. They're sending me home tomorrow."

"Bloody hell," says Mikael. "You were lucky to get off that lightly."

"So they tell me," he says.

"Hirak. Aren't you the ones refusing to have the wind farm on your land? According to the minutes of the last municipal exec meeting, that is."

"Yep, that's right. A ludicrous refusal in the greater scheme of things. Regardless of what we say, we'll have to give up the reindeer if it goes ahead. Not that it really matters much," adds Per-Henrik, and turns onto his back. "Reindeer have no future, anyway."

"That's depressing," says Mikael. "Isn't there some law to stop them building it?"

"The municipality says the way the windmills are being built won't encroach on the reindeer grazing grounds. And that there are other areas we can use instead."

"And are there other areas?"

"Yes, but they'd involve transporting the reindeer there by truck and helicopter, which we simply can't stretch to, financially. The municipality thinks it's done its duty by pointing to a solution. They couldn't care less that it's an unrealistic one. But how about you—what are you going to do, now that they're sending you home and your daughter's thrown you out?"

"It'll sort itself out. There are hotels, I assume, if nothing else."

"Pardon my curiosity," says Per-Henrik, "but I couldn't help overhearing. Henry Salo isn't exactly unknown around here. And I've read the news, about the shooting and so on. It feels unreal for that to happen in Gasskas. Do you have any leads as to where the boy could be?"

Mikael shakes his head. "No, unfortunately."

"Speak of the devil," says Per-Henrik, and retreats behind his curtain.

"Henry!" says Mikael. "I wasn't expecting you."

"Well, here I am," Salo says. "I had a bit of business in Boden. How are you?"

"OK. They're discharging me this afternoon."

"Good, good. Terrible thing to happen. I expected a bit of drunken brawling, but submachine guns fired at the ceiling and Lukas . . . then Lukas . . ." He sits on the edge of Mikael's bed and buries his face in his hands.

"Hey, take it easy," says Mikael. "I . . . the police will find him."

"Bastards," he says, "going for a child. Do you think it's my fault?"

"Well, what do *you* think?"

"I'm a local government official. People think I have power, but I just carry through whatever the politicians have decided on. Build wind farms, start mines, close nursery schools. This must be about something else. The papers are even speculating about a dispute over child custody." He rocks back and forth. "We've got to get our boy back home. He hasn't hurt anyone."

"Have you any theory at all on who could have done this?" says Mikael.

"People always get a bit resentful if things don't go their way, don't they? But not off the top of my head, no."

"And if you look further into that skull of yours?" says Mikael.

"I'm tempted to ask you the same question," says Salo. "I mean, it's certainly a coincidence. You come up, the owners of the land start making trouble, Pernilla gets all tetchy and Lukas goes missing."

"So it's my fault now?" says Mikael.

"I'm not saying that, but there is talk. People thought you asked some pretty strange questions at the lodge meeting. Maybe I didn't tell you what the Tigertooth Order's motto is: 'Tolerance, brotherhood and acceptance.' Open to all shades of opinion, in other words."

Tolerance, brotherhood and ignorance. "I'm a journalist, Henry, and you must realize that your club prompts questions about nepotism and undemocratic decision-making."

"Yes, but you're missing the point. We keep within the bounds of the law. There's no sacrilege in discussing things before they come up on the politicians' agendas. Knowing the lay of the land saves money for businesses that are already taxed to the hilt."

"Before the publicly elected officials—and that includes women— have had their say?"

"Yeah, yeah," says Salo, getting to his feet. "I only wanted to warn you. Put down your pen and go home if you can't find anything more useful to do. Pernilla's beside herself with worry, just so you know."

51

"Master detective Kalle Blomkvist . . . So this is where you're holed up, in a hospital in Norrland. Can't you even go to a wedding without ending up in some action movie?"

A long time. Or no time at all, depending how you look at it. But he's pleased. More than pleased. Moved, perhaps. Relieved, at any rate.

"Lisbeth! Jesus, am I glad to see you. How did you know I was here?"

"You sent a few incoherent messages, which isn't like you. Yours tend to sound more like 'Starchy old gent seeks companion.' So I thought I'd better check what had happened to the great detective. Make sure he hadn't had a stroke or gone senile."

Per-Henrik, too, has perked up at the sight of the strange figure still loitering in the doorway, unsure whether to sit down or leave.

"There's a chair under Micke's stuff," he says.

"Good job someone here is polite."

"Per-Henrik shot himself in the stomach. And I got shot in the shoulder."

"The nutcase ward," says Lisbeth, but she is not unfamiliar with the person in the bed next to Blomkvist's. She has put some time into investigating the Hirak family. "Are you Märta Hirak's brother?" she asks, seeing a hard look appear on Per-Henrik's face as she speaks.

"Yes," he says. "I guess I am."

"You *guess*?" says Lisbeth. "Then you probably know that Märta has a daughter none of you care about, even though she's lost both her mother and her grandmother."

"It's more complicated than that," he says.

"Not for me," she replies, and gives Mikael a poke. "Come on, you can't just lie there. We've got a shitload to do. I've already made a start, in fact."

"They're discharging me this afternoon, but Pernilla—"

"Has thrown you out, yes, I know. And that's understandable. You can be pretty hard work, you know. But joking aside, you didn't answer so I rang her after I got your weird messages."

"She's angry," he says.

"Terrified," says Lisbeth.

"Unfair."

"Honest. Where are you going to stay?"

"Don't know. At a hotel, I suppose."

You're not coming to stay with us, that's for sure. No way would I let that happen. I'll help you, but then it's bye-bye for good.

Stay in the feeling, Lisbeth. He hurt you once. But you still like him. You can let it go now.

Shut up, Mrs. Ågren!

"You're welcome to stay with us," says Per-Henrik. "We've got room."

"Though apparently not for Svala," says Lisbeth.

Mikael puts a hand on her arm.

"Thank you, Per-Henrik. I'd be pleased to take you up on the offer."

"And as for Svala . . ." says Per-Henrik, and pauses mid-sentence for so long that Lisbeth gets up to go, "why don't the two of you come and see us out at the farm?"

It is painful for him to say the words, Lisbeth can understand that. In her book, the whole lot of them can go to hell, for all she cares, but this is about Svala. The girl needs a home. The Hiraks can't be the worst option.

"He seems to like you," says Mikael.

"Who doesn't like a charmer?" she says.

"Hang on a minute, I'll walk you out."

They walk along the corridor and sit on a bench by the lifts.

"OK, then, Kalle Blomkvist, where do we start?"

52

What are you blubbering about?
  They're after me now.
  But you've got the key.
  The key to what?
  The key to everything.

Thinking like Mammamärta is the same as being at rock bottom. Finding a way out, but never *the* way out.

Svala has been thinking about Mammamärta a lot. She understands the choices her mother has made. Some of them to protect Svala. Others to protect herself.

The path is there in front of her. All Svala has to do is choose. Either to remain the child she has never been. Or to make her own decisions.

Heian shodan, nidan and *sandan*. In the pattern of the kata there is no space for thoughts. Only the body's striving for balance.

She showers, gets dressed, puts the key card in her back pocket and closes the hotel door behind her. Got to start somewhere.

"I want to see Henry Salo," she says. "I haven't got an appointment, but could you please call his extension? I'm Svala Hirak, please pass on my regards."

Never forget to be courteous, says Mammamärta. Courtesy opens doors.

"You can sit here while you wait," says the receptionist. "He'll be down to fetch you shortly."

Henry Salo looks more approachable than last time, and more tired. He breathes heavily as they go up the two flights of stairs to his office. He closes the door and invites her to sit down.

They are not especially alike, Märta and her kid. The name makes his stomach hurt. *You can do what you like with her.* Imagine if that's precisely what Branco now intends to do. Can he really be that crazy? A businessman with an international reputation?

"What can I do for you?" he says.

"I broke into your house."

"I'm afraid you've lost me. Today, you mean?"

"No, a while ago."

"But we haven't had a break-in. Nothing's missing."

"Yes, it is," she says, "but you might not have noticed. I know that you know my mother. Märta Hirak."

"Yes, I do. We were childhood friends. How is she?"

"I don't know. She's disappeared. I thought you might know where she is."

Miss you.

"What makes you think that? We're not in touch."

"But you know Pappy Peder. Peder Sandberg."

"I know who he is," says Salo, and pours two cups of coffee. "Because you do drink coffee, I suppose?"

She does.

"Would you like a sandwich?" he says. "Cheese or liver pâté?"

"Cheese, please."

They drink and eat and think. She wants something. Knows something.

"Why did you want to talk to me?" says Henry.

"If we could get back to the break-in," she says, rummaging in her backpack. She produces a monkey with tufty fur and asks for a pair of scissors.

"You stole a toy monkey from Lukas?" he says.

This is bizarre. But the girl is serious. He gets the scissors.

She cuts a little hole and pulls out a pastille box. She shakes it under his nose and asks if he knows what it is.

"I haven't got time for this," he says. "Get to the point."

"The safe in your dead-animal zoo," she says. "Behind twenty-two dark blue suits."

"That's not possible," he says. "Only I know the code."

"You do and I do," she says. "FQZ0081VG. I know you got the key from Mammamärta. And if she gave you a key, then it means she trusts you. I don't know why. Every time I read anything about you it makes me think: untrustworthy."

She has a very strange way of expressing herself. Not like a child her age. For the freakishly precocious there are only two paths. She will either die young or go a very long way indeed. Right now, she has him on a hook.

"I love your mother," he says. It comes out so unexpectedly that it makes them both jump.

"Are you having an affair with her?" asks Svala. "I thought you just got married. Pernilla, or whatever her name is."

"Märta and I were together a long time ago, but things got in the way."

A six-foot-five albino monster, to be precise, but he can't say that to the girl. For the person sitting opposite him to have been begotten by that repugnant human hulk is inconceivable.

"Your mother is . . . Well, what is she? Special."

"Men seem to think so," she says, and returns to the key. "What lock does it fit?"

"I couldn't tell you," he says. "That is, I don't know."

Is he lying? Of course he is. Lying to children is easy. All adults do that.

"So you're not going to tell me which lock it's for?"

"No," he says. "It's bad enough that you've stolen it. Maybe I should ring the police?"

"Or I should." Svala digs in her backpack again. "We have a mutual acquaintance," she says. "Marianne Lekatt."

And now that he thinks about it, he's seen that backpack before. A girlie, pale blue thing on the kitchen settle. It looked out of place. That was what struck him, that it looked out of place in the shabby old kitchen, but he didn't get around to asking.

"I was there," she says, holding out her phone. "Sorry about the sound. If you tell me where the key goes, I'll delete the file. Otherwise I will forward it."

Outside the window, the river is coiling like a gray grass snake through the town. Perhaps the time has come. How easy it would be to free himself from all this. One step from a rock is all it would take.

"OK," he says.

"No lies," she says.

He sighs. "No lies. I don't know exactly what it's for," he says, and this is true. "If you want my view, it looks like a key to a PO box. Or possibly a safe-deposit box. Your mother asked me to look after it."

"Did she say anything else?" asks Svala.

"No," he says, which is almost true.

Märta lies on his arm and runs her fingers through his hair. Soft afternoon darkness suffuses the room. A moment of peace. He can count them all.

"Can I ask you a favor?" she says, switching on the bedside light. She is grave. So beautiful at that moment that he falls apart.

"Anything you like," he says.

"It isn't a big favor," she says, and puts the key into his hand. "Can you look after this for me? Lock it away somewhere, or hide it?"

"What's it for?" he says.

"That doesn't matter," she says. "But if I die. When I die. I want you to give it to Svala. It only means something to her."

"OK," says Svala, "I believe you." She holds up her phone and deletes the video clip. "You're using the wrong tactics on Marianne, incidentally. She's such a nice person. You don't know her."

Bloody kid, thinks she knows it all. The very thought of the old woman makes him angry again. It's all her fault. This whole goddamn mess begins and ends with her.

"Just one last thing. Do you know where Mammamärta is?"

He shakes his head. "I'm afraid not," he says. "If I did, I'd go get her and bring her home."

53

"No tire kicking, thank you very much. Forty-two thousand, that's my final price. It's a few years old, but forty-five thousand miles is nothing for a diesel."

"Forty thousand, not a krona more," says Lisbeth. "If it doesn't last the month, I know where you live."

"You can Swish," he says, and reels off the number.

"I don't think so," says Lisbeth, and gives him a little lecture on the risks of linking services to bank accounts. Or, even worse, linking different entities with one another.

He stares out over the yard and lights a cigarette.

"Do you want it or not?"

The cost of the Ranger will be charged to her account for unforeseen events. For a couple of years at least, she has evidently received a salary each month and some interest on her shares. Armansky must appreciate her services.

"Will they last the winter?"

"For a woman driver, two at least."

Woman yourself, she doesn't say; they need a car. She hands over the wad of notes and lets him count them. Once they've signed the documents and shaken hands, he gives her back five hundred kronor.

"You counted wrong," he says.

"I know," she says.

He shakes his head and mutters something about womenfolk.

"By the way," says Lisbeth, "that snowmobile over there, is that for sale, too?"

"You must be joking," he says. "I'd rather sell my wife."

"Good job you haven't got one, then," Lisbeth whispers to Svala.

"Why did you have to be so nasty?" says Svala as they bump away down the dirt track. "He was only trying to sell the car. His mum died last week. She was Grandma's friend, Ann-Britt."

"You could have told me that before we got there," says Lisbeth. "Do you know the way to the Hiraks'?"

"Do budgies live in cages?"

"I thought you'd never been there," says Lisbeth.

"Just because I've never met them doesn't mean I haven't been there," says Svala, turning right at the crossroads.

Lisbeth has the next question on the tip of her tongue, but stops herself. Stirring up feelings might make her start thinking about her own. In some situations, most of them in fact, it's better to do the feeling afterward. Or not at all.

"The brakes feel good," says Svala. "And the gearbox is fine, too."

She's pulled the seat as far forward as it will go. Her head barely reaches above the steering wheel. Driving instructor Lisbeth doesn't have to remind her to keep checking her mirrors. Svala has driven before.

"There's no risk of us meeting the police, is there?"

"As if it would matter," says Svala. "You seem to know how to handle them."

And what the hell does the kid mean by that?

"I'm assuming you haven't heard of TikTok."

"Of course I have," says Lisbeth. "It's a place where children hang out."

"I thought you were a computer nerd," says Svala. "And worked in security."

"What's that got to do with it?"

"TikTok," she says. "There are two clips of you and Jessica Harnesk in the leading roles. We all know who she is. She comes into school at least once a year to talk about drugs. Everybody likes her. Especially when it means they miss maths."

"Stop!" says Lisbeth. "Now. Pull into that lay-by. Now. And turn off the engine."

"We'll freeze."

"I don't give a shit. Switch off the engine and repeat what you just said."

"In one clip you're both dancing and in the other one you're sitting on a sofa," says Svala, getting out her phone.

You know where pike swim in the reeds
And the fox sneaks on the porch
And the hooch is on the bubble in the garage
That's the place I damn well want to call my home

"We were dancing," ventures Lisbeth. "So what?"

"It doesn't bother me, but seeing as you're my auntie, it's kind of embarrassing."

She angles the phone so that Lisbeth can see.

Those lips . . . And the rest . . . being an unknown person in an unknown town. So much to talk about. The easiness. The freedom.

"Who put it up there?"

"Someone called Henkebacken."

Thanks. Now he'll never give up.

Maybe it's time you started setting your own boundaries.

"Perhaps we ought to change places," says Svala. "You do realize how stupid it is to let a child drive. I'll never get approved for a driving license later if they catch us at it now."

"OK," says Lisbeth. She grabs the girl's chin and turns her face toward her. "It's like this: I'm not your mum. I happen to be your aunt—entirely involuntarily, I might add. You wanted to drive. You got your way. Take responsibility for your own bloody actions and don't try to pin them on other people like some snotty brat."

"You should have said no."

"You should never have asked."

54

The Hiraks' place looks like most of the farms around Gasskas. A red house with white corners, a smaller building at right angles to it, a cowshed that has seen better days and a dog pen from which three spitzes start barking madly as soon as they get out of the car.

The girl is hesitant. She pulls up her hood and keeps her eyes to the ground.

Lisbeth looks around. The house is in darkness. No one seems to be at home. The girl looks lost. *Sorry, I know how it feels. I'll try harder.*

"Let's ring at the door, then," says Lisbeth, but nobody answers. "That's odd. We said four, didn't we?"

"There's a light on in the byre."

"The byre?" says Lisbeth.

"The cowshed," she says, stressing every syllable, and follows some footsteps to a half-open door.

Flayed animal carcasses are strung up above them. But the strangest sight of all is Mikael Blomkvist in a blood-red plastic apron, busily jointing a dead reindeer. Not without help. Per-Henrik Hirak has all his focus on the knife in Mikael's hand. "Hello," Per-Henrik says, glancing up briefly before switching his attention straight back to the animal.

"I've been roped in as a butcher's apprentice, as you see," says Mikael. "Not the easiest gig for a Stockholm vegetarian."

"I've told you before, only wimps are vegetarians," says Lisbeth.

"If you cut the topside too thick, you'll miss the eye of round," says Svala.

"Perhaps you should hand over the knife to the experts?" says Per-Henrik to Mikael with a nod at Svala.

"There's an apron over there. The cow and calf strayed into traffic. The cow needs jointing, too."

Unna gehtsul várrista, várrista, várrista.
Unna gehtsul várrista, ietján váldáv duv.

Mammamärta, I don't know what to do.

But, Little Snail, you know how to do it. Start by dividing the body into two sides so you can take out the fillet straightaway. Next, cut off the saddle between the vertebrae and the restaurants can have their favorite piece.

The body is heavy. She has to struggle with the thigh bone. She staggers and finally gets it onto the bench.

Use your thumb now and take out the sirloin tip.

She lines up the joints beside the fillet. Topside, sirloin, knuckle, eye of round, silverside.

Her arms feel weak, one finger is bleeding.

"I'll do the other side," says Per-Henrik. "You can strip off the stewing meat. And you," he says, his words directed at Lisbeth. "You look as though you can wield a knife. As for Mikael, we'll have to put him on the bagging up." He throws over a marker. "Today's date, name of the joint and owner. In this case put Märta. Or maybe Svala," he says, and looks at her. "Write Svala."

You are a Lapp and you have your reindeer.

Your name is Sami.

Sami-Sami, you have your own marking. Don't forget it.

Can't you come back instead of talking inside my head?

Soon. I've just got a few things to fix first, and then I'll be there.

Laura Hirak, Märta's younger sister, breaks flatbreads in half and puts them in boiling broth. She ladles a piece of meat onto a plate and places the flatbread, which has softened and swelled like a pudding, alongside it.

"And we eat the soaked bread with lots of butter on," she says, putting the plate down in front of Svala. "Eat the meat first so you know you'll have room for it."

"I don't eat meat," says Svala.

"I can understand that," says Laura. "I wouldn't eat chicken or shop-bought meat, either, but this is reindeer. You can't get more natural food than that."

"This animal didn't ask to die and become food for humans," says Svala, cutting a bit of the limp flatbread.

"We're grateful we've got any reindeer left at all," says Elias, Märta's elder brother. "Your father did his best to—"

"We can leave that for another time," interrupts Laura. "It isn't the girl's fault."

"No, but she's got his genes," he says. "And Märta's."

"What isn't the girl's fault?" asks Lisbeth. "Now you've said this much, you'll have to tell us the rest."

The siblings look at each other. Why not lance the boil?

"Well, then," says Elias. "Märta, her mother, that is, wasn't like the rest of us. Instead of settling down, she wanted to see the world. It was our father's fault. He put fancies into her head. Maintained she had talents she shouldn't waste and that she was meant for more than just an ordinary life."

"Sounds like a discerning parent," says Lisbeth, and gets an irritated glare in return.

"Märta was—"

"Do we have to talk about her as if she's dead?" interrupts Svala.

"Isn't she, then?" says Elias.

Svala stands up so violently that her chair topples backward, pulls on her boots, grabs her jacket and slams the door behind her.

"Was that necessary?" says Laura.

"In my view, yes."

"Then you can tell them the rest. I'm going to see where the girl's got to."

"Exactly," says Lisbeth. "I want to know all about the miseries of the Hirak family that are apparently Svala's fault. Pretty good going for a thirteen-year-old."

"Not hers," says Per-Henrik. "Märta's and the old man's. She did as he said and went off to become something special. She came back a few years later, a fully fledged drug addict, in the company of the girl's father, Ronald Niedermann. They'd met in Stockholm. They turned up here one day and demanded Märta's share of the farm, even though our parents were still alive. They needed money. Dad always had a soft spot for Märta and he found it hard to refuse. She cooked up some story about a business they were going to start and he opened his wallet. Not that it was very fat. Nobody gets rich keeping reindeer, but he must have put some by over the years. Soon after, they went back to Stockholm and we heard nothing for a couple of years, but one day she was dumped out there in the yard, beaten half to death. There was barely a part of her body that wasn't black and blue, broken or lacerated. We let her live here. She got on top of her drug habit and found a job with the council. She stopped all that drivel about artistic dreams, thank goodness. She restarted her relationship with Henry and turned back into her old self."

"The same Henry . . . ?" says Mikael.

"Yes," says Per-Henrik. "Salo. They go back a long way. They were inseparable as children. Dad wasn't particularly happy that they were together again. The gypsy kid on the hill, he called him, but there wasn't anything much wrong with Henry. Not then, anyway. Everything would have been fine if she hadn't turned out to be pregnant. Did a paternity test and Niedermann drew the longer straw. That was when all hell broke loose."

55

Svala works her hand through the chain-link fence of the dog pen. The laika keeps its distance, but Norrbotten spitzes enjoy being noticed. Alert to the laika's every move, she opens the gate and sits down on an upturned food bucket. The spitzes compete for her attention. She gives them a nice scratch and they lick her in return. Out of the corner of her eye she can see the laika approaching.

Laura stops dead when she sees the girl in the dog pen. Someone should have warned her, but who could have known she would take it into her head to go in there? The old bitch should have been put down long ago. Now she doesn't dare to shout to the girl to get out as fast as she can. Any sudden movement could make the bitch attack.

From only a few feet away, Svala puts out her hand.

"You're scared," she says. "But you'll be brave enough to lick my hand. Your master doesn't seem very nice. I can understand you wanting to bite him. Mammamärta used to talk about you. When she's back we'll come get you and take you home."

To Laura's surprise, the bitch sits down beside the girl. Rests her head in her lap and lets the girl stroke her.

Unna gehtsul várrista, várrista, várrista.

Unna gehtsul várrista, ietján váldáv duv.

"I only know Little Snail," says Svala.

Laura approaches them quietly. The laika growls.

"She hates you all," says Svala.

"Very likely," says Laura. "So does Märta. She should have taken her dog with her."

"She wouldn't have had a good life with us," says Svala. "Pap Peder is scared of dogs. You knew my real dad, right?"

"I wouldn't exactly say 'knew,'" says Laura.

"What was he like?"

"He came back to get you. He wanted you to grow up with his family in Germany. You were just a newborn. My brothers managed to chase him off, but he wouldn't give up. He was . . . how shall I put it . . . intimidating. Then summer came. The reindeer separation was in full swing and the reindeer were gathered for the marking of the calves. Märta," Laura says hesitantly, "had disappeared and left you here with us. She wrote a note and left it on the kitchen table. *Look after the baby.*"

"Who looked after me?" says Svala.

"I did," says Laura. "I had you in a birch-bark carrier on my back. It got late, and we all went back home to our own chores," she goes on. "Dad never told us he'd had a phone call from Niedermann a few days before. When we got back the next day, the reindeer were lying on the ground. Some had been shot, others had been stabbed. Quite a few were still alive but badly wounded. It was as if a pack of wolves had gone through the grazing ground. It was horrific. We lost almost all our stock."

"But Mammamärta must have come back?" says Svala.

"Yes, she did," says Laura, "when your dad died. But she had Peder Sandberg with her in his place. She claimed he'd saved her, and you, too. They'd come to take you home. The old man and your uncles tried to stop her. Peder Sandberg was notorious even then, but she told us she was in some kind of debt to him on account of Niedermann."

"Did Pap Peder kill my dad?" she says.

"Not according to Märta. He went to his own death, was all she would say. You screamed until you were red in the face. '*Li, li,*' you screamed, *No, no,* when Märta tried to pick you up."

"Did I speak Sami?" asks Svala, her voice full of surprise.

"Of course. And very well, what's more. You were only a few months old when you said your first word."

"What was it?" says Svala.

"*Eadni,*" says Laura. "Mother."

"That's odd," says Svala, "because Mammamärta wasn't there." Laura says nothing. Her eyes are moist as she turns to Svala.

"Elias's last words to Märta were harsh. 'If you go now, you're not welcome back. Neither you nor the girl.'"

"You threw us out," says Svala.

"I realize it must be hard to understand, but Märta attracted misfortune. We couldn't afford to lose more than we already had."

"And me?"

"You," she says, trying to stroke reluctant Svala's arm. "I've always hoped you would come back."

The laika slouches off to the water bowl. The other dogs are stretched out on the ground. Rain clouds are moving in across the river and the ravens fight over scraps from the butchered carcasses.

"You can understand why I don't feel particularly liked here," says Svala, getting up. "I think we're going home now."

56

Gaskassen—YOUR PART OF THE WORLD

Mikael Blomkvist shakes his head and strolls in at the front entrance of the local paper. Finds his way up to the newsroom and then to the editor in chief, who is sitting with his feet up on the desk in his inner sanctum beyond the open-plan offices.

"Well, hello there, Blomkvist. Good of you to come. Can we get you a coffee?" He presses a button on the house phone and a few minutes later they each have a cup in their hand.

"So," says Jan Stenberg, "things are happening in this town. Have you heard any more about the boy?"

"Sadly not," says Mikael. "The police don't seem to have come up with any leads. How hard can it be?"

"The forest is deep," says Stenberg, "and the world is big, but it all depends on why they took him, of course."

"Certainly," says Mikael. "What's on the programme for me here?"

"Entirely up to you," Stenberg says. "The team is raring to go."

One team member is so raring to go that he's as absorbed in the trotting-sport magazine as Mormons reading the Bible and doesn't even look up when Mikael introduces himself.

"I've been at *Millennium* magazine since the early 1990s," he says, and someone puts their hand up.

"Hasn't that ceased publication?"

"The print edition, yes, but now there's a podcast. And it's online, too, of course."

"Yes, I know," says the hand-raiser, "but I haven't heard you or seen your name for ages."

He clears his throat. "That's right, I've been on extended leave. We'll have to see what happens next year. What about here, then? Which of you is in charge of the digging assignments?"

"That would be you, wouldn't it, Anna? You like gardening," says the voice behind the sports magazine, getting a laugh from the others.

"We haven't got anyone like that," says the Anna in question. "We all chip in as best we can."

"And how's it going, do you reckon?"

"Last week we had a thing about the financing behind Gasskas IK. It was good."

"The article, or the financing of the ice hockey club?" He's read it. Gasskas IK has stable finances, buoyed by support from local businesses and the municipal council. The article wasn't bad as far as it went, but it was superficial and excessively positive. The journalist made do with obvious answers. An investigative assignment reduced to a humdrum hack job.

"Both," says Anna.

"Can you give me more?" asks Mikael. "How do you think the reporting of the kidnap story is going?"

It feels unreal to be talking about Lukas. As if he was just anybody.

"Initially we had two reporters on it, but now it's just me."

"And what's your name?"

"Janne Bolin."

"Hi, Janne. And what's your current approach? I assume you're still keeping abreast of where the police have got to?"

"You bet we are," he says. "We've been camping outside Salo's house along with the kids from *Expressen*, but he's keeping a very low profile. Your daughter, too. Pernilla or whatever her name is."

Whatever her name is.

"They want to be left in peace, I daresay," says Mikael. "Is there nothing else to go on?"

"No," says Bolin. "The police keep holding press conferences with their prettiest young policewomen at the lectern, but nothing new has emerged that Flashback hasn't already written about."

"And what's Flashback writing about that you people with your local knowledge can filter down to something tangible?"

"Mainly about people who've gone missing and a police force that doesn't seem to care," says Anna. "Not if the disappearances are drug related, at any event. Gasskas is to Norrland what Järvafältet is to Stockholm. Criminal networks are left to get on with their activities in peace here, as they are there, it's just that things are less spectacular.

There's no shooting. The young people simply vanish into a sinkhole. Occasionally one will turn up head-down in a bog, but most are never found."

"Purely from a journalist's point of view, what do you think of that take?"

"I think Flashback sucks," says Bolin.

"No smoke without fire," says Anna.

"Precisely," says Mikael. "If I were you, I'd follow up on a few of their posts."

The morning slips by. On the dot of twelve, they all go to lunch. Mikael stays on, sitting at a borrowed computer usually used by the trainees and browses the archives. First he does a search on Henry Salo and gets over three thousand hits. To narrow it down, he puts a minus in front of "Salo" and brackets around "Henry." Still several hundred hits. Most of them from the early 2000s and about one of Gasskas's big hockey stars, the Canadian Paul Henry.

He changes method, counts backward and searches by year instead. At five to one he finds what he's looking for. July, 3, 1991. Headline: BOY LOSES FINGERS IN WOOD-SPLITTER INCIDENT. Subheading: *Minors taken into care after suspicion of neglect.*

Bark. Henry's name before he was adopted. Joar Bark. His brother.

He makes a note of the name and closes the search window as the journalists trickle back in.

"OK," he says. "Apart from the kidnapping, what events have you written about in the last month?"

"The refugee girl who went missing, she got a few headlines," says Janne Bolin. "And other than that there's been a lot about the indoor market and the closing of the maternity unit. And hockey, obviously. Things are going pretty well for Gasskas. Second place in the league. If they can keep it up, we've got a chance of making it into the SHL."

"And the plans for the mine, of course," says Anna. "But for that we've used a lot of TT Agency material. Same for the wind farm. There isn't that much to write about until the construction starts."

"How do you see it going from there?" says Mikael.

"Once the wind farm's in place, we'll be able to report on the opening ceremony, but the only stuff going on at the moment is project planning."

"What about the locals who live around the construction site?" says Mikael. "The protests from the environmentalists and those refusing to allow it on their land, aren't you interested in them? Or the Mimer mine project and all the hubbub over that?"

"Not so much," says Anna. "People seem pretty fed up with Greta Thunberg and her lot."

"And whose fault is that?" says Mikael.

"Her own," says Janne. "Nobody up here's got time for her nagging. People have no choice but to use their cars. And the idea that we should all be driving electric could only have been hatched by some teenager with rich parents."

Mikael takes a few moments to compose himself. This is worse than he was expecting.

"OK," he says. "If I were to tell you it's the media's fault rather than the politicians' that people aren't talking about climate change anymore, what would you say then?"

"How do you mean?" asks Anna.

"I mean that you're like a flock of sheep," he says, waving that day's paper, "who all graze the same patch until the whole troop of you move on to the next one. It's crime and punishment on the agenda at the moment, am I right?"

"That's important," says Janne. "We ran a feature on summer cottage break-ins last week. People are very anxious."

"Even in Gasskas?"

The journalists exchange sideways looks. "Perhaps not here," says Anna.

"Heck yes, even here," says Janne. "All these immigrants have moved in and God only knows what they'll come up with to get out of working."

"Are you a racist?" says Mikael, taking the bull by the balls.

"You can call it what you like," he says, "but I don't want Gasskas to turn into some ghetto like bloody Rinkeby."

"You don't?" says Mikael. "Hmm, maybe we should talk about the Svavelsjö Motorcycle Club, then?"

"The thing about them," says Anna, "is that they collected a hundred and forty thousand kronor for the Children's Cancer Fund last summer. I know they look like nasty pieces of work, but who does that sort of thing? Not criminals, at any rate."

"What if it's all a front?" says Mikael.

But then it is three o'clock and coffee and Danish pastries are calling them away.

"What's the password for the archive?" Mikael asks before they go. "I want to see if I can pull up some good topics for you."

Anna replies, " 'Playupgasskas,' all lowercase."

After the break he takes them through an example about electricity prices and recurring pieces on people forced to freeze through the winter.

"It's bloody awful," says Janne Bolin. "Pensioners who've worked all their lives and can't afford to pay their electricity bills. What kind of country have we ended up living in?"

"You're right," says Mikael, "but why not try to get to the bottom of the issue and ask why electricity prices have doubled, even though you live in the region that generates the majority of the country's electric power?"

"Cut off the rest of Sweden at the Dala River," says Janne Bolin. "And let our resources stay here. That's my proposal."

"Very original," says Mikael. "I'm amazed you didn't go into politics."

Once Janne Bolin has gone off to his dental appointment, the air is easier to breathe. Although the investigative journalism day got off to a sticky start, Mikael feels he has won over a couple of the younger reporters who, while perhaps not starry-eyed about him—because they've never actually heard of *Millennium*—nonetheless seem interested in what he's got to say. By the end of the day they've drawn up a plan for a thorough piece of investigative work that also encompasses Salo and the Tigertooth Order, with keywords highlighted in red, words like "corruption," "infringement of competition laws," "undemocratic decisions" and finally "KGB, the Municipal Gasskas Companies."

"Don't forget," Mikael says, pulling on his leather jacket over his other one, "the quality of the questions determines the quality of the answers. Don't make do with simple answers simply to get the job done. Ask for more time if that's what will take you forward. Ask uncomfortable questions. Even a denial is an answer. A hesitation is an opening and a lie is a smoke screen to hide something else. Next time we'll talk about the importance of credible sources and maybe even loyal ones. Toodle pip!" *Toodle pip.* Where the hell did that come from? A nod would have done just fine.

57

He takes the stairs two at a time, cuts across the square and goes into the hotel, makes for the bar and orders a beer that is soon easing the pain in his shoulder and bringing his pulse down. He needs this.

"Mikael Blomkvist. It's been a long time."

He turns. The possibility has already occurred to him. It would be strange for them not to run into each other. So here he is. Face-to-face with Hans Faste. Carrying a bit more weight than before and looking older, but with the same vacant eyes and skewed, stuck-on smile as if one side of his face is paralyzed. Enough to slow anyone's pulse.

"I thought I spotted you a couple of days ago," says Mikael. "What brings you up here? Did Stockholm get too dull?"

"Ho ho. No, I got a job running the Serious Crime Unit. They needed an experienced officer to hold their hand."

"And they found you?" says Mikael.

"A man has his contracts," he says, "er, I mean 'contacts.' The wife's from here."

"It's been a real baptism by fire for you, then. Is there anything new on the kidnap?"

"Nothing I'd tell a hack."

"I'm not asking as a journalist," says Mikael. "The boy is my grandson."

"Christ. I saw your name in the paper, sure enough, but didn't make the connection. So it was you who got shot?" he says. "Let's drink to your recovery!"

"It was only a scratch. It's surprising you haven't detained anybody, isn't it?" says Mikael. "I think your colleagues should start wondering whether you're a suitable boss if your people can't find even the slightest lead?"

"That's rather uncharitable of you," says Faste. "We're engaged in a professional police operation which is going to lead us to those responsible."

"Sorry," says Mikael, trying a different approach. "It's just that I'm feeling a bit upset about what's happened." Which is true—more than true. Lukas is in his thoughts day and night, as is the frustration that all trails seem to end right outside Raimo's.

"I can understand that," says Faste, looking sincerely sorry. "We lost our youngest grandchild to cancer last year. It was tough, really tough, so I know how you feel."

Mikael raises an inward eyebrow. People can surprise you.

"A month after that I got gallstones," says Faste. "That was a blow as well. After all we'd been through."

"Life can be hard."

"Life is hard, as the farmer said to the pig."

Mikael has suppressed his memory of Faste's laugh. A kind of girlish giggle fettered inside a sixty-three-year-old police officer's body. Scary.

"But no leads?" says Mikael.

"Only loony nonsense," says Faste, wiping his eyes after his outburst.

"Fancy another one?" says Mikael.

"Thanks. That's decent of you," he says, licking the froth off his top lip.

"What are the loonies saying, then?" asks Mikael, hoping that Faste won't find it funny.

"A seeress who's been looking at the stars. A guy in the old people's home who says he saw the Wagner Group marching up toward Björkberget. A dopehead who says various people he knows have gone missing and the police couldn't care less. That sort of thing."

"The seeress," says Mikael, "what did she see in the stars?"

"Stars," says Faste. "Very revealing, but I've got to get off home now. Carola has my dinner waiting."

"Enjoy," says Mikael, and heads to reception. "A single room for two nights, please."

Five past four in the morning. Every night, always at the same dawn hour, he is woken by some thought that sticks up its snout and demands to be heard.

Stars. A white delivery van. He digs into his memory. Forces his way through the taste of blood and the sound of shots. A sliding door swooshes shut and the van pulls away. Stars. A star.

He gets up. Boils the kettle, shakes the instant coffee into his toothbrush mug and goes back to bed. Logs into *Gaskassen*, a dubious 259 kronor a month, and scrolls through the news.

TIP WINNERS WITH TROTTING-SPORT MILLIONAIRE—
TUCK IN BEHIND BOSSE LUNDQVIST

FIFTY-FIVE BEARS SHOT IN THE COUNTY

POLICE SILENT ON KIDNAP CASE

For Mikael, this confirms what he already knows. Where Lukas's kidnappers are concerned, the police have no concrete leads to go on.

"We are currently at a sensitive stage of our investigation," says Hans Faste, group leader for Serious Crime. "We have received a great deal of information from the public and are processing this. Several of the tip-offs are of interest to us. We are extremely hopeful that we will find the boy within the next few days. For operational reasons I'm afraid we are unable to tell you any more at the present time."

Unlike Lisbeth Salander, who also wakes early, he does neither push-ups nor sit-ups. He showers, gets dressed, makes himself another cup of instant and finds her number.

"Are you awake?"

"I am now."

"Do you want to come with me to Storforsen? I need to go back to the beginning."

"Where are you?"

"City Hotel."

The days went by. Piece by piece they solved the Vanger puzzle. And at nights . . . No. That was a long time ago.

Well done, Lisbeth, this is progress.

"Outside the main entrance at nine," she says and hangs up.

58

Lisbeth skips the hotel breakfast. Domesticated chat with Blomkvist over bread rolls doesn't tempt her. She uses the time to think and to fill up the car. She hesitates before she sends a text to Jessica. <Want to meet up later, this evening?> The answer comes straight back. <I'd like that, if I can get away from work.>

At a quarter to nine, the Ranger is in front of the hotel.

A few minutes later Mikael jumps in. The windscreen wipers swipe away the sleety rain, which settles in slippery streaks across the road surface.

"You've got winter tires, I suppose?" he says.

"You drive if you're going to whine," says Lisbeth. "Presuming you've taken your test since last time?"

"All good. And I'm not whining, just asking."

"Now tell me," she says. "You were burbling on about stars. The Dog Star, the Plow and so on."

They're standing outside Raimo's, looking out over the majestic rapids. But Mikael's brain is at a standstill.

"This is about where I got to, before they fired," he says, pointing up to the exit road. "They must have been parked behind the catering van. How would you be thinking? You've kidnapped a child and don't want to risk meeting other cars."

Lisbeth brings up a map on her phone and zooms in on the area.

"Northwest, mostly forest and tracks for forestry vehicles."

They take the road that follows the river upstream, passing turnouts with mailboxes and trash cans that look residential, and then turn left up a barely discernible tractor track.

"Someone's driven this way, at least," says Lisbeth.

"Could have been hunters or anybody," says Mikael.

After a few hundred yards they're brought to a halt by a barrier across the track.

"Locked," reports Mikael.

"Locked is for amateurs," says Lisbeth. She opens her Leatherman sheath and selects one of the multi-tools. "Click," she says, puts the padlock in her jacket pocket and swings the barrier aside.

"It looks like something military," says Mikael.

They drive on past a building with visible holes in the roof and a shed made of green corrugated iron. The track gets worse and worse, and comes to an abrupt end at the riverbank.

"Let's take a stroll," says Lisbeth.

Grateful for her winter boots from Santa Land, she squelches up to the trees and smiles to herself. Mikael slithers after her in ordinary shoes that are soon soaked through. *Typical Stockholmer, hopeless outdoors.*

They pick their way along a path that is indistinct but has seen enough use not to get overgrown. It slopes steeply uphill. Mikael is panting along behind her.

"Feeling a bit out of condition, Blomkvist?"

"I'm fine," he says. "Just keep going."

At the top, the view opens out. A checkerboard of forest and more forest punctuated by barer patches extends as far as the eye can see, but there are no buildings. No smoke from chimneys or other signs of life.

"Beautiful but deserted," says Mikael. "Do you understand how people can live up here?"

"They can get away from other people, at least," says Lisbeth, studying the map again.

"It's fucking cold, too." He pushes away the impulse to move closer to her. Maybe put his arm around her. Draw in her strange scent and kiss her. Feel her lip ring against his teeth, suck it in and . . .

Stop that! You use women for affirmation—that's why you never fall properly in love.

Erika Berger, why are you piping up out of nowhere?

But she's right. He wants Lisbeth to see him. See the man, his true self.

"They could have continued by water," says Lisbeth. "Or they went some other way entirely."

"Probably. We could just be wasting our time."

"I've checked up on Salo's biggest current project, the wind farm, and the companies that are in the cards for the construction contracts," says Lisbeth. "Fortum in Finland is almost ludicrously transparent. The Dutch are a bit more discreet, but fully visible when you start rooting around. The third one, on the other hand, the Branco Group, is fascinating."

"Oh?" says Mikael. "In what way?"

"The company scarcely exists. I put Plague onto digging, but all he's come up with so far is what anyone can find with a basic Google search. That's to say, impersonal office pictures, people shaking hands and so on."

"You seem elated," he says. *Lisbeth Salander. Crazy, wonderful, peculiar person. How the hell could I blow my chances with you?*

"I like new problems," she says. "They keep the old ones at bay."

"They must have had to submit a financial statement to the council," says Mikael. "The documents should be available to the public, if so. I'll pay a visit this afternoon."

"I doubt you'll get anywhere," she says. "Big companies are bound to demand confidentiality if they're going to share their figures. We found a fair amount on Salo, on the other hand. He seems to have gambling debts. Quite big ones. But it looks like his prayers were answered the other day. Six hundred thousand landed in his account. Unfortunately we can't find out who paid it in."

"Aren't you ever afraid of getting caught when you go snooping into people's private lives?"

"You should see what I've found on you," she says, giving him a punch on the shoulder.

"Ow. For God's sake, Salander."

"Sorry."

On the way back to the barrier, they stop by the buildings. A cracked sign hanging at an angle warns the unauthorized that they do not have access. The area is fenced off and the multi-tool comes in handy again.

The dwelling is more than abandoned. A tree is winding its way in through the door. The wallpaper is hanging off in long lengths.

"Odd that they've left the furniture behind," says Lisbeth, opening a cupboard. "Even the crockery."

"But no Lukas." The boy's hand in his. The curly hair tickling his face.

You back off from Henry. It isn't his fault Lukas is missing. It could just as well be yours.

Pernilla's angry outburst lies like a wet woolen blanket over his whole existence. He wants to meet her halfway and try to ignore Salo's potential guilt, but he can't. The obvious motivation behind the kidnapping is Salo's business interests. He has to take this further, even if it poses a threat to the already fragile father-daughter relationship. He is a semi-rotten dad, but if he can't even be Mikael Blomkvist, then he's nothing.

Lisbeth pulls open the door of the corrugated-iron shed. It takes a while for their eyes to get used to the dark.

"The van," says Mikael, resorting to the flashlight on his phone. "How the hell did the police miss this?"

"Despite having such a competent boss . . ." says Lisbeth. She pulls her sweater sleeve down over her hand and opens the front door of the van. Apart from a packet of chewing gum between the seats, it is empty.

The sliding door jams. Between them they manage to yank it open. Empty there, too. Mikael shines his flashlight across the seats and floor.

"Hang on," says Lisbeth. "Shine it between the seats again." She feels for something in the beam of light and fishes out a small piece of metal.

"An anchor," he says.

This necklace will protect you against most things.

But not everything.

"Didn't you have some sailor's charm?" says Lisbeth.

"Yes," says Mikael. "I gave it to Lukas this summer."

He's got to get out. Get air. Breathe. Think.

Lisbeth takes a few pictures before she shuts the door of the shed and locks the bolt back in place.

Mikael is already in the car.

"We're going to find him," says Lisbeth. He makes a snuffling sound and leans his head against the window.

"He was with me over the summer. I didn't want to have him at first, it felt like hard work looking after somebody else's child."

"Pernilla's child, your grandchild, and not just somebody's," says Lisbeth.

"Yes, and when she came to fetch him, he didn't want to go."

"Strange kid," she says, rummaging around for a paper napkin.

"I know," he says, and blows his nose. "Sorry, I never cry normally. Nor do you, eh?"

When did you last cry?
I don't remember.
When, now what was his name again, your legal guardian, Holger Palmgren, died?
No.
Your mother?
No.
A good cry can be cathartic.
I'm sure you're right, Mrs. Ågren.

"With a bit of luck the cops will be able to find some fingerprints. Put 'DXC711' into your license plate app."

"Sirius Flowers, a florist in Luleå," says Mikael.

"There's your star," she says.

59

At his request, the Cleaner has been brought a new batch of newspapers, a packet of O'boy drinking chocolate, some fresh milk and a pound of sweets.

"I've never had anything to do with children," he says to the Delivery Man. "What do you do with a child?"

"I dunno. Cozy Fridays, maybe."

The Cleaner cuts the cable ties from around the boy's ankles and lets him sit up. He sets out some breakfast and pours himself a cup of coffee.

The boy drinks O'boy and cuts himself a small slice of sausage. The Cleaner takes the opportunity to do some firearms maintenance. He gets out his Glock and removes the magazine. Takes apart the mainspring and firing pin and examines the parts thoroughly. Wipes them with a rag and slots them back together.

The fire is crackling in the stove. The comfortable, homey feeling spreads through the hut. It is Friday, and cozy.

"We're going on an outing today. If you try to run away, I'll kill you straight off."

The boy slurps the last of his chocolate drink. An expiring fly bounces slowly against the windowpane. The eczema on the Cleaner's elbow is as itchy as a mosquito bite. He has read about snake-venom ointment somewhere, and who knows? They might come across a viper, along with a hare or fox.

They walk to the first eagle's nest. The boy goes in front. The Cleaner doesn't know what his name is. He's said it several times, but he doesn't remember. Doesn't want to remember. "The boy" will do just fine as a name. They get on well together.

He puts a hand on his shoulder. "Wait," he whispers, and points up to the crowns of the spruces. There are twigs and sticks woven together into a sort of basket, hanging from the forked branches. The nest sways in the wind. Melting snow is dripping from the trees.

"Does anyone live there?" the boy whispers back.

"No, not now. The female lays eggs in March. She makes sure to sit on every egg for thirty-eight days before it hatches. If I hadn't helped them with food, half the chicks would have died."

"Why are we whispering?" asks the boy.

"So we don't frighten them. They're close by. Come on and I'll show you."

They walk a bit further. The boy has no proper clothes. To keep warm, he's wearing the Cleaner's Helly Hansen over his party clothes, with a length of rope tied to make a belt. His feet stumble along in the Cleaner's sneakers, padded out with some pillow stuffing.

The Cleaner gestures to him to stop. For his part, he is occupied with emptying the bucket in the forest clearing.

The boy could run. There is a road somewhere. He stays where he is. The stench of the meat blows toward him. Tears come into his eyes. The smell turns his stomach. He grits his teeth. Stands waiting for the next signal.

"Come here," says the Cleaner, and crawls in under a spruce. The boy crawls after him. "Sit on my jacket." The Cleaner spreads it out for them both.

The boy presses his legs against his to keep warm.

The Cleaner's hand is hanging in the air above them. The first eagle lands on the meat. The arm lands around the boy. He presses himself into the Cleaner's armpit.

"Are you cold?" says the Cleaner, and rubs his arm.

"A bit."

First one eagle, then two. A third is fighting for its place in the hierarchy.

"Aren't they beautiful?" whispers the Cleaner, passing the binoculars.

"Yes," the boy whispers back. "I'd like to do a drawing of them. Could you take a photo?"

The Cleaner gets out his phone. Turns it one way and then the other.

"I'll show you," whispers the boy. "You press here."

As quickly as they flew in, the show is over. The eagles take off into the sky and they walk home.

The Cleaner makes a new fire in the stove. He takes the cardboard packaging off the roll of plastic wrap and hands it to the boy with a stump of pencil. Then he gets out the bag of sweets, opens it and turns down the edges, and puts it on the table.

"What sort do you like best?"

"The sour ones," says the boy. "My mum is nice," he goes on. "She should never have got married. We were fine when it was just her and me."

The Cleaner pours a drop of whisky into the wooden cup.

"Henry's better than you think," he says, which makes the boy look up.

"Henry," he says, "do you know him?"

The moment. The sense of solidarity. The unexpected trust.

"Henry's my big brother," he says and instantly regrets it.

Now there's no going back. And since you can't take back words, he might as well go on.

"You can see it as a story," says the Cleaner. The boy draws while he tells the story. He pours himself another drop of whisky and gathers his words. He has never said them out loud. But they have always been playing, like a record that never ends.

"My brother," he says, "was the stronger of us two. The strongest of us all. I was nothing but skin and bone. Pretty much like you. A skinny little weakling. Our father was a devil. Our mother was a butterfly. *Run, Joar, run into the forest.* And I ran. Hours later, I plucked up the courage to come back. Henry was sitting on the front porch. The devil was gone. But our mother . . . Well, it doesn't matter. It was a long time ago. It's time for you to go to bed."

The boy stares at his feet.

"Yes," says the Cleaner, "you've got to."

He fixes the cable ties around the boy's ankles.

The boy turns and puts the pillow over his head.

In a forest hut built in 1880, the log walls have absorbed a lot of tears.

The next morning, the landscape is white. About eight inches have fallen during the night. Although it is still snowing, a low winter sun is shining through the trees. The Cleaner takes his coffee cup out with him. Pisses against a tree and lets his thoughts from the previous night slowly resurface.

The boy is sleeping. The boy fell asleep. For his part, he's poured himself the last few drops of whisky and browsed through the past week's issues of *Gaskassen*. Reads the death announcements in scrupulous detail and fantasizes about a new life.

He has it good. Better than most. But it is still time to take some initiative.

Nobody knows who he is. Not Henry, not anyone else from the town. Nobody but the boy.

He goes in and wakes him.

Cuts off the cable ties and shoves him toward the door.

Does he see the bare feet tramping through the snow?

No.

Does he see the gooseflesh on the cold arms?

No.

Does he hear the imploring voice?

No.

Does he see the sea eagle diving on the boy and digging its claws into his shoulders?

Yes.

And he hears the scream. The beak pecking the back of the boy's head and the scream.

A life for a life.

A shot is fired.

A bird falls to the ground.

A boy is bleeding.

The Cleaner picks up the body and carries it into the cabin.

He does not know whether the boy is alive.

But everything he had been intending to do before the sea eagle came is gone.

He heats some water.

Bathes the wounds and bandages them with some T-shirt fabric torn into strips.

He holds the bag of sweets under the boy's nose and prays for his life.

"God," he says, "I am no child-murderer. At least let the boy live."

60

There are advantages to paying attention in current affairs and social studies lessons.

"Excuse me," she says to the receptionist. "We're doing a group project at school. I'd like to look at any documents relating to the political decisions concerning the wind farm."

"Sure," says the girl behind the glass. "You're not the only person to make that request today. Some journalist from Stockholm was here a little while ago. I'm not sure what his interest in this dump can be, but never mind. Personally, I'm moving out as soon as I can. I'm just getting some extra hours in. Do you want the e-mail correspondence, or will the minutes of the council meetings be enough?"

"Bring me the lot," says Svala. "Our teacher thinks the class should take more interest in civic engagement. I need to get my average grade up a bit."

"Sounds as though you've got Evert Nilsson teaching you," says the girl with an ambivalent smile.

"Well guessed. Not exactly the most generous teacher when it comes to grading."

"No, but he's good."

Which he is, she supposes, for the lazy and disenchanted. Svala has grown tired of arguing with him. It usually ends with him asking her to be quiet.

After Svala has spent a long half hour with a women's magazine, the girl returns with a paper carrier bag that looks as if it contains enough reading for a while to come.

"Have fun," she says. "And say hi to Mr. Nilsson."

Svala goes over to the library. After some hesitation, she sends a text to Lisbeth. <Group work at the library. I'll be home late.>

She really ought to tell her aunt the whole thing from beginning to end. The more she knows, the harder it's going to be for Svala to do what she has to. The list is not long: 1. Find Mammamärta. 2. Inform on Pappy Peder.

It takes her all afternoon to go through the contents of the bag. *I'm doing it for you, Marianne.* The plans to allocate land to one of the largest wind farm construction projects in the world have been underway for several years. She sets aside any information of potential interest, such as records of protests and appeals against a variety of decisions.

Essentially it is not the municipality but the KGB that is sitting on the tastiest morsels, and she cannot get at those. The KGB comes under the Companies Act. Apart from standard annual reports, financial and general, all the detail lies beyond public access. Of all that is said and written, there is only one e-mail, dated October 25, that she does not understand.

From Henry Salo to the Branco Group, and then their answer: *"The clock is ticking."*

Not that it matters. There is no need for her to understand everything. She has sussed out the most important thing: Marianne Lekatt has the law on her side.

A PO box or safe-deposit box. Svala goes to the station.

"I've got to empty our PO box, but I've forgotten the number," she says, showing the key to someone who looks like a member of staff.

"That isn't a PO box key," he says. "Not here in Gasskas, at any rate."

"Thanks anyway," she says, and goes down to the station concourse. The railbus to Boden is about to depart. Another is just coming in from Luleå. In the general melee, nobody pays heed to the girl going along the rows of left-luggage lockers, trying out a key.

Nobody but one. Mikael Blomkvist. His thoughts go once more to Lisbeth. He really would like to get to know her. Not just as some kind of emergency relief worker who turns up when he needs her help.

"Hello," he says. "You seem to be looking for someone. Can I help?"

"No," she says, "but thanks anyway."

"We've both got the same carrier bag to lug around, haven't we? Sorry, I probably shouldn't poke my nose into your business."

"Are you going to write about the wind farm?" she asks.

"Yes. And you?"

"School project. An essay."

"Have you got a title for it?" he says. She has several.

"'Undemocratic Decision-Making Processes in the Sale of Wind Farm Rights.' 'Feather in the Cap for Greedy Municipal Boss.' Or what do you think of this one: 'Murder and Blackmail, the Price of Wind Farm Construction'?"

Mikael Blomkvist gives a whistle. "Not bad headlines," he says. "I'll have to change my angle. If you fancy something to drink, we can go and sit in the café."

She hesitates. He could potentially be useful, but the risk is that it will all take too long and she will be stuck there listening politely while the old guy expounds on things.

"No thanks, I need to get home. But I found what I was looking for. You can have my notes," she says, rummaging in the carrier bag.

As he walks away and rounds the corner of 7-Eleven, she turns her attention to the bottom row. Not feeling particularly hopeful. Most of the lockers are empty; there are keys in all the locks apart from the two furthest in. She can feel instantly that it fits. She checks all around her before she opens the locker door. No journalist, nor anybody else taking an interest in her.

A cardboard box, like a shoebox. She gives it a little prod to assess its weight. Not heavy. The lid is stuck on with silver duct tape. She pulls the carrier bag toward her and shoves the box down into it. Then she leaves the station and walks into the town center. In Nygatan she has second thoughts and goes back in the opposite direction.

A short way behind, a journalist is setting off after her, but she is too tired and hungry to be fully on her guard.

Her sneakers are too slippery for the slushy sidewalks. She should have put her winter boots on. But wearing out your winter boots before the serious snow has even arrived is like driving with winter tires in summer. Old Gasskas saying, very likely coined by Mammamärta or some other single mother with an appetite for parasitic men and white wine.

Svala's belly wants to think about food, so she tries to come up with words to distract her from the strong smell of pizza coming out the door of Buongiorno.

Forest. Earth. Forest. Earth.
The ground holds me down.
The trees pull me up.
In between there is nothing but air.
Forest. Earth. Forest. Earth.
So I can breathe.

She has found herself heading automatically toward Tjädervägen instead of City Hotel. Buongiorno is probably a place to avoid. She pulls her hood down over her face. She looks like any other freezing teenager, but clearly not to everybody.

"Wait!" She would recognize that voice even if he were standing by her gravestone talking to her. Pappy Peder.

She continues walking. Faster now.

"For Christ's sake, kid, I said wait."

With his potbelly and smoke-ruined lungs he is no sprinter, but then nor is she in her non-grippy shoes with the carrier bag cutting into the palm of her hand.

When he is so close that she can hear the emphysema wheezing at the back of her neck, she turns to face him.

"What do you want?" she says.

"Just to talk."

"No," she says, and starts walking again. "We've got nothing to talk about." Or is that stupid? He might let something slip about Mammamärta. "Talk about what?" she says.

"It's been a while since we last saw each other. I just want to know how you are."

When reality beats fiction.

"You've moved, right?" he says.

"Sorry we forgot to send you a new-address card," she says, and starts walking.

He grabs her arm so hard that she drops the carrier bag and has to stop.

"Your mum's taken this thing that belongs to me. Maybe you know what I mean."

"I'm not a mind reader."

"The hard drive. My hard drive."

Does she know anything about a hard drive? No. She takes a firmer hold of the bag.

Sandberg tries something else. "Your mum owes me money. If you don't tell me where it is, you'll have to work to pay off the debt." He makes a circle with his left hand and jabs his index finger in and out.

She turns away. "Are you playing dumb, or what?" she says, and feels his grip on her arm tighten. "You've already set your anabolic meat mountains on me."

His confusion is genuine. He does not know what she's talking about.

"Jörgen and Buddha," she says, and explains slowly and clearly what they forced her to do and how they kept watch on the flat.

He lets go of her. And it's just as well for him that he does. Mikael Blomkvist is standing under the balustrade of Pizzeria Buongiorno, keeping a close eye on the chain of events. When the dodgy guy starts pulling her by the arm, he puts down his carrier bag and is poised to run and intervene. But when the guy lets go of her and goes back in to his pizza a few minutes later, Mikael slinks in and orders a beer at the bar. With his back to the guy's table, where a companion with the same aura of charm spreads good cheer by belching loudly after every swig of beer, he can hear what is being said.

"The kid doesn't know," says Peder Sandberg to the other man.

"You've gone soft," says the man. "You should have hurt her a bit more. That's the way to talk to girls."

"Not this one," grumbles Sandberg. "She doesn't feel pain. You can dislocate her arm and she won't bat an eyelid. Believe me, I've tried. She mentioned you, by the way."

"Doesn't surprise me," says the other man. "Girls usually do."

Before Jörgen can blink, Peder Sandberg has grabbed him by the hair and is smacking his face into his pizza. Blood from his nose combines with tomato sauce. A family with children grab their coats and escape into the street.

"We're going for a little drive," says Sandberg, and pushes the other man ahead of him toward a matte-lacquered BMW with tinted windows that is parked outside.

Through the window Mikael can see him shove the bloody-faced guy into the back seat and get in beside him. Mikael takes a picture. He gets half the license plate in the shot.

<Do you know them?> he texts to Lisbeth.

<One is Svala's stepdad. Is she there?>

<On her way home, I think.>

61

When Jörgen realizes they are on the way to Vaukaliden, a place where nothing good ever happens, he starts to beg. First to beg, then to cry.

"Shut up," says Sandberg, holding back the impulse to thwack his face into the front seat for good measure. He doesn't want to mess up the car. "Nothing's going to happen to you if you do as I say. Turn down to Max Burger—we're picking up the Russian as well," he says with a light punch to the driver's shoulder.

The driver has no name. He just drives. Unless you ask Svala, of course. Then his name is H. and his descriptors are Elvis sideburns and trousers that show his bum crack. It follows that the Russian also has a letter: J. Quiet, red hair, sunglasses in winter. Under E., Jörgen's letter, there is only one word: fat.

"Sooo," says Sandberg when they've picked up the Russian and reached the highest point of Vaukaliden. "Seems you guys have been going it alone."

"What d'you mean, alone?" says Jörgen, and gets a sharp elbow in the side. "We didn't mean anything by it. We were only playing a game, thought the kid would be able to fix Salo's safe. Her mum owed us money, like you said. We wanted our cut, that was all."

"So you targeted my family. Just like that. Without asking me. A child, what's more."

"The safe was empty. Of course we would have shared it with you."

"And where's Buddha?" says Sandberg, pressing a knife to Jörgen's throat.

"He went off into the woods. Ran after the kid and disappeared. I waited a while. When he didn't come, I pushed off. I didn't want to risk being found, did I?"

"Shut your trap, you fucking genius. Salo's never had any money, for Christ's sake."

"You told us," says Jörgen with the voice of a tearful child, "that he had a safe, so we thought—"

"That's enough," says the Russian, and drags Jörgen out of the car. Unlike Sandberg, he has never been much of a knife guy. He relies on his own body and *zastan*. Because whatever they may call him, he's not Russian; he's Bosnian.

They walk toward a sheer drop known locally as Finn's Fall, after a blind-drunk Finn who lost his balance sometime in the 1950s.

At the bottom of the sheer drop is the river. Just now so black that it is invisible to the eye. A falling body will bounce off the rock wall and plop straight into the water.

"I've told it like it is, I swear, Peder, for God's sake, I don't want to die, you have to understand that it was just a game. Listen, I've got a daughter, I know it was wrong, I'm so sorry. I mean it, I promise. Sorry."

"Shut it," shouts Peder Sandberg, and presses the point of the knife harder against his throat. It is already sticking into the pig neck, a couple of inches so they can bleed him like a slaughtered animal.

The Russian is so excited that he lets off a shot.

"We only wanted a bit of fun," whispers Jörgen, pushing Peder to the utter limit of his non-elastic patience. Without hesitation. Without consideration for the fact that he has known Jörgen since their first year at school and is godfather to his daughter, he pulls out the knife and shoves him over the edge.

His fleshy deposits protect him from the first impact with the ancient rock. Thus his body descends through the air fully conscious until his head collides with the next protrusion and he is dispatched straight into a life reincarnated as a rabbit.

A dog walker thinks it's a strange time for hunting.

A woman in the service flats asks if the Russians have invaded.

If Svala had been with them, she would have extracted her notebook from the monkey and drawn a new line.

E.: Deceased.

62

Is it day or night? Märta Hirak doesn't know. Nor how long she's been here. They have moved her, she knows that much. The cushions and scented candles have gone. The air is heavy and damp. As if she were in an earth cellar.

The darkness behind the duct tape is total. Occasionally they take it off. A bowl of soup or a plate of macaroni. They evidently do not want her to die. Even though she feels as if she is on her way there. Her thoughts wander back in time. She cannot bring herself to stay in the present. Her language, too. There is safety in the old words.

The reindeer circle around them in the enclosure. They follow one another, around and around. Always counterclockwise.

The Sami village has gathered for the reindeer separation. Men, women, children. Everybody is needed and they make good progress with what has to be done. Before autumn comes, new calves have to be marked, some of the animals have to be treated against reindeer warble fly and others picked out for slaughter. The summer work is over; after marking, they will be transported eastward to plentiful grazing so they are ready when real winter comes.

It's the first year Märta is carrying her own lasso, but she has been practicing since she was a child. Now she is fourteen, aims for the right marking and calculates the distance. Her fathom, her salla, measures a yard and a half. It is the salla that determines how far she can throw.

She starts cautiously, with a calf. Her first throw misses, but not her second. Now the struggle begins. The calf is fighting for its freedom; Märta fights to force it into the fold.

Many reindeer later, her arms aching from the exertion, she sits around the fire with the others. She knows the lasso is a man's tool. It is inappropriate for Märta to have had that honor. Märta herself sits quietly, but inside her a clear voice is objecting. I want to be part of this, it says. I am not inferior to my brothers. I have my own marking. Let me take care of my own herd.

"Isn't it hard enough to preserve our traditions without the womenfolk being as willful as Stockholm feminists?" says Elias. Four years older, he already has authority. *Women have their tasks and men theirs. The lasso is the man's tool, full stop.*

Later, when the fire has almost gone out and most of them have left, her father turns to her and says, "You acquitted yourself well today."

Dad. What happened?

Märta shakes off old memories. What are they now but old, and memories?

"Hello there, I'm talking to you," says Varg. As he rips off the tape, the skin around her mouth comes, too. She tries to grimace, form words.

"Sorry," says Märta. "I didn't hear."

"We're going to have a little talk, you and me," he says, pulling her up to a standing position.

If only she could see.

"You don't need eyes to talk," he says, kicking her ahead of him.

Varg, is that his name? *Varg* means "wolf." The wolf lies in wait for the reindeer. Runs after the calf, as do the wolverine, lynx and bear. They will be shot. She can take consolation from that.

She is made to sit down on a chair.

Hands on the table.

The sound. Of chopping. So familiar, and yet. "Oops!" She gives a scream as the knife goes through her finger. Pulls her hands toward her and a blow strikes the back of her head instead.

"Fingers on the table, you." A different voice. A woman. The chopping starts again. With every chop her growing dread. *Not my hands.* "Oops! Oh dear, I slipped again." She forces her hands to stay where they are. *Chop, chop, chop.*

A door opens. Not being able to see heightens the sounds. Wheels, a rolling sound, a cart, perhaps. No, a wheelchair.

"I'll take over here. And bring something to wipe up with. I don't want this goddamn mess on my shirt. Hello, Märta," says the voice, calmer now.

She gets out a hello.

"It seems you've got something that doesn't belong to you."

"Like what?"

"A hard drive."

She is lying in his arms. The sun is on its way down. The room is burning like fire. Fire was his body and hers. He twists her hair around one finger. Lets go of it and starts again. Outside, the world goes on. In here, there is no world. No her, no Henry. Just a few hours' respite. She gets up, puts her clothes on. Takes something out of her pocket. A key. Can I ask you a favor? Anything at all.

Märta realizes there's no point in lying. That moron Peder, of course. He's seen his chance to get his own back. So predictable.

"It's gone," she says, and gets the expected blow to the back of her head. She's starting to feel them now. "I threw it in the river. Nobody knows the password, anyway." Another blow, harder this time.

"Perhaps you'd like some tea," he says. She does not answer. She visualizes a film covering her face. And here it comes. *Splash.* He's enjoying himself for sure. She whimpers for his sake. The pain is what he enjoys.

"Must be a real drag not having any legs," she says. "Is it cerebral palsy or was your mum so drugged up that she missed out a whole stage of your development?" She's taking a risk. If they knock her out straightaway, then she can't answer. They will never know.

A miscalculation. He laughs.

"She's very funny, this one," he says. The others laugh obediently. The woman's laugh is hoarse. She makes a mental note.

"There's always a choice," says the wheelchair. "In your case, two. One: you tell us where the hard drive is. Two: we kill the girl. Svala, wasn't it?"

She can also choose not to speak. Right now it feels like a good strategy.

Is it day or night? She doesn't know. Is she alive? She doesn't know. Henry is stroking her back. *It will always be you and me.*

63

"We live here now, and that's that," says Lisbeth, taking a Coke from the minibar and putting Märta's diary on the bedside table. "I'd like to read some more when I get back."

"I feel like a prisoner here," says Svala. "We can't even do any cooking."

"You can come and go as you please, but watch out for long-haired men in leather vests. And what's wrong with room service?"

"I fancy chilling out in front of the TV," says Svala. "Can't you stay home and watch a film with me?"

"I will, I'm just popping out for a while first," she says. "I won't be late. *Apocalypse Now* is on TV4. Have you seen it?"

"No. Are you meeting that cop again?"

"Part of my all-around education," says Lisbeth. "See you later."

The Ranger purrs like a cat through the town. The expectation purrs like a tiger. She parks outside the police station. Ten minutes later, Jessica rings to apologize.

"A couple of colleagues are off sick, it's been a crazy day," she says, and lowers her voice. "Faste's decided we're going to investigate the kidnapping ourselves and not call in National Operations. He's damn well getting worse. He's put the trainee onto things he has no experience in, simply so he's in somebody's good books. We're getting nowhere."

"I'm happy to help. Get your stuff together, I'm waiting downstairs."

"I'm sorry, Lisbeth, but I just can't. There are people here who've worked triple shifts and need some sleep."

"Well, we're going to work, too. One last little task. You won't regret it."

"What's it about?"

"I'll tell you when I see you."

"OK, boss," says Jessica, handing Lisbeth a coffee in a paper cup. "Where are we going? Fine by me if you say home to sleep."

"Soon. First we're partying with the Svavelsjö gang. It's open house there tonight."

"The Svavelsjö gang—are you out of your mind?"

"You've read my autobiography online, so you ought to know I have a special relationship with them."

"I must have missed that part," she says. "We keep a close eye on them, we drop by all the time. The only thing we've seen so far is a gang of wannabes washing motorbikes, but going unarmed and in plain clothes sounds like a really bad idea."

"Go get your shooter, then, if that makes you feel any safer. I'll wait."

"Police officer on secret mission with Lisbeth Salander. I'd lose my job the minute they found out."

"Oh, come on. We're only going to a party."

"No guns, in that case," she says. "Off duty. Unarmed. An idiot seeking out the scum for a study visit."

"We're only going to stand at the bar and look decorative."

"I like you," says Jessica. "In fact, I think I'm a little bit in love with you." *The hair. The mouth. The Barbie legs.* "But I'm assuming you wouldn't choose to party with the dregs of society without good reason."

"They have a connection to Salo, albeit indirectly."

"What are you basing that on?"

"Salo's business interests. Even the police must have made that link as far as the kidnapping is concerned."

"Of course, but we haven't found anything to link him to Svavelsjö. He's a conceited prat, but there are plenty of those around and it doesn't necessarily mean they're criminals."

"Salo doesn't need to be a criminal to fuck things up. He wants to save the wind farm deal. The Svavelsjö lot will take any job that's going. How are things with your delightful ex-husband, by the way?"

"He's been admitted to the psychiatric clinic. He called and threatened to take his own life, so we sent a car. I didn't know things were that bad. OK, I get that he was jealous, but wanting to end it all?"

"Everyone feels that way now and again," says Lisbeth. "And sometimes there's help to be had."

"He's at Sunderbyn, not in Switzerland."

"Have you seen the TikTok videos?" says Lisbeth.

"He took them down," she says. "He's not a . . ."

"Bad person," supplies Lisbeth. "Maybe not, maybe just a jealous prick who thinks you ought to be alone for the rest of your life so things don't get too trying for him. If that isn't being bad, then I don't know what is."

"I give in," says Jessica, and yawns. "We can go to bed early, too."

"Just this last thing," says Lisbeth. "Then we'll go back to your place."

"Or to yours. Where are you living now?"

"At the hotel with the kid."

"The kid, oh yeah . . ." says Jessica.

Lisbeth drives through the gate at Berget and parks as close to the door as she can, alongside old jalopies, quad bikes and motorcycles.

"Yours is quite something, too," says Jessica, patting the Ranger on the bonnet.

"Just trying to fit in," says Lisbeth.

Which they do. To begin with, anyway. With their leather jackets, black Levi's and boots, they're not dressed like the other women dancing in different degrees of what might be defined as sexy leather, but at least they're neutral.

They cross the dance floor, past the leather vests and other rabble whose names and dates of birth Jessica could recite at will.

"That's being a small-town cop for you," she says. "We know our hooligans. But what do you see us doing now? You haven't got some other agenda, have you?"

Has she? No. Well, yes.

"Only that I'm sick of seeing their ugly mugs outside the hotel. They want to get at Svala. We need to find Märta. She isn't here—I've already checked the place out—but maybe some hanger-on will say something they shouldn't, to make themselves look important."

Jessica is already regretting that she agreed to come along. She's no private investigator; she's a regular police officer, hopefully with a future once Hans Faste retires or dies prematurely out of the blue. Unlike Lisbeth, she's no thrill-seeker, either. She just wants an ordinary life and a chance to be a good mother. She likes Lisbeth and is drawn to her like a flour beetle to a pantry, but Lisbeth as a part of her home life? Hard to imagine.

"And speaking of Faste," says Lisbeth, "there are leads on the Lukas front that the police don't know about."

"The kidnapped boy?" says Jessica. "In that case I want to know about them."

"Of course," says Lisbeth. "If you help me, I'll help you. But we need to get a drink first."

"You're driving."

"Yes," says Lisbeth, and buys two beers. "Stop giving me that god-damn cop look. We're here for a party."

It must be the exhaustion. She should have been able to work it out even in her sleep. Peder Sandberg.

"Can we go?" says Jessica, but it's too late now.

"Jessica Harnesk. I didn't expect to run into you here. Have you swapped sides?" He laughs out loud at his own comment and pushes a strand of hair back from her face.

"Stop that," she says. "If you don't want to go straight to the monkey cage, you'd better back off right now."

"Ooh," he says. "Now I'm scared."

"Who's this dickhead?" says Lisbeth, even though she already knows.

"Peder Sandberg," says Jessica.

"Her previous ex," he says, raising a beer bottle to Jessica.

"We never got together."

"Oh yes, we did. A real little wildcat in bed, nobody would have thought you'd end up in the police."

Come on, let's go down to the river. I'm fed up with the others pretending they actually know how to dance. Are you cold in that dress? Here, have my jacket.

"I read this thing the other day," says Lisbeth. "Somewhat naively writ-ten, but it sounded just like you. Maybe it even *was* about you. Yes," she says, "that's right. Pappy Peder Sandberg, it must be you."

"Oh yeah?" he says. "And that mini-devil is the author, no doubt. That little creep wouldn't even be alive if it weren't for me."

"Precisely. You have done the odd bit of good, I'm sure, even if it was a long time ago. But the mini-devil, as you call her, happens to be brilliant at drawing maps. I daresay you realize what might happen to you if the police found out about that. Oops," says Lisbeth and claps her hand to her mouth. "I forgot, the police are already here."

Come on, the changing room's open, we can go in there.

I've got to go home now. Mum's sitting up waiting.

Your mum's spreading her legs at Svartluten. You're not much better yourself, I bet.

The same hands, the same eyes. Another time, a different power dynamic. She realizes she has been waiting for this moment. Longed for an opportunity to get back at him. Not as a cop. As a woman.

"I'd watch myself, if I were you," says Peder Sandberg. "There are plenty in here who'd enjoy taking down a cop."

"Yawn," says Jessica. "Why don't you get back to impressing the little boys?"

"Today, ideally," says Lisbeth, poking him in the shoulder. He sticks his face close to hers and then things move very fast. His hand grabs Lisbeth between the legs and roughly propels her backward.

It catches her unawares. With everything she knows about Sandberg and the genetic clones that preceded him, she ought to have been prepared. Her head slams into the improvised bar counter of old tires and corrugated iron. Now his hand is around her throat. *Get your arm above his hands and smash him in the temple with your elbow.* But with the lack of air comes the panic. The tunnel vision. The feeling of simply wanting to let go. Within seconds comes unconsciousness, even if death takes a few minutes longer.

You're a bushi, *Lisbeth, a warrior. If you've lost your* katana, *use your own sword.*

At the same moment Jessica manages to loosen his stranglehold on Lisbeth's neck, Lisbeth forms her forefinger and middle finger into a rigid V and spears his eyes with a perfect *nihon-nukite.*

There it is again, the dependable old autonomous reflex that equips the body to shield its vital parts. As he lets go of her neck to protect his eyes, she delivers an upward *ura-zuki*. Incapable of controlling his own body's response, Peder Sandberg doubles up.

With Sandberg temporarily out of action, she can allow herself a bit of entertainment. She angles her hand and aims a springy *shuto-uchi* at the fleshy folds of his neck, making him sink to the floor in a heap of bewildered pain.

"Krav Maga," says the cop.

"Karate. It doesn't take much," says Lisbeth to Jessica. "You can incapacitate a jerk with your open hand, as long as you aim for the right places."

I know you want to. Don't make a fuss. There. Good. Ahh. You fucking whore, that was nice, wasn't it?

"Fascinating, but perhaps he needs one last reminder," says Jessica, giving Sandberg a kick up the arse that sends him flying onto the dance floor. But rather than letting him nurse his wounds and humiliation, she kicks him again and again. The good-time crowd gathers around in a bellowing ring: "Kill him, kill him, kill him."

In the end it is Lisbeth who pulls Jessica away from Sandberg's whimpering body.

"Don't kill him, just scare him. And there we have the great leader, too," says Lisbeth, with a wave at Sonny Nieminen. "Time to leave now, before his brain cells start jumping into the right sequence along memory lane. Hopefully the message has got through."

That's right, Sonny. Don't forget the past. The jail years. The rise and fall of the club. And above all: don't forget Lisbeth Salander.

He clenches his fists.

"Drive," says Jessica, and keeps her eyes on the road ahead until Lisbeth pulls up outside her house. Switches off the engine and lets silence do its work.

Something happened. What?

Lisbeth pulls Jessica to her. Breathes in the scent of the tangled hair. Runs her hands over the winglike shoulder blades.

You've been through things that you cannot deal with yourself. If you can put words to them, you've come a good way along the road.

Thanks, Mrs. Ågren, but no thanks. Some people only understand the language of violence.

"Tell me," she says.

Jessica sits up. Tugs her sleeves down over her hands.

"He raped me, that's the thing. It was a long time ago. At the school prom. He boasted about it afterward to anyone who would listen, which seemed to be the whole of Gasskas."

"And you?"

"I guess I did what girls generally do: kept my mouth shut and went through hell. It felt good to pay him back. Almost too good. If you hadn't been there, I would have kicked him to death."

"You can always get a job with me if you get the sack. The pay's better, too."

Jessica shakes her head, opens the car door and lets in the night chill.

"Incidentally, that stuff you said to Sandberg about letters and a map, what was all that?"

"Nothing. I lied. Do you want me to come in with you?"

"No, I'll ring you some other day."

The hair, the mouth and the Barbie legs let themselves in and close the front door behind them.

I think I'm a little bit in love with you.

Same here.

Before driving back to the hotel, she looks up the coordinates of the place they found the getaway van and composes a text. Adds a heart, deletes it and presses send.

64

They sit in the double bed and read aloud from Märta Hirak's diary, which is a series of short, sporadic entries dating from 2010 onward.

"Where did you find the diary?"

"The key," says Svala, and goes on reading. "Nearly my entire life. And Mum's. I don't know how she could bear it."

How did Lisbeth's own mother bear it? Why didn't she ask for help, take her children with her and move out?

"She was scared," says Lisbeth. "Fear does things to people. Forces them to make irrational decisions just to survive."

"Even if their children are the ones who suffer?" Svala says.

Move out, hope for society's protection. He would always have found them.

"Yes, even then."

Some of the entries are about Peder Sandberg's assaults on the girl. Lisbeth tries to stay calm. Perhaps she shouldn't have stopped Jessica from finishing the job.

"Do you think it was Pap Peder who murdered my real dad?" says Svala.

The question is natural. But the answer . . . However genuinely she had intended to tell Svala, the truth refuses to come out.

She can't tell her about Niedermann's death without giving her the rest. The girl has quite enough imbeciles around her. The less she knows, the better off she will be.

"I don't know," she says. "It was a long time ago, but I don't think you need grieve over losing him. He was a hardened criminal. Peder Sandberg is a kiddies' sandbox compared to him."

"Funny how you know so much all of a sudden," Svala says.

"He worked for Zalachenko. There were a lot of people wanting to get at him."

"What sort of work did he do for him?"

"He was his bodyguard, you could say. But tell me what sort of person Märta is," says Lisbeth, to divert the conversation away from the swamp.

"Like you, in a way. Small and cocky, but more fun."

"Thanks!"

"You never laugh. Mum laughs nearly all the time. If only she hadn't chosen Henry Salo," says Svala.

"He's crazy in a different way," says Lisbeth.

"But he still loves Mammamärta," she says.

"How do you know?"

"He told me. When I went to see him at his office."

"Why did you do that?"

She hesitates before answering.

"Do you know who Marianne Lekatt is?"

"The woman who doesn't want the wind farm on her land?"

"That's her. I happened to be there, in the bathroom. He turned up and threatened her."

"How do you mean, threatened?"

"First he shouted at her, told her he and his family would be in for it if she didn't release her land to the wind farm project. And when she said it served him right, he pushed her over and she hit her head on the stove. I filmed it."

"What were you doing at Lekatt's?"

"We're friends," she says.

"And why did you go see Salo?"

"I wanted him to tell me what the key was for."

"Did he know?"

"No, and I believed him."

"Can I see the film?"

"I deleted it. That was the deal."

Oh well. A deleted file can always be retrieved.

"I'm doubtful whether the diary contains anything that would serve as valid evidence against Sandberg, even though Märta is convinced it does. Was that really all there was in the left-luggage locker, Svala?"

Svala reaches for the monkey. "Have you got a knife?"

"Are there fish sticks in the sea?" says Lisbeth, opening the Leatherman sheath on her belt.

"Jesus," says Svala. "Seriously. You clearly aren't aware of the 1988 knife laws . . ."

And you ought not to be, either.

Svala unpicks the seam and puts her hand in. "If you tell anyone about the monkey, I'll never speak to you again," she says.

"A hard drive," says Lisbeth, studying it from all angles. "Do you know what's on it?"

"I took it to the gaming store."

"Shit! And?"

"It's got a cryptocurrency account on it. But without the password, no one can get in. I've tried everything I can think of. I'm sure only Mum knows it. I'll have to wait until she gets home," she says, and locks herself in the bathroom.

<Hotel bar in ten?>

<OK.>

65

"So this is what we know," says Lisbeth over a beer with Mikael Blomkvist.

"Hang on," he says. "I need to write this down."

"It must be a pain being gaga at such a young age . . . I never have to take notes."

"Rub it in."

"Young, young, young. Gaga, gaga, gaga."

"Right, where do we start?"

"Lukas's kidnap. Is he the target?"

"A secondary one, at any rate."

"In that case he ought to be somewhere in the immediate area. It would be too risky to transport him very far."

Don't be scared. We're going to find you.

"I've noted that down."

"People around Salo, then? Your darling daughter, Pernilla, for example. What do you know about her?"

"Too little," he admits.

"Thought as much. It might be best for me to talk to her. She likes me."

"Everybody likes you, don't they?"

"Yeah, yeah. What about Salo, then?" she says, tempted to bring up the Lekatt video.

"Extensive circle of acquaintances. We'd better start from the center. The heart, as he would call it."

"The municipality."

"Yes, and above all its current business dealings. There's a lot hidden away in the KGB. They come under the Companies Act and don't have to account to the public in any detail, except through standard annual reports. Their correspondence isn't official, for example."

"Want to take a bet?" says Lisbeth.

"Noted."

"What does your gut instinct say?"

"Salo," says Mikael. "And the company that doesn't exist, Branco Group."

The time has come to mention Lekatt. She gives him the exact same words that Svala used about Salo: the fact that someone might be threatening him.

"Makes sense," says Mikael. "Incidentally, Svala gave me a whole stack of notes. She ought to get a job at *Gaskassen*. Talk about attention to detail. She seems mainly interested in Lekatt, but she came across an e-mail from Branco, too. He and Salo seem to communicate via some alternative device. Presumably the e-mail was printed and archived by mistake."

"What did it say?" says Lisbeth.

"'The clock is ticking.'"

He's behaving oddly. Asks me weird questions about people I meet at work.

It sounds as if he's scared.

Never mind that . . . Do you want to see the pool out back?

"That brings us back to Branco," says Lisbeth. "But it's beyond me why some patch of land can be important enough to kidnap a child for?"

"It's quite an extensive bit of real estate, in fact," says Mikael. "Over a thousand acres."

"But still. There must be something special about Branco Group."

"I've been offering a bit of spiritual guidance at *Gaskassen*. Their homework is to put the municipal council under the microscope."

"Great," says Lisbeth, "but if even Hacker Republic can't unearth anything, it seems unlikely the local hacks will."

"No, but we can leave the simple stuff to them and concentrate on the big picture. Try to get something out of the police," he says. "I couldn't help noticing that you have a good contact there."

"What do you mean by that?"

"TikTok."

"You've been ogling some kids' app? Gross."

"You've clearly been doing the same."

"What I do in private is none of your business."

"True, but you've got a police contact, anyway. Use it."

"Well, you can use Faste, in that case. You two seem to be at about the same level," says Lisbeth, getting to her feet.

"Do stay. Sit, please. I'm sorry if I went too far. We need to finish working out our strategy."

"I've already got it in my head. I'm going to pay Salo a little visit; that should get things moving."

"Noted."

"Dickhead."

"Also noted."

66

Lisbeth takes a detour to the hotel room to check whether the kid is hungry. She wouldn't mind something herself . . . a pizza, maybe . . . but the room is empty. Though Svala has left a note.

> *Doing homework with a friend who lives outside town. I might sleep over. Will let you know if so.*

Sounds a bit fishy, but good if it's true. Lisbeth has never heard her mention a friend. On the contrary, any time she asks, Svala snaps her head off.

She picks up her laptop. Nothing new from Plague, but plenty from the Milton intranet. She reads through the report from the security breach at the Ministry for Social Affairs and her laughter bubbles up.

Look, Svala, I'm laughing!

Dick and Pick stage a raid to test the gullibility of the staff. They stroll in, each with a standard-issue tool case, and say they've come to fix a few computers that are acting up. They have to show their IDs, admittedly, but no one asks them who authorized their visit. Everything is theirs for the taking.

They work their way systematically through about ten computers, planting a bit of spyware and a few other nice little surprises. Their task complete, they walk out with all the ministry's confidential information essentially in the palms of their hands. But because they're the good guys, they gather the staff together and tell them what has happened. Everyone is appalled, of course. But this does nothing to prevent a duo of bad guys sauntering in a mere two days later and claiming to be from Milton Security. They, too, have to show their IDs, after which they go through the same sort of procedure and leave the office with a polite goodbye. Three hours later, de Deus receives his first threatening letter.

She tries to concentrate on her work but gives up. Her thoughts keep revolving around Salo and Branco.

Hi Dragan, do you know of a company called Branco Group, involved in security among other things? Thought you might at least have heard of them. I'm helping Gasskas Municipal Council with a few things.

Hi Lisbeth, Branco rings a vague bell, to do with watches, as it happens. I have a slight weakness for Rolexes, as you know. Typical immigrant, I know, but one has to spend one's money on something. A few years ago a very special Daytona that had belonged to Paul Newman went on sale at auction in New York. I happened to be there, as did the man who bought it. I went over to congratulate him afterward and introduced myself, and so did he. He turned out to be a Swede called Marcus Branco. A pleasant fellow. Confined to a wheelchair by thalidomide. We had a cup of tea together and a little chat about cybersecurity. I don't think he said exactly what line of work he was in. This is just a hunch, as you can hear, but bearing in mind the price, around $15 million, he must have been some kind of top dog. Good luck with Branco and with the girl as well. Best, Dragan A.

Lisbeth considers hacking Svala's phone herself, but decides to farm out the job to Plague. The kid would be livid if she found out. She'd be bound to start mouthing off about violation of integrity or, worse still, clam up for a few days to punish her.

<Need to get hold of a deleted video. 073 435 88 91. Urgent.>

While she has the number in front of her, she thinks she might as well try Svala. No answer.

<Sorry to disturb your studies. Just wanted to say there'll be pizza for dinner. Yum!>

<Sleeping here. Pizza sounds good, let's do it tomorrow.>

And where is here? she's about to type, but thinks better of it. She trusts the girl; it isn't that. She's not the type to drink moonshine or smoke surreptitious cigarettes and hang out with older boys. Just the opposite; she always seems to have a clear reason for anything she does.

In the same moment it strikes her that the monkey which usually

guards the bedpost is gone. She checks the bathroom and the other bedroom. No monkey and no diary.

<Were you afraid I'd steal the monkey?☺>

<Someone's helping me mend it.☺☺☺>

Lisbeth's shoulders relax. Everything is alright. She connects to
Plague. No answer yet.

She rings Jessica for the third time. No answer there, either.

<Want to meet up?>

<I'm working.>

Damn. She's sulking. Lisbeth tries to figure out why. Something she
said, something she did? Another message pings in immediately.

<Got to prioritize work. We'll have to meet another
time.>

She throws the phone onto the bed and takes a shower. Not because
she needs one—it's only been three or four days—more to help pass the
time.

Plague to Wasp: <Showtime.>

The sound isn't the best. Lisbeth gets out her Sennheiser headphones
to cut through the crackle. Just as the girl has grasped, there's the indica-
tion of a threat to Salo and his family. But there's something else that she
doesn't at first understand. She goes back to the beginning and listens
over and over again.

67

"Hello. Lisbeth Salander, Milton Security."

"Right. What can I do for you?" says Salo, and gestures to her to take a seat. He is sitting behind a large desk, swiveling on his chair. Behind him stretch shelves full of files. There is perfection in the tidiness of the piles of paper. His suit is crumpled. A rank smell of sweat and old alcohol permeates the room.

"I'm an expert in cybersecurity. At the moment I'm helping the Gasskas police with information about the disappearance of your son, Lukas. I have some questions."

"Fire away," says Salo. "Do you want coffee?"

"No, thank you. The investigation has revealed that there's some kind of threat directed at your family. Or perhaps primarily at you."

"I don't know anything about that," says Salo.

"To do with the wind farm construction?"

"That's a major project. There's a lot at stake. Naturally there are always differences of opinion—it would be strange if there weren't—but a threat? No. I've already told the police all I know. Several times over. The boy's disappearance is a mystery to me, too."

"What's your own take?" she says.

Well, what, indeed? He studies the peculiar woman opposite him. Impossible to guess her age. Skinny and bedraggled. Dressed like a teenager with hair dyed black and a ring in her nose. Somewhere between fourteen and forty-four. She looks unreal.

```
<66.301252, 20.387050.>
<7 p.m. Come alone.>
```

"Do you have any identification?" he says.

Lisbeth hands over her Milton ID card.

"Oh, it's you. I heard you were playing detective with the hack."

Salo pours himself a glass of water from a carafe and drops three Treo tablets into it. The headache, the fatigue have parked themselves in his body like a virus. At home, Pernilla sits weeping interminably. At the office, colleagues are running around like nervous prey, convinced that their young, too, are in the risk zone, which perhaps they are. "Go to the police," is his advice. "The police exist to protect us."

Salo is a man of action. The one who makes things happen. A problem solver. But right now, all he wants is for this creature in his room to leave so he can lock the door and get back to the visitor's sofa and his bottle. Unfortunately, the day is not yet over. *Come alone.*

"Was that all?" he says. "There are things I need to do."

She gets out her phone. It takes only a few seconds for him to realize what she's playing to him. *That little devil. You can't even rely on a child.*

"You went to see Marianne Lekatt," says Lisbeth.

"Yes," he says, "to talk."

"Funny sort of talking. To me it sounds more as if you're issuing a threat," she says, and turns up the sound.

"Stop that," he says. "It sounds worse than it is."

"I realize that, and it doesn't bother me if you twist the landowners' arms to make them sell to the wind farm project."

" 'Grant the use of,' " says Salo. "They're not selling, they're granting us the use of the land and earning a few hundred thousand a year in return. Without having to lift a finger."

"Thanks for the information, but the interesting bit is something entirely different," says Lisbeth, holding the phone closer to him. *"They're after me. You've got to release the land. Do it for my sake."*

"So," she says, closing the video. "Either you tell me the whole story, or it'll be movie night for the police tonight."

He gets up and paces the room. He stops by the window. The water level in the river is high. The thought makes him feel safe. How easy it would be. To go up to Storforsen. Step off the rock and be united with the surging mass of water.

"This is about your son," she says. "Don't you want him to be found?"

Does he? What he wants more than anything is to have Pernilla back, instead of that human wreck at home. To be spared the accusations that it's all his fault. What a way to start a bloody marriage!

"Of course I do," he says, "but I've got to do things my way."

"You're going to do a deal with the kidnappers?"

"I told you, I've no idea who they are," says Salo. "Do what you like with the video."

"One last question and then I'll go. Why should Lekatt do it *for your sake*?"

He turns. Runs his hand through his hair as he's caught in the creature's emotionally neutral gaze.

"Because she's my mother," he says.

68

Salo checks the coordinates for at least the third time and drives out of the council garage. Apart from a few timber trucks heading in the opposite direction on their way to Karlsborg or Piteå, the road is deserted. He passes Lake Kallak and takes a left toward Kåbdalis.

He has checked the map. The place is not unknown to him. He sometimes goes there. Chucks his small-bore rifle into the boot of the car and picks off a capercaillie that has found its way to the dirt track to peck at the grit.

The van is at the far end of the clearing where the timber trucks turn. A black Transporter. He parks beside it and winds down the window.

"You asked for a meeting. Here I am. What do you want?"

"Get out of the car."

A voice he does not know. His mouth goes dry. His legs are unsteady. Salo is not a small man. This guy is at least a head taller than him. Black clothes and a face covering. It's absurd. Some Wagner type in safe little Gasskas. A place where people leave the key in the lock and never have to look behind them when they're out at night. How the hell did it come to this?

"You evidently haven't been taking this situation seriously," says the man.

"I've done all I could," says Salo. "Where's the boy?"

"What boy?"

Salo gasps. His pulse is pounding in his throat. His voice cracks. "Lukas."

"The question is what we're going to do with you. Since you didn't get the landowners to change their minds, we've no use for you any longer," he says, taking Salo by the scruff of the neck. "But we happen to be quite a decent crew, so we thought we'd give you another little choice." He pulls Salo with him to the back doors. A woman has gotten out of the van. The same black clothes. Only the eyes offer any clues. *Move him.* She shines a flashlight into his face and opens the doors.

Blinded by the glare, he does not initially know what he is looking at. A cage? A dog?

"Voilà," says the man. "Say hello to someone you know."

Salo turns away and throws up.

"Eugh, that's not a very nice greeting for someone you love," he says, and manhandles Salo back toward the cage. The body is not moving. The face is a bloodied mess, as if they plunged the head into boiling water. But he can still see who it is. He gives a sob. Tries to force his hand between the bars of the cage to reach hers.

Not Märta, not his Märta.

"As you can see, Romeo, we've been kind enough to let her live. Not much of a life, but still . . . As you may remember, it was you who told us we could do what we liked with her and we've certainly done that," he says, and chuckles. "We get why you like her so much."

Saturday. Their father is coming home. Henry and Joar are keeping a lookout. Hiding in the garage, waiting for the car. Their father gets out. Henry raises the hammer.

With a bellow he shoves aside the woman and punches the man. Once and then twice. He doesn't know where the punches land. The woman's laughter is as raw as a November morning in Murjek. Then it all goes black.

A long time later, he has no idea how long, he opens the car door and throws up again. The Transporter has gone. Subzero temperatures have turned the mist on the windows to ice. He scrapes the windscreen and lets the tears flow.

Instead of turning back to Gasskas, he goes on to Storforsen. Turns off before the hotel and drives up to the rapids. Sprints across the narrow wooden bridges. Slips and slides across the rocks until he reaches the outermost point. Climbs over the safety rail and looks down into the thundering water.

God. We've spoken before. You want me to live and sort out the mess, but I can't do it. Do You hear me? I can't do this any longer. First Lukas, then Märta. They're going to take me, too.

What turned me into the person I am? All I wanted was a bit of appreciation, don't You understand? Everything I do is in the best interests of this place, the best interests of my family, but nobody sees it. So for that reason, God, I've had enough.

Then his phone rings.

God almighty, call me some other time. He loses his thread. Gets out his phone. Pernilla.

"Where are you?" she says.

"At the rapids."

"What are you doing there?"

"I'm going to jump."

"Henry. Get away from there. Back away from the water. Do it now."

"No," he says. "It's too late. Too late for everything. I'm sorry, Pilla. It isn't your fault."

"First Lukas and then you. Don't you get how goddamned selfish that is?"

"Yes, but that's how it is."

"No," she says. "I won't let you."

She was angry. Took it out on Mikael. But she isn't stupid, even if everybody takes it for granted that she's the nice one. The reliable one. The one who's there for other people.

It's tragic that Henry is thinking this way, but in the current situation it's an advantage. He makes no great effort to conceal his secrets from her. She ransacks his desk. Makes copies. Goes through his pockets for business cards and phone numbers. Checks his private e-mail when he falls asleep on the sofa and has forgotten to log out.

If he dies, Lukas won't come back.

She runs to the car, accelerates away and heads for Storforsen. At least half an hour's drive. The snow is coming down thickly. Maybe longer.

She keeps talking. Says all sorts of things. It doesn't matter what. Sometimes he responds. "Are you still there? . . . Henry?" "Yes." "Do you remember when we met?" "Yes," he says. "Tell me," she says. "How did we meet?"

"You were on tour with a choir. I was in the audience."

"Go on, tell me more. What happened next?" She is shouting the words now, and the roar of the rapids is all around her. The snow makes the path to the river hard to negotiate. Got to make it in time.

"You were so beautiful," he says. "And good."

"The hell I was," she shouts. "I'm not good. I'm an ordinary human being . . . Don't jump," she shouts through the roar of the water. She climbs over the barrier and tries not to look down. "I'm behind you."

"No," he says. "You don't get it."

"Maybe not, but if you jump, I'm jumping, too."

"You've got Lukas. He's alive."

"How do you know?"

"They said it. When I was playing God and exchanged one life for another."

"They?" she shouts. "Who the hell are they?"

He gives up. Clearly today is not his time.

"Back away," he shouts back. "I'm coming." He struggles over the barrier. He wants to hold her, be held. They are soaked through and shivering. Without the adrenaline, the rocks are slippery and the evening is impenetrable, black. He wants to tell her everything. Share the fear. Feel safe.

They warm themselves up in Pernilla's car. Hold their hands up to the fan. The skin slowly grows back on Salo's body and the images fade.

"I heard you both. When you rang her."

"Who?" he says.

"Märta Hirak. I saw the number and read your texts."

The body. The blood. The cage.

"Märta was a mistake. An isolated fling. She turned up one day with a key. We had a couple of drinks and before we knew it—"

"Stop! That's enough." *I'll turn you in, you bastard, you can be sure of that.*

His headache has eased. Telling the truth brings him closer to peace of mind. For the first time in months, he experiences a kind of calm. "We'll get Lukas back," he says, putting his hand on hers.

She withdraws her hand and engages a gear. "Are you sleeping at home tonight?"

"Do you want me to?" he says, getting out of the car. He only just shuts the door before she pulls away.

69

Svala gets off the bus in Harads. She walks in the direction of Britta's Treehotel.

"Hi," she says. "My dad's booked the Seventh Room. Peder Sandberg. He's coming a bit later."

"Welcome to the hotel," says the receptionist, checking the booking. "Quite right. Two nights. Would you like me to wait to take the payment until he gets here?"

Svala hesitates. It's tempting, but it would be stupid. She can't risk the staff starting to dig around.

"No. He's given me the money," she says, and puts twenty-three thousand kronor on the counter.

Last time she came in the back way, through the forest. She made sure to melt into a group of visiting tourists and went with them from lodge to lodge, learning almost all there was to know about architects, lighting and, crucially, how far off the ground each of the lodges was.

Twenty-three thousand is virtually half the monkey's savings. The Seventh Room is the largest lodge and is thirty feet up, a U-shaped construction among the spruces. A coarse-meshed net, like a hanging terrace, is stretched between the two protruding bedroom sections. She opens the balcony door, balances her way out onto the net, lies down on her stomach and watches the world below. She has plenty of time. It will be dark.

Half an hour before the time she is due to meet Pappy Peder, she takes the path down to reception and hands in one of the keys. "I'm checking out now," she says, "but Dad will be staying till tomorrow. I've managed to get a ticket for the match. He's giving me a lift into Gasskas and then he'll come back and check in."

Peder Sandberg is lying low. Which does not mean that his brain has stopped thinking evil thoughts. Quite the opposite. He is fantasizing about revenge. He can't let go of the humiliation. Him on all fours. The police bitch's kicks landing on his body. That first kick, from behind, is something he cannot bear to think about. Karate Kid makes him feel physically sick. But worst of all was the others. The Svavelsjö gang standing in a circle laughing at him. And not only then. Now, later and forever.

It has been a few days now and his balls have stopped aching, but there's something about his ribs. Broken, probably. Coughing is out of the question. There's no risk of him laughing, at least. He picks up his Glock, takes a two-handed grip and sees in his mind's eye the bodies exploding in a hail of bullets. Arms, legs and guts. The last bullets splatter brains across the wall. He is feeling better already.

He is so engrossed in thoughts of vengeance that he almost forgets he has an assignment.

You're actually only worthy of cleaning toilets, but I'm giving you another chance. Get hold of the girl, whatever her name is. Svala. That's the one. Make her hand over the hard drive and take her out.

You mean shoot her? he asks to make sure he has understood his instructions.

Precisely, says Sonny, as long as you get hold of the hard drive. Or do whatever you like, as long as she disappears. Let's start with that. After the kid there'll be a bigger assignment, but we'll come to that later.

He'd rather shoot police bitches. Not that he cares about the little devil, but he does have a few grains of decency in his body.

<Have info about your mum. Got time to meet?>

<5 p.m. at Buongiorno?> she texts.

<OK.>

Moron.

At three she drops by the pizzeria.

"Svala, haven't seen you for ages. How are you? Are you hungry?"

"No thanks, I've just eaten. Can you give Peder this?" she says, pressing a handwritten note into a flour-white hand.

"Sure," he says, and asks after Mammamärta.

"Er," says Svala, and is suddenly in a hurry.

It doesn't normally affect her like that. She's good at swallowing things. Perhaps it's to do with this place. She could see her sitting there laughing. See them together, herself and Mammamärta.

It is all his fault. Faults exist to be rectified.

Peder Sandberg is not stupid. As he sees it, he's fucking clever. He drives up a track for forestry vehicles a little way behind the Treehotel, locks the car, puts the keys on the front tire so he won't drop them anywhere and moves toward the treetop lodges. The hotel is world-famous. Not just because of Justin Bieber and other nobodies who want to play bird-ies. This is where spies being hunted nationwide were able to elude the Security Service. That's the sort of thing Peder Sandberg doesn't forget. One day he will be famous, too. He is well on the way.

The police bitch. Just chill. Her time will come. Meeting with Branco next week. Admittedly without telling Sonny, but nobody's ever died of double-dealing. *We need somebody like you.* Of course, who doesn't?

The Seventh Room is the lodge at the far end. He has googled to make sure. What a dumb kid. It couldn't be better. Alone in a hotel room. Not that he's planning to shoot her there. *That* would be stupid. But under cover of darkness, nobody will see them leave.

Svala checks the time. Five to eight. She starts up the coffee machine and empties a packet of Singoalla cookies onto a plate. One last check.

> Hi Amineh, I've read about you. You were thirteen when you ran away from your family and became a Peshmerga fighter. I am thirteen too. I am not running away from my family, they are running away from me. Tonight I am meeting my stepfather. He is misogyny and repression of human rights all rolled up in one person. I hope I can be as brave as you.

> Hi Svala, thank you for your message. It made me sad to read it. No thirteen-year-old should have to fight like you. In the eyes of the law you are a child. But I understand you and I know that in some situations we have no choice. Take care of yourself. Amineh.

. . .

Does Peder Sandberg have a choice?

Of course he does. As frenetically as he tries to be worst, he could try to be best. An individual always has choices. The destructive ones present themselves most readily because they do not require mutual understanding. The fighter in us, or the hunter if we want to shift the object to fauna, is a genetically inherited function, whereas unconditional love, altruism and general compassion are acquired, and also take more energy.

So how can a thoroughgoing change in society be achieved? We must start with the corrupt political leaders who advocate globalism, multiculturalism and mass immigration. Below them in political systems, in the apparatus of state and in the political parties, they have many underlings who must be eliminated. Yes, my friends, eliminated. No one is getting close to the real question. How is the earth to survive?

Hi Marcus, I saw your TED Talk. Unbelievably inspiring. Do you have an organization that people can join? Or, like, films you can recommend?

Peder, keep your eyes open. There are a lot of us who think like you. We are on the move, organizing ourselves and infiltrating wider society. Our time is soon. Marcus.

Going up steps puts you at a disadvantage, but up he must go. Up to a child who is happy to meet her stepfather. He has nothing to lose. The fact is, and he has to admit it, he will be glad to see the freaky kid again. She's crazy, but who isn't? Say what you like about Svala, but if she is as Märta claims, she will meet him halfway. No struggle or fuss. Death does not need to be complicated.

Is it, Marcus?!

That's right, Peder. Some people are not meant to live.

A knock at the door. The handle goes down. Her pulse rate goes up. It's obvious that he's after something.

"It's been a while," he says, looking around. "Not a bad little place you've moved into. Have you robbed some pensioner?"

"I saved up," she says. "Do you want coffee?"

"Why not," he says, taking apart a sandwich cookie and licking off the jam. "A chip off the old block," he says with a broad smile that reveals the gaps in his teeth. "Your mum has clearly taught you a thing or two."

"Yes, she has," Svala says, and opens the diary. "I'd like to read something out to you."

"Fine, as long as it's not the Bible."

Mammamärta's bible.

March 4, 2016. Some trouble with a dealer in Kalix. Peder wants me to go with him. When I ask why, he says, "So I can learn something new." We get to a flat. It's evening. A boy of about five or six answers the door. Peder sits down in the kitchen to talk to the father, that is, the dealer. The boy and I watch kids' programmes. There's a row. The boy is alarmed. I shut him in the bedroom so he won't hear. He bursts into tears.

"What is this shit?" says Peder.

"Wait," says Svala, and goes on reading.

Peder ties the dealer to a kitchen chair and starts from the top. He cuts off an earlobe. Then the other one. He screams, begs for mercy, promises to pay and so on. The boy is screaming, too. I ask Peder to stop. OK, he says, and draws a gun. Points it at me, holds out the knife and says I can choose, either to continue cutting or to be shot. I chose to be shot, but he can't bring himself to do it. We leave the flat. Later he takes it out on Svala instead. We spend the night in the ER.

She shuts the diary. "Two hundred pages," she says, "copied at the library and hidden in a safe place."

"What do you want?" says Peder.

"What do you think I want?" she says.

"Money, of course. How much?"

"I don't want your disgusting money. I want to know where my mother is," she says. "If you don't tell me, the diary will go to the police. Especially if you kill me. If that happens, there's no way back for you."

She has already noticed that he is armed. Nothing unusual in that. She simply has to stay a step ahead. Peder is no strategist. Anger is what drives his actions. What's more, he's a coward and he hates heights. He never even dares to go out on the balcony.

"A diary doesn't prove anything," he says. "Anybody could have written this rubbish."

"I have other proof," she says, which is true. The monkey contains many secrets. It's just a question of drawing the right card at the right time.

Sandberg laughs and points the gun at her. "We're going for a little ride, you and me. First we'll go get the hard drive, and then that'll be the end of your fun and games."

"You'll have to catch me first," she says, and takes several quick steps out onto the net. She has been practicing. She knows how to compensate for the movement of the net. She knows he will hesitate at the door. She takes out her phone and points the camera in his direction. *Say cheese, Pappy Peder.* The flash captures him in a perfect pose with his gun, his manic look and everything. Sent.

"It would be stupid to shoot me here," she says. "People will hear. There are French tourists in the Bird's Nest a few trees away. If you manage to catch me, I promise to come quietly."

The ground billows below him when he makes the mistake of looking down. He hates her. He hates the whole damn situation. He has shown himself to be soft and is being punished. He's been drinking coffee and listening to fairy tales instead of nabbing her right at the start. He could shoot her here and now, but the darkness and the swaying net mean there's a good risk he will miss. He is not exactly a sniper. He prefers to shoot people at close quarters. His silencer is on the bed at home. The shot will be heard all over fucking Harads. He takes a few steps toward her, the net is more rigid than he thought. Ha ha, she probably thought he wouldn't dare.

She moves in an arc. She keeps close to the lodge and aims for the opposite door, which leads to the other wing of the U-shape. Pap Peder will try to intercept her. That's what she's counting on, anyway. And if he doesn't? Her only plan B is the photo she's just sent to Lisbeth, but the road here is twisting and Gasskas is at least half an hour away. She stops. He is close now. She is ready.

Play for time. Get the enemy off-balance.

"If you tell me where Mum is, I'll give you the diary and the copies," she says.

As if he knows where the whore might be. She had something brewing, he knows that. Thanks to him, her plan was foiled.

"She wanted to be with the big boys, I suppose," he says, "but I don't think it turned out very well."

"And who are they?" she says. "Those biker jerks?"

If his ribs weren't so infernally painful, he would have laughed.

"Now shut your mouth," he says. "You're not going to get away. Let's go in, drive back to town and get it over and done with. I've nothing against you, really. To me you're just a job. It'll be quick and painless."

"As you're here to shoot me anyway, you might have the decency to tell me. Looks like I won't be blabbing, doesn't it?"

A stubborn little devil. Like her mother.

"I don't care if you believe me or not," he says. "I don't know what their names are."

"Or where they're based?"

"Somewhere nobody's going to look," he says. "She should have stuck with me." He takes one step backward and then another.

Damn. Think. Exploit his weakness. Make him angry.

"Mum was with Henry Salo," she says.

"Old news," he says.

"I mean the whole time you and she were together. She went behind your back. Slept with Salo whenever she could."

Good. He's taking a step forward.

"I've always known," says Svala. "We often joke about you. How dense you are not to have noticed that she's got Salo's ring on her finger. Märta and Henry. Forever. Everybody knows they're an item. Everybody except you, obviously." He is sticking close to the wall, making his way around in the same way she did. His heavy breathing, only a few feet away. *Fuck.* She needs to get him out into the middle.

He raises his gun. Rage versus reason. Now there's no going back.

She makes a run for the door. Exactly as she has calculated, he comes straight across the netting to cut her off. But as she covers the final feet to safety, she slips and loses her footing.

He grabs her by the hair and pulls her upright. As he tries to shove her through the door, she jabs an elbow into his ribs. In the flash of pain, his brain boils. He seizes her arm and twists it up behind her back, like in the old playground game.

Does that hurt?

No!

And that?

No!

How about this?

Bang. The ligament cracks like a shot in the night as her arm is ripped from its socket. They stop for a second.

Mae-geri. A front kick, the first move a beginner learns, and in the right situation one of the most effective. Providing it is done the right way. Lift the knee, snap the leg forward, focus the power on the striking surface and let the hip do the job in a strong rolling movement.

Again. Better. The hotel room is their dojo. The cushions their punching pads.

You're a natural, says Lisbeth, tying a bathrobe belt around her waist and bowing.

One-armed rag doll Svala Hirak makes full use of centrifugal force, prepares for *mae-geri* and lands it in the part of the body with a name that sounds like a Greek seaside hotel: solar plexus. Pap Peder's final trip to the sun takes him in a wide arc, over the glass barrier that runs around the edge of the netting.

A two-hundred-pound body falling thirty feet does not scream. It lands obligingly on a rock and breaks its neck.

Allow no fear. You are a warrior. No thinking. Just do what you must.

The arm is not hurting. Vittangi disease has its advantages. Joint problems and atrophy are later symptoms. But the arm is unusable. Her left, what is more.

She stuffs the diary into her backpack, squeezes dish soap onto a dishcloth and wipes the keycard and the handle of the coffee machine.

Switches off the lights and closes the door. She pauses for a moment and listens. The forest is silent. She goes briskly down the winding steps.

She has spent a large part of her thirteen-year-old life considering how to escape Pap Peder. Now he is lying there. Neutralized and out of her life forever. It is not joy. It is not sorrow. It is necessity.

He should have made do with the diary. How am I to find you now, Mammamärta?

Unless anyone deliberately goes to the base of the Seventh Room, the body will not be found until tomorrow. But what if some dogged tourist does just that? She tries lifting him by the leg, but realizes he is too heavy to be moved with one arm. The pistol is sticking out from under his belly. She removes the magazine and stows the separate parts of the weapon in her backpack. She gets the keycard out of her back pocket, presses it a few times against his limp fingers and slides it into his coat pocket.

The sound of a twig snapping. She stops and holds her breath. Another sound. *Damn it.* If they find her here, she's had it. Footsteps. They move away. Return. She flattens herself to the ground and crawls in the opposite direction. If only she can get to the edge of the forest she will be safe.

A whisper. Her name. "Svala? Are you there?"

Lisbeth. She gets up and pulls her aunt into the darkness beneath the lodge.

"Mind you don't trip over the shitheap," she says.

"It looks dead," says Lisbeth, and Svala nods. "Are you sure?" She nods again.

The Peshmerga fighter slips into the protective darkness of the forest.

After a brief visit to the ER and with her arm provisionally replaced in its socket, Svala gets there just in time for the third period. Three to one Gasskas in the match against Björklöven.

At 10:40 she tucks herself up in bed with the monkey. Using her phone as a ruler, she makes a new column under the letter A.

Deceased.

70

Salo goes up to his office. Lies down on the chesterfield and tries to gather his thoughts.

He ought to be focused on Marcus Branco and how to stay one step ahead. That's the sort of thing Salo does. And yet it is the girl he thinks about. Her and Märta. How different life could have been.

Above all, he thinks about Marianne Lekatt. It is entirely the girl's fault.

She's such a nice person.

When his father is away working, his mother dances on the table. Comes alive, laughs, spends time with her sons. They go out to pick mushrooms and berries. Help each other with the animals, in a unified battle against the poverty that always has one foot in the door.

Why has he forgotten the good parts? Because it makes the betrayal easier to bear.

She was a victim, too.

But she abandoned them. Went into her own world and left them outside.

A person who cannot forgive grows bitter.

That kid always has to know best. He gets up, pulls on his boots and takes the path to the mountain for the first time since he moved here.

He has forgotten how the forest can be.

The forest is a place where he goes hunting, an essential battleground with vegetation of varying degrees of hindrance. All at once he is aware of other things. A solitary pine that has rooted itself in a cleft in the rocks and is stretching its scraggy arms toward the light. An ant heap in the form of a sugarloaf, marsh Labrador tea that is still green and fragrant when he touches it.

Bit by bit it unfolds and speaks to him, saying: *The forest survives everything as long as it is left to its own devices. The forest gives to those who see.*

Thoughts of all the bad stuff that frames his existence are erased. The path intermittently disappears. One step at a time forces other thoughts aside; they cannot be accommodated under slippery boot soles.

Instead of rounding the hill, which is the easiest way, he goes up to the highest point and sits down where they always used to sit, he and Joar. Like eagles with oversight of the farm and the people who lived there. A few angry steps across the yard were all it took to tell them whether they could go home or not.

This is where Branco Group wants to build. Right at the top, where there is most wind. Their mountain, his and Joar's.

Moisture soaks through the fabric of his trousers and he continues on the steeper but shorter route down to the house. Dusk falls. The temperature sinks below zero. There is no light visible. No smoke rising from the chimney.

Now that he has finally summoned the courage to meet her as a human being, that human being is not there. *Damn.*

He goes up the front steps. Tries the door. Open.

The word "hello" is ingrained like a reflex action still lingering from childhood. If "hello" is answered, it's safe to come in.

No one answers. He takes off his boots, hangs his jacket on a hook. Puts on the light in the hall and opens the kitchen door a crack.

The first thing he sees are the legs. They look as if they've got tangled in a kitchen chair.

"Mum," he says. A forgotten word.

A mum who is beyond first aid is stretched out on a rag rug, woven from strips of his childhood. Red hair spread out across the blue pattern.

He sits down beside her. Turns her face toward him, what is left of it after a bullet has hit her forehead and, he can only hope, killed Marianne Lekatt instantaneously.

Salo shuffles over to the sink. He leans against the pantry door and tries to work out what to do. The most natural course of action would be to ring the police. He has nothing to do with her death. Yet here he sits feeling anything but innocent. It makes no difference who did this. He has gambled, staked his own mother and now she is dead. He is to blame.

71

Somewhere nobody's going to look . . .

Lisbeth checks on the girl. She is still asleep. It turned into a late night. Eventually she got the whole story out of her. *Somewhere nobody's going to look.* The blackmail plan and the hole in the netting.

Lisbeth is dubious about that particular aspect of Svala's account. It seems extraordinary for a luxury hotel not to keep a rigorous check on health and safety, but what the hell. Sometimes a half-truth is easier to live with. Sandberg's departure from this life is no loss.

Somewhere nobody's going to look . . .

The phrase gnaws at Lisbeth all the way to the library.

Mikael Blomkvist is not alone. Lisbeth can see telltale signs from a distance. A cop. The town seems to be crawling with them. And she's right: Birna Guðmundurdottir extends a hand. "I'm with the Serious Crime Unit," she says. "Mikael tells me he and you are trying to map out the people behind the kidnap."

"Among other things," says Lisbeth.

"I didn't catch your name," she says.

"I didn't give it," says Lisbeth. She has no time for Mikael Blomkvist's acquaintances. She gets herself a cup of coffee from the vending machine and asks a librarian the way to the map room.

"Wait, Lisbeth," says Mikael. "Can't we go through the material one more time. There are a few things I want to add."

"Do you know a Marcus Branco?" Lisbeth asks the woman.

"No," she says. "We know one of the companies tendering for the wind farm is Branco Group, but a Marcus? No."

"Why do you ask?" says Mikael.

"I got a sort of tip-off from Armansky."

"No other news?" he says.

Not in front of that police girl, at any rate.

"I'll be in the map room. Come and join me when you're through with her."

She starts from scratch with a standard 1:10,000-scale property map of the area. Houses, roads, lakes and so on. All around the municipality there are huge numbers of little roads leading to individual houses, often beside lakes. Physically investigating every last shack would be impossible. She has to find some other starting point.

Instead of fetching the next scale of map, she asks to borrow paper and something to write with.

Where would nobody look?

Sewage tunnels
Uninhabited buildings
Abandoned mines
In the attic of the municipal council offices
In the police station basement

And then she stops. It is winter, after all. She crosses them all out except for the last two. Then she crosses those out as well but reinstates uninhabited buildings.

An uninhabited building need not just be a residential property with the heating turned off.

Storehouse
Garage
Industrial

She chews her pencil and tries to think constructively. The municipality is the smallest in the region in terms of area. But large enough for people never to be found when they go missing. The dead ones, at least. The seven who are recorded in Märta's diary, for example. They were the ones she had been intending to put Blomkvist onto. She can hear the woman's laughter even here. Doesn't she know you're supposed to be quiet in a library?

Lisbeth checks *Expressen* and *Gaskassen*. No dead males found in Harads. Yet. Clever kid, paying for two nights. Whoever assigned Sandberg to bumping off Svala is going to feel even more motivated once his body is found. The kid is in danger. The question is whether giving them the hard drive would be enough. Lisbeth has already copied the file over to her own laptop. Without the password, the hard drive is no more than scrap metal. Which should imply, if Lisbeth is correct in her thinking, that whoever has Märta hasn't managed to get the password out of her. The question remains: Is she alive?

And Lisbeth has completely run out of inventive ideas. She scrunches up the sheet of paper and shuffles aimlessly through the assortment of other maps. She does not know what she is looking for. *Not.* The question is what might *not* feature on a map.

"Excuse me," says Lisbeth to an elderly man a few seats along. "There are maps of everything, aren't there, from population numbers to heights above sea level, houses, factories, hospitals and so on. Is there anything that would never be on a map?"

"Now there's a question," he says. "Let me think."

Lisbeth sends a surreptitious glance in Mikael's direction. He's in his seat, bent over his phone. She does another quick search on Harads. Still no news, even though it's nearly one o'clock.

If only she could go home. Put the key in the lock and shut out the world. Curl up in a window and watch the traffic flowing across the bridge in a never-ending stream as the pizza grease runs down her chin.

"Hmm," says the man. "You wanted to know about maps. The only thing I can think of is military installations, bunkers and the like. Not even military buildings that are decommissioned would be on a map, as far as I know."

"Are there any of those in Gasskas?" she says.

"Given how close we are to the bases at Boden and Älvsbyn, I would expect there to be a few scattered around."

"But nothing specific?" says Lisbeth.

"I have a vague memory from my childhood. Someone my parents knew bought a place in the forest and got a bunker in the bargain, but I don't remember the location."

Lisbeth spreads out the property map again.

"Try," she says. "If it was a farm or something, there'll be a road to it, won't there?"

"Can't be sure of that. Some villages, especially those where only a few people lived, didn't get roads until the late 1950s. There were paths, of course, and tracks for horses and carts."

He runs his finger across the map. Mumbles to himself and reels off place names. "Somewhere in this area, I reckon," he says, making a ring around virtually the entire municipality.

Her patience is nearly at an end. Soon another day will have passed without any progress.

"OK," she says, "how about guessing, then, off the top of your head? It doesn't have to be right, just say something."

"Here," he says, his brown-stained index finger making a snus mark out in the middle of nowhere.

When the man has gone and the librarian is looking the other way, she folds up the map and tucks it inside her jacket.

"I'm off now," she says to Mikael, who has swapped his phone for his laptop.

"Did you know that Marianne Lekatt is Salo's biological mother?"

"Yes, he told me."

"You'll have seen the news as well, then."

"No. What?"

"She's been killed. Shot. Found dead on her kitchen floor."

"Who found her?" asks Lisbeth. The day suddenly has a point to it again.

"Henry Salo."

72

The message comes in the middle of the night. He sees it the next morning.

`<Clean away the object.>`

The boy is asleep. He has slept for most of the past twenty-four hours. The Cleaner checks on him. Gets a little water into him but no food.

The wounds from the eagle attack are not healing, and why should they? The beak hacked into his head. The claws gripped his body in an attempt to carry him off. A sea eagle can take flight with a reindeer calf. In the predatory order of things, the boy is perhaps not meant to survive.

Rather than making coffee, which is his usual routine, he goes out. The snow has decided to settle. The month has changed to November. There is a quarter drum of meat left. The last blowout.

The sky is clear. A capercaillie is startled and flaps away. He has a decision to make.

The calls of the sea eagle are a mystery to the Cleaner. According to the bird book, the species is relatively quiet, except in the breeding season, when it gives a shrill screech like that of a black woodpecker.

The Cleaner's eagles screech when they detect the hunks of meat he has spread on the feeding tray. *What a lot,* they screech, *enough for everybody!*

One, two, three. The eagles have landed. But instead of lying in his hiding place as usual, he goes back to the hut and starts to clean.

He cleans to obliterate his own traces. Cleans and lets the tears flow. Cleans in the knowledge that at least half the current local population of eagles will die without supplementary feeding. Cleans and thinks of his two years in the log cabin. The bodies that have come and moved on in the form of eagle chicks, which have hatched and tried their first faltering wingbeats about ten weeks later.

Apart from the boy.

Even for people like the Cleaner, there have to be exceptions.

His mind is made up. The boy needs care. Lukas.

There is only one person he can turn to. Henry Bark. Or Henry Salo, as he is now called.

The voice. *My big brother.* The way he has always found it hard to distinguish between *s* and *f* since his front teeth . . . *Burn in hell, you old bastard.*

"I've got something you want," says a voice.

"Who is this? Hello?"

"Joar," the voice finally says. "Suggest a place."

"What is it you've got that I want?" asks Salo.

"You'll have to wait and see. Suggest a place," repeats the voice.

Salo puts down his phone. It could very well be a trap. He weighs the advantages and disadvantages. Life going on without Joar, or an opportunity to become whole again.

"How do I know you're Joar?"

"You've got a birthmark between your shoulders."

Anybody could know that. Henry Salo is not ashamed of his body.

"Our horse was called Pontus and the puppy the old man ran over with the tractor was called Finn."

"There's a cabin between Vaikijaur and Kvikkjokk," says Salo. "I'll send the coordinates."

"I'm leaving now."

"I'll see you there."

"Come alone, or you'll be sorry. My brother or not."

Ever since the Cleaner came to the cabin, he has known that there will be an end. The same way he came to an end in Afghanistan. In Syria. *In Mali.*

The boy has been loaded. The cabin is in flames. The remains: bones, craniums, DNA. Who knows?

A cleaner comes and goes. Keeps a community clean for a while and moves on to dirtier places.

The boy is tucked into a wooden crate. Others might call it a coffin. The Cleaner pulls the crate along by hand, covering the miles to the quad bike. The vehicle is snowed in. A car would have been preferable, even a snowmobile, but at least he has a trailer and snow chains for the wheels. He had planned to sit on the reindeer skin but he spreads it over the boy and then puts on the lid. He couples the trailer to the bike, straps on the crate and drives out onto the road.

After ten miles or so, he stops in a lay-by to check on the boy. He loosens the straps and opens the lid a little way. The boy is asleep, because surely it is only sleep? His face is still. *Hello. Wake up. I mean you no harm. I was only following orders.* He shifts slightly. Opens his eyes and closes them again. Snowflakes melt on his face. The Cleaner dries his cheeks, closes the lid and drives on. Halfway he stops again to fill up with petrol from a jerrican.

Evening is turning to night. Fires are burning low. People sit huddled up to one another. Through the binoculars he can see them individually. There are allegedly rebels among them. Women, children and old people are all he can see. But no men.

There must be some mistake? Operation to be carried out as planned.

A single drum beats out the rhythm. The notes of a kora keep them on course for the village. Automatic fire is impersonal. It spreads. Nobody knows who is shooting whom. Soon afterward they withdraw. Sleep for a few hours. Come back the morning after. He pokes a body with his rifle butt. The woman falls to one side. Beneath her, a pair of eyes open. The young gaze of a girl. Her eyes are not afraid. Shoot me, they say. Shoot me now.

"Stay dead," says Joar. "Stay dead."

73

Henry Salo's life is in chaos. So is the weather. SMHI, the Swedish weather service, has issued a storm warning. There is a risk that blizzards on the road to Kvikkjokk will make it impassable. He drives as fast as he can. There are snowdrifts across the road by the time he reaches Jokkmokk, but he has no choice. At least he's not driving an electric car. Still over sixty miles to go. Half a tank of fuel. For the third time he tries getting through to Pernilla.

The subscriber is not able to take your call at present, but you can . . . He throws the phone onto the passenger seat and switches on the radio.

"The British mining company Mimer has got the go-ahead for its plans to set up an opencast mine just south of the disused Gasskas mine.

"The decision has come in spite of vocal opposition from a wide range of protesters, including local residents and the environmental movement. UNESCO has also made its views known, claiming that the mine violates the rights of the indigenous Sami people. The decision is unprecedented in that the County Administrative Board had turned down the Mimer application.

"The government and the Mining Inspectorate of Sweden have chosen to override the earlier decision. Sven-Åke Nordlund, as Minister of Industry, how do you justify that?

"'Both Sweden and the world need new, safe mines if we are to be able, going forward, to guarantee access to rare earth metals, which are needed among other things for the production of batteries for electric cars. The switch to green industrial practices is one of the most important developments in our society today. Mimer Mining has agreed to terms and conditions that are unique and guarantee that reindeer herding will not be impacted.'

"Immediately after the announcement, climate activist Greta Thunberg tweeted that the government decision brings shame on Sweden and amounts to a racially motivated assault . . ."

And there he switches off.

Bloody Lapps and eco-nazis. At every fucking turn. Why can't they understand that all he wants is what's best for the municipality?

The phone rings again. The same number. The voice. *Little brother.* Deep. Dark.

"I'm turning at Vaikijaur now." The storm whines down the line. "How much further is it?"

"Twenty-five miles to Björknäs and then you turn right toward Nautijaur—" The line goes dead.

Joar was nine when they were separated. Now he's thirty-nine. The question is, what has happened in the meantime?

Henry forces himself to think about the present and Branco surfaces again. The deadline has expired. Märta was just the start, then Lukas, and now? Presumably Pernilla and him last of all. He calls her. Wants to hear her voice even though she hates him now. If worse comes to worst, it could be the last time. The thought won't go away. Thirty years without contact with Joar. He could be anyone at all by now.

"You created this mess, and now it's up to you to sort it out. I can't stay here any longer," she says.

"Where are you going?" he says.

"I'm going with Olofsson to . . ." Without even hearing where they're going, he has already anticipated it all. Details, words, greetings, hints. How the hell could he have been so blind?

"You and Olofsson?" he says.

"Damn you," says Pernilla, and gives a sob. "All I want is to get Lukas back."

Christ, not more tears. He can't cope.

"He's a bit old for you, isn't he?"

"Bloody idiot," she says, and hangs up.

For the last five miles the car can only crawl along through the drifts. He keeps switching the headlights between high and low beams. The windscreen wipers are struggling with wet, sticky snow. Every so often he has to stop and knock off the clumps. He can forget the little stub of road up to the house. The vehicle tracks are already snowed over. For the last few steps he is forging his way through drifts three feet high. A faint light is shining from the window of the cabin.

74

Somewhere, in the middle of nowhere, in a virtually roadless landscape of forest, lakes, streams and mountains, a man is sitting in a wheelchair feeling pleased with himself. He has fit a lot into his day. Taught the doll a few new subtleties. Had tea with Märta Hirak. He checks his watch again. He does it significantly more often than timekeeping requires. Maybe that is what happens when you have arms but no legs. Or is it because of the special provenance of the watch? He's not even right-handed, but putting a watch on his right wrist feels wrong. Paul Newman would never have done that.

The others will join him soon. He stays where he is, enjoying the quiet. Opens a couple of bottles of champagne, straightens the plates of canapés and prepares his speech.

This evening they're having a party in the Eagle's Nest. Their twenty-fifth anniversary, in fact. He wishes they could celebrate other things, too, but that time will come, he is sure. Various irritants have already been gotten out of the way. Others will be dealt with in their turn.

They have dressed up. They nod at Marcus a little formally before taking their seats around the semicircular marble table, which today has a cloth on it, in honor of the occasion.

"We had a vision, even as children," says Branco, and pauses theatrically. "We wanted to earn money. And we wanted to see the world. Together we have been through fire and war. Some of you in a very literal sense. I still remember that magical night in Nicosia. The roof terrace, the food, the wine and the mild night air. That was where we defined who we wanted to be and how we were going to get there. We had reached a crossroads, a point at which it was time to draw a line under the past and look forward. The activities of the Branco Group companies have proved highly successful since then. A solid combination of property, mines, security and entertainment. Yet we have never been content, always striving to move forward. You wondered why we should be coming north when the rest of our operations were spread across the globe and I replied, 'We are going back to our roots.'"

Varg, Järv, Björn, Ulf and Lo. Other than Lo, they have known each other since they were ten years old. Done business ever since they could work out percentages. Saved, invested, developed. They are different from one another and yet alike. Varg is a warrior with his heart and soul. Järv is quiet and possibly the smartest of them all. Björn is the technological wiz. Ulf is their firearms fetishist. And then Lo. His eyes rest on her. He has never met a more faithful woman. It is rather a shame that she will never serve a man. Except for him, of course. Or have children, for that matter.

"Cancer" is the first thing she says. In answer to the question about why she has chosen a different sort of life. A life with them. "My mother, her sister, my sister. So then I had everything removed. Twenty-four and useless as a woman, at least in a reproductive sense. But that's not how I see it. There's no biological clock ticking in me. My life isn't ruled by hormones. I have a freedom that other women don't."

In actual fact Lo is not the only one of them who cannot reproduce. In a collective act of solidarity, they have all been sterilized. Children and family simply don't fit in with their lifestyle.

"As usual, I thought I would start the evening with a lecture," says Marcus. "A lecture on the future, you might say."

Varg clears his throat. "Sorry," he says, "but would it be alright to take one of these sandwiches? I'm starving."

If Marcus Branco had known Varg less well, he would have been furious. Varg may not be the sharpest tool in the shed, but he wins the prize for perseverance. Oh, and loyalty, too, of course. He also has a side that the others lack. He is empathetic. For that reason, he is the only one of the Knights in whom Branco confides on a completely different little subject. The destruction of the earth.

Like all great men, Branco feels a need to give his ideas concrete form in writing. But without readers, without an audience. They sometimes get together, just the two of them. Marcus reads aloud and Varg, with his slow-witted brain, questions every last particle until the message is as clear as glass. Once he has understood, there is no going back. He is on Marcus's side. Even though he calls him both Hitler and an activist for the Green Party.

"Basically, the Green Party and Greta Thunberg are right," says Branco. "The human race is well on its way to destroying the earth, which is the very prerequisite for life. If the earth is to avoid destruction, there's no way around it. Climate threat isn't an invention of scientists and attention-seeking girls; it's reality. Human beings and the human need for warmth, food, transport and life's comforts are the biggest threats to this earth and, paradoxically, even to the human race. This may sound brutal," he says, "but for the earth to survive, a large proportion of the human race has to die. Transposed into soft politician's prose, it sounds more or less like this." He brings forward his beloved flip chart and pointer.

1. The fertile generations now living are the last ones. Human beings must stop reproducing until the earth regains its balance.

2. Companies that promote fossil-fuel emissions and exceed emission limits must be penalized financially and banned from conducting business.

3. The public must be prohibited from using any vehicle that contributes to fossil-fuel emissions above zero.

4. Only climate-neutral energy may be used.

5. If force is needed to make the world see the gravity of the situation, then force must be used.

"Are we going into politics?" says Järv with surprise in his voice. "I thought you hated politicians."

"And I do, but as you all know, there are fresh winds blowing today. People have grown tired of being nannied. I think there's an opening here."

There are more points on Marcus's list. The death penalty, for instance. But he is not planning to become a new Kim Jong-un. The focus is not on him personally. He is an anonymous figure and always has been. The fact that he has no legs has nothing to do with it. The lack of certain physical extremities has made him mentally stronger.

He is a born leader. Good leaders do not need admiration; they need obedience.

In Hitler's world, he would have been one of the first to the gas chambers. A freak without legs. A worthless cripple. An Untermensch.

"But listen, everybody, we're not just here to talk entertainment—we've got to eat and drink as well! So *skål* to the rest of our lives," says Branco, raising his glass. "It's going to be fantastic."

Ulf relieves Björn. Somebody has to hold the fort. From the monitors in the conference room they have sight only of their immediate surroundings. In case anyone pays them a visit, which has never happened.

From the control room, on a mezzanine floor just up from the entry level, you can switch between different camera views. The bunker, the interior of the house apart from Marcus's private suite, the reception room, the cells and the outside terrain, an area of a few thousand acres enclosed by a fence.

But instead of following procedure, Ulf takes a stroll down to the cells. He is bored with the Hirak whore. There's something unsavory about drug addicts. And she's starting to look more dead than alive. He doesn't know why Marcus insists on keeping her.

"She amuses me," he says. "And she hasn't cried once."

The doll, on the other hand, is as inviting as a mocha cream cake, an exotic forbidden fruit with the innocent expression and firm flesh of a child.

He likes to freeze the picture when she's lying on her lonely bunk, sobbing. She arouses tenderness in him, an urge to hold her for real. Stroke her smooth brown skin and whisper soothing words in her ear. He sometimes goes down just so he can talk to her. Changes her sheets so he can stay longer.

"Are you awake?" he whispers through the hatch in the door. No sign of movement. A bit louder this time: "Are you awake?"

Finally. She has been waiting.

She turns over and looks at him. "What do you want?"

"Can I come in?" he says, looking around to make sure that no one else has strayed into the darker reaches of the bunker. He taps in the code and opens the door.

"Are you cold?" He sits down beside her.

Easy now, you'll only get one chance.

"You've always been nice to me," she says, "not like the others."

"There's not much wrong with them," he says, "they're just doing their job."

"That woman's the worst," says Sophia.

"She's a tough customer," says Ulf.

"But not you," she says, leaning toward him.

The first days she is too scared to think. The legless monster—she doesn't know what else to call him—enjoys her being at a disadvantage, but only up to a point. He wants fire and passion. She goes along with it. Obeys his slightest gesture. Gives him pleasure. Puts her fingers in her throat as soon as he leaves.

You are the only one in your family who survived. A witness. In that lies your responsibility not to die.

Sooner or later the monster will tire of her, she knows this. When one of the others, the one now sitting on the bed, starts hanging about her cell, she sees an opportunity.

"What's your name?" she asks.

"My name means 'fang,'" he says. So she calls him Jaws. Jaws brings food. Sophia feigns Stockholm syndrome. Luckily he does not dare to go all the way. In the panting final stages of his arousal, he forgets to take the food tray.

Jaws moves closer to her. Puts his arm around her. Takes her hand and moves it to his crotch. She strokes him through the fabric, undoes his fly, asks him to pull down his trousers so she can reach properly, feels around under her mattress with her other hand, pulls his erection hard up against his stomach and he whimpers with pleasure. She gives a couple more tugs, and now his eyes are closed. In the last, intensive movement, just as he is about to come, she grips the fork and sticks it into his scrotum, yanks it out and stabs with it again and again. His neck, his eye and finally his heart, if he had one. But it is not enough. She presses the pillow over his face. Sees his legs twitch one last time. Takes the knife from the sheath at his belt.

Observes that the blade is sharp before she steals out through the cell door, which he has left ajar for practical reasons, so he can make a rapid exit.

The idea that she might try to run away from his amorous advances has not even occurred to him.

75

The off-road vehicle parked beside the cabin is a Can-Am, with a trailer. Henry can see faint footprints and the marks left by something being dragged up the steps.

He is not one for firearms. Although hunting fills his autumn weekends, he barely knows the make of his shotgun and has certainly never felt inclined to get himself a handgun. He regrets that now.

Life is full of paradoxes. Wanting to die one minute and to live the next, for instance. More than anything he wants to have control over his own demise. Not to disappear like some dopehead kid in Brancoland, or for that matter at his own holiday cabin.

The warmth indoors washes over him. The fire crackles, the soft light of the paraffin lamps lights up the kitchen table and at that table sits a man who looks more or less like himself. Except that his hair is not slicked back like Prince Daniel.

The Cleaner stands up. Twists his hands as though he doesn't quite know what to do with them and Henry is reassured. He undoes his parka, tosses his cap onto the hat rack, takes the kitchen floor in five strides and throws his arms around his brother.

Run, Joar, run.

I'm not running anymore. We've got to kill him.

Their father's car pulls up in front of the house. They are waiting in the garage. Joar raises the hammer. Lets out a battle cry and . . . trips on his own shoelace.

How long? He doesn't know. In the end it is Joar who struggles out of Henry's arms. He sits down and Henry takes the chair opposite.

"Tell me," says Henry, and Joar tells him.

"Tell me," says Joar, and Henry tells him.

Two brothers. Two lives.

"You said on the phone that you've got something I want," says Henry.

"That depends," says Joar, and nods toward the bedroom.

He has removed the lid. Folded back the reindeer skin. The boy no longer responds when he strokes the hair back from his forehead.

"Oh my God. Lukas! How the hell? Was it you all the time? You must have known where he was."

"Not to begin with. I'm just a cleaner," says Joar.

"Weird sort of cleaning company you must work for," says Henry.

"He's alive," says Joar, "but he may not be for much longer. The eagles saw him as prey."

"Eagles?" says Henry. "What the hell have you done?"

"Not me, the sea eagles. You can take the boy with you, but on one condition. Björkberget. Whatever Branco demands, it's a no. Do you get it? He's not having our mountain. Mum has the right to do what she wants."

"So you don't know . . ." says Henry.

"Know what?"

"She's dead. And she's left The Holt to you."

Memories flash through the room. Thirty years is a long time. Or sometimes nothing at all.

"Branco will make sure he gets his way," says Henry. "Lukas is just the start. You inherit the place, but if you don't agree to their plans, you'll be on their list, too."

I have my own list.

Lukas shifts, gives a whimper and opens his eyes. Stretches out a hand to Joar and asks for water. Fresh snow melts in a wooden scoop. The boy drinks and goes back to sleep.

Pernilla would never forgive him.

"We can talk about that later," says Henry. "I need to get him to the hospital."

And what the hell do I say there? That I found him in a coffin?

Joar takes him by the arm. "There's one more thing. You never saw me. When I leave here, it's the last time we see each other."

"Then you'll have to take care of Branco," says Henry. "It's the least you can do."

Joar looks at him with the same sorrowful, boyish eyes as he did then.

"Branco is just a name. I work for him. I don't know him."

One brother drives toward the unknown. Another to the hospital at

Sunderbyn. A coffin burns in the Tulikivi stove. A boy is delirious with fever. His mother weeps in someone else's arms.

Henry, aren't you ever afraid?

No, it doesn't help.

Next time we'll kill him.

Yes, we will. Now go to sleep.

76

Although afternoon is drawing toward evening, Lisbeth decides to take the car and scope out the northeastern part of Gasskas municipality.

"I want to come, too," says Svala. "It's my mum who's missing."

"You've got a test tomorrow. And don't forget to put your gym clothes in."

She smiles at her own comment. It can be entertaining to play the parent. And like any other sporty mum with a curling practice to get to, she leaves a hundred-krona note for takeout.

She tunes in to the local radio station and smiles again. No, not smiles, laughs out loud.

"A man in his thirties was found dead yesterday at the Treehotel in Harads. According to Hans Faste, head of Serious Crime, the death is being treated as an accident. The man is believed to have fallen from a height of ten meters and died of the injuries he sustained."

She finds it rather less funny when Svala's text arrives.

<Your girlfriend rang. Asked lots of questions about Pap Peder.>

And soon afterward the same so-called girlfriend rings Lisbeth as well. It has been a while since they last spoke. Lisbeth has grown tired of asking because she always gets the same answer. *Sorry, I'm working.*

"I just spoke to Svala. Assume you've heard that Peder Sandberg is dead?"

"Bless his filthy soul," says Lisbeth.

"And you don't know anything, either, of course?"

"Only that he took a pasting from a redheaded woman with Barbie legs."

"Lay off," says Jessica. The evening with the Svavelsjö gang is still hanging uncomfortably in the air. Not because Sandberg got himself a thrashing, but rather because of the memories he took such pleasure in stirring back to life. The rape, the shame afterward, the pregnancy, the abortion. The distress of a fifteen-year-old forced to cope on her own.

Your mum's spreading her legs at Svartluten. She wanted to kick him to death. Kick the leer that has haunted her all through her life. The words that cannot be forgotten, as certain words never can.

"Is Svala involved?" she asks. "According to the hotel, a teenage girl checked in to the same accommodation and paid cash."

"Svala was at hockey. I picked her up at the rink afterward. And anyway, don't you think Sandberg has enough enemies among his own kind?"

"Absolutely, but we found something in his inside pocket. A diary that Märta Hirak seems to have kept."

Clever kid. Soon I won't have anything left to teach you.

"It's a real shame that other people are taking a fall because of this. Just like him, you might say."

"Isn't it? What are you up to yourself? Do you fancy meeting up?"

Lisbeth has opened the map from the library on her lap and is studying the snus-brown fingerprint, which appears to be in the middle of a bog. It's a gamble, but she has to start somewhere.

"Sorry," she says. "I'm working. But we can speak later."

The sense of solitude is spread before her like a wasteland. Forest interspersed with bogland and lakes, but no settlement and barely any roads. She doesn't know what she is looking for or where to start. Some old fellow's childhood memory is all she has to go on.

The Fortifications Agency ought to know. If they sold the property sometime in the 1950s, it must be in their records. I'll follow up on it and get back to you.

Mikael Blomkvist. She has heard nothing from him yet.

Who's that cop Blomkvist's messing around with?

You mean Birna? Blonde, cheerful, attractive?

In other words, everything Lisbeth is not.

She pulls into a lay-by and checks the map again. The old man could have entirely misremembered.

While he waits for Birna—Lisbeth is not barking up completely the wrong tree—Mikael Blomkvist finds a seat in a corner of Pizzeria Buongiorno and has a beer. When Birna texts to say she's running half an hour late, he once again brings up the coordinates IB sent him. They take him to Henry Salo and Pernilla's house. A few months before they moved there. He rings Lisbeth's number.

"Hello there. What are you up to?"

It's amazing how everybody has to know what she's doing.

"I'm doing some recon, that's all. It's getting dark."

"That map the old guy got you interested in. Can you take a photo of it?"

"I guess so, but why?"

"I'll let you know later, but just send it, OK?"

"What are you doing yourself?" she asks, but he says he has to go.

"We'll keep in touch. Don't forget to send it."

A few seconds later it arrives, a map with fold lines and a snus stain in the middle of nowhere.

Mikael zooms in on the area on Google Maps. He goes over it click by click and starts to think he could be right. He rings Lisbeth, who dismisses the call. Rings her again, but then Birna comes in.

Newly washed golden curls bounce on her shoulders.

Her smile has all the bubble of a hot spring. Damn attractive.

And yet he can't help thinking of Lisbeth. The opposite. The most elemental person he has ever met. If Birna is a spring, then Lisbeth is a volcano. As hot as lava. As hard as Archean rock.

"Excuse me," he says, "I've just got to make a quick call."

77

Sophia Konaré tries to get her bearings. She stops outside the other woman's cell but realizes she will never be able to get the door open from the outside. They have met but never spoken to each other. Sophia on her way to the monster. The other woman on her way from him.

The light, daylight. The monster's bedroom has some kind of window. But to get there, she has to cross all those other spaces. Offices or whatever they are. People moving about, making calls, sitting at computers and appearing to do jobs like anybody else.

The cells are somewhere out of the way, she knows that. They tend to come for her toward evening. Sometimes she stays all night. Lying awake beside the monster's sleeping body. Her disgust isn't caused by the fact that he has no legs. Mali is full of maimed people. It is more the knowing what goes on in his sick mind. He is the scientist. She is the guinea pig.

Once his lust has found its outlet and is temporarily satisfied, he likes to talk. To orate. To roll over onto her arm and let his words fill the darkness with an even greater darkness. A lot about time, the time that is almost nigh, and the world's need to unite under a common leader.

"You see, doll," he says, "we all grow up thinking we are little cogs in a huge machine. That we all have some kind of significance, regardless of who we are and how we look. But that isn't right. With medicines, technology, medical skill, gene manipulation and so on, we take away nature's process of natural selection. Earth only has room for a limited number of individuals. The question is, which of us get to live, and which of us don't?"

Perhaps that is precisely what she has done. Helped the earth to eradicate a part of the human race that brings nothing to the table.

One of the cells has a dead man lying in it. As dead as she will be if he is discovered before she can get out. *My family,* as the monster calls the others. *That's right, isn't it, doll? You have to agree that family is the most important thing.*

She stops. Hears voices in lively conversation with one another, like at a party. Step-by-step she makes her way toward the sound. Catches sight of them. Leans forward and counts. All of them except one. Only a pane of glass between them and her. She has to get past it. Without being seen, preferably. Further along the corridor, beyond the window, there are a set of stairs and a lift. If she is lucky, they lead up to freedom. If she is unlucky, back to hell.

Varg gets up and goes toward the glass doors. His turn to relieve Ulf. He glances at the outdoor camera view on the monitor. Notes that a herd of reindeer is disturbing the sensors again. They'll have to get the technology sorted out. The last two years, uneventful on the security front, have made them complacent. He will have to bring it up at the morning meeting. He presses down the door handle. Turns to cast a final affectionate glance at the others. The champagne bubbles are making him feel happy. It has never been them against the world. The opposite, more like.

Sophia backs into the darkest part of the corridor. She has missed the moment she needed. The alternative is to go down into the tunnels. The very thought makes her shiver. And then? Without shoes or outdoor wear? A skimpy, little-girl nightie with teddies on it is all she has to shield her from the winter cold. That's the way he likes to see her, the monster. Like an innocent piece of meat in a Bamse bear nightdress.

The second day they took her on a sightseeing tour in the underworld. She lost her bearings after the third corner, which was presumably what they intended. At every turn, more doors, stairs, huge rooms, ladders, tunnels.

Even if she can get down there it is highly unlikely she will find her way out. She has to take a chance. As the lift door closes, she dashes past the glass doors like a streak seen out of the corner of Lo's eye. She wrenches open the fire door and runs up the stone steps until she comes to two more doors.

Her instinct tells her right. But still she turns left. Down some steps, taking them two at a time, and suddenly there is only one armor-plated barrier between her and freedom. A fingerprint later she is out.

She runs. The last time she saw the ground outside it was bare. Now, the snow comes partway up her calves. The nightdress flutters around her thighs. She stumbles, gets up, tells herself to hurry, falls over again. Like a gnu that has become separated from the herd, she seeks the refuge of the forest.

Her brain tells her to lie down and sleep. She carries on running. The way she has always run. Fast, barefoot and with a clear goal in sight.

Lisbeth Salander is about to turn and drive back to Gasskas when she sees something glinting a few feet along a disused tractor track. She opens the window, gets her binoculars from the glove compartment, focuses on the lower part of the pine tree and moves the telescopic sight slowly up the trunk. A camera. A goddamned camera. Positioned so the risk of its discovery is minimal. If she had not been watching a squirrel dart through the branches, she would never have noticed it. If there is one, there are very likely more.

She tries to think strategically. If there are cameras only along the tractor track, she will not yet have been seen. But if there's one trained on the lay-by, too, then she has had it. She dares not take the chance. She engages gear and drives the mile to the next one.

Here there is no tractor track or path to orientate by. What is more, it is nearly dark. Only the moon and the snow brighten up the surroundings. Walk, or come back when it is light? She does the same as everyone else in Norrland: puts the car key on the front wheel, switches on her headlamp, jumps over the ditch, snips her way through a game-proof fence, or whatever it is, and plunges in among the trees.

A mile through forest. The snow is not deep. The cold has hardened the surface to a crust, but not so hard that it always holds. Sometimes her foot goes through.

Sweat runs down her back. According to the map, she will soon come to a bog. Hopefully a frozen one. Every so often she stops to listen.

Varg notes that Ulf is not at the control panel. Lazy fucker, sneaking to the bathroom in the middle of his watch. But anybody can get caught short. In eight seconds when the real-time pictures from the cells and other spaces are updated he will sound the alarm, which will automatically lock all the exits.

He zooms in on the picture from the doll's cell. The first time, everything looks normal. The second time, he sees the hand. He gets on the intercom between the conference room and the control room and sounds a general alarm, triggering the automatic locking system. Now it takes a fingerprint to get out. *Why the hell don't we have that as standard procedure?*

"The doll's missing. Suspected intruder. Ulf most likely dead. Arm yourselves and spread out. I'll take the outside."

They are under threat, but Varg can't help feeling the arousal. Life in the bunker is monotonous and quite dull. He is a soldier. A *universal soldier,* whose varied life at the epicenter of assorted hotbeds of war has now been reduced to office routine.

Not even Märta can avoid the commotion. Someone throws open her cell door, pulls off her blanket and leaves the cell as quickly as they have come. She is too weak to put the blanket back into place, but her thoughts are as clear as the water of the stream at Njakaure.

You devils. Now your time has come. Wasn't that what he said, the evil one? That the time would soon be right. Well, here's your Apocalypse. Now!

Sophia no longer knows which direction she is going in. Her strength is starting to fail her, the cold finds its way into her consciousness, making her steps slower and her thoughts truncated. Initially all she could hear was the crack of the trees in the cold and the rushing of the wind. There are other sounds now, growing ever clearer. Footsteps. And heavy breathing. A phone ringtone and then a voice. *Gnu move in herds. There is safety in numbers. A solitary animal soon becomes a target for predators.*

Varg follows her tracks. He is going to find her. Barefoot and without clothes. Not even a hunted animal can run indefinitely. Suddenly the tracks divide, or rather cross each other. She is not alone. He kneels down to see better. One track has shoes, the other is barefoot.

No hunt without a hunter. Lisbeth follows the tracks a little way. Moves behind a tree and waits.

Aunt Lisbeth, there's something I've got to tell you.

The girl sits down on her bed. The monkey is next to her.

You know when I broke into Salo's house?

Yes.

I lied. The car hadn't gone when I came out. F. chased me through the forest. Fired his gun at me. It was him or me.

Don't worry, the raven will take care of him.

Lisbeth Raven Salander.

She never does locate a body, but she finds the murder weapon, the branch with dried blood on it. She takes it with her to the car with the intention of dumping it somewhere. But then that bloody irritating M. rings and it gets left in the boot. There's a meaning to everything.

From her position she sees something start to move. Very probably a man. The figure moves forward. Stops, crouches, runs a hand over the tracks, gets up and moves forward again.

A bit further, a bit further—now! The blow to the back of his neck hurls him facedown into the snow. *To think that someone gave birth to you and maybe fed you from their breast once upon a time.*

She does not have time to react when the sideswipe comes. Though her blow must nearly have knocked him out, he manages to roll over and kick her legs from under her. Now Lisbeth is the one with her nose in the snow and he is back on his feet. The branch is out of reach.

"Up," he says, pointing his gun at her. She kneels, raises her arms to signal *Don't shoot.*

Is it a child, or perhaps a dwarf?

"Who are you?"

"I was out for a walk," she says.

"Oh, sure," he says, and gives a laugh. "And somewhere just over there the doll is on the ground and freezing to death because of you. Nice work!"

"Can I get up?" she says. Not the right time to be cocky. She needs to find a new opportunity. And double quick.

"Exactly what I was going to suggest. We're going to walk a bit further, you and me. You like walks, after all."

They walk, retracing his steps. She goes in front. A sudden lunge when he is least expecting it could resolve the situation. She has to get him closer to her. She slows down, the moon following them through the treetops.

"Shit!" Her foot goes sideways and she loses her balance.

"For Christ's sake," he spits, pulling her up by an arm.

A gentleman, thanks for that, Branco, you've drilled them well, those apes of yours.

She spins around and knocks the revolver out of his hand with a *shuto-uke*. He reacts exactly as she expects and tries to lock her arms.

Think about what you need, Lisbeth. Karate's good, but in close combat Krav Maga is outstanding.

With the speed of a ferret, she extracts herself from his grasp.

If you have the right hold, one arm around the front of the neck and the other in a fist at the back, you can cut off the oxygen supply.

Thanks for the tip, Jessica, but I'm not tall enough.

Instead she delivers a *migi-ashi-fumikomi* to his knee joint as her elbow jabs a *yoko-empi* into his temple.

The knee breaks with a nice little plop. Unless he has another gun in his underpants, he is essentially defunct, at least for now. She takes his revolver and runs back, following the trail of shoeless footsteps.

There is something compassionate about the snow. It makes her warm, like the forest tarn where they go bathing in summer. Someone who has always dreamed of the sea, swimming naked in a tarn. Fatma is there, and Amina, Mum, her little brother. And Dad? You forgot me that time. Have you come to rescue me?

Lisbeth hoists the girl onto her shoulder. *The doll. I'm going to make you all pay for the doll.* Carries her like an animal carcass through the forest. Their only chance. If there is *one* enemy, there will be more. *The car. Please don't let them have got to the car.* She has to set the girl down several times and get a fresh grip. The moon is shining on the roof of the car. She grapples with the game-proof fence to get them through. Let sleeping Brancos lie.

78

Henry Salo's thoughts are inscrutable but his first impulse is natural. He rings Pernilla. *The subscriber is not able to take . . .* Jealousy writhes in him like a twisted gut. *Olofsson, you lecherous old arsehole.*

Her son is lying on the back seat, still tucked up in the reindeer skin. Salo has no idea if he's driving around with a corpse, or where he's going. Gällivare is actually the nearest hospital. But when he emerges onto the E45, he finds that the snowplow has not cleared the northbound carriageway. It must have turned at Vaikijaur and gone back to Jokkmokk. Only the faint tracks of a quad bike are visible in that direction. He dares not chance it; he will have to go to Sunderbyn, south of Boden.

Or will he? The question is, what will happen when Branco finds out the boy has been set free. Who will he go for at that point? Märta, of course . . . He has already exchanged her life for Lukas's once. Is it time to trade again? Salo is not cynical, but practical. While Branco is still unaware that the boy has been found, the situation remains unchanged.

Everybody is looking for the boy. The hack, that creature he goes around with, the police, the media . . . Blomkvist is not open to bribery. But let the police do something useful for a change.

"Gasskas Police. Birna Guðmundurdottir."

"Henry Salo here."

"Henry. What's up?"

As arranged, they meet at the hospital. The boy is alive. The boy's mother still cannot be reached.

"Switching off your phone when your child is missing. Who does that?" says Salo.

"I'll contact her via Messenger. Right, then, tell me," says Birna, putting aside their coffee cups and getting out her notebook and pen. "How did you find him?"

"I got a phone call. From someone, but I don't know who it was. When I got up to the cabin, the boy was lying in the bed. There was even a fire going in the stove. But only Lukas was there. And the snow had blown over all the tracks."

"Why didn't you call the ambulance service and police right away?"

He is prepared. He has to give her something for her to understand the gravity of the situation.

"There's a threat hanging over my entire family. And if it gets out that the boy's been found, then Pernilla will very likely be the next target." *Which she deserves, actually.*

"Or you," says Birna. "In other words—you know who's behind Lukas's kidnap." She is making an effort to keep her voice calm. *He knows. He's known all along. Kept quiet to save his own skin. The total scumbag.*

With his elbows propped on his knees and his head hanging between his legs, he really is a pitiful sight. His admission that Märta Hirak is in the same hands has not improved matters.

"So Lukas was kidnapped because of the wind farm project? And Märta Hirak, too, but you didn't bother telling the police what you know."

"As you can probably imagine, they threatened other things if I went to the police. I thought I could sort it all out myself, with the landowners and the politicians."

"What's this about the landowners?"

"If only they'd agreed to the use of their land, none of this would have happened." *Afraid it would, Salo, dear boy. The wind farm is only the beginning. We will need a loyal assistant in the future, too.*

"Which makes you the main suspect for the murder of Marianne Lekatt."

"Me?" says Henry, now bolt upright in his chair. "No, that's insane. It was me who found her. She was my biological mother."

"Plenty to argue in favor, in other words. I'm sure you understand that you'll have to come with me to the police station. I've called for backup. While we're waiting, you can think about how you're going to explain the payment of six hundred thousand kronor into your bank account."

But what happens next is that Pernilla arrives with Olofsson in tow. Salo clenches his fists. Pernilla does not even look at him. Olofsson gabbles some kind of apology and follows Pernilla into the room where Lukas is lying.

"My wife," says Salo to Birna.

"You'd be hard put to find a better one. You should go in and talk to her."

Salo goes in and Olofsson leaves the room.

"How the hell did that happen?" he says. "Did you have to be with him, of all people?"

"You know nothing. Just be quiet," says Pernilla, fully focused on her son. His head of curls on the pillow. As safe and secure as an innocent child.

" 'Thank you, Henry, for finding Lukas,' " says Salo.

She turns. Gets to her feet. Comes toward him. Clears her throat and spits straight in his face. "Exchanged one life for another, was that what you said? As if you were some sort of fucking God."

Just then, the boy sits up in bed. "Hello, Mum. Where's Grandad?"

79

Lisbeth bundles the girl into the front seat and drives a few miles before daring to stop. She transfers her own boots to the girl and wraps her in a quilted jacket and a blanket. With the heating on full blast and a few mouthfuls of flat Coca-Cola, Sophia recovers enough to whisper. Her words are labored and Lisbeth tries hard not to hurry her, and what she describes is a very peculiar place.

"Wait a moment," says Lisbeth, and rings Mikael Blomkvist. No answer. She hesitates and calls Svala on the car's hands-free device. Nobody can hold their tongue like she can.

"Hi there. Have you got something to write on?"

"Where are you?"

"I'll tell you later."

The kidnapped girl's voice is faint and husky. "It's like a maze, with no windows," the girl says. "Apart from the monster's room, which has windows in the roof."

"What makes him a monster?"

"He's evil," she says. "And his body . . . is like some strange animal's. He has no legs, just feet that grow straight out of his trunk." She sobs and lets the tears flow for a while before she goes on. "But . . . between the feet . . ." Then she starts to cry again.

"He raped you," says Lisbeth and the girl nods.

Lisbeth has worked out who she is. She has read about her. The girl from the refugee center. Sophia Konaré. She ought to hold her. Comfort her. Say that she knows what it's like, that they have the experience in common, but time is not on her side. The girl needs medical attention and Lisbeth has things to do.

"Take it nice and easy," says Lisbeth. "Have some more Coke. When you're ready, I'd like to know more about the building. Under the ground, you said. A bunker?"

"With cells and corridors linking the different rooms, I think."

"How many people are there?"

"Including the monster, six—er, five."

"Who was the sixth?"

She seems reluctant to answer. Finally she says, "My salvation, my way out of there."

"Who are they, do you think?"

Stay dead, stay dead.

The girl's head keeps drifting to one side. Sleep. The same men as always. The ones who save with one hand and kill with the other.

"One more question," says Lisbeth. "You mentioned cells. Did you see anybody else in there?"

"A woman," says Sophia, scarcely audible. "White. Dark-haired. I don't know if she's still alive."

"Was her name Märta?" says Svala, almost shouting now. "You must know what her name was, at least?"

"I don't know," says the girl. "I don't know."

"See you soon," says Lisbeth and ends the call to Svala.

Around twelve miles later, she turns into Sunderbyn hospital. It's hard to rouse the girl. Unwillingly she sits up, mumbling something about the woman. "Sorry," she says, "sorry."

"It's not your fault," says Lisbeth. *You devils.* "We'll do our best to find her, but to make sure nothing goes wrong, it's important for us to stick to the same story. OK?" *We'll get you. One by one we'll get you.*

"OK," says the girl. She reluctantly takes off the jacket and boots. Gets out in the south parking lot and staggers off toward the main entrance.

80

"SMHI has issued a warning of continuing adverse weather conditions today in large areas of inland Lappland. The storm that reached the mountains yesterday is now moving east. Strong winds and heavy snowfall are expected and the public is advised to keep off the roads if at all possible.

"But before we end this morning's bulletin, we're going to listen again to the words of Hans Faste from the Gasskas Serious Crime Unit on the subject of the eighteen-year-old Malian girl who went missing from Fridhem Refugee Center in mid-October and has now been found:

"'The course of events was as follows: A motorist spotted the girl walking along the highway between Murjek and Kirtik. She was barefoot and had no outdoor clothes.

"'The police have conducted a series of searches since her disappearance, but everything so far points to the girl having left the center of her own free will. She claims to have spent the intervening time with a man of the same age from Gällivare. The police wish to contact the unknown motorist who found the girl and drove her to Sunderbyn hospital.'"

Lisbeth turns off the radio. Good. Now the police can start looking on the wrong side of the municipal boundary or not at all. Sooner or later they'll get some tasty scraps, but for now she can't risk the police barging in on Branco and sabotaging the possibility of getting Märta Hirak out alive. She texts Jessica Harnesk. <Keep watch on Sophia. I'll get back to you.>

The answer comes instantly: <This is a police matter. Where are you? Tell me what's happened!>

It is not only Lisbeth who listens to the Hans Faste piece on the radio. Marcus Branco hears it, too.

The Knights have gathered for a minute's silence. Luckily Varg is thick-skulled and will be fine. But with a broken knee, he is more of a problem than an asset.

Ulf, on the other hand, is being commemorated by the drinking of tea from Fujian province and an analysis of the events of the evening.

The CCTV images from outside show only one discrepancy, most likely caused by reindeer. They know the way the doll went through the forest, but not who her accomplice was.

"It could be sheer chance," says Järv, looking around at them. "Could she have got Ulf to involve someone from outside?"

"Ulf," says Branco, "why him?"

"He was besotted with her, in love."

"In love?" says Branco. "How embarrassing."

Sheer chance, Branco. You know what sheer chance can do. You weren't born in 1961 like most of the other thalidomide cases in Sweden. No, you were born in 1987 to a Brazilian mother suffering from some unspecified immunodeficiency.

As early as 1965, Brazil reintroduces what was known in Sweden as Neurosedyn under the name Thalidomide, for its anti-angiogenic and immunomodulatory properties. Your mother buys the tablets on the black market. Gets pregnant and gives birth to you. A child with no legs, unnaturally long arms and a sexual organ so disproportionately large that it compares favorably with that of a horse. Hardly surprising the doll calls you monster.

"Crisis protocols," says Branco. "You know the drill."

"What do we do with the whore?" asks Lo.

"Is she still alive?"

"Yes, but never mind her for now," says Järv. "You all need to see this first."

KIDNAPPED BOY FOUND

The boy who was taken by armed men from a wedding party at Raimo's Bar in Storforsen has been found alive at a cabin near Kvikkjokk.

There are unconfirmed reports that it was the boy's stepfather, municipal council head Henry Salo, who found him. The Gasskas Police have chosen to play down this development out of consideration for the family. *Gaskassen* has, however, been able to obtain an exclusive comment from Hans Faste, head of Serious Crime.

"An extensive search has been conducted, resulting in a positive breakthrough. I am not able to go into any detail; however, I highly commend the work of my excellent colleagues."

"You decided not to call in the National Operations Department but to use your own resources to solve the case. Is this proof that a small police unit can achieve great things?"

"Very much so," says Hans Faste. "It was our local knowledge in combination with our experience that made all the difference."

"Contact the Delivery Man," says Branco. "Make sure he finds the Cleaner." In a monotone he issues a series of orders. To do with Salo and Salo's wife. Then he glides to the lift and descends to the cells. Or the "hotel," as they call their accommodation among themselves. He taps in the code, wheels his chair in and closes the door behind him. He is not going to repeat Ulf's mistake.

The blanket has slipped off. He picks it up and slings it over the back of the wheelchair.

Is she alive? He gets out his reaching aid. A long stick with a grabber, not unlike a street cleaner's litter-picker. He grabs her arm and raises it.

"Oozy," he says. "The mouth sore seems to have spread. I think we'll have to consider you unviable soon," he says. "But let me tell you one thing, Märta. According to the selection criteria that I use to categorize the world when I give you my little lectures, you would have been in with a good chance of survival. You're poor, have no car, don't eat meat and so on. That is to say, you consume minimal amounts of the earth's resources. And by the way, Märta, thank you for being a good listener."

He spreads the blanket over her body. Pats her on the leg in one last farewell.

81

It all happened over a few weeks, one late autumn in Gasskas. It is like a fairy tale. A myth retold so many times that the improbable becomes the truth. Like hunting tales told around the campfire, or a fisherman's account of his catch.

Certain individuals play major roles: Henry Salo, Marcus Branco and Mikael Blomkvist, for example. Others—Sonny Nieminen, Jessica Harnesk and Peder Sandberg—fulfill functions without taking up a great deal of space. They are only human beings, but they all have their background stories, the things that make them exactly who they are.

Lisbeth Salander and Svala Hirak have had a life in common for thirteen years without being aware of each other's existence. They have each gradually moved along a predetermined path toward the point where the two intersect. The question is whether this is where it ends. Or whether the intersection is just the beginning.

In the beginning it was men who applied makeup. Warriors who camouflaged themselves or painted themselves with blood, earth and ashes to express their tribal allegiance.

In a hotel room at the top of City Hotel, commonly known as the City, a thirteen-year-old girl prepares herself for the final battle. She opens her laptop and googles "Lisbeth Salander + makeup + tutorial." Starts with her face. Covers it in white powder and then does her eyes. Applies the kohl to her eyelids. Draws bold lines of kohl beneath and above the eyes. To finish off, she paints her lips black. There is not much she can do about her hair, hopelessly straight and white-blond. Or about her complete lack of piercings. She ties a black scarf around her forehead and scrutinizes herself in the mirror. It is not her. It is Lisbeth. It is both of them.

Some floors below, Lisbeth sits at a bar table studying building plans.

And OK, this is in part thanks to Mikael Blomkvist. He identified the property that the Fortifications Agency sold to Anders Johansson in 1951. Five thousand acres of forest, mostly pine and spruce, but that was as far as he got. It was only when Lisbeth worked her way deeper into the secret spaces of the military that she found the bunker.

Things are urgent, but it takes planning to get inside what she assumes to be Branco's stronghold. If Sophia's information is correct, he has around him four sidekicks with military training who will not only be armed, but very likely in good physical shape. Minus one who presumably finds it hard to walk after his forest encounter.

It is a remarkable construction. Built in stages from 1910 onward, on a mountainside that slopes steeply at the front and is flat at the back. The perfect fortress for a discreet businessman and his shady activities, whatever they are. Hacker Republic still has not been able to find a back door into the company, but it is only a matter of time. She has to give the Branco Group credit for that. They are a textbook example of good cybersecurity. Or are they? The thought has been gnawing away inside her although she has done her best to dismiss it. Plague. Something isn't quite right. She can see it plainly now. Branco ought not to have been a problem. Not a permanent one, anyway. Everybody exists somewhere, as do companies and even the secret police, people with new identities and so on. Sooner or later they leave a trail. Plague, if anyone, should have found him.

For now she contents herself with sending a message.

Wasp to Plague: `<Is everything OK?>`

`<This might not be the time>` he writes back `<but we've found a minimal opening into Branco. Seems to have been involved in an environmental scandal centered on a mine in Patagonia some years ago.>`

She relaxes her shoulders and comes back to reality. According to the plans, there are two entrances. Probably also another, a more recent addition that leads to the more modern living quarters and is accessed by fingerprint recognition, according to Sophia.

She saves the maps as images on her phone, finishes her Coke and takes the lift up to the seventh floor.

For one second, no longer than that. *Camilla. Herself.* Then reality catches up and Svala is any old teenager who has gone bananas with the makeup. "No," she says, "you're not coming."

"Oh yes, I am. It's my job to bring Mammamärta home. And anyway, you need a driver."

"I thought we'd finished that discussion," says Lisbeth, sounding like any other authoritarian arsehole.

"There's been a foot of snow since yesterday. We're going to need a snowmobile."

"*I'm* going to need a snowmobile, you mean."

"So you're planning to join one of those tourist trips around Kåbda-lis, are you, all in a procession?"

"No, but according to the operating instructions, all you have to do is put your foot down."

"Oh, sorry, I forgot you were a Stockholmer. But good luck with the fresh snow," says Svala, taking off the sweater with leather elbow patches and heading for the bathroom.

"Wait," says Lisbeth. "What's that?"

"Dragons are cool, but Shotokan tigers are even cooler."

Lisbeth is forcefully reminded of why she never wanted to have children.

"What ink slinger lets a child get tattooed without their parents' permission?"

"None, I assume, but you wrote a very nice permission letter."

82

"Do you remember me?" says Lisbeth. "I was the one who bought the Ranger off you."

"How could I forget?"

"I know you don't want to sell your wife, but I need to borrow your snowmobile."

"No," says the man. "There's going to be even more fresh snow by the weekend."

All this bloody fuss about fresh snow.

"I realize it feels like a lot of trouble, but I'll pay well. Five thousand for twenty-four hours. OK?"

"Five thousand." He laughs. "That's a bit over-the-top, isn't it? Three will do. But twenty-four hours and no more."

"Not a minute longer, I promise, but you'll have to drive it there. The Ranger hasn't got a tow bar."

"Yes, it was my mother's," says the man gloomily.

Lisbeth casts around for something consoling to lighten the mood. "But it's a nice color, anyway."

"If you hadn't told me you worked in computers, I'd have guessed you were a psychologist," observes Svala, trying out the driver's seat. "It's cool that it's a Summit. I got bored with Pap Peder's old Bearcat. It's a snowmobile for fucking geriatrics."

"Don't swear," says Lisbeth. Finally a bit of payback.

The nearer they get to the meeting point, the more quietly they go. Mikael Blomkvist has sent various texts and so has Jessica Harnesk. The gist of them all is: *Don't do anything hasty. Let the police do their job.*

She wonders how much Harnesk knows. Could Sophia have said something? She'd be surprised. Blomkvist? Possibly. He has a habit of sticking his nose into other people's business, although she has to admit this has sometimes had its uses, historically speaking.

The last thing she does is to contact Plague. Just to be on the safe side.

<Send the info to Blomkvist> she writes. <Same address as before. Probably the same log-in details too.>

The Ranger-snowmobile man arrives and then drives off again.

They are parked about six miles from the bunker.

Inside the Eagle's Nest, a succession of crisis meetings is being held. For once Branco is not sure of his next move. Things are starting to go against them in a way they had not bargained for and he finds it hard to solve the equation. This is no longer about Salo and the wind farm, but an external threat to the whole Branco Group. They have detected advanced attempts to infiltrate their systems. Which luckily they've been able to ward off. And although nobody says it straight-out, he can sense that they think it's his fault. *The dolls. He should have done without the dolls. Particularly the last one.*

Which leads onto the next point: the doll's escape.

There is not a great deal to say about the escape beyond the unpredictability of the human factor and a desperate (and, in Marcus Branco's eyes, ungrateful) Sophia Konaré. But after that. Varg's wretched return, crawling like a beast.

He feels he's getting to the crux of the matter: the person in the forest. A diminutive karate monster "out for a walk." Who the hell is she? And not only that: who sent her?

"All information secured and deleted," Järv informs him from the control room. "And that leaves us with a more profane problem: the whore. Tell us we can dispose of her now."

83

"*Bassai dai*," Lisbeth says, looking at Svala.

"Breaching the fortress."

She has seen that look before. Not wanted to dwell on it. It is everything Lisbeth wants to forget. Zala, Niedermann, Camilla. The strangely pale blue, almost-white eyes. Always ready for violence, and Svala is no exception. The bold strokes of the kohl pencil heighten the cold but also the darkness in which Lisbeth suspects she lives. As they all do. Otherwise, they would never have ended up in this mess.

"You can never change the path of fate, only choose which side to walk on," says Svala.

Lisbeth puts down the sun visor and adjusts the mirror slightly. Sticks her hand in her inner pocket. Produces a bit of blood, earth and ash and paints on the soul of a warrior.

"You look like Noomi Rapace," says Svala.

"Who?"

"Doesn't matter," says Svala, and turns down the proffered can of Coca-Cola.

"Can I give you some advice?" says Lisbeth. "If you have to fight."

The girl nods.

"You only get one chance. I know I taught you that a karateka never strikes first. That is true. Karate is above all defensive. But in combat . . ." The girl's arms are as skinny as a half pound of spaghetti. She's a natural in her white bathrobe belt.

"Remember, your opponent is at their weakest at the moment they make their attack." *Sen no sen.* "You are a warrior, Svala. Not a soldier. A warrior. A *bushi*. But today you're a driver," she says. "You stay in the forest until I come back out. Got that?"

Svala rests her forehead against Lisbeth's. "You're good," she says. "Weird but good. And while we're sitting here, not knowing if we're going to survive, you could answer a few questions, right?"

"Sure," says Lisbeth.

"How did my grandfather die?"

"He was shot."

"By you?"

"No, by the police."

"And Camilla?"

"Suicide."

The last question hangs in the air.

"We need to get going," says Lisbeth.

"Did you kill him?" says Svala.

"In a way," says Lisbeth.

In a way.

84

When evening has once again fallen over Gasskas to protect those who hunt in darkness, they set off.

The plan is to go in from the northwest. The lashing snow reduces visibility, but that cuts both ways. The wind eats up the sound of the engine. They will be able to get relatively close without being heard.

Lisbeth suspects there is another approach road that is not on the map. The one Branco himself uses to go in and out of the property. They should avoid that one, unless Plague has managed to knock out the CCTV. She has asked. He hasn't replied.

The snowmobile weaves jerkily between the trees. As the kid said, it's no game for beginners. Svala stands up with one knee on the seat so she can see better. She shifts her body weight as a counterbalance when required, and with the skill of a seasoned driver she manages to keep the runners from cutting down into the snow. Mile by mile, Lisbeth's internally memorized map is not perfect but it is all they have. With what they judge to be a few hundred yards to go, Svala switches off the engine. Lisbeth checks her phone; no coverage except the emergency services number. They have to shout to hear each other above the storm.

"There are snowshoes in the saddlebag," shouts Svala. Lisbeth fastens the straps around her boots and slides down from the snowmobile.

Svala pulls off her mitt, puts her hand inside her jacket, takes out the gun she salvaged from the forest and hands it to Lisbeth.

"Do you know how to use it?" she says.

This kid never ceases to amaze her.

"Might be best for you to hang on to it yourself."

"No need. I've got my own. Pap Peder's. It's about time he did something useful."

Are you there, Mammamärta? I can't feel you anymore.

They look at each other. Thumbs-up. Step-by-step, Lisbeth disappears in among the trees in the direction of the bunker. Svala counts to a hundred, then turns the snowmobile and drives in a wide circle to approach the place from the opposite side.

Sorry, Aunt Lisbeth, but this is my Mammamärta we're talking about. I'm not going to sit here waiting like an innocent child.

And you didn't expect me to, either.

The first barrier to overcome is the getting in. By studying the Fortifications Agency's pictures of better-known military buildings around the so-called "Lock of the North," Boden Fortress, she concludes that a strong pair of bolt cutters should do the trick, even if dynamite would have been preferable.

According to the plans, the main building is almost half a mile beyond the entrance Lisbeth is aiming for. Around the highest terrain, the gusting wind has peeled the snow from the granite. She takes off the snowshoes, straps them to her backpack and moves toward her target.

It is virtually impossible to spot that there is a way down to a bunker here. The door is more like a hatch. Fortunately, all that secures it is a heavy-duty padlock. She tests it first with one of the tools from her Leatherman, but the padlock has a code and does not respond to mechanical manipulation. Not against the clock, anyway. The cutters have to work hard but finally they get through the metal.

I would have fixed it for you. You know I'm good at numbers.

Stay away.

What is there in a bunker built more than a hundred years ago? Waterlogged chambers? The remains of a telegraph station, bunk beds, medical supplies? Corridors that have fallen in? She has found no information to indicate what its function was. Like many other military defense installations, it is unofficial. Barely in the authority's own archives. It has only one name: H9.

She angles her headlamp downward and tries to visualize what lies ahead. She plants her feet inside, closes the hatch behind her and feels an instant anxiety. The sounds from outside, the whining storm, the cracking of branches, everything suddenly stops. No sounds find their way in here and none will find their way out, either.

Stay calm. Breathe. Stay calm. She illuminates the walls, as far as the light from her flashlight will reach. The room is empty except for a rusty shovel with a broken handle and an ancient boiler in one corner. She tracks the pipes along the ceiling. Water has left a tidemark a good way up the walls. She pulls off her glove. Fresh moisture on her fingers. The pungent smell of mold catches in her throat.

Pass through a corridor. Risk of blocked fire door.

The light in front of her, the darkness behind her. Step-by-step. She stops. Listens. Opens the door to the corridor and continues on.

On one side, a brick wall has collapsed. More chunks of brick give way when she staggers slightly and puts out a hand to steady herself. The impulse to turn around, to run back, crawl back up to the world and get away from here is almost overwhelming. *Do it, Lisbeth, you don't need to be a superhero. Go back, leave it to the police.* The voice is enticing. But it is precisely what makes her get a grip. She's not letting any damn therapist set the agenda. She's here because it's urgent. Märta Hirak could already be dead, but if she isn't . . . if she isn't, then Lisbeth's her only chance.

Three rock chambers in a row. Estimated size: 300 by 600 feet. Status unknown.

The fire door is stiff but it gives. Now she's in the middle chamber. Her headlamp flickers, goes out and comes back to life again. The temperature must be about forty degrees. Like in a mine or an earth cellar. For a while, curiosity wins out over fear. Here, too, the damp comes through the natural rock surface of the walls, blasted out of the ancient primary rock. The chamber is as big as an aircraft hangar. Step-by-step. When she is almost at the other side, she stops and listens again. The darkness has its own sound of heartbeats and breathing.

Complicated middle section on different levels, steps and rooms linked by various corridors. Select one side and stick to it.

She runs her fingers around the edges of the doorway. Presses her body against what should open to give her access. Damn, the door is walled up. Now she will have to go back, find her way to one of the flanking rock chambers and look for another door. Her headlamp flickers again. Without light she is in serious trouble.

She turns it off to save the battery. Panic is threatening to take over again when she hears the voices. They seem to be coming from above.

Via a ventilation system or through a loudspeaker. Not that she can hear what they're saying, but voices, all the bloody same. She must be close.

Eeny, meeny, miny, moe. The hangar on the right or the left. Left. In the middle there is a door. People lived here. Soldiers. Officers. Weeks and months without daylight, like the others who built it. Year in, year out, in dust, damp, rockfalls and hell.

You're privileged, Lisbeth. Just keep going.

The next door opens as easily as if it has just been oiled. Almost too easily. Light is filtering down. Spreading clarity over the chaos of options. And what then? The priority is to find Märta Hirak. Slowly, soundlessly, she is moving toward the voices and the light, when all at once the light goes off and the voices stop.

She switches on her headlamp. Dead. Takes it off and tries to shake some light into it. Still dead. Rather than use the flashlight on her phone, she tries to remember what the set of steps looked like. That, too, seems to have collapsed at one point. What is she to think, already ten steps up? She feels her way forward. Catches her hand on a nail. This won't work. She gets out her phone. Of her five contacts, three have texted her. At some point she must have had a signal, but there definitely isn't one now. There is no phone tower that can reach the grave. She sweeps the light from her phone over the steps, decides on a strategy and picks her way to the top step.

On the other side of the door, small rooms of varying sizes. According to Sophia, linked to the living quarters by a lift.

If there is anyone standing on the other side, she has had it. She opens the door a little way. Nobody.

Another second's light from her phone gives her just enough time to make out that she is in the cells. *The hotel.* Modern doors with peepholes. The cells themselves are flooded with white light. First one. Empty. Next one. Also empty. In the third, a man's body is doubled up with a pillow over its head. *Your salvation, Sophia.* In the fourth and last cell there is a woman lying under a blanket. Märta Hirak. Lisbeth cannot tell if she is asleep or . . . She stops. Hears the voices again. More distinctly now. *Report. Destruct. Code name: Tingvalla.* And then some words that she understands at a deeper level. *Packet sniffing. SQL. Zero-click exploit. Spoofing. Buffer overflow.*

She walks toward the voices. If they are going to get her anyway, at least she'll have heard what they're saying.

"Everything's ready. Departure at twenty-one hundred."

"Shit, look what the cat's brought in. A mouse?"

"Looks more like Halloween. Trick or treat?"

"Ow, let me go!"

Svala.

Without hesitation Lisbeth pulls the gun from her jacket, opens the door a crack to get her bearings, and when eyes turn toward her she kicks it wide open and aims in their direction.

Two people. A woman and a man. She has not set eyes on them before.

"Let go of the girl!" she says, and Svala backs toward Lisbeth. "Keep going," she hisses to Svala, "out the door."

The woman remains passive. Her companion walks slowly toward Lisbeth.

"Suit yourself," she says, and fires a shot that narrowly misses the man. "Next one will be a bull's-eye."

"OK, OK," he says, and raises his hands.

"Get out of the room," says Lisbeth. "I'm going to count to three. One, two—"

Suddenly all hell breaks loose. A third figure appears out of nowhere. Initially she thinks it's Branco because he's in a wheelchair. At the Hawking chair's top speed he advances toward her, shooting wildly but not hitting much.

Keep cool and concentrate. Hold your breath, take aim, fire.

He screams as the bullet hits his shoulder. He loses control of the wheelchair, crashes into the wall but regains control and makes off toward the lift. Only the woman is left. *Unarmed. What a pity for you, bitch.*

Lisbeth backs off until she reaches the door she came in by.

"Don't try to come after us," she says.

"No danger of that. You're going to die like rats down there," says the woman before she turns and follows the man. That is when Lisbeth registers the smell of burning. The moment she closes the door to the cell corridor, the conference room explodes. The smoke is already finding its way under the door. They need to get out of the bunker right now. The first cell is open. Svala has her mother in her arms. She is stroking her hair.

"Is she alive?" Lisbeth asks.

Svala nods.

"We'll have to leave her, or we're all going to die."

"I'm not leaving her here," says Svala, and starts coughing.

The smoke thickens. Lisbeth lifts Märta off the bed. At that moment, the power goes off.

"Use the light on your phone," shouts Lisbeth, and rolls Märta Hirak in the blanket.

"It's got no charge," Svala shouts back.

For the second time in twenty-four hours, Lisbeth hoists a woman onto her shoulder to save her from Marcus Branco. To save her, Svala and herself.

"Keep hold of my jacket." Lisbeth's instructions are short and clear. "Get my phone out of the backpack and use the flashlight on that."

The light barely penetrates the smoke. They make their way to the next door. Märta Hirak's head hits the frame. The smoke comes with them like a tail.

"There's a fall of rubble in the middle of the steps. Keep to the left." Or was it the right? But then . . . then it was the right, surely? She has remembered correctly. A few more feet and they're able to close the fire door behind them. Another explosion goes off above. They have to get out.

"Take Märta," says Lisbeth. The girl cradles her mother, whispers something, hauls her onto her shoulder, focuses on the point she is aiming for and sets off across the chamber. Half-pound-spaghetti arms and on reindeer-calf legs. Six hundred feet with barely any light to guide them. *Secrets of the elite forces, get out and hide.*

At the door in the middle, before they tackle the corridor with the collapsed wall, they swap over again. Märta is a dead weight. Is she even breathing?

"Not far now." The girl is panting heavily. She stumbles just as Lisbeth did, saves herself with her hand and sets off another fall. First just a few bricks, then more and more. Instinctively Lisbeth pushes the girl ahead of her and then heaves the three of them over the rubble to the other side. A few seconds later the entire wall collapses like a house of cards.

"That was close," says Svala, shining light on the death they have just cheated.

At the way out, the one she entered by, Lisbeth sets Märta down. Shakes life back into her own arms and puts her shoulder to the hatch. Nothing happens. She braces herself and heaves with all her might. Not a millimeter.

The smell of smoke is in their clothes. Maybe it is on its way toward them. She can't tell. Someone has locked the hatch from outside. Someone is laughing out there, *the woman,* she has put her lips to the lock and shouts so loudly that they cannot help but hear.

"Burn, you goddamned rats, you'll soon be burning in hell."

"Not without you," Svala shouts back. "We're going to find you. Wherever you are we're going to find you. Don't forget that, you . . . devils," she adds quietly.

Lisbeth sinks to the rock floor. Leans against the damp, moldy wall and tries to think. They could try to shoot their way out. Completely pointless, she assumes. The bolt is made of iron. The risk of rebound is greater than the chance of success.

She turns to Svala. "How the hell did you get in? I get the cell, it has a coded lock, but the outer door? Sophia said it had a fingerprint scanner."

Svala coughs and coughs and coughs again.

Lisbeth slaps her on the back.

"It doesn't help," she wheezes. "I've got asthma. Left my inhaler at the hotel." Her breathing is coming in deep gasps. She takes off her backpack and rummages among her things. Only two have ever truly been hers: the laptop and the monkey.

"Open the monkey," she says to Lisbeth, and puts an arm around her mother.

Lisbeth unfolds a knife and releases the contents onto her lap. The last thing to roll out is a grenade.

"Seriously, Svala, where did you find this?"

"I got it from Mammamärta a long time ago." She looks at her mother.

Tucks the blanket around her shoulder. "And I still want to know how my father died."

"OK," says Lisbeth, her voice hardening. "Your father, my half brother, was a real arsehole. He'd do anything your grandfather told him to. Threaten people, extort money, commit murder. Like you, he could feel no pain, but when he stole money from the Svavelsjö gang, he went too far. He was after me at the same time. That was another of Zalachenko's commissions. Can you see, Svala, how sick it was for my own father to give my brother the job of killing me? So I set a trap. He walked into it, but it could easily have been me. To make it all stop, I rang Sonny Nieminen. It was his crew who killed your dad, not me."

"You could have said that from the beginning."

"What's this, then?" says Lisbeth, holding up a cigarette packet. "Not a great idea to smoke with asthma."

Lisbeth shakes the packet. But instead of cigarettes, what falls out is a finger. Lisbeth recoils in disgust. The skin is gray, almost white. Except at the severed end, where the bone is sticking out.

"Ulf's finger. That was how I got in," says Svala. "I got it from Sophia. Maybe this is news to you, but we know each other. She's a reader, like me. I took the bus to Sunderbyn. Who can resist an innocent thirteen-year-old? Not even your policewoman."

Now it could well be time to call her.

Lisbeth puts back everything except the grenade and the finger.

"Do you know how a grenade works?" she asks.

Svala shakes her head. "We'd better google," she says, and reads out loud. "Hand grenade, military abbreviation HGR, is a grenade launched at its target by a manual throw. Hand grenades are made to different specifications for a variety of uses but are classically designed with explosive capacity for offensive use within a small radius. Other types of grenades have concealing capacity (smoke effect) for momentary or continuous smoke cover."

"We've had quite enough smoke already."

"With a conventional egg-shaped grenade, the user grips it in one hand and holds firm the cotter pin, which secures the safety lever. The user removes the pin before throwing, and once the grenade leaves the hand the lever is released, allowing the striker to trigger a primer that ignites a fuse or delay element, which burns down to the detonator and explodes the main charge."

"OK," says Lisbeth. "I'm the grenade thrower."

"You've only got three seconds to run after you pull out the pin."

Together they lift Märta and carry her limp body as far from the point of impact as they possibly can. Perhaps it is already too late.

"The grenade has to land close to the target, otherwise it won't work," says Svala in a voice that is fighting for oxygen.

"I know," says Lisbeth, and they hold each other's gaze. "And if we don't see each other again . . ."

"Just do it," croaks Svala. "Better to be blown to bits than to be burned alive."

Cotter pin, release, three seconds, throw, run. Lisbeth hurls herself over Svala like a human shield. The sound of the explosion in the empty rock chamber, the pressure wave and fragments of stone battering their bodies. One last tremor runs through the rock floor. Then all is silent.

Light snowflakes are sailing down to the ground. The moon wanders across the indigo sky. A helicopter rises into the air. An eagle's nest burns until only the bedrock is left. A girl gets to her feet, legs trembling. Crawls out through a wall that has been blasted to pieces. Receives a lifeless mother, sits down in the snow and strokes the hair out of her face.

"Mamma, we're safe now. We got out. I read your diary. Pap Peder's dead and if you can only remember the password for the hard drive we can get away from this place. You and me, Mamma, that sounds good, doesn't it?"

A Mammamärta opens her eyes. Although they are just slits in the swollen flesh they can look. That look is saying something. As if it were lips, it is forming a word.

"I can't hear," says Svala and pulls her closer. "Say it again."

A swallow can fly at forty miles an hour. The girl sits motionless with Mammamärta on her lap. The final breaths come jerkily. Move away like a fleeing herd of reindeer.

Lisbeth Salander puts her arm around Svala. They sit like that until they hear the sirens down on the road.

85

"Well, now," says Mikael Blomkvist, holding up the latest edition of *Gaskassen*. "Perhaps this isn't what any of you were expecting when we first met. Nor me, if I'm honest."

The coffee thermos is doing the rounds of the editorial office. Jan Stenberg is lapping up the praise in much the same way as he is the pearl sugar on his cinnamon bun.

"I said, didn't I," he says, "that *Gaskassen* is at least as good as the national media at digging up interesting news, and here's the proof."

The portrait photos of those identified by DNA from the bones left by the Cleaner's sea eagle banquets are lined up like a rogues' gallery on the front page. The Cleaner himself would very likely maintain that most of them deserved their place on the rubbish dump, but no one knows who he is or what role he played. That is why he is accorded no quotations in the article.

But the Cleaner reads the paper, too. He plows through every page until he finds the name. The boy. Lukas. He's alive. Doing fine. *No, it wasn't that bad and he didn't feel scared. They ate sweets and watched the sea eagles.* It was obvious. The only inland population of sea eagles. All they had to do was ring the Society for Nature Conservation and the remains of the cabin were located. The cabin, but not the Cleaner. The boy's description could have applied to any middle-aged hunter. A man about the same age as his dad, Henry. Green cap. Orange sweater. Did he recognize him or find out his name? No.

Apart from Lukas, there are also some remarks from Henry Salo. The dramatic course of events: the cabin in Kvikkjokk, the snowstorm and the car journey to Sunderbyn.

Does he know who left the boy there? No.

He shouldn't, but he simply can't stop himself. Joar drives down to Lake Njakaure, unlocks the barrier and parks the quad bike a little way into the forest. He puts his small-bore rifle over his shoulder, straps on his Tegsnäs hunting skis and sets off for the last few miles.

It is a beautiful day. A few degrees below freezing. The snow is glistening like a picture. He opens his backpack, takes out a plastic bag, empties the contents onto the ground and slips in under his usual spruce.

It usually takes a minute or two. When a quarter of an hour has passed, he gives up. There is something wrong. Not a sea eagle in sight.

The meat will have to stay where it is. The fox and the raven will be glad, anyway. He turns his skis and heads for the nest. Even from a distance he can see that something is wrong. The ancient firs that have proudly borne the nest aloft are now lying on the ground, stripped of bark. Nothing is left of the nest but bits of the twiggy basketwork. It's a nature preserve, for God's sake.

The Cleaner looks around him one last time before he turns sharply and skis back in his own tracks. His thoughts are moving forward, too. Never remember, never regret.

Mikael Blomkvist pauses over the photo on the far left: Malin Bengtsson, IB's daughter. They could have made so much more of the material had there been time. The coordinates in her phone, for example, which with the inversion of a couple of digits indicated Branco's HQ rather than Henry Salo's house. They will have to hold their nerve. Mikael senses that there will be more opportunities to make Marcus Branco's acquaintance. *You won't be able to resist that story, Erika Berger.*

"But what about the rest, then?" asks Mikael Blomkvist in a private call with Stenberg. "The bribes, the wind power, the suspected blackmail and so on. Don't you think *Gaskassen*'s readers are interested in the affairs of the municipal boss?"

"He hasn't been found guilty of anything," says Stenberg. "One might think you're trying to drop your own son-in-law in it. Henry's a bit unconventional, but we can't just write speculatively."

"We wouldn't want that, would we?" says Mikael. He puts his leather jacket on over his other one and checks the time. The train to Stockholm leaves in a couple of hours. First he's off to meet Salander for a last drink at the City.

"Meeting night tonight," he says to Stenberg. "My best to the guys at the lodge. Maybe see you around."

"Where are we now?" says Mikael. He passes Lisbeth a Coca-Cola and takes a swig of his beer.

"How do you mean?"

"We aren't exactly done with Branco, are we? I read Plague's message."

"Speaking of Plague," she begins, and then thinks better of it. This is nothing that need concern him. If there is a shred of doubt it is something she will have to deal with herself. "I'm feeling very much done with Branco right now," she says instead. "My ears are still ringing."

"Can we go through it all one last time?" he says.

"No," she says. "I can't face it. How did it go with your Icelandic lady friend, by the way?"

"Oh, you know, it went the way these things usually do. I'm going home today. Might arrange to see her in Stockholm sometime. How about you?"

"Cops aren't really my scene. They're on the wrong side, you might say."

"Meaning?"

"Just something a kid told me once. You can't change the path you walk, you can only change the side you walk on."

The conversation flows as sluggishly as the rubbish in the River Ganges. If a window was open, it is definitely shut now.

"And . . . the kid . . . what's happening with her?"

They drive out to the Hiraks' one last time. Sitting in the back seat are the monkey and the backpack and Svala's few possessions. She herself has her arms tightly wrapped around Mammamärta and Grandma.

Laura is in the dog pen. Per-Henrik swings in from the forest on a snowmobile. Elias is probably doing his own thing somewhere.

Lisbeth switches off the Ranger. "You haven't changed your mind, then?" she says.

"About Stockholm? I don't know, but I've got to start somewhere. I'll come down for the Easter holidays."

"You'll get to eat some fucking good pizzas, I can tell you that. And don't forget the karate, Svala-san."

"I won't, if you stop swearing."

Laura shuts up the dogs' cage and walks toward the car. Per-Henrik comes slithering across the icy yard to join them. Elias turns up on a kicksled.

"I'll be off, then," says Lisbeth.

"Not yet. You've got to come to the funeral first."

With snow inside their boots they all tramp up to the highest point of Björkberget.

The landscape spreads out below them, without beginning or end. Here and there, smoke rises from chimneys.

"Poor Marianne Lekatt," says Svala, letting her grandmother's ashes fly down toward her house.

"Someone's got the fire going down there, at any rate," says Elias. "Maybe we've got new neighbors."

Svala has saved Mammamärta's urn for last. She cradles it in her arms for a long time before twisting off the lid and letting the wind scatter the ashes at will. "Fly free, *Eadni,*" she says. *Fly fast, like the swallow on the stages of its journey. Hover like the sea eagle above the earth. My Eadnimärta.*

EPILOGUE

```
<Hi Lisbeth, hope all is good with you. Just want to
wish you a Happy Christmas. Mikael.>
  <Thanks, see you around sometime.>
  <Great, what are you doing tomorrow?>
  <Don't push your luck.>
  <Life is short. Loch Ness, 7 p.m.?>
  <OK, Dickhead.>
```

Because, yes, that is how it is. Life is a singular gift. Particularly when the gift comes direct from Santa in Rovaniemi. Svala hands in the notification slip. Receives her parcel, goes into Pizzeria Buongiorno, orders a Vegetariana with extra cheese and a Coca-Cola.

Slowly she undoes the Christmassy string. Picks off the sticky tape, unwraps the paper and holds the book like a precious treasure in her hands.

Svala H.
AAMULLA TULI YÖ

Oh hell, now she'll have to learn Finnish, too.

A NOTE ON THE AUTHOR AND TRANSLATOR

KARIN SMIRNOFF was born in Umeå, a small hamlet in northern Sweden, near where she now lives and a short drive from where Stieg Larsson himself grew up. She worked as a journalist before quitting her job to buy a wood factory. Her debut novel, *My Brother,* was nominated for the prestigious August Prize and has been optioned for TV by the producers behind *The Bridge*. *The Girl in the Eagle's Talons* is the first in her new trilogy based on Stieg Larsson's Millennium books, and is being translated into more than thirty languages.

SARAH DEATH studied Swedish at Cambridge University and University College London. She is a three-time winner of the George Bernard Shaw Prize, most recently in 2021 for *Letters from Tove,* the correspondence of Tove Jansson. She has also been awarded the Swedish Academy Translation Prize 2008 and the Royal Order of the Polar Star 2014.

A NOTE ON THE TYPE

This book was set in Minion, a typeface produced by the Adobe Corporation specifically for the Macintosh personal computer and released in 1990. Designed by Robert Slimbach, Minion combines the classic characteristics of old-style faces with the full complement of weights required for modern typesetting.

Typeset by Scribe, Philadelphia, Pennsylvania

Printed and bound by Berryville Graphics, Berryville, Virginia

Designed by M. Kristen Bearse